Also by Starling Lawrence

LEGACIES

M o n t e n e g r o

Montenegro

a novel by

STARLING LAWRENCE

Farrar Straus Giroux

New York

Farrar, Straus and Giroux
19 Union Square West, New York 10003

Copyright © 1997 by Starling Lawrence
All rights reserved
Distributed in Canada by Douglas & McIntyre Ltd.
Printed in the United States of America
First edition, 1997

Library of Congress Cataloging-in-Publication Data
Lawrence, Starling.
    Montenegro / Lawrence Starling. — 1st ed.
        p.   cm.
    ISBN 0-374-21407-7 (cloth : alk. paper)
    1. Montenegro — History — Fiction.   I. Title.
PS3562.A9155M66   1997
813'.54 — dc21

for L. C., always

Let come these things men thought could never be;
Let Hell devour; let Satan swing his scythe:
Still graveyard turf shall bring forth many a flower,
For coming kindreds in Time's later Hour!

— from *Gorski Vijenac* (*The Mountain Wreath*)
by Peter Njegoš, Prince-Bishop of Montenegro, 1830–51

Montenegro

Prologue

Connecticut, 1988

"LET THERE BE LIGHT," he said, in a tone between mockery and reverence. And there was light: a single beam of it, at this one moment of the midmorning, finding the gap where ice had taken a limb off the big maple, and illuminating only his hands as they lay on his chest. The window was open, admitting a soft breeze, and the sun catching the edge of his ring was reflected in an arabesque of thin gold that seemed to cut the cloth of the coverlet.

His hands looked very much the same as they always had, and very much like each other, but whereas one still worked, the other did not, and this was a surprise and a disappointment to him. For although he was old, he did not think of himself as old.

All his life he had been a vigorous man, performing feats of strength and endurance in his youth which now seemed incredible even to him across that distance in space and time. And in his eighty-fifth year he had astonished his grandson by pulling his body up to the beam in the study and holding himself there for several seconds. "A chin-up," his grandson had said in a wondering tone of voice.

He had not so much escaped the indignities of old age as he had shrugged them off, secure in the illusion of inexhaustible resources. Like many old people, and not a few of the merely middle-aged, he was more comfortable with the idea of the past than with the reality of the present. He did not brood on loss, but he greatly regretted that there was no one with whom he could share the riches locked in his memory.

His grandson was a pleasant young man, and would listen politely to any story served up to him. But he had never seen the mountains of the old man's youth, could not have survived a week in such a place, and even the way he spoke the word *Montenegro* was a sign that he understood none of the mystery of it, or the longing. His son was dead, dead long ago, and his wife of more than sixty years seemed less familiar to him than the nurse, a pleasant and professional young woman with a fine carriage to her head and proud eyes. His wife had never been proud, but often distant, and never more so than now, when she was obsessed with the tedious complexities of the present, and took consolation not from moments of remembered joy or hope but from a grim expectation of eternal life. She did not like to listen to the stories with which he could charm a perfect stranger, for they reminded her that he was raised in a heathen land, and still dwelled there in his mind.

His condition was painless. He had endured pain in his lifetime and would gladly do so now, though it seemed inappropriate to take any pride in his own stoicism when there was the example of his father, who had ploughed and hoed a farm and vineyard out of the rocks of the Balkans on the stump of a leg lost in the war against the Turks, in 1878. Still, he himself had been beaten until his back broke, and he had never once cried out. The pain of that wound had come back to him from time to time during the long years of his exile, so that at times he could not lift his arms above his shoulders. But there was no pain now, and he could not even tell where that knot of muscle might be that had formed over the cracked bone. Whatever had taken the life out of his left hand had taken the pain as well.

The doctor did not say he was dying, which had been his first question as soon as he had regained the power of speech four days after falling down in his study. He had taken a whole shelf of books down with him, along with the patent model of the Peacock Turbine that was, as his wife had told him nearly every Tuesday for half a century, impossible to dust.

"Do you expect me to get in there and clean out every one of those little things, those . . . vanes? Clara won't do it, and I don't have the time. We could give it to the Church." His fall had rendered this impasse moot. Clara would have swept the pieces of the hated engine into a plastic bag, perhaps even thrown them away. If it had been spared, he would see to it when he regained his strength.

But whatever the doctor said, something had changed during those four days that he had lain here speechless and practically immobile. He was no longer in perfect control of what he remembered, and the familiar figures of his past now appeared to him in surprising ways.

He had thought of his mother nearly every day of his long life, and sometimes she seemed almost to have a physical presence, particularly when he was telling some stranger how he had come to America, what his life on the desperate farthest slope of Montenegro had been like, how she had given the last years of her life to make this dream come true: that her son would go to America and become a famous scientist. He had often told the story—for he loved stories and was good at telling them—of how his mother took as her bible on the New World a tattered magazine with many pictures and a flowery text (not a word of which she understood) on the Columbian Exposition in a place called Chicago; or how she had made him learn English from a book after the work in the fields was done and the animals bedded down; how she made him read aloud to her so that she would understand a few words when he wrote to her from America, always in English. And she had appeared to him in dreams, exactly as he had seen her on that last day, crushed by the fallen beam, forcing him to look at her, into her eyes, though in his helpless rage and shame he would rather have torn his own eyes out, to look at her while she spoke to him, saying over and again that one word: *America.*

That was his mother's message to him, the one thing that she had wanted him to remember about her, and the one thing that he must do for himself in her memory. And against all odds, in defiance of the Turks and the Austrians, of his father's implacable will, of the will, it seemed then, of the mountains themselves that cracked and broke around him as he and the English struggled towards the sea, he had done it. His conscience was clear, or clear enough that he could bear these visitations, these dreams that might otherwise have broken him.

Now it was different. She was dressed neither in the torn and bloodstained clothes of the last day, nor in the severe black skirt and shawl which she had worn almost every day of his life, and which seemed perfectly adapted to milking a goat or giving birth to a child, but in white and scarlet and silver, as if arrayed for some magnificent celebration. Or might these be the raiments of paradise? With her eyes she asked a question that could not be answered by the simple version of his life that had served him for so many years, and that question seemed to be *Have you led a good life?* It was a strange time to begin considering such a question: he had never thought about it.

The English visited him as well, not the tall, graceful young man that he remembered, but fixed and confirmed now in middle age, with youth and arrogance and wonder all fled from his features. And this was strange, because the English—Harwell, that was his name— had died during the Serbian retreat through the mountains in the Great War, or so he had been told in a letter from Harwell's orderly, a letter which had travelled halfway around the world to find him. Harwell, still in those splendid boots, now spoke to him with gentle irony of the curious turns his own life had taken after he had so rashly turned his back on England. He looked about him in amazement at the furniture and the objects on the desk, as if to say, "Without me, where would you have ended? What would have become of you?"

And, most awkwardly, he saw again the girl, Aliye, who had loved him and died because of it, and whose face had haunted him until the day he first laid eyes on his wife, who never knew how exactly she reminded him of the dead girl.

Aliye's face was just as it had been, and the simple perfection of her body burned through the folds and gathers of the black cloth as it always had. She did not speak to him, but held out her hand in a gesture of welcome that seemed also to ask this question: *Do you love me?* The more he thought about it, the more convinced he was that she, Aliye, wanted him to come to her, had forgiven him, and he had no choice but to do as she desired. And from this perception—his volition or acceptance seemed to have nothing to do with it—he understood that he must now be dying, whatever the doctor said.

"Mr. Peacock?" There was a crisp rapping at the door. The nurse had brought to the job a sense of propriety that seemed more suited to a first-class hotel than to this, well, this deathbed.

"There is no need to knock. I am always here, and almost always awake." He liked her, and liked to talk to her, even though he knew that her interest was a professional obligation. Anyway, he was grateful, for when she had first come he had been incapable of speech. He had wanted to talk to her, wanted her to sit on the bed.

"We have a surprise for you this morning, Mr. Peacock. Mrs. Peacock and I have a surprise for you." And in they came, the nurse in white and Harriet in black, the pair of them looking like figures in an allegorical tableau.

"I am happy to see you," he said, and they both smiled, the nurse rather more successfully. She arranged the pillows behind him and put her arms around him to hoist him up onto the mound. His lungs filled with the odor of linen, the odor of her, clean certainly, but with a sharp, pleasing suggestion of flesh that set him to wondering if he had ever made love to a woman with hair of this extraordinary color, the gold of icons. What a pity she must put that cap on it.

"I am so glad to see you looking better, Thomas. I thought the Lord had called you." He smiled reassuringly at his wife and reflected on her obstinacy. His name was not Thomas, but Toma. He had explained this to Harriet, just once, it is true, and now so many years ago, but something of such evident importance should need no repetition. He thought that either she would remember the correct inflection, or he would grow accustomed to hers, but he was disappointed on both fronts.

The surprise turned out to be a breakfast of eggs and an English muffin with fresh orange juice, all in honor of his apparent, or desired, recovery. He guessed that the nurse, his white angel, had busied herself with the oranges and the muffin, while his wife, with the best intentions, had burdened the pan of eggs with a handful of herbs from the plot just beside the kitchen door: marjoram, oregano, rosemary, all bruised and thrown in with the stems still attached, and the whole covered with parsley at the end. It was pretty enough, but stank so that he was afraid he might not be able to eat it. She was like a deaf person when it came to smells. Well, he would try. He would turn his mind to the time when the English had fed him partridge eggs on their flight to the coast, and he, unable to move hand or foot, had eaten them greedily, shells and all.

When he had done what he could with breakfast the nurse announced that it was time for Mr. Peacock's bath. "Will you stay, Mrs.

Peacock? Afterwards we are going to have another story about . . . about where Mr. Peacock grew up. He's been telling me all about it." Harriet gave him a sharp glance, and the nurse a kinder one. No, she would not stay, having so many things to attend to, what with the upcoming church fair. She would take the tray to the kitchen.

"I am praying for you, Thomas." These words were spoken with love. She loved him when she prayed for him, but he could say nothing back to her. Was there not a man in her Bible called Doubting Thomas? He would think about this connection.

After the door closed behind the black angel, the white one removed the pillows and stripped back the blanket and top sheet from his bed. He listened to the water running in the bathroom and tried to remember the last time he had been washed by a woman. He closed his eyes, searching for a path back through the tangle of sensations to the moment when he had fallen. His heart raced, then skipped several beats. Was he dying now?

"Everything's fine, Mr. Peacock," said the white angel as she slipped a rubber sheet under him and removed his pajamas, practically in one motion. "This will be over before you know it, and you can tell me another story about the old days. Could you lift up, please? Don't hold your breath now. You can talk to me if that makes it easier."

Talking would make nothing easier, so he stared at the rough plaster of the ceiling and tried to think of anything that would distract him from the cool circles her hands and the soap made on his skin. The sour odor of the sickbed, of his unwashed, naked body, rose reassuringly to him. He still smelled like a man. Then he looked down at himself, as if it might be the body of a stranger and he a doctor, or the white angel's assistant. He still looked like a man: old muscles, no longer corded along his arms and across his belly, but muscles nonetheless, their shape and even their color faintly visible through the milk-white skin. There on his thigh was the ugly wound where the Austrian had gotten him: a couple of inches to the left and he would have left his balls in the dying man's hand, as the other had surely intended.

Just as he was reflecting on the miraculous preservation of his manhood, the white angel reached this same destination in her progress from toe to head. She grasped his organ boldly from its nest of grizzled hair and attacked it with her sponge. She paused, took more water from the enamel basin, and registered no surprise to find the thing growing in her hand.

"Well, Mr. Peacock," she said, giving him an appreciative squeeze, "you must have been quite something in the old days. It doesn't bother me at all, I assure you. Just put it out of your mind." And she let it drop onto his stomach like an old sausage, as if the Austrian had succeeded in his task after all.

When the bath was over, and the bedclothes and pillows put back to his satisfaction, she came and sat beside him. There was plenty of room for both of them, as this was the bed he had ordered from that old drunken cabinetmaker on the day that Harriet had agreed at last to marry him. A breeze through the open window—it had been closed during his bath—brought the scent of turned earth and the bruised herbs from the garden, mixing now, as it curled past his head, with the smell of furniture polish from the headboard. He gazed on the nape of her neck, at the hair pulled savagely up under the cap. He was saddened by the cap. Before long the hair she twisted every morning would turn a flatter, brownish color, then white, and no man would wish her to take it down. But today . . .

She took his hand, the one that did not work, and began to massage the muscles of his palm with her small, strong thumb. Then she made a circle with the tips of her fingers and brought them to bear on his fingers, one by one, up and down the length of them.

"Can you feel that, Mr. Peacock?" Yes, he could feel it. Aliye had held his hand like that on the last day, when he would not allow himself to touch her. They had lain in the cool shadow of the great rock overlooking a tiny sloping vineyard cleared out of the stony waste. They lay there for most of the afternoon and he did not remember a single word they spoke, or if they spoke at all. Everything was decided: he could not change what was going to happen—what he thought was going to happen—except by being a different person altogether, and even this he did not understand at the time.

The English had seen them there, riding his horse along the rim of their bower, probably in pursuit of one of his strange little plants, no bigger than the palm of your hand. They must have seemed to him, to the English, like two tired children, and she held his hand, just like this, and took each of his fingers, one by one, in the tips of hers.

"Oh, Mr. Peacock, we're doing much better today. Now I want you to squeeze my hand. That's right, yes. And harder now, harder still . . . I assure you, Mr. Peacock, you're not going to hurt me!" She regarded him with an expression of naive merriment. "As hard as you can."

He let out a sighing breath, and she glanced again at his face, her smile gone. "That's enough for now, I think. Perhaps we'll try again later." She went back to the gentle massage of the muscles, working on the heel of his hand. "It must be time for your story. I wish Mrs. Peacock had stayed to hear it, but perhaps she's heard them all before. I hope I have time to hear them all. I mean, before you're up and around and don't need me anymore."

And since his mind had so recently been on Aliye, she who beckoned to him but would not speak, he followed the path of memory from that moment in the stony field as if it were indeed a tale he had intended to tell all along, a tale that would make perfect sense to this kind, stupid young woman, who didn't know the difference between the Serb and the Turk, and who couldn't have found his country on a map. And he realized as he was telling it that it was a story waiting for him as well, as if he himself had not known what had happened until the moment of this telling.

They walked back from the vineyard in silence, for once not caring who saw them coming or going, and when they reached the point where she must go to the left and he to the right, Aliye, having steeled her mind to do what she would do, did not so much as glance at him. He called to her softly then, and still she paid him no heed, as if she had not heard, had never known him and would never know him. He called once more, her name tearing his throat.

She seemed to age as she walked away from him, for the sway of her walk was muted, then lost in the black cloth, and she might be just another Mahometan woman walking to the market, or to the well. In his foolishness, absorbed in the grief he was discovering and losing practically in the same moment, he thought he was looking at the woman she would become, and his breathing became calmer. Later, and for many years, he would be haunted by the cruel falsehood of this glimpse of the future. Aliye. He repeated her name softly and added, "I did love you."

The Austrian soldiers had taken him soon after his parting from Aliye, riding right up to his father's house, smashing a trellis that the English had constructed for his mother at the corner of the house. He remembered a flowering vine wrapped around the leg of that white-stockinged bay that Captain Schellendorf rode. They did not tell him by what right they seized him, a free citizen of Montenegro, nor on what charge, saying only that the peace had been disturbed, and a murder, perhaps, committed. He would be questioned; if innocent, released.

He knew nothing of murder, and nothing of Austrian jails, but before they even laid a hand on him or took his clothes away he knew he was their property, and that it would take a miracle to deliver him from such a place. And so he began to pray to Saint Sava, as he had heard that Serb warriors must do in their time of need, and invoked the name of King Lazar, who had met his enemies and found a brave death without victory on the Field of Kosovo, five hundred years earlier, but not so many miles from the rough stones on which he now crouched. He prayed instead of answering their questions, which enraged the guards, and he sang aloud when they began to beat him. Finally, he had prayed at the top of his lungs so that he might not hear the softer sounds from the next room, the drunken oaths of encouragement, the lewd whispers of Schellendorf, and his yelp of pain.

At last Saint Sava had come to him, in the quiet that was like a tomb, riding on a white horse as a symbol of victory, and had delivered him from his enemies. The coming of the saint was announced by a sudden trembling of the earth that had destroyed the jail, and his horse stepped effortlessly through the rubble of the wall. With his sword the saint had pointed to the long splinter of wood, sheared off a beam, that was to become his own terrible sword, and he followed the glimmer of the saint and his horse through the dark streets that still pitched and shuddered beneath him. The cobblestones heaved from the ground like broken teeth and he stumbled often, but he was able to find the hospital bed where Schellendorf lay, and there he took his revenge.

The saint deserted him then, having shown him what was to be done, and so he was alone with the man he must kill. He sang now, sang the verses of *The Mountain Wreath* as he had heard his father sing them, knowing that this man was not the Turk, the ancient enemy of his people, but one who had destroyed and defiled his life so completely that he must be killed like a Turk.

He would have taken the head as well except that Schellendorf, more dead than alive, had somehow wrenched his sweat- or blood-slick wrist loose from the corded linen that bound him to the iron bed, seized a bottle from the table, smashed it, and thrust it into his thigh. Schellendorf had died then, a savage grimace on his face, and it was all he could do to bind the wound with a torn sheet and drag himself through the confusion of the darkened garrison town, hoping that no one would pay attention to another wounded man.

When he stopped talking there was an absolute stillness in the room, as if neither he nor the white angel were breathing, and so he took her hand in his good one, the right one, and placed it again on his thigh, on the glazed flesh where the bottle had entered and left its shards. His manhood rose, more urgently now, like a snake trapped beneath her wrist, beating there. Her hand, though, was as dead as his own.

"These are the most terrible things I have ever heard in my life," she managed to say at last. "How can you . . . Why are you telling me this?" She did not look at him, but at the floor, or at her feet.

"I tell you this because it is my life. This is what I am." And with his other hand he knocked the cap from her head in an unhurried, awkward motion. Pins clattered on the floor and her hair fell around her face. She was weeping now, making no sound, flinching as if she were being beaten.

"Ah," he said, smoothing out her hair with the fingers that did not work. He had never seen hair like this. The tenderness of the gesture, or perhaps the sound of his voice, roused her to a sense of herself and where she was. For a long moment she looked at him, her face a mask in which he could read neither recognition nor emotion of any kind. She tore her hand from his grasp and backed away from the bed, keeping her eyes on him all the while as if he might follow her.

Then she was gone, and in her haste she had stripped away the covers. Where were his pajamas? Had she forgotten to put them back on? It did not matter, and he did not try to raise himself up and catch the corner of the sheet there by his knee. He was not cold. His body was illuminated in a curious, pleasing way, but when his hand went to his breast, as it often did, he found nothing, not even the beaded ribbon around his neck, and he knew himself to be naked indeed. His hand groped on the night table; a plastic bottle of pills clattered to the floor, but his fingers closed around the precious object, that flat, worn cross of plaited silk that was as familiar to him as his own body. He sighed and closed his eyes. Sleep might come now, or revelations, or even the angel of death, but he had no fear.

Chapter One

Cattaro, February 1908

HARWELL HAD ALWAYS prided himself on being a good sailor and a perfectly rational man, but he had been so miserably and unaccountably seasick since the steamer left Trieste two days earlier that it was difficult to accept this affliction as anything other than an omen. Much of his boyhood was spent racing small boats on the Norfolk Broads, and the Channel crossing, with its chops and cross seas, was familiar, even welcome to him. He once read three chapters of a Russian novel in the course of a Channel storm so violent that even the steward in the first-class lounge had to excuse himself.

For these two wretched days, however, he had scarcely left the deck, hoping that the vicious wind, the bora, howling the length of the Adriatic, might clear his head and settle his stomach. The wind set the old Ungaro-Croatian steamer into a continuous shuddering roll as soon as she cast off; it drove the smoke straight over the bows like a pennant pointing south, covering the deck and his clothes with a fine grit; and when he was sick, which had happened more times than he could remember, eddies of this same wind flung his vomit back on him, spattering his trousers and shoes. He remembered with disgust a plate of macaroni he had eaten just before boarding the ship. He had no notion of what the sauce had been, and he had never liked that sort of food anyway. He determined never to eat it again.

It was dawn now, or nearly so, for the light was trapped behind that great mountain, which he could see only in outline. He had spent the night in a deck chair, muffled in two blankets. The steward had been alarmed at the idea of providing either the chair or the blankets at such a late hour, and had demanded security of two sovereigns and all the Italian coins in his pocket. Harwell, already in low spirits, was first annoyed, then offended, for the steward clearly doubted his sanity. Why would a man about to jump overboard need a deck chair? And would he conceivably take it with him over the side? Well, he had been warm enough, or nearly so, and he had even managed to sleep for a while. He had woken once and glimpsed, across the broken sea, the lights of Ragusa, that ancient city which he had hoped to see in the daylight, her ramparts set against the unforgiving mountains of Illyria.

He leaned now on the rail, for he was exhausted still, and felt the vibrations of the steamer altering as she steered a majestic curve out of the violent waters of the Adriatic, through the narrows, and into that vast, sheltered bay, the Bocche di Cattaro. The dark mountain, his destination, now limned with light, lay dead ahead, and ghostly white villages defined the shoreline. The wind had dropped, and he was surrounded by clouds of clamoring gulls. He breathed deeply and contemplated the possibility of breakfast.

The steward seemed surprised to see Harwell still alive, but made a swift recovery, hoping to preserve last night's deposit as this morning's gratuity. At last the man surrendered the two gold coins, holding back the Italian ones, which Harwell let him keep.

The cabin stank so that the sickness nearly came back over him, but he managed to change out of those filthy trousers and scrape the worst off his shoes. He packed quickly, cursing himself for having too much luggage, and found a place for his shoes in the side of one valise where they would not do too much damage. The trousers were impossible. He thrust them under the pillow, muttering that the steward could jolly well earn his tip.

Dressed in breeches and the beautifully burnished Maxwell boots his mother had given him as a going-away present, assured by the steward that his luggage would meet him on the quay, he set off in search of breakfast. But the door of the dining room was still locked: perhaps he was the only passenger disembarking at Cattaro? Sustained rattling of the brass handles eventually provoked a response. A sleepy waiter opened the door and set a place on the table that had only recently been his bed.

Harwell perceived a cruel irony in the fact that whereas he had been offered all sorts of food when he wasn't able to eat it, he now found only two brittle rolls and a pot of last night's coffee, partly warmed. There would be worse before long, he supposed, surprising himself with this gloomy reflection. He was a young man neither of great family nor of great intellectual achievements, but of energetic enthusiasm for whatever tomorrow might bring. And this trip—he hardly presumed to call it a mission—which was starting so unpromisingly, had seemed the perfect thing, seemed to suit him exactly. Harwell, little given to analysis or examination of motive, knew this in his bones, and it had been confirmed for him by Raymond the last time they met.

"You are extraordinarily lucky, Bron," Raymond said, as if he were about to complete his thought. Instead, there ensued a silence that lasted until Harwell looked over to catch that long, fine face, now half in shadow, closed in upon some reflection that would not be shared. Raymond was shifting his glass back and forth on the arm of his chair, an almost imperceptible motion that set the firelight to playing in the tiny amber lake of his brandy.

"Lucky," he went on at last, "because whether you know it or not, you have found something to do that will engage you completely, and a part of the world you will never tire of."

"Come with me then!" Harwell was surprised by his own voice. "Just the two of us. I'm told the mountains there are like nothing you've ever seen, or perhaps even imagined. Have you ever heard of the Sandžak of Novi Pazar? Quite a colorful place it sounds, perhaps even a bit dangerous. You can load my rifles for me as we hold off the remnants of an Ottoman army and the hordes of the Albanian bandit princes. You have two weeks. More than enough for a man of your parts to learn Serbo-Croat, and I'll put in a word with Lord—" Raymond's raised finger stopped Harwell just short of an indiscretion: it would be awkward for a man of Raymond's party and government connections to know too precisely what Auberon Harwell would be doing in the Balkans, or even who would be sending him. *I'm not cut out for this work*, Harwell thought. The cover story about the alpine flora of the dolomitic karst was too thin to be essayed with such an old friend.

"I think you'll find, were you to stray anywhere near the Sandžak of Novi Pazar or Bosnia, that the Austrians give you more to think about than the pitiful old Turk or the Albanian rabble. And they shoot back, or so I'm told." Raymond's melancholy was gone, and he was himself again: bantering, self-deprecating, his humorous in-direction distracting one from the astonishing depth of learning, of information. Harwell wondered how he could bear to be separated from his friend.

"Anyway, Bron, I don't think I'd be much use to you in this ad-venture. I'm much better at dead languages than living ones, and any grouse in Perthshire can tell you how hopeless I am with a firearm. Even your Albanian bandit, I think, prefers a fair fight."

"And has it not even crossed your mind, the idea of simply shutting the door behind you and . . ."

"Oh, yes. Indeed it has."

"Well, then? For God's sake, it's not a decision about how you'll spend the rest of your life; it's a holiday."

"Is it that? I should be surprised if that were so, and disappointed. For you, I mean. I think you underestimate the attractiveness of one good Englishman: you will shine like Phoebus himself against that chaos, and I shouldn't be surprised if you become a very great man indeed, vizier to Prince Nikola and his Montenegrin headhunters, or perhaps even king of Albania."

Harwell snorted. The brandy went up his nose.

"You laugh, Bron, but stranger things have happened. They made poor old Otto king of Greece not so very long ago, and he was only a minor German, quite insignificant compared to yourself."

"And you wouldn't . . ."

"No. I mean I would, but I couldn't. I am arguing three cases at this moment, and I believe there is talk of my standing at the next election. Most persuasively, it appears I must be married, and you will believe me when I tell you that there is no terror in all the Balkans to compare with my Cynthia when her passions are excited." Raymond allowed himself a smile at this evocation, a very gentle smile, thought Harwell.

"And besides, dear Bron, it will be so much more thrilling for you if you do it alone, whatever it is the unmentionable Lord P has you up to." He raised his glass. "So here's to your adventure," and in Greek he continued, " 'We give you glory: it is yours to win.' May the spirit of Dr. Jowett, along with the shade of Homer, watch over you so that your exploits reflect credit on Balliol."

They drank off what remained in their glasses as a seal to their mutual affection and admiration, but the glow of that moment lasted only until Harwell bade Raymond good night.

He did not see his friend again for the fortnight before his departure, nor did he have any real letter from him, only a note full of hollow gaiety explaining his absence when Harwell boarded the train for Dover. In the strange light admitted by the vaults of glass high above, he said his goodbyes. He kissed his mother's cool cheek, and shook his father's hand, surprised by its strength. "Auberon . . ." The rest of the paternal benediction was lost in a great belch of steam. Harwell climbed onto the train and waved cheerfully, wondering if Raymond would miss him in the months to come. It rained all the way to Dover, and he was able to read almost half the book Raymond had sent with his note: Captain Sir William Hoste, Nelson's brave lieutenant, accounting for his extraordinary exploits in the Adriatic. On the flyleaf was Raymond's own name and congratulations on the occasion of his sixteenth birthday in the year 1898. Beneath it now, again, the quotation, the exhortation, from Homer.

Although the sun had yet to rise above the humped shoulders of the mountain, and a damp, windless chill lingered over the port of Cattaro, Harwell was so elated to have his feet on dry land again that he might have skipped for joy, were he not conscious of the attention of the two Austrian port officers. There was his luggage beside him on the quay—he had counted the pieces with care—and there, on the steep headland across this narrow arm of the bay, was a patch of sunlight on an outcropping of stone studded with bright yellow flowers. Soon that same sun would reach the level ground where he stood, and warm him. The wretched steamer slid away from the quay and hooted once, a valediction that echoed from the mountains before dying away.

The procedure of the Austrian customs was, to Harwell's thinking, aggravatingly tedious, and quite ridiculous when one considered that just this insignificant bit of land along the coast belonged to Austria. In half an hour, or however long it took him to secure transportation, he would be shut of these meaty fellows in their coarse blue tunics and caps.

"Auberon Augustus Harwell." They managed, in repeating his name like the echoing mountains, to mispronounce or misinflect every syllable of it. The larger of the two, the one with good teeth, seemed to be in charge. He riffled through the passport contemptuously, as if he needed only to glance at it to know it contained nothing but lies.

"Auberon Augustus Harwell, why do you come here? You are a tourist perhaps?" The smaller one, with bad teeth, smiled hugely. Harwell had prepared himself for this moment, but now found himself unsure of his audience. What business was it of theirs to question an English traveller?

"Yes, it is just as you say. A tourist." He wished he had had time to brush up his German as well, but the infernal Serbo-Croat had drained him of all patience for foreign languages.

"And what will you be looking at here in Dalmatia, so far from your England? You see that Cattaro is a very small place indeed." The Austrian indicated with a sweep of his hand the little port and the heights above. Harwell followed the gesture with his eyes, taking in for the first time the old ramparts that ran zigzag up the nearly vertical face to a fortification at the top of a precipice. The sight of the mountainside, now bathed in light, and the blue sky above, was thrilling to him. He could not imagine what lay beyond, and he was impatient to be finished with this foolishness.

"I will not be staying in Cattaro, nor in Dalmatia. I plan to travel in Montenegro, and I have a particular interest in flowers. I shall be staying two months, perhaps three."

"Flowers?" The large one turned to his companion. "Are there flowers in Montenegro?" The other man, still smiling idiotically, shrugged his shoulders. "We don't know if there are any flowers in Montenegro, so you may be disappointed. But there are many wicked people there, and it is dangerous for any traveller. Many bandits. Perhaps you should not go. There will be another ship, an Austrian ship, tomorrow."

Harwell thought they might simply be playing a joke with him. The boredom of this place must be overwhelming, even to such marginal intelligences. Or they wanted a bribe. Of these two possibilities he found the motive of financial gain less offensive. He thought of the other piece of paper in his pocket, the one that Lord P, in Raymond's coy designation, had given to him at the end of their interview with the cryptic remark that it should be used only in case of great emergency, and best not used at all. "It has been signed by Baron Aehrenthal himself, and should you need to use it, this paper will unlock almost any door in the Balkans, but at the expense of every favor owed to me by the Austrian Embassy in London. It is not certain that Aehrenthal even knows what he has signed. You will therefore not be careless with it." This, thought Harwell, did not qualify as a great emergency. He reached for his wallet.

"Gentlemen, I'm sure there is a solution to this difficulty. There are port fees perhaps?"

The Austrians took the money—the two gold sovereigns that the steward had been denied—but did not thank him or indicate that the money was anything other than what he had suggested. Nor was his ordeal over.

"Now we will see about your luggage. A great deal of luggage, perhaps, for a tourist, and in such a place? There is unrest in these parts, as I'm sure you are aware, and particularly in the territory beyond Montenegro, in Bosnia and the Sandžak. Will you be going to such places? Or will the flowers of Montenegro be your only interest?"

"I have no idea; it will depend. In any case, I believe the Sandžak of Novi Pazar belongs to the Ottoman Empire, as does Bosnia." Harwell's comment was foolish, and he regretted it immediately.

"Belongs, as you say, to the Turk," said the officer, with a dismissive downturn at the corner of his mouth, "but it is Austria, I mean to say the Austro-Hungarian Empire, that keeps the peace there. No one else can do it, and so we, here in Cattaro, must be very careful, very careful indeed. You will open the big one first."

Harwell was grateful for the chance to break off the lecture: there was nothing to be gained by discussing the politics of the Balkans with an Austrian. There in the top of his valise, wadded up into a stinking ball, was the pair of trousers he had thought to leave behind on the steamer. He would gladly have wrung the neck of that spiteful bastard of a steward: the smell of vomit would by now have infected every other article in the bag.

"So, we are not so careful in our packing." The Austrian made the same face as when he had dismissed the authority of the Ottoman Empire, and his wordless colleague now laughed aloud. Harwell, in his fury, could not think of the German word he needed, and so he seized the trousers and stalked to the edge of the quay, where he threw them into the water.

The officers went through each bag, making him unpack his belongings onto a long, dirty table. They admired his evening clothes, fingered his shirts and the stiff white collars, turned every page of Linnaeus' *Species Plantarum* as if they expected to find incriminating papers there, and managed to tear an illustration folio of Haworth's *Saxifragëarum Enumeratio*. Then they came to Waldstein's volume.

"A German book." This was said approvingly.

"Yes, a German book, though written in Latin, as you can see. He was a very considerable expert. Please be careful of that one; it is very old, and it does not belong to me." Had Lord P envisioned such a situation when he had taken the book from the shelf in his library? In any case, Waldstein had saved the day, and the inspection of his luggage was now over. Harwell determined that he would read the book at the next opportunity, or at least as much as his Latin would allow.

"We are satisfied," said the Austrian as Harwell latched his baggage, "but we see you have no firearms, not even a pistol."

"Indeed not. You would not have been amused to find a pistol in my luggage, I think."

"Well, you have a point. We must be very strict about such matters. Not so many years ago Prince Danilo, the uncle of this present fellow, was shot and killed here in Cattaro by a visiting Montenegrin, one of his own people. All the same, you must have a pistol at least if you plan to survive your journeys up there." He jerked his head to indicate the mountain at his back. "And you are English, yes? Not one of these savages. Gerhard, show him your pistol."

The smaller man took the leather case from his belt and laid it on the table in front of Harwell.

"Take it out, Gerhard. Show him how it works, what good care you have taken of it." Harwell watched, but made no move to touch the pistol, wondering if this might be a trap of some sort.

"What do you want me to do?" he asked at last.

"I want you to buy this pistol. For your own safety."

Harwell took a five-pound note from his wallet, and the stiff, new paper with its tracings of blue and gray inks reminded him of everything he had left behind. It was a ridiculous sum of money to pay for such a thing, even if it had been new. The Austrian bowed, and gave him extra bullets. He pocketed the banknote. Gerhard's smile was gone.

"I would advise you not to travel at night, and also to take the Austrian road up the mountain. You will see then what Austria can do for this part of the world, and why they need us. Gerhard, run and find the porter for him."

Harwell had intended to heed the warning about travelling by night, and he knew that Cetinje, the capital, was a good six or seven hours' journey away, up over the top of this rock face that crowded the port against the water. But to his astonishment he found that there was not a single carriage for hire in all of Cattaro, not so much as a chaise. A large party connected to the Russian Legation had arrived yesterday and set off for Cetinje with much luggage and even crates of furniture, all of which, explained the liveryman in some awkward variant of the German tongue, had to be taken immediately up there. Here he made an extravagant, disgusted gesture indicating the mountain. There were no carriages to be had. Harwell might wait for the coach, which might arrive shortly after noon, or he might choose to buy a horse, perhaps two with all that luggage. There were excellent horses to be had, he said, bowing obsequiously.

After taking his own measure of this excellence—hammerheaded little brutes for the most part—Harwell decided he would wait for the coach, and set off to see what Cattaro had to offer an English tourist. The old town was surrounded by a market, tiny stalls and tents against the crumbling walls that couldn't have been defended against a band of determined schoolboys. Through the bright throng he walked, smiling politely as stately women with gold coins in their headdresses offered him dates, and oranges, and freshly killed chickens, then across the tiny drawbridge spanning a moat. Here he was required to pay a toll, as the old keeper told him, to keep the machinery working. Harwell reflected on the utter insignificance of this place, however picturesque, and the improbability of grown men fighting over it. And yet, in the past one hundred years, Cattaro had been owned, or occupied, by the Austrians, the Turks, the French, the Montenegrins, and, for one brief but glorious moment, the English. There may have been others he had forgotten.

Everything in the town was on a diminished scale—the houses, the cobbled streets, even the twelfth-century cathedral of Sveti Tripun. A plaque in French informed him that this particular saint was the patron of horticulture, which Harwell took as a favorable omen. "Well done, Tryphon," he said, putting a shilling in the box next to the sign.

Wherever he looked, the eye was drawn back to the fact of the mountain, that grander edifice, shadowing all else even in broad daylight. A wall of rock, some thousand or fifteen hundred feet, rose directly behind the cathedral, and as Harwell looked up between the twin towers he saw a tiny chapel or shrine cut into the face of the cliff far above. It was such heights as these that Hoste and his sailors had scaled in December of 1813, dragging the cannon from their ships behind them, and so induced the surrender of the French garrison. The account he had read was thrilling enough, but the evidence now took his breath away. Like the French commandant before him, he could not quite believe his eyes.

At noon he ate heartily at a hotel on what passed for the main street: soup, some sort of seasoned stew, and a cold roast chicken. It was not good food, but he was very hungry, and as he was afraid to eat imprudently on his very empty stomach, he asked the waiter to wrap the rest of the chicken in a cloth, a clean cloth. He drank coffee afterwards, and gazed up at the blue sky above the town and its narrow arm of water. The place was like a coffin, he thought, and he would not spend the night here.

At one o'clock he returned to the livery to find that the coach had not returned. Perhaps there was a problem—it was a very steep road, after all—and even if the coach came now, there was no certainty that it would start back up the mountain before the next day. At two o'clock Harwell decided he had no choice but to purchase a horse,

which he would need in any case for the roadless wastes beyond
Cetinje, and he settled on a little mare with a dished face and signs
of spirit—Arabian blood, unless he was mistaken. Perhaps she was
too small? *Sire, she is stronger than you would imagine.* The off-side
eye was slightly cast, was she blind? *Sire, it is no matter; she knows
the road well, and I have given you an excellent price, as God knows.*
He purchased another horse, a perfectly placid one, for his baggage,
and at a quarter past three, sweating from the exertion of tying everything down, he was ready to leave.

"Where is the road?" Harwell, now mounted, felt a surge of excitement, and tried not to let it show in his voice.

"Sire, there are two roads. Over there"—he pointed to the left,
seemingly at the rock face itself—"over there is the old way, what we
call the Ladder of Cattaro."

"It must be too steep for the horses, surely."

"Not in the least, Sire, but you would have to walk." Harwell
wiggled his toes in the new boots, feeling the two spots that might
already be blistered from his stroll around Cattaro.

"And the other road, the new one?"

"Over there, Sire. The Austrians are very proud of their road. Go
with God."

Chapter Two

HALFWAY UP THE MOUNTAIN Harwell was overtaken by a brief rain squall, which chilled him, but delighted him too, perhaps because he had at last washed the dust of the old Europe from his boots, and he was now baptized into the new, this other world. Below him, virtually at his feet, lay the little port of Cattaro, with its olive groves stretching south towards Albania, all obscured now by the rain and a rising mist or fog. Ahead and above, while he could not yet see the top of his mountain, the landscape was unfolding into a succession of long, bleak ridges of the limestone karst that hemmed the Adriatic on its eastern shore. It was a rough gray stone, forbidding to the touch, and it would not hold water, he had read. Whole rivers there in the land above disappeared into the karst after running for a few miles, to issue forth in jets and geysers many leagues away, and one, although he had not seen this, ran underground into the bay itself, where it made the water boil with the swirling mushrooms of its strong current. The little yellow flowers that he had noted early in the morning were everywhere around him here, a species of primula, he thought.

Harwell assumed he was halfway to the top because he had been counting the hairpin turns on this astonishing road, and he knew there were twenty-seven of them. He had just coaxed his reluctant packhorse around the thirteenth, and there, south of the port, he saw the first few turns that presented a vast white M to the traveller on high, a private tribute, it was said, by the Austrian engineers to their empress. A fragrant steam rose from the shoulders of his mare, though her enthusiasm for the climb seemed undiminished. The packhorse, carrying the equivalent of a heavy man, was breathing hard and eating the yellow flowers at every opportunity. The mist now grew thick, and he urged his horse closer to the safety of the rock, for although there was a guardrail on the outside of the road, it was broken in many places, and he had seen the wreckage of vehicles in the bleak gullies below. Sometimes a white rock or a garland of flowers marked these gaps in the railing.

He had expected the mist to burn off or blow away as he climbed: surely it was a freak of that passing shower? But the mist—he could call it a proper fog now—grew steadily worse, and five or six turns farther on he was beginning to worry about seeing the road properly from the slight elevation of his saddle. If he were to walk, only until the damned fog lifted, he could keep one hand on the rock and know that he was at least ten or twelve feet from the precipice.

As he contemplated his situation, he heard the sound of a rock falling into the road not far ahead of him. He had seen no other travellers since leaving Cattaro, and so he unlatched the holster and let his hand rest on the cold metal of the pistol grip.

"Who goes there?" he called out loudly, in German. There was no answer, and after a few moments of straining to hear a sound that was not there, he let the feisty little mare go ahead at her own pace. Ten steps farther on someone laughed, almost in his ear.

"*Dobro veče, gospodine englez.* Welcome to Montenegro." Harwell did not answer, uncertain whether he had understood what was said, and his mare edged crabwise away from the voice and towards the railing. He drew the pistol and pointed it where he thought the man might be. The other spoke again, this time in French.

"Good evening to you. I did not mean to disturb the English gentleman. I threw the stone to warn you." Still Harwell could not see the man.

"And how did you know I was an English gentleman? Are there not people of every sort on this road?"

"It is as you say, but you were whistling, and only the English whistle for themselves."

"I most certainly was not whistling."

"Would I invent such an unimportant thing, dear sir? It was one of your hymns, I believe, a charming one. The name may come to me yet." Harwell, mortified, sighed heavily. At least the man did not sound dangerous.

"Please come down into the road, if you would be so kind. I don't like talking to someone I cannot see." Laughter again, and then the man was suddenly beside him, very tall, with dark hair and a great black beard, beaded with the mist. He seemed not so very much older than Harwell.

"Perhaps you are afraid of the dark? I assure you there is nothing to fear in our country, not for a man such as yourself."

"Why should I be afraid of you? You do not appear to be armed." Harwell held the reins and the lead in his left hand; his right hand rested awkwardly on the other wrist, with the pistol pointed at the man's head. There was something about this fellow that the mare did not like.

"Indeed not, for I am on my way to Kotor, and the Austrians would insist on taking my pistol from me. It is better to leave it here at home. They might take away my fine pistol, with its silver filigree of the hound chasing the stag, and give me back one of theirs, one such as yours."

"I have been told that people do not travel on this road alone, or after dark. Your business in Cattaro must be important, unless, perhaps, you are a bandit."

"Kotor, not Cattaro, if you please," said the black-bearded man. "It is a name which honors our right to that place, to the sea."

"Your business in Kotor, then."

"My business is my business, and if you must shoot me, please take my heart, and not my face, or my mother will never forgive you. In any case, you should know that there are no bandits in this country, only free men."

"The Austrians have a different story to tell." Harwell, beginning to feel embarrassed by the pistol, dropped his aim a few inches to the man's chest. The mare would not be still, and even the packhorse began to pull back against the lead rope, so that he hadn't a hope of hitting the man in the head anyway.

"The Austrians . . ." Here the man spat. "You will never know Montenegro if you listen to the lies of the Austrians, and they will never have Montenegro for themselves, even if they can buy our king. My name is Mirko Petrović. But you should put your pistol away now, for if I were a bandit I would already have killed you and taken whatever I wanted."

"Perhaps it is the pistol that prevents you?"

Rich laughter greeted this suggestion. "Let me tell you how it would be." The man's hands were hooked comfortably onto a colorful sash or girdle that Harwell could just distinguish in the light that was left. He had the air of one who is about to tell a joke.

"It is growing late to be travelling on this or any road, and the weather is a further uncertainty. Your horse knows the road, but you yourself do not, and this makes her nervous. You are a good horseman, I would judge, and the sun never shone on such a pair of boots, but perhaps you are not comfortable in our mountains. Not even an Austrian road can alter the steepness of them." Here he spoke a word to the mare in Serbo-Croat that Harwell did not catch, perhaps to calm her, for she seemed to fear him.

"There. Now you can hold your pistol on me more easily, yes? But even so, although you seem to have the advantage of the weapon and your mount, everything could change in an instant." He laughed, and Harwell said nothing. "You do not believe me?"

"I think you . . ." And in the middle of his reply, Harwell saw that he was speaking to thin air, and then the mare was trying to buck and kick at the same time. The pistol, falling from his hand as he tried to steady himself, was caught in midair by Mirko, who now stood on the other side of the horse, quite close to the edge of the road.

"Christ!" muttered Harwell, his heart hammering at his ribs. In Mirko's right hand was a great crooked knife, which must have been hidden in the folds of the girdle. With his other hand he offered the pistol to Harwell.

"We are all Christians here, although we in Montenegro call upon Him only in our churches. Take the pistol and put it away now, for it will surely break if it falls to the ground." Harwell did as he was told, and mumbled an apology for his blasphemy.

"I am sorry if I have frightened your horse, but I do not think you would have believed me without proof. Had I been in earnest, I would have drawn my *hanjar* across her belly, not merely tickled her with the back of it. With her guts spilling onto the road, you would have been hard put to keep your seat, much less shoot me, and then there is the edge of the road to consider." Mirko put the knife back into its hidden sheath. "You are fortunate, then, to be among Christians, friends, shall we say. And I repeat, there are no bandits in Montenegro, only free men. You will know now how to answer the lies of any Austrian."

"Thank you." Harwell tried to gather his wits. Why was he grateful to this man? "Thank you for your advice. I had better get along if I am to reach Cetinje this evening. Though in this weather . . ."

"The weather will be clear after you reach the pass, but quite cold I would think. In any case, you will find your way." Harwell considered how broad this Mirko was in the shoulders, how huge a man to have made such an agile move.

"And is there no place to stop, in case . . ."

"No, there is no stopping on this road in the dark." Here Mirko paused. "And you will meet no one. But be careful all the same."

"Thank you again, and goodbye."

Mirko put his hand on the bridle. "And your name? I have told you mine."

"How terribly rude of me. I am called Harwell, Auberon Harwell."

"Auberon Harwell. It has no meaning in our language, but I am glad to know you. Have you anything to drink?"

From his saddlebag Harwell produced a chased silver flask and offered it to Mirko, who took a long swallow, then another.

"Like your name, this is unfamiliar to me, but pleasing enough, though it is not as strong as our *rakija*."

"It is called whiskey."

"Whiskey, then. To your long life, Auberon Harwell," and he drank again, offering the flask back to Harwell. "Will you give me your boots?"

"What?"

"Your boots. I would like to have your boots. They are very grand. Surely you can get others in your country? Or perhaps you have others in your luggage?"

"No, that is impossible. They are a present from my mother." Here Mirko nodded in sympathetic agreement.

"Your mother. We shall drink to her, and to mine." And they drank.

"Perhaps you would like to keep the flask?" asked Harwell. "It belonged to my mother's family, but I do not need it."

Mirko considered the flask. "No, alas, I have no place to carry it, as you can see, and it would be a pity to melt such work down into silver. Perhaps you should give me money." Harwell regretted his haste in putting the pistol away.

"Do you need money, then?"

"Need? Perhaps not for myself. But I must go to Kotor, and the Austrians may ask me for money, for bribes. It is a very expensive place for us."

Harwell felt his face flush, prickling in the damp mist. "You have not told me your business there."

"And I have not asked after yours, out of courtesy. But let us say that anything you give me will preserve the freedom of Montenegro. The English are great lovers of liberty, I think."

Harwell unbuttoned his coat with his free hand and extracted two notes from the inner pocket. He had no idea how much money he was giving away, for he kept his eyes on Mirko. It felt as if it might be two five-pound notes. He hoped it was not more than that.

"Thank you," said Mirko, crackling the new paper appreciatively. "Go slowly, and may God go with you. Farewell." He released his grasp on the bridle.

"Goodbye," said Harwell, and when the Montenegrin stepped away from him into the fog, he realized he could see nothing beyond his mare's ears, neither the wall to his left nor the edge of the road to his right. Slowly indeed. The mare would know the way.

He had lost track of the number of turns, but there could not be many more, and the air grew colder now as the crepuscular fog darkened into evening. The mare did indeed know the way, and seemed calmed by this new responsibility, for Harwell had let the reins fall slack, and neither checked her nor urged her on. With her head lowered, she walked deliberately up what Harwell prayed was the middle of the road.

Suddenly the vapors of the bay vanished, or rather Harwell rode out of the top of the cloud and was dazzled by the evening star and the intense violet-black sky surrounding it. Behind him, to the west, was a curious blush as the sun sank behind the fog and the sea. In a little while the waning half-moon would rise, and he would have all the light he needed; even now he could see the blanched gravel of the road well enough to urge his mount on a little faster.

But the mare would not move. He should have known something was wrong by the set of her ears as he was admiring the starry prospect. She snorted, sidestepped, turned in a sharp circle, and seemed inclined to go anywhere, even off the edge of the road, rather than farther up the mountain. Harwell, sweating from his exertion, dismounted in a fury, and only then caught the cloying stench. He listened to the silence ahead, then clucked to the mare, who allowed him to lead her.

The dark shape on the white road must be a horse, and as soon as Harwell could see that, he knew also that he was walking in a shallow stream of blood. He stepped closer to the rock to get away from it, and there against the wall was another dark shape, though smaller. Both his horses now were fidgeting, trying to get away from the reek of blood, and so Harwell had some difficulty lighting his match. If he let slip the rein and the lead rope, God only knew where the horses would end up.

He barely glanced at the horse, having foreseen that long, clean slice across the belly and the trampled mass of entrails. The poor brute must have died in terror of its own blood. What he wished to see was the man's face. He had no illusions that he might still be alive.

The knife had made a clean job of the man's neck, but that did not explain the corpse's expression, a rictus of lunatic glee. Harwell's only other experience of death was a Latin master who had passed from this world to the next in mid-conjugation, chalk in hand, a peaceful event. But what a fool he had been, making jokes about his adventure with Raymond, or asking Lord P if he would be in any physical danger. The old man had smiled, meaning perhaps you will find it if you want it. He felt humiliated as well by the courtly badinage of that villain who was now in Cattaro, spending his money, or nearly there and warmed by happy anticipation.

The corpse was well dressed, but not English, a reassuringly foreign face with heavy features that seemed unused to such expressions of hilarity. With time enough and light, he might have found other clues, even though the papers would have vanished with the money. He dropped the match and led the horses on a few paces, then remounted, trying to think what he might have done differently, what lesson there was to be learned in all this. His despairing conclusion was that he had been foolish and fortunate.

Now the road flattened perceptibly, leading along a narrow col with the land dropping away on either side, and Harwell knew the pass was near, for he could feel a breath of wind cold on his face. He looked back and saw that the afternoon's vaporous cloud had vanished altogether, and the waters of the bay spread north and west far, far below, with the Adriatic a blackness beyond the headland. The lights of Cattaro, such as they might be, were hidden from him.

When he was through the pass, and the terrors of the ascent shut away by a sudden turning in the road, Harwell's heart lifted, in spite of the cold, for there beyond him was the landscape that he could never have imagined, still and whitened by the light of a low moon. Around and away as far as he could see stretched a colorless wilderness of rock bent and teased into fantastic forms, unrelieved by any mantling of dark forest. A monotony of rock, he thought, trying to define it, and more like a vast, frozen sea, some fable of an Arctic traveller, than any mountains he had seen. He wondered if by daylight the rock would reveal some subtler colors, and wondered also if he would be able to find words to express the excitement he felt in a letter to Raymond.

The wind was gone now and the cold, airless and palpable as a garment, settled on him while he rested the horses. When he moved on, their shod hooves made a clear ringing on the stones. The road bent back to the left, skirting the rim of a sudden and steep valley, a *polje*, where he could just make out a different texture or shadowing that might be stubble or bare, ploughed land. In the spring, water would collect in this pocket of the karst and drain slowly, like a clogged bath, leaving enough soil for pasture or some hardy crop. The whole life of this land must be hidden away in such corners, he thought.

A dog barked below, and he saw a lightless house or barn there partway up the slope, its roof a dark symmetry against the rock. He urged the horses ahead a little faster, but from the sound of the dog he knew it must be angling up the rocky hillside to cut off their arc on the road. The barking did not sound angry, or particularly menacing, but he wanted no company. He wanted a warm bed and a good dinner.

The dog was a small, indeterminate thing with white markings that fairly glowed in the moonlight, and it seemed to think the horses were a great adventure offered up by the night. It barked, not savagely but playfully, and made for the heels of the packhorse, which bucked once and bolted ahead, tearing the rope from Harwell's hand. Words of command and fine Anglo-Saxon curses had no effect whatever, and at last Harwell rode the mare straight at the dog, hoping to frighten it. He would shoot it if he had to, if he could hit such a target in this light.

But it was all a game to the dog, and before Harwell quite knew what was happening, the dog had darted into the jumble of rocks at the side of the road and was a stone's throw behind him, chasing the poor packhorse into the night. He heard barks and a terrified whinnying, then nothing at all.

He found the dog lying in the road, panting, waiting for the game to begin again. The packhorse lay motionless where it had run off the road, probably catching its leg somewhere in that treacherous ground. In his despairing fury Harwell dismounted to fetch the dog a great kick in the ribs, and so sent it yelping back down the hillside.

Perhaps, he thought, it has hit its head and is stunned. But when he lit his match he saw that the horse was watching him without making any effort to get up or even to move, and that the right foreleg had broken with such violence that a splinter of bone showed there. The horse's breathing made slow jets of steam in the night air. He cursed, then caught his tongue, knowing that he would only succeed in alarming the injured animal. "Good boy," he said, "good boy." Then he unholstered the pistol, cocked it, and shot the horse in the head. Now he could curse to his heart's content.

The mare stood where he had left her, and consented to be caught. He tied her reins by the long lead to the dead animal, giving her enough rope so that she could forage in the stones for whatever grass grew there. Seeing her eat, he realized that he was himself hungry, starving, in fact, and so he sat on a cold rock and finished his chicken and drank the last of the whiskey that he had nearly given away. He would attempt nothing in the dark, for he would need light to sort his things and decide what must be left behind, and light to pack what he would take on the mare. He would sleep now.

He took the saddlebags as a pillow, and made himself as small as he could inside his coat. In an hour or so he crawled over and settled himself against the belly of the dead horse, which was still warm.

Chapter Three

THE TOWN OF CETINJE drowsed in a midmorning sun that promised spring, a hope that only yesterday had seemed impossible. For two weeks the cruel bora had held the town in its grip, and though the snow was gone, that damp and penetrating wind made any excursion an agony. And yet, thought Lydia Wadham, surveying the bare, freshly raked yard of the Ženski Crnogorski, the Girls' Institute, and yet there will soon be flowers.

Miss Wadham was not given to staring out the window, and was quick to discourage any such tendencies in her pupils. The class proceeded much as it usually did—today an oral exercise in the irregular verbs and their troubling parts—and most of the dark heads were bent over the desks as the girls chanted in unison, "He goes, he went, he has gone . . ." But the window was open, and although Miss Wadham tried to listen for any slurring of the words, she was distracted by that breeze, confusingly warm and cool, that grazed her cheek and made her wonder what might bloom in this unfamiliar land.

Last spring . . . Well, there had been no spring for her in the damp confines of the Bible college in Birmingham, only the endless anxiety of her studies, letters from her mother chronicling the slow failure of her father's lungs, and the depressing sights and smells of the dormitory, which housed nineteen other plain, earnest women more like herself than she could bear to think about. The funds for the missionary work in Macedonia had also failed: there was vague talk of a decline in collections and of unfortunate investments, but her father, in the last letter he was ever to write to her, told her flatly that the money had been stolen and with it his hopes for her; and had she not by an extraordinary coincidence seen the notice for this position in a yellowing newspaper, she might now be a governess to someone's brats, or living with her mother in Kidderminster, and taking in sewing. At least in Kidderminster there had been roses, and springtimes back beyond the great divide of her father's death that seemed to have no care other than the naming and cutting of flowers. It was too cold, surely, for roses in this place, real English roses, but there by the fence the green fingers of crocuses broke the crust of soil, and in the corner was a budded bush, leafless still, that might be an azalea. The very thought of flowers made her flush with pleasure, and she remembered . . .

"*Englez . . . Englez . . .*" She thought at first that the words might be coming from behind her, a murmuring in the classroom, but when she turned abruptly she saw only the tall Petrović girl, second cousin to the prince and very conscious of that fact, staring back at her, or past her, a slow smile taking possession of her face. The other girls fell silent one by one and took to staring out the window, following the example of Zara Petrović, who now spoke in slow, faultless English.

"Miss Wadham, please look. He comes. Your countryman has come."

Miss Wadham was astonished by this perfect phrasing from a pupil who had given no signs of absorbing anything at all for the past several months, and by the meaning of the words. She turned again, trying to ignore the giggles and shuffling of feet behind her; and because the Girls' Institute had been a gift to the people of Montenegro from the empress of Russia, and necessarily splendid, its windows were tall, and wider than the span of her arms, so that she and her pupils had an excellent view of the strange spectacle in the road.

The yellow-haired man leading the horse was unmistakably English, even if he had not been surrounded by a handful of boys, urchins really, proclaiming this fact at the top of their lungs. His face at this distance seemed young, but the shuffling gait was that of an old man . . . Perhaps he was hurt? The cut of his coat, the weary reserve in that face, even the gesture of impatience he made when the boys came too close to the horse's heels, all this seemed so familiar to her that she could not keep herself from pushing wide the windows and calling out to him.

"Do you need help, sir?" And then, because he seemed not to hear her clearly above the din of the boys, she called out to them in their own language: "Stop it! Leave him alone! You are a disgrace to your country!" He turned then, a great smile lighting his face in the sudden quiet of the street, and she repeated her question to him.

"I must find the Grand Hotel, if you would be so kind."

"At the end of this street, on the left. It is the only one. Do you need a doctor?"

"Thank you, no . . ."

"Would you like to come in?" She had no idea what had come over her.

"You are too kind, but I think for now, the hotel. Thank you for your help. You are English, I believe?"

"Yes, English."

Here the boys, who had fallen silent at her command, pointed at her and chanted: "*Engleskinja . . . Engleskinja . . .*"

"Give them no money. The boys, I mean. I . . . Good day, then."

As she was shutting the window she heard one of the girls whisper, again with quite creditable pronunciation, the absurd phrase "She loves him."

The bathtub was of puzzlingly minimalist dimensions for this land of giants. The men Harwell had encountered on his slow progress up the wide main street of Cetinje had all been of nearly his own height, some taller, though none as broad as Mirko. They were dressed in little red jackets with gold buttons, and long, colorful tunics, bound at the waist with bright sashes that held an arsenal of pistols and knives. They regarded him gravely, nodded to him in their black-and-red caps. If he walked slowly enough he could more or less hide the limp, but he felt as if he were walking on coals. He saw no women other than the English girl in the window of that curious stone building on the outskirts of town. What on earth could she be doing in a place like this?

The water was cooling now, for the tub was of galvanized metal and not a proper porcelain one, though the wooden rim was neatly fitted. He found that by propping his feet upon the wall he could submerge his torso, and he luxuriated in the heat on his back and shoulders. He had soaked his feet—the water had taken a tinge of pink—and then washed them with the brutish brown soap supplied by the Grand Hotel. He looked at them now, livid and puckered from their long immersion, and at the quite remarkable set of blisters. How long, he wondered, before he could wear those boots again? or take up his journey to the eastern frontier? What mad vanity had prevented him from changing into something more convenient when he was shifting his belongings from the dead horse? Well, there were worse places than this old hotel to spend a few days. He soaped himself lazily and thought again of the English girl leaning out the window. Why had he not asked her name? He wished that he had seen her face more clearly.

"*Topla voda!*" The bellow at the door of the bath took Harwell completely by surprise, and without any further ceremony a dwarfish woman dressed in black barged in and dumped the steaming contents of her basin into the bath. "*Dobro?*"

"Yes, it is good," he managed to say, trying to cover himself with his hands. "Thank you. *Drago mi je bilo.*" In fact he resented extremely this interruption of his gently erotic reflections on the English girl. The water was excruciatingly hot, and he shifted his weight to mix the scalding layer with the rest.

The woman paid no attention to his nakedness, but was very upset by his feet, and particularly by their placement on the panelling of the wall. She seized his leg, muttering to herself all the while, and bent it so that his foot rested on the rim of the tub, then began to wipe the panelling. "*Ne . . . ne,*" she said, wagging her finger at him.

She pointed at his feet. "*Lekar?*" He shook his head: he did not need a doctor. She picked up his right foot, much the way he would have checked his hunter's foot for stones, and shook her head, muttering to herself an incomprehensible stream of syllables in which he caught only the word for "foreigner." She left the room, indicating that he was not to move from his bath, and returned a few moments later with a pot of purplish paste that she offered to apply to his feet.

Now it was Harwell's turn to say *"Ne . . . ne,"* as politely as he could manage in that language, and to promise, in words and signs, that he would use the valuable paste presently. And what time would dinner be served? Dinner would be ready whenever the English gentleman had finished with his feet.

Warm, relaxed, and freshly shaved, Harwell negotiated the narrow passageway and then the odd little staircase, taking it one step at a time to preserve his dignity. His dress shoes did not pinch his feet, and the salve seemed to have at least an anesthetic effect. A vigorous shaking and brushing of his coat had restored some of its elegance, but the repacking of his baggage in this morning's frost had been very trying, and the tails were undeniably wrinkled. He tugged at his white piqué waistcoat, mercifully uncrumpled, and stepped down into the lounge of the Grand Hotel.

He dined alone—a reasonable soup, followed by a bony little fish and a guinea fowl—but there were other guests in the dining room. In another corner, at adjacent tables, sat two grave gentlemen who were speaking what sounded very much like English. When he was finished eating, and wondering whether brandy would be medicinal or a mere indulgence, the waiter presented him with the card of His Britannic Majesty's Minister, the Honorable Sir Percy Foote, O.B.E. Harwell looked up and saw the florid little man gesturing to him.

"Mr. Harwell, it is my honor to introduce you to His Excellency Baron von Tripp, my Austro-Hungarian colleague, or perhaps confrère, in what we might call the diplomatic service of our respective countries."

Harwell bowed and shook hands with both men, observing that they seemed quite drunk at such an early hour of the evening, and the English diplomat particularly so. He sat and accepted a glass of brandy. He had planned to pass through Cetinje and on to the Sandžak of Novi Pazar without disturbing Sir Percy in his conduct of official business, and certainly without answering informal questions on the nature of his own.

"You are already something of a celebrity here, Mr. Harwell, perhaps in spite of yourself."

Harwell made a deprecating gesture and cleared his throat. He hoped this was not true.

"You must forgive our curiosity," continued Sir Percy, "but our proper European guests, here in this little tinderbox of the Balkans, are few, and they tend to travel by carriage or even the occasional automobile, but not by foot, and not leaving a trail of baggage and slaughter in their wake."

"The man," Harwell began, not sure if it was wise to respond at all, "the man was already . . ."

"Of course he was dead already. Englishmen do not go about cutting people with knives, like foreigners. I was merely pulling your leg." Sir Percy laughed merrily; the baron did not even smile.

"The deceased was an Austrian national," he interjected in excellent, sour English. "We will be looking into the situation, and perhaps you will be making a statement to the local authorities." Harwell sighed, and the British minister filled his glass, spilling a quantity of M. Ragnaud's formidable cognac on the cloth.

"Come, sir, we are not on official business here. This hotel is neutral ground, as it were, and Mr. Harwell is our guest. Perhaps we should hear what plans he has made for his stay in Montenegro; perhaps he will write a colorful novel of his experiences in Prince Nikola's land."

"I wish it were in my power to do such a thing," replied Harwell, "but writing is beyond me, I'm afraid, and I am here simply as a traveller, or a tourist, as the fellow in Kotor put it."

"But, my dear fellow, if you are a tourist you must have taken the wrong ship in Trieste. You could have gone to Venice, or anywhere on the western shore of the Adriatic, or Corfu, and found paintings, and gentle landscapes, and such food! Tell me, my dear Baron von Tripp, have you ever eaten the scampi at the Danieli in Venice?"

"The scampi," the baron reflected, "yes, the scampi."

"Here, you see, we do our best, and I think the Grand Hotel is all very well in its own way. A first-rate second-rate sort of place, wouldn't you agree?" Sir Percy covered his mouth, and belched.

"The guinea fowl surpassed my expectations: it was much better than what I ate last night, and probably a good deal better . . . better than the food elsewhere in Montenegro."

"Certainly better than in the wilder regions."

"Wilder regions," echoed the baron. "Too wild for Europeans, I think."

Harwell smiled weakly, and shrugged. "Do you gentlemen dine here often? I would have thought . . ."

"Ah!" The baron drew himself up straighter on the banquette, interested in the conversation for the first time. "You are wondering about the propriety of our arrangement. You have only to look closely, and you will see that the ministers of Great Britain and Austria-Hungary are not, in fact, dining together." He pointed at the half inch or so that separated the two tables, and ran his finger along it for emphasis. He smiled at Harwell. "Everything is quite correct."

"Impeccably so," agreed Sir Percy. "It does sometimes happen that we encounter one another here on a Tuesday evening, that being our respective cooks' night off, and we play a game of chess before dinner, sometimes a game afterwards. I never win at chess after dinner. Joachim, have I ever beaten you at chess after dinner?"

"Never. Not even a draw."

"Sometimes our colleague the Russian minister comes as well, but he sits at your table, so that he cannot even be suspected of dining informally with us. We do not invite him to play chess with us, because neither of us can beat him. Over there, just within earshot, I should imagine, are two minor Italians who show up whenever we do. We rather suspect that they have been sent to mind us, hoping to catch us in an indiscretion of some sort. Is that not our opinion, Joachim?"

"Yes, and it is my further opinion that this slender information is retailed elsewhere, to the Porte, for example, where they are desperate for news of Turkey's neighbors, and even"—here the baron's voice dropped almost to a whisper—"even to the palace here. That man will stoop to anything. We pay him entirely too much money, and for what? I have told Aehrenthal this myself."

Harwell's mind fretted back and forth over questions he could not pose. The man was surely Prince Nikola? He hoped his face was a perfect blank.

"But we have strayed from the subject of your own interests in Montenegro." Sir Percy raised his glass to Harwell. "You were going to tell us, informally, of course, what brings you here."

"I am told that there are some quite astonishing works of art right here in Cetinje, at the monastery, frescoes, icons . . . ?"

"Sadly, no. Your Baedeker overlooks, or treats with discretion, the fact that much of it was burnt or carried away by Mahmut Pasha, the last uninvited Turk to visit Cetinje, in 1780-something. But only a few years after that he paid the price, with his own head. *That* object you may certainly see at the monastery, if it interests you."

"The head? A hundred years later?"

"I assure you they take such trophies very seriously here. More permanent than captured battle standards, in a way, and infinitely more impressive. There's the Orthodox church at the other end of town, you may have seen it on your way in, and round it they have a quite impressive railing made of captured Turkish cannons, from 1858 and '67, and whenever they have a dustup, that's where they put the fresh heads. I confess I haven't checked lately. Mahmut Pasha Busatlija, though, is too valuable an item for public display, and so he is kept at the monastery. An icon, if you will."

"I had no idea . . . I mean one hears of it, but tends to dismiss it as ancient history, along with impalement and other such . . ."

"Barbarities. Yes, well, it is an interesting place, but not altogether civilized. Not yet, and perhaps not ever. In any case, you will want to see the fresco of the Blue-Eyed Christ at Morača, and perhaps the Dormition of the Virgin at . . ."

"I thank you, Sir Percy, but although I may stop at the monasteries for lodging, and will perhaps look in upon the Blue-Eyed Christ, I am hardly an expert." Harwell thought there was less damage in establishing his ignorance at the outset.

"No frescoes? No icons? What then, my dear Mr. Harwell? What on earth could make this trip worth your while?"

Harwell cleared his throat. "I am particularly interested in flowers."

It had gone pretty well. Or well enough. Harwell was applying more purple medicine to his feet and trying to remember, through the fumes of more brandy than he could possibly have intended to drink, exactly what he had said. His feet, though alarmingly discolored, no longer hurt him. He regarded them solemnly. "I look like a blue-footed booby," he said aloud, then louder still: "I *am* a blue-footed booby."

He had been lucky, once again. Sir Percy's knowledge and interest, apparently encyclopedic on all other points, failed him when it came to the flora of Montenegro, and Harwell's readings in Haworth allowed him to stay two steps ahead of Sir Percy in the matter of saxifrages, their distribution, and the possibility of undiscovered, or at least unclassified, species in the high karst region or the Brda to the east. The baron had grunted at the mention of flowers, as if he could not believe his ears. Quite exactly as if he could not believe his ears.

Harwell rose and hobbled over to the bed, leaving curious tracks on the pale wood floor, then on the little carpet. He rummaged in the untidy mound of his belongings, trying to find Haworth's volume. He wished to check and see if there really was a plant named *Saxifraga dalmatica*, as he had alleged earlier in the evening. The Haworth was nowhere to be found. He would look again in the morning.

The conversation had been by turns shocking, provoking, and even humorous, but always interesting. Sir Percy was clearly no great admirer of the mercurial Montenegrins—"an unstable people" he had called them—and their precious history of five hundred years' resistance to the yoke of the Ottoman Empire he dismissed with an impatient gesture as chronic discontent. Here the baron had supplied the helpful phrase "Jacobinism of the *Untermensch*."

One of Harwell's disadvantages, laying aside his inexperience and the awkwardness of trying to conceal much of what he *did* know, was that as the evening wore on—they never did get to that second game of chess—he had more trouble saying what he meant, even remembering what he meant, and in the organization of his thoughts. Harwell, in short, had got drunk, while Sir Percy and the baron, having already arrived at that plateau, carried straight on through the second bottle without any apparent effect.

Harwell listened to his host with all the patience and deference he could muster, but brandy tended to bring out an argumentative streak in him. Raymond had once told him this (and he had disputed it, aware that he might be falling into some sort of logical trap). At one point he interrupted Sir Percy and demanded to know why the Montenegrins should not be regarded as heroes and defenders of the faith for their gallant resistance when all the other lands between the Danube and the Bosporus had submitted to the Turks?

Sir Percy, taking no offense, observed that *their* faith was not exactly *our* faith, in point of fact, and the Turks were, in their own way, godly enough. As for heroism, it all depended on what one had to lose. Sir Percy invited Harwell to keep his eyes open as he travelled. Whereas the Christian populations, the *rayahs*, of Bosnia, or Serbia, or Macedonia lived in relatively fertile lands that supported agriculture and industry of a sort under any ruler, here they lived on rocks, *ate* the rocks for all he could see, and fought among themselves until the Turks tried to organize their affairs, at which point they became patriots and heroes.

Moreover, and surely Harwell could see the point, one had to be a realist, had to recognize that the world divided quite naturally into rulers and those who were ruled. That was the way God had ordained things, and that was the way the world had worked since the beginning of time. The Turks, for all their regrettable excesses and personal vices, were rulers. The Austrians had their own noble traditions of empire (here Sir Percy touched his glass to the baron's). And could Harwell, as a loyal subject of the Crown, overlook the obligations of empire, the ruler to the ruled, and vice versa? The Montenegrins fit very awkwardly into this universal scheme. They had proved to be quite worthless as subjects, and they were now well and truly independent, God bless them. But it was only common sense to recognize that they would be even more hopeless, more dangerously chaotic, on any larger scale, and the sensible policy was to contain them in their barren mountains, to discourage any notions of empire. Empire? One had only to glance at the map, said Sir Percy, to see that the Sandžak of Novi Pazar, the northernmost finger of Turkey-in-Europe, was all that divided the Montenegrins from their brothers in Serbia. *Sandžak of Novi Pazar* was a curious designation, was it not? Like having to say the *Duchy of Devonshire* at every turn. Quite emblematic of the inefficiencies of Ottoman administration. Fortunately, this bit of real estate was now in competent hands. The baron smiled and inclined his head graciously in Sir Percy's direction.

This was an awkward turn for the conversation to take, and even if Harwell could have sorted out his opinions on the rights and wrongs of empire, on the rights of man and the nature of liberty, he would have had to do so without any mention of the Sandžak, or Montenegro's expansionist fantasies, or the determined and self-interested Austro-Hungarian resistance to that expansion. Quite a hopeless task, even for a sober Auberon Harwell. How he wished that Raymond were there to dissect the rhetoric of this soft, simpering little man and the taciturn bully on whom he fawned. But Raymond was not there, and so Harwell made excuses for his feet and retired, having accepted an invitation to dine two days hence at the newly redecorated British Legation.

He sat now at the writing table and took a sheet of the hotel's paper, a shade of blue that tended towards the color of his foot medicine. He would summon Raymond, or invoke his presence, or at least punish him gently for not being here where he was needed, rather than arguing the subtleties of boundary waters and fishing rights at The Hague. He wrote.

The Grand Hotel
Cetinje
26.ii.1908

My dear Raymond:

It is quite late, and I am not entirely sober, and although it is not so cold as it was, there is a wind tonight driving rain against my windows and making the upper stories of this quaint hostelry creak and groan in a lively manner, so that you might almost think your correspondent were old Bulwer-Lytton and not my humble self.

I shall tell you two facts about this astonishing country that will amuse you. The first is that the chief literary work of the principality—in fact it constitutes practically a national anthem—is an heroic song entitled Gorski Vijenac*—The Mountain Wreath—by a former ruler, one Peter Njegoš, a prince or a bishop, I forget which. His subject is an event that occurred on Christmas Eve sometime in the early 18th century, when the God-fearing Christian Serbs of this place rose up and killed every last one of their Mahometan brethren who refused to accept the cross. This, as who should say, cleansing, is coyly referred to as the Montenegrin Vespers, and Njegoš's poem is pretty well the modern equivalent of the* Chanson de Roland. *Grown men bellow verses at each other on every occasion, and behave as if they cannot wait to have another crack at the sons of the Prophet. To duplicate this sensation in England, one would have to imagine a Tennyson, of royal blood, writing with approval and at tremendous length of the persecution of the English Catholics when they were hung, drawn, and quartered at Tyburn.*

Beyond the improbability of such a poetic creation you must conceive of mothers—yours? mine?—reading such ghoulish stuff to infants in the nursery, and old Jowett setting the Balliol scholars to learn its thousands of lines by Michaelmas term and to Hell with Pindar, Homer, and that lot.

The second item, on a lighter note, is that at the most recent convocation of Prince Nikola's notables of the realm, the minister of finance, seized, perhaps, by the spirit of Njegoš, delivered his entire address on the upcoming budget in impromptu blank verse, which met with approval, and even applause.

Before you form too absolute a notion of the conditions of life in Montenegro, before you book passage to join me in my quest, I must tell you that I have not witnessed these things with my own eyes, and am relying on reports from a source that I should not name, and whose deeply conventional opinions may have colored any facts that he . . .

Harwell laid down his pen. He found it difficult to be both amusing and discreet at the same time, and wondered whether it was wise to include a word such as "quest." For all he knew, his letters from this place would find their way to the desk of Sir Percy, perhaps Prince Nikola. He was too tired to finish the letter now: his mind would be clear in the morning. And if he were to go for a walk, the weather and his feet permitting, a description of the severed heads on the church railing would make a fine closing flourish to his letter.

He pushed the pile of his belongings over to the far side of the bed and crawled under the covers. He dreamed of sunlight, cascades of tiny, bright flowers issuing from the warm rocks, and snakes.

Chapter Four

AS ALWAYS, when required to dress for an unfamiliar occasion, Lydia Wadham worried that her best might fall somewhere short of the mark. She had been invited to the British Legation twice before, and had certainly worn this black silk on one of those evenings, feeling then, as now, that being so plainly dressed had the effect of calling attention to herself, though of the wrong sort. Lydia had no string of pearls as did the glamorous Princess Vera there, also dressed in black, and surrounded by interesting men from the various embassies and legations. But then, she reflected, her own dear father had not been a prince.

She did not really enjoy coming to this place, grateful as she knew she should be, and she did not enjoy the company of Sir Percy Foote. She was here tonight, she knew, because she was the one marginally acceptable Briton available to Sir Percy beyond the legation staff, aside from Mr. Grout, that insinuating little man who occasionally turned up and brought the smell of his tannery with him. Her tenuous connection with the empress of Russia, patron of the Girls' Institute, probably enabled Sir Percy to overlook her other liabilities. She could only hope that she would not be seated by him at dinner.

After exchanging some pleasantries on the coming of spring with the kind, tedious Lady Foote, Lydia had made her escape from the

Russian minister, who overwhelmed her with his enthusiasm and strong breath. She was alone now, which was her usual fate at these gatherings, and she recognized this as her own choice. The making of small talk was unbearable: the world had not offered her a sufficient store of lighthearted subjects to be touched on and then forgotten. But as a silent observer, without the distractions of conversation or male admiration, she had a clear view of the room—a gaudy little bandbox, hung in swags of yellow and blue cloth that clashed with every other color there—and of everybody in it.

The Russian and Austrian ministers, she noted, stalked the periphery of the gathering like great black birds of prey, never once encountering each other. They reminded her of figures on a cuckoo clock, one forever doing the precise opposite of his counterpart. Such silliness, she supposed, was part of their job: if Russia advances, Austria must withdraw; if one signs a treaty with Montenegro, the other must court its enemies. Sir Percy—she had learned this much in the few months of her residence—was inclined personally towards the Austrian position, and towards the Austrian minister himself, with whom he was said to be on intimate terms; but on this occasion the host of the party observed a strict neutrality, and he was now calling for more champagne for Mme Veliganov. But the center of interest was undoubtedly the wife of the French chargé d'affaires, Mme de Mercure, whose rich peals of laughter and daring décolleté compelled one's unwilling attention. The name was as implausible as the bosom, thought Lydia, closing her eyes and blushing at her own boldness.

When she opened her eyes again the French woman was still there, now gazing up in seductive mockery at a tall young man who blushed crimson to the roots of his pale hair. Lydia recognized him as her Englishman, her countryman, and sympathized with his distress. That ghastly woman. Still, he must learn not to stare. She was about to approach him, rescue him from his situation, when the prince's equerry intervened, and led him to where his master stood. Lydia moved to a point just beyond their circle, where she could hear what was said.

She had not noticed Prince Nikola before. He was dressed not in the ceremonial costume of the Montenegrins but in a plain black coat, perhaps out of deference to his host, and whereas the equerry stood tall and striking in those flowing colors, the prince seemed aged and diminished, rather like an unhappy stuffed animal. He greeted Harwell, holding one hand behind his back.

"Welcome, Mr. Harwell, welcome to our country and to our capital," said the prince, in English. "I am sorry that your arrival should have been marked by such awkward circumstances, but I have a surprise for you." And from behind his back he produced a book, which he held out to Harwell.

"Your Highness is too kind. I was certain I had lost this volume in . . . on the mountain." Harwell opened the book, which was somewhat the worse for wear but intact. An illustration of the *Saxifraga ferdinandi-coburgi* shone forth as bright as any silk.

"May you never be parted from it again. And now, Mr. Harwell, may I introduce you to Miss"—the equerry whispered in his ear— "Miss Wadham."

Lydia, surprised by the prince's attention to her, and at last confronted by this elegant young man, stared stupidly at him. "Mr. Harwell," she managed at last, "do tell me how you came to be so interested in flowers."

It happened, through the kindness, or pity, of Lady Foote, that Lydia Wadham was seated beside Auberon Harwell at dinner. And Harwell made a display of his botanical learning for her sake—for he had quite thoroughly digested the information in Linnaeus and Waldstein, and would apply himself to the serendipitously restored Haworth; he described his meeting with the renowned traveller and plant hunter Reginald Farrer, a friend of the family; and while he was telling her all this she was trying to make connections between such plants as he hoped to encounter, imperfectly described, and those which Draško had told her would blossom here in Cetinje, or in the high karst to the west, or in the mountains away to the east, the Brda. She had only Draško's word for these marvels, and so she asked Harwell if he would be so kind as to let her look at his books.

Harwell would be only too happy to do so, would bring them, at her convenience, to . . . was it a school, that imposing stone building? She had a certain charm that comprised both diffidence and boldness, and he was impressed with what she knew about the land and its language. It was very pleasant to speak English with this sympathetic young woman, even if there were broad hints of Birmingham in her voice; and if she was a less commanding presence than Mme de Mercure or the local princess, there was an attractive intelligence in her eyes and a flattering persistence to her questions.

The clatter of the dinner went on around them, and Harwell tried briefly to make conversation with the very deaf lady on his left, who spoke only German. But in addition to her advantages of youth and language, Lydia had a sense of humor. When he described his ordeal on the Lovćen road, his brush with death at the hands of a highwayman, he let slip the name, and a slow smile built on her face.

"I assure you I do not exaggerate. The fellow up the road was dead as a post."

She did not doubt his word in the least, only . . . only that Petrović was the name of the ruling dynasty in Montenegro, and Mirko, the prince's late uncle, its most celebrated warrior, victor over the Turks at Grahovo, et cetera. To claim such an assailant, did he see, was rather like boasting that the Duke of Wellington had burgled his house, or run off with his hat.

And she had actually laughed—a very pretty sound—at his whispered suggestion that he might find severed heads on the railing of the church. That was surely Sir Percy pulling his leg. No heads at all? No, the prince was quite firm on that point. Whatever private thoughts Nikola might have on the practice, this was to be a European capital, and such trophies would impede progress on all other fronts. Of course, out and away from the capital, on the frontier, life was different, and there, perhaps, he would find . . .

"You have been there, then?"

"Where?"

"The eastern regions, towards the Sandžak of Novi Pazar?"

"No. Gracious, what a thought. Quite a wonderful thought. Only my mother would suspect that I spend my time travelling in such exciting places. Unfortunately, I am bound to Cetinje, and to my indifferent scholars."

"Perhaps you would be a better explorer than I, with your command of the vernacular and the history. Once you have read my books, I could send you in pursuit of the saxifrages and I could stay here to play chess with the diplomatists and be the object of their gentle mockery." Harwell was not used to making jokes with young women, or proposing such flights of fancy. He hoped that he had not made an improper suggestion. He blushed.

Lydia pressed her advantage. "When you come, I mean if you would be so kind as to bring your books to me, I would be able to introduce you to a girl, a most cunning child, whose family lives just there where you are going."

"Where?" His perfectly stupid question coincided with a lull in the dinner conversations, and to prevent Lydia from answering he grasped her hand under the tablecloth and squeezed it.

"In the farthest reaches of the principality, Mr. Harwell, and sur-rounded, no doubt, by botanical treasures."

In the afternoon of the next day Harwell arrived at the Girls' In-stitute with his three books under his arm, having taken an indirect route in order to see the Orthodox church and its railings with his own eyes. How could he have been so gullible as to take Sir Percy's nonsense seriously?

The books were laid out on Lydia's desk in the schoolroom—there was the window where he had first seen her—and the child was sent for. She was twelve years old, he guessed, and cunning indeed, dark and straight and solemn. Her brows formed a single delicate line to frame her eyes, and her long, elegant hands seemed to embarrass her. She was named Natalia Pekočević (how would he ever keep track of such names? Well, it sounded something like "Peacock"), but that was practically all he learned by his halting, ungrammatical, and necessarily indirect inquiries, until Lydia told her that the En-glish gentleman would be travelling in the direction of her village, and would wish to carry a good report of her to her father, her mother, her brother.

Then he could scarcely stop the flow of information, and had to ask Lydia to help him negotiate this torrent. Yes, she lived in the farthest corner of Montenegro, at least three days from the capital, and so close to the border that in fact it ran right through the middle of their farm, and Papa was angry about that, and would fix it some-time soon now. And was it in the mountains where her parents lived? Yes, just on the edge of the mountains, overlooking the gentler land below, which was better for growing things. Did they have neighbors? Not so many, only Turks or Albanians. And there were flowers? Yes, many flowers, though perhaps it was still winter there. But when it came time to plough, and she drove the oxen down the road to the field, the ditches would be full of flowers, although she did not know their names. And if he was interested in flowers, her brother Toma would show him where the different kinds grew, or would take him up into the mountains to hunt the goats, or away to the burial places of the old religion. Here he looked inquiringly at Lydia.

"The Bogomils. An interesting heresy."

Harwell, his head full of questions that could be neither asked nor answered, listened patiently while the child recited the name of every last animal in the family's possession, including some already deceased. Then Lydia stood and put her arm around Natalia's shoulders, and spoke in English.

"I am sure that Natalia wishes she could travel with you to show you these things herself, but she also wishes to be a scholar, and for that she must stay here with me, and study. Off with you now." When Natalia was gone she added: "A most unusual family. I have met them only briefly, but Draško knows the whole history. You must ask him."

Harwell himself departed soon afterwards, leaving in Lydia's care two of his three precious books. He would return, of course, to fetch them.

They sat in a violet dusk, the tea growing cold in the cups, and for what seemed like many minutes now, measured in heartbeats, not a word, not the rattle of a saucer had broken the absolute peace of her little sitting room. It was not that they were at a loss for words: they had found much to say this afternoon, both before and after the departure of Mlle Belinskaya, Lydia's colleague and almost friend who had been invited to preserve the decorum of this occasion, and had soon perceived her hostess's true desire to be left alone with her caller. What harm could come of it, Lydia asked herself, glowing in the contemplation of that question. Who would even know? Now they sat, gazing on the bright squares of the window while, beyond, a thickening light fell from the mountains and filled the stony plain of Cetinje. She had lived here for six months and had never seen a comparable light; and in all the twenty-four years of her life she found no frame of reference for her feelings just now.

"I suppose I should be going." Harwell shifted his weight carefully in the armchair—it was a modest thing in proportion to his oarsman's frame—so that he did not have to look over his shoulder to catch the spectacle of sky. He had been unnerved by the expectant silence, and, having broken it, regretted the words.

Lydia smiled to herself at his awkwardness and knew that there was no force behind the words. He did not want to go, she knew that much, and yet the possibility that he would stand, brush the crumbs of cake from his trousers with those huge hands, and disappear into his adventure in the east . . . this thought turned in her like a blind knife. She had, on many occasions in the past several months, found herself wondering at the force of habit: why it was necessary to hold her fork the way she did, or tuck her hair into her cloth cap at night. Why now it seemed necessary to Mr. Harwell to propose the one thing that neither of them wanted him to do.

The thought of what she ought to do, and what he ought to do, and what possibilities arose if they paid no attention to these considerations, this thought made her heart beat faster with a thrill of dread and anticipation, and so her hand stole to the crevice in her settee and drew forth the waxed packet of dark Turkish tobacco and the little papers. He seemed to be a man of secrets, and now he would know hers.

Her fingers were practiced, and she was wetting the paper with her tongue to secure the cigarette when he glanced at her and realized what she was doing. The expression on his face was fleeting and involuntary. "You will not be offended?" He shook his head, demurred, but she knew he had never seen a woman smoke before.

On that day in late autumn, a cold and sodden day when she had forced herself to take a walk towards evening, after having waited hours for the weather to clear, she had entered the grounds of the Institute by the back gate. She was miserably wet and practically immobilized by the wind and cold, because she had not paid attention to the road, had confused one path with another there in the shadow of Mount Lovćen, and it was practically dark by the time she recognized the now familiar chimney pots. Ordinarily, she would have walked around to the front of the building, but the little gate was there at hand, the one the servants used in their comings and goings, and so she passed through it and followed the wet stones around the corner of the gardener's shed, from which there emanated a crack of light across her path, and a deliciously unfamiliar smell of tobacco.

She pushed the door open just far enough to see inside, where the gardener, a leathery man with sad creases in his face, was exhaling a plume of smoke in satisfaction over his pots of freshly divided chrysanthemums glowing there in the lantern light. Their eyes met, and she knew at once that he was afraid of her, for his hand started towards his mouth, as if he would have hidden the cigarette. She closed the door behind her—there was a blessed stove in the corner as well as the lantern—and filled her lungs with the happy combination of tobacco smoke and the scent of bruised chrysanthemums. She pointed at his cigarette.

"What do you call this?"

"*Yenidje*," he said, and handed the glowing stub to her.

This was the beginning of their friendship. The Girls' Institute, he explained, had very strict rules for the conduct and moral improvement of its charges, and the absolute disapproval of alcohol and tobacco, unambiguously stated in the charter of the empress of Russia, had been extended to cover the staff and servants of the Institute by its current director. At the mention of this official, the difficult and determined Mlle Petrovna, the gardener made a dismissive gesture and Lydia Wadham responded with a conspiratorial smile. The gardener, hoping to secure himself in this exposed position, rolled her a cigarette of her own.

Of course she had never smoked before, and she coughed explosively at her first efforts, until the gardener showed her how to take just a little of the fragrant smoke and draw it in with a full breath. This was not the local tobacco, he said, but pure *yenidje*, from Turkey, the only true gift of the Turks to his people. She did not understand much of what he said at first, but she had an ear for languages, and had learned a fair amount of Greek before the mission plans evaporated. In time, over many cigarettes, he told her about this country and about his work, giving her the names of flowers she could not hope to see for months, and the names of heroes who had been dead for centuries. And at last he had purchased for her in the bazaar her own supply of the *yenidje*.

Lydia offered the cigarette to Harwell, who took it from her and put his lips where hers had lately been. A cloud of sudden smoke wreathed his head, as if this thing were a cigar to be reduced by manly efforts, not inhaled carefully. She would teach him.

"May I make one for you? It would give me the greatest pleasure." And although he did not particularly want to smoke just now, he nodded his head in agreement, willing, anxious, to see the pearls of her teeth and the tip of her tongue in this exercise. When she was finished making his cigarette, she lit it with a match and drew once, so that he would see how it should be done. Then she rose to light her lamp and to set out a small dish of spirits of ammonia, which would, in a few minutes, obliterate all traces of the smoke, and preserve her secret.

Surveying the fine jet of smoke he had made of the last of his cigarette and feeling just a bit light-headed, Harwell suddenly remembered his books. They were right there on the table, and he had not noticed them for the past two hours.

"I wonder, Miss Wadham . . ."

"Lydia, please. You were going to call me Lydia."

"Lydia, then, most willingly. I was going to ask a favor of you."

"You have lent me your books. What could I refuse you?"

"Two favors, perhaps, if my credit is so great. First, I have some baggage that I must leave behind, items that would be worse than useless where I am going, and I am not sure that I should trust my belongings to the hotel."

"They would be quite safe with me."

"Thank you. And the second thing is . . . I have a letter, quite an important letter, and I would like it to go to England without delay and without . . . well, in all security. I gave a letter to the captain at the hotel the other day, and he looked at it with the most undisguised curiosity. Perhaps you could enclose this in your next letter to your mother?" Lydia took the envelope from him.

"What an unusual color."

"Not what I should have chosen for myself, but beggars . . ."

"And this Lord Polgrove must be a relative of yours, then?" Harwell flinched to hear the name spoken aloud. Before he could find the words to respond, Lydia had reached for a book, the Linnaeus, and opened it to show the bookplate with Polgrove's name written there. "It is a wonder that anyone would lend so valuable a book to be sent on a journey such as yours."

"He is my patron, so to speak, certainly no relative."

"A famous man, in his own way."

"Famous?" Harwell felt the color draining from his face. "I would not have thought so."

"Unless I am mistaken, there was an article about the alpine collection of this same Lord Polgrove in the *London Illustrated News* about a year ago, perhaps more. Is there not some extraordinary feature, a newsworthy feature to his collection, a mountain of some sort?"

"Of course, the Matterhorn, or a scale model that must be thirty or forty feet high. The head gardener told me that his lordship insists on doing the planting himself, even on the highest elevations, where they secure him by ropes and pulleys. I have never seen the thing in bloom, but it must be quite a spectacle."

"It was most impressive in the photographs. Forgive my curiosity, my undisguised curiosity," she added, her eyes cast down.

"Your most welcome curiosity," he said, and took her hand.

"Before I forget, Mr. Harwell, Auberon, I have, by the greatest coincidence, a letter for you. It arrived only this morning, enclosed in a letter to me from Mr. Baxter, the one person in our missionary organization in whom I should place any confidence. It seems that your doubts about the mails here are quite widely held."

She handed the second book to Harwell, with a cream-colored envelope stuck into the flyleaf. His lordship's hand was, unfortunately, thoroughly distinctive. Harwell slipped the letter into his pocket without any comment other than his thanks.

She walked with him to the door, through a dim hall that echoed the absence of the scholars, who were now safely at their supper. She went out into the night and looked for stars.

"You will be cold."

"I do not mind," she said, taking his hand. "Where will you sleep, when you leave Cetinje?"

"Under the stars, I expect. It is a little warmer now, thank God, and I have already borne the worst that Montenegro has to offer. I am told one gets used to sleeping on the ground."

"And for food?"

"Well, as the good Sir Percy has observed, this land abounds in monasteries. Surely they will not turn away a man in need, particularly if he can pay for his supper. And I have bought a fowling piece. Quite an extraordinary weapon, if I can puzzle out its operation."

"Ah, if only . . ." She was glad that he could not see her face.

"Only what?"

"If only women could have the adventures that men can have. A horse, a pot for tea, and a fowling piece, nothing more."

"You make it sound like a story with a happy ending, whereas in fact anything might happen. My horse could break its leg, or I might have my throat cut by the Duke of Wellington, or be bitten by a snake."

"Exactly so. I'm afraid it sounds quite irresistible." She laughed nervously, embarrassed by the turn the conversation had taken. Her unspoken thoughts put a silence between them.

"May I write to you from where I am going, asking this same favor of you?"

"Of course you may, only you must write to me as well, a true letter, or I may burn the other out of spite. You will tell me what it is like there where little Natalia lives, and send me sketchings of the flowers, the ones that are not good enough for Lord Polgrove, or the ones you have spilled water on." And feeling him standing there, not touching her, but so close that she could sense the heat of him through her thin dress, she added, "And yet I will not have seen these things for myself. Could you not take me with you? I would . . ."

"You cannot . . . You have your . . ."

"I have nothing. There is nothing for me here that matters to me at all."

Hearing the agitation in her voice, the edge of hysteria, Harwell took her in his arms. There she shivered against him, then reached up to pull his face down to her hot mouth.

"Take me with you, I say." This she whispered into his shirtfront, gasping for air. They kissed again, enveloped in an intimacy that astonished them both. His hands found the lobes of her ears, the rich forest of hair at the nape of her neck. Her arms stole around his waist beneath his coat, and he shivered once in that cool circle of her flesh.

A noise at the side of the building startled them: possibly the banging of a shutter. Standing back from him, straightening her hair, she felt the true chill of the night. What would he say?

"I leave tomorrow, or perhaps the next day. Your offer stands?"

"Offer? Oh that, yes, of course. I thought you meant . . ."

"No, Lydia, it is impossible. I cannot take you with me."

"And can you so easily leave me behind?"

"No, no. I mean . . ."

"Go then, if you must. I shall be here."

"Good night. Perhaps I shall see you before I leave."

"Perhaps. Good night."

After her supper, as she was brushing her hair and preparing for bed, Lydia placed her hand on her neck where his had lain so briefly, trying to imagine what it felt like to him. Only one other man had kissed her, a divinity student who had also just smoked a cigarette. She remembered that taste of tobacco, but everything else was different. Everything. Perhaps he would not leave her behind after all.

Chapter Five

ON A BRIGHT, WARM DAY, under a sky the color of cornflowers, Auberon Harwell rode out of Cetinje, headed west rather than east, on a circuitous route that must take him past the Girls' Institute. Last night's gentle rain had confirmed the arrival of spring, and in every field and garden plot a pyre of plum branches smoldered, filling the air with a sweet haze that put him half in mind of his childhood, of the deep days of summer, when hornets guarded the ripening peaches, and of winter, when the hollowed drum of some fallen fruit tree burned in the nursery grate. And yet, as he rode with this freight of pleasant memories, he marked the utter strangeness that surrounded him, whether in the whitened rocks that waited for him beyond the town, or just at hand, where the fires were fed by bent women muffled in black, and his passing noted with no countryman's wave or muttered greeting but the blank appraising stare of unshaven men on ladders who paused from their work with those great cruel hooks.

Harwell rode alone, leading an ass that had been his last purchase in the market of Cetinje, and the subject of a prolonged negotiation punctuated by impatient gestures on the part of the Greek merchant, and many cups of thick, sweet coffee. The ass was a forgiving beast, and had stood for hours in the stable yard of the Grand Hotel while

Harwell struggled with the canvas and the rope, trying to fit his expanded cargo onto that meager back. It was his own patience that gave way first, for he prided himself on his knowledge of knots, and yet even he could see that his succession of bowlines, half hitches, and hand-over-hands was inadequate to this task. At last the hostler had taken pity on him and showed him how the awkward, lumpy load might be secured by long diagonals of rope that came together in something that resembled no knot he had ever seen, a loose, four-cornered arrangement that would yield to any motion of the pack or the ass and yet not slip. He had tipped the hostler handsomely and salved his pride with the thought that he had at least chosen well: here was an ass that would be bitten to death by curs before running onto the rocks.

The ass now followed willingly, if slowly, and paid no attention to the puddles in the road which his mare took pains to skirt. One part of Harwell's mind was devoted to the bright surface of the world on this fine midmorning, while another, deeper part wound and rewound the ropes in the hostler's intricate pattern. He was concentrating on this mental exercise to such a degree, and trying not to succumb to doubts that he could repeat this marvel tomorrow, that the Girls' Institute seemed to rise out of the very stones at the side of the road and surprised him in the blinking of an eye. The mare came to a halt, as if she knew the reason for the circuitous route Harwell had chosen.

In his breast pocket Harwell had Lydia's note, now several days old, and when he shifted his weight to dismount he was reminded of that presence by the rasp of paper against cloth. The letter had been written in the wake of his abrupt departure from the Girls' Institute on that starred evening, written in that same spare sitting room, before caution or second thoughts could slow her pen.

The thoughts had tumbled from some deep place in her, with such a power of feeling that the words and sentences seemed inadequate vessels to contain such meaning. "Forgive my directness," she had written by way of apology, "but I have no experience in these things; and while I know that women ought not to behave with the freedom that is allowed to men, and that forwardness in matters of the heart is taken for immodesty, still we are not in England, and that is my excuse. I can imagine myself at Kidderminster, and your coming to call there: what a civilizing and constricting power would reside in the furniture of that room, in the smell of the roses, in the rattle of a cart on the cobbles, not even to mention the presence of my mother! I would be all blushes and maidenly reserve, and the idea of offering you a cigarette, much less lighting it for you, would strike me dead in my chair. But here we are on what feels like the very edge of civilization, of the known world, and there is more excitement, more freedom in such a place than if I lived three lifetimes in Kidderminster. The great adventure is yours, and the danger which goes with it. If I were to go with you, the danger would not matter at all, but the idea of not knowing where you are and how you are seems unbearable." She told him how it felt to receive his kiss, and how his back had warmed her hands under his coat; she said that their parting, following so suddenly on her discovery of a bliss that had transfigured her, was like a physical blow; she described the room in which she sat, now dark and empty, but resonant still with the pleasures of his presence, lighted by her memories of that afternoon which would remain with her always. And she told him that there were other thoughts besides, which could not be committed to paper, but must wait and be whispered to him when next he held her. Let that moment be soon, if he had any feeling for her, or even pity.

The letter had arrived when Harwell was breakfasting in the Grand Hotel, and he had read it hastily while the mutton chop cooled on his plate, and then again, slowly, with a second pot of coffee. He felt the flush in his face, and was glad that there were no other guests in the dining room. To calm himself he asked for the local paper, *The Voice of the Montenegrin,* and spent the next half hour struggling with two paragraphs about the rumored construction of a Montenegrin branch of the trans-Balkan railway, from Belgrade to the Adriatic, straight through the Sandžak and Montenegro. There was a phrase there that might mean Austria and Italy had guaranteed the financing of this project, subject to the sultan's approval, or that they had been asked to guarantee it. This would be an important distinction, certainly in the eyes of Lord Polgrove.

He had returned to the hotel late in the day, after an excursion to the market, where he encountered the knowledgeable gardener Draško, and then a brisk walk to the heights behind the monastery where the tomb of Danilo, the prince's unfortunate predecessor, lay open to the elements under a curious stone cupola. He called for a bath, and when he had made himself thoroughly comfortable by planting his much improved feet on the panelled wall, he read Lydia's letter yet again, taking care not to wet the pages. He read it very deliberately this time, remembering the smell of her hair when her head was pressed to his chest, and the tickle of fine down on her neck. He thought of himself as a man of the world, and had just enough experience with women of a certain class to make such a claim plausible; but of a thinking, feeling being whose ardor might match his own he had no experience at all. The combination of the warm water and the thought of those things she could not bring herself to write created an urgency in his loins such as he had seldom known. There, that hand might be hers, and that feathering, wondering touch . . . and so he surrendered to his pleasure.

The mare was not fond of standing still, and she signaled her impatience by a tossing of her head that sent sprays of foam into the sunlight, for she also worried the bit in her mouth. Harwell scanned the building and grounds for signs of life and found none until Draško appeared around the corner, pushing a wheelbarrow full of manure. He nodded to the visitor and set the barrow down next to a bed of freshly turned earth near the gate.

Where were the scholars, asked Harwell, staring at the blank window, and where was the English teacher? A holiday, replied Draško, a holiday for everyone but himself, and they had all gone off up there—a wave of the hand in the direction of the snowy peak of Lovćen—to celebrate the feast of the empress's patron saint. Even the cook had the day off. Did the English teacher know he was coming? Draško's expression hovered between grievance and concern.

"No, no, she knew only that I was leaving soon. I myself did not know the exact day." Thus Harwell absolved Lydia of any blame in this matter; but he did remember writing her a note—a pale and shallow response to hers—in which he fixed this morning as the likely date of his departure, and made a small joke of hoping that she would again protect him from the ragtag and bobtail. Had he found a way to put his own feelings into words, words that flowed on the page, trembled there as if they might leap into the reader's eye and heart, might she not have found a way to excuse herself from this alpine picnic?

Perhaps it was better this way after all. He would need all the hours left in the day to reach the river, and he knew that any conversation between them, even one conducted in broad daylight, must revive the subject of her impossible offer, her . . . well, her scandalous offer. Was this why he had not found time to call on her again, though there was much he could have learned from her yet about this land and the one beyond?

He had made good use of Draško, though he was quite sure the gardener had been sent to find him in the market, and had spent one afternoon in the stable yard of the Grand Hotel, showing him the engravings in Lord Polgrove's books. He had noted which species Draško knew, either as shown on the page or with slight variation, such as a darker eye to that dianthus, or a woollier stem to the androsace. And when he came to a particular kabschia saxifrage, named for that German princeling most loathed by Lord Polgrove, Draško made a gesture, throwing his hand at the mountains to the east, and repeating, "But red, red, much redder than this."

Draško stood before him at the gate now, stood straighter and taller in his role of host-by-default, and rolled himself a cigarette. When he had lit it he blew a plume of arrogant smoke in the direction of the building. "Will you leave word for the English teacher?"

"Tell her, please, that my baggage will be delivered today from the hotel, and that I am sorry to have missed her. Tell her also that I will soon write to her, a proper letter." Draško nodded approvingly at the thought of such a letter. "And thank you, Draško, for your help, and the kindness you have shown me."

"My help and my knowledge are small compared to your journey. Danilo Pekočević will be as a beacon in that darkness. If you find him, all will be well with you."

"Until we meet again, goodbye."

"May God keep you in his hand."

The sun glared off the white rocks as the road climbed through the karst formation to the east of the capital. Harwell had no dark spectacles, and when his head began to ache he had to ride with one hand shading his eyes, an awkward maneuver, as that same hand held the ass's lead. He stopped once to look back at the town, a patchwork of tile roofs and greening fields in the wilderness of rock, and noted its vulnerability to any enemy that might penetrate this far into the territory of the Montenegrins. "Free men in their own minds, but in fact slaves to geography," Sir Percy had said of them. "An army of children could take such a place." Harwell had no answer to that, then or now.

When the mare staled, and then the ass, Harwell was reminded of his own need, and he dismounted to unbutton his flies. At that moment, with his mind perfectly concentrated on this simple animal task, the army of which he had lately thought appeared to him as dots of color descending the far flank of Lovćen. That would be the school party, returning from the expedition, the celebration of their saint. One of those dots, a gray or a black one, no doubt, would be Lydia Wadham. He buttoned his trousers in haste, though the procession was so very distant, and laughed at his own clumsiness. Would his binoculars show him Lydia? No, for by the time he found the case and focused the glasses, the party had vanished into a dark swath of conifers, and did not reappear.

This is foolishness, he said aloud to himself. He remounted and rode on, and in a short while he crested the valley wall, and the plain of Cetinje was shut away behind the white rocks.

The road now began a long descent through a landscape gentler and more fruitful than the harsh plateau of the capital. The fields were broader and no longer hemmed in by rock, and in the untilled pastures goats and even a few dwarfish cows grazed among brilliant archipelagoes of violets, daisies, and aconite. He saw a few people, mostly women, bent over their tasks in the fields, and from the shadows of rocks at the verge of the pastureland, shepherd boys eyed him insolently. Ahead of him somewhere lay the town of Rieka, the winter quarters of the royal family, which he would skirt if he could. There was nothing here that would interest Lord Polgrove, nothing that was not already known to him.

With his mind lulled by this pleasant and unremarkable landscape, and by the motions of his mount, Harwell thought again of Lydia, of the suddenness of their mutual discovery, and the botched timing of his departure. Nothing was settled between them, although her note had begged him for some clear sign. Was there, in fact, anything to be settled?

There was a girl in England, whose parents were known to his, and because they had suffered together the awkwardness of hunt balls, where they had worn hand-me-down clothes, and the boredom of Sunday dinners, where his father and hers had talked of sheep dipping and the depressed price of wool, they knew each other well enough to exchange the occasional letter. He had kissed her, more than once, and even felt what might be her breast beneath several layers of cloth and some discouraging whalebone. Her letters were nothing like the one he carried in his breast pocket. They were the sweet musings of a schoolgirl, deliberately sweet, for her mother had probably told her how to write them, and he imagined that if he received a letter from her twenty-five years hence it would contain nothing but these same enthusiastic and inconsequential reflections. It had been made plain to him, by many indirect signs from his mother and one carefully scripted lunch with his father, that marrying this girl would be a very acceptable project.

He had no feelings towards Daphne, pretty as she was, even beautiful, and pleasant, and rich. "Let us not forget rich," said his friend Howard, playing the devil's advocate. "What shall I do, then?" asked Harwell in the anxiety that enveloped him following the conversation with his father.

"I think you would come to resent deeply any advice I might give you on this point, Bron, and so I choose not to compromise our friendship. I might be wrong, in any case." Howard, whose idleness, backed by the immense wealth of the Cecils, had assumed Olympian proportions since he had come down from Oxford, found only amusement in his friend's confusion. "But I perceive a duty to help you decide the matter one way or the other. Either you love her, or you don't."

That night, following a performance of an Oscar Wilde play in the Haymarket, Howard had entertained him to an excellent supper, and then taken him to a certain house near Shepherd Market said to have been frequented by the Prince of Wales in his sporting middle age, and what happened there confirmed Auberon Harwell in his confusion.

They were received by three young women in a sitting room with pretty chintz fabrics and Turkey carpets, a room lit by gas and a log fire, for it was already November and they had come in out of a cold rain. After the first bottle of champagne the gaslights were extinguished, and there was only the illumination from the grate, which fixed certain details of the proceedings in his memory and imagination as if they had been branded there.

One of their hostesses was so immediately familiar with Howard that Harwell guessed at some prior acquaintance, and it was Kate's cheerful forwardness, and her singing voice, that overcame Harwell's reservations.

"Sing for us, Katie," suggested the tall girl seated on Harwell's left, whose features, in repose, had the aspect of a beautiful artifact.

"If you please, Katie," added Howard. "It would give us all such pleasure to hear you."

Kate, having drunk a good deal of the second bottle of champagne, obliged with ballads of the west country, sung in a clear, low voice that hinted at glories and powers inappropriate to such simple tunes, then with certain songs of a bawdier nature which made even Harwell smile, and, finally, with a hymn, shockingly beautiful in that setting, the more so as she was gently unbuttoning Howard's clothes as she sang.

"Enough of music now," said Kate, pouring more champagne for Howard, "or we'll all fall asleep before the fun." And with that she pulled Howard to his feet and then knelt before him. Reaching into his unbuttoned trousers she coaxed forth his manhood, and left it swelling idly in the firelight to Harwell's fascinated and horrified gaze while she reached behind her for the champagne bottle. "No secrets between friends," she whispered to her audience.

With a few practiced strokes of her hand she brought Howard to a state of bursting readiness, then rolled back the foreskin and blew on the glistening flesh. From the bottle she poured a sudden, careless draught of champagne which drenched his sex and puddled on the carpet below. Howard's indrawn breath was a loud noise in the silence, and when she took his entire sex in her mouth he cried aloud. With her nose and cheeks pressed right to the dark opening of his trousers, Kate shook her head like a terrier with a rat, then withdrew to contemplate her handiwork through half-closed eyes.

Howard staggered and might have fallen had Kate not risen to steady him. She bent to whisper something into the ear of the girl to Harwell's left, then she led Howard away through a door to the side of the fireplace.

Harwell had never experienced or witnessed such a thing, knew of it only as one among a multitude of fabulous and perhaps physically impossible acts whispered about in the bathhouse or the darkened dormitories of his public school. He had been told, more lately and on more reliable information, that prostitutes, if one paid them extra, would do that for one as a kind of distasteful favor.

With Howard and Kate gone, Harwell experienced a tidal pull of reservation and shame that might have extricated him from this room, this house, altogether, had he not been compromised by the disarray of his own clothing. The girl on his left had kissed him once on the mouth and then set casually about the task of unbuttoning the pearl studs of his shirtfront. The small, dark girl to his right, hardly more than a child, he would have guessed, had unbuttoned his flies, and her hand now played teasingly, knowingly, with his exposed parts. There was something curiously old and young about her face as her lip curled in concentration, or when she lifted her eyes to smile at him. The graceful dark brows, the darker eyes, the unfamiliar planes in her face: a Gypsy, perhaps.

The one on his left caught his nipple deliberately between the nails of her thumb and middle finger, held him there until he made a little sound, then offered her finger to be kissed. "Stand, now, Ariana," she said, "and take off your clothes."

Ariana turned her back to Harwell and indicated the row of hooks and eyes there with a pretty, shy gesture over her shoulder. He unfastened them carefully, his hands curiously calm, and when she stood she was naked except for her garter belt and stockings. Her legs, and the curve of her buttocks and back, limned in the firelight, made a deep impression of beauty, of animal grace, on Harwell's mind, and when he later tried to order the events of this fantastic evening in his memory, this one image was always the point of departure and return.

The other girl, whose name he never learned, ordered him to kneel before Ariana and kiss that violent bush of black hair. When he had done this, and felt Ariana trembling in his cupped hands and against his mouth, he was told to stand and remove his own clothes. He obeyed, for that level, unsmiling gaze unnerved him, and she ran her hands approvingly over his body, as if checking the conformation of a horse.

They left the sitting room by another door, and Harwell found himself in a sparely furnished chamber just cool enough to raise goose bumps on his flesh. There were devices here that he had never seen before, and to the simplest of these, a stout wooden frame that filled one end of the room, his wrists and ankles were fastened so that he stood like the spread eagle. The tall girl slapped him once on the buttocks and took his stones in her cool fingers, while Ariana knelt to perform a gentler version of Kate's trick.

He was conscious only of Ariana's mouth, all his being centered there, and when the other hit him with a switch across the back of his legs, he cried out in surprise.

"No," he said, trying to control his voice.

"Yes" was the rejoinder, and she eased the tip of the switch between his legs, tapping him lightly there where she had caressed him. "Yes," she said again, and held a glass of champagne to his lips.

He was beaten then, not as hard as his housemaster would have done, but with infinitely greater imagination. And while this continued Ariana held him and soothed him, sometimes climbing him as she might an oak to press her cheek to his and her cool body to his fire. In this she was artful, for while she often grazed his shaft with her arm, or cheek, or belly, the touch was momentary, and he was not allowed to enter her or spend himself.

They gave him more champagne then, and Ariana put her hand on the nape of his neck while she held the glass. The other, whose clothing was in perfect array, kissed him again on the mouth, a lingering and suggestive kiss this time. She took a netting that hung from a hook and attached its other end to the far wall, adjusting it to hang just at Harwell's waist. Into this sling, a kind of hammock, she secured Ariana by the wrists and ankles, so that she, too, was a prisoner.

The slightest pressure on the hammock brought Ariana's sex, spread wide by the positioning of her legs, into an instant of shivering contact with his own, and Harwell strained forward against the ropes. He watched then as those elegant hands played with Ariana's body, making her tremble or flinch. Ariana panted, her head thrown back against the breast of the girl behind her, and when the hand that had been foraging between her thighs was presented to her mouth, she kissed it, then bit the fingers.

At last Ariana was presented to Harwell as a kind of offering. Long white arms stretched the length of Ariana's torso, the white hands gripped her hips, raised them slightly, and so impaled her slowly upon him. There was a moment of stillness, during which no one drew breath, and then the gentle rocking of the hammock achieved a perfect, weightless friction which he hoped might last forever. In those few minutes, or seconds, before the cataract of pleasure took him, Harwell found himself looking into the eyes of the girl standing behind Ariana. A half-smile played on those features, rapt and remote, and it was as if he made love to her, as if Ariana's willing body were an instrument of her desire, and his.

In the days and nights that followed, Harwell was not himself, forgetting to eat, spending long hours in his bed but sleeping little. He might have talked with Raymond—or he might not—but in any case Raymond was away in Scotland inspecting the fisheries. Letters from Daphne and from his parents went unanswered, and when he asked Mr. Bromfield if he might take a couple of days off, the solicitor replied, with more kindness than he would have expected, that the idea had merit. *Ogilvy v. the Beverston Hunt* had been dragging its way through the courts for eighteen months now, and a week's delay in Harwell's brief on soil compaction would hardly signify.

For two days Harwell haunted the alleys and arcades of Shepherd Market, became a familiar wraith to certain fruit sellers there, and an object of curiosity, then derision, to the streetwalkers whose route more or less mirrored his own. *Got it up yet, sir? Meanin' your courage, o' course.*

He took no notice of them, for their mockeries were gentle compared to his own thoughts. He was hoping to meet Ariana, however briefly, in a setting where light and air would dispel the memory of what lay behind that red door, which, however long he watched it, never opened during the daylight hours. A constable asked him what business he had on this street, and Harwell produced his card. On his next round the constable winked at him.

At last he found her, recognized her from behind even though she was wrapped in a woolen coat and a pearl-gray shawl, and he waited while she deliberated on the oranges she held in her hand. When he spoke her name, it was her companion, Kate, who looked around sharply at him. Her face in this light was older, her hair a less convincing shade of orange.

"Well, sir, a pleasure to see you again, I'm sure."

"I was hoping to speak with Ariana."

"Oh, sir, that's not possible, I'm sorry to say."

"I don't want anything from her, I just want to talk to her." It was as if they were discussing someone who was not present, for Ariana had stiffened at the sound of her name but still had not turned around.

"As I said, sir, it's not a question of wanting. She can't do it, and that's that."

"Is she foreign?"

"Foreign? Yes, sir, she's that, but it's not like she don't understand you . . . Oh, for the love of Christ! Show him, Ariana!"

Ariana turned then, and though her face was without any particular expression, every feature radiated a blank misery that struck him with the force of a blow.

"Open up, Ariana, and have done with it!"

She opened her mouth and he saw that she had no tongue, or only the ragged, purple stump of one lurking there beyond the brilliant arc of her teeth. She closed her mouth and watched his face until he had to look away.

"How . . . ?" he began, but could not get beyond the word.

"How? How would I know, sir?" Kate's voice had an edge of anger in it. "Maybe that's what you get for being foreign. But I'll tell you this: a man done that to her, and you can bet on it. Come along, then, Ariana. Good day to you, sir, and perhaps we'll be seeing you again, in business hours."

Harwell put his hand out to touch Ariana, whose eyes had devoured everything written on his face; and she, mistaking the gesture, seized his hand and shook it awkwardly, as if pumping water. When they had gone, the greengrocer asked if he intended to pay for them bloody oranges which he'd already gone and weighed.

Harwell's return to Mr. Bromfield's chambers was short-lived, for it was not long after this that he received the summons from Lord Polgrove and the offer of a very different kind of work, for which, he was assured by Raymond, God had set him on this earth. He finished the brief on soil compaction—the heavy weapon in Squire Ogilvy's contest with the careless patricians of the hunt—in a burst of energy that surprised both him and Mr. Bromfield. A month later he was gone from London, having written Daphne an awkward note to inform her of his suddenly changed plans, of the uncertainties of the future, et cetera, et cetera. Perhaps it would have been better, he reflected later, and kinder, to have further reduced this information to the simple truth that he would not marry her.

He would never marry: that was an even simpler truth that occurred to him as he surveyed these broad, sunlit orchards stretching away and down towards the plain below. His resolve was a closed door between himself and the nightmare of his last months in London, and if he would not marry, then he had no right whatsoever to lead Lydia Wadham on, to feed her hopes. And in order to insulate himself more surely from those hopes, he imagined a Sunday dinner in the long dining room at Newton Court, with his parents, and Raymond, listening in forced politeness to some anecdote of Lydia's, delivered in that accent that was not her fault, of course, but could hardly be ignored.

He reached the river in the long light just before the sun dipped behind the pass, and found a level, grassy area a few hundred yards north of the ford. He unsaddled the mare, and unpacked the ass, taking a careful last look at the ropes and the knot, then hobbled each with rawhide and the tiny bells he had purchased from the tinker. They could graze here to their hearts' content, and if they tried to make off he could find them in the dark.

A little farther up the river, where a slow bend encircled a marshy meadow, he took two teal with one shot from his fowling piece—it could hardly be called a shotgun—and found his way back to camp with the aid of that curl of smoke rising above the thickets of scrub. Smoke? He had not lit a fire.

He approached as quietly as he knew how, with the fowling piece cocked, and expelled a great breath of relief when he recognized that thin back and the jut of chin as Draško, who was busy feeding twigs into the blaze. "*Dobro veče*," he called out.

Draško rose and made his salutation, looking weary, as well he might, for there was no horse in sight, and he must have walked or run the many miles from Cetinje. He carried only a small bag slung over one shoulder, and when the fire had caught to his satisfaction, he drew forth a pair of worn slippers and put them on his bare feet, sighing gently.

"You wore no shoes?" Harwell was unable to believe what he could plainly see.

"I would not ruin them. Such a road . . ." Draško's voice trailed off.

"Why have you come?"

"The English teacher, Gospodjitsa Lydia, sends you her greetings," said Draško amiably. "She was wishing to see you, and to give you these things." And now he drew forth from the bag a small, bright kettle and a pouch of tobacco. Harwell turned each one over in his hands, not knowing what to say, and offered the tobacco to Draško, who shook his head. "After we have eaten."

Harwell dressed his ducks, taking care not to tear the fat over the breast when he plucked them, and Draško caught two trout with his hand in the dark water where the river undercut its bank. Cleaning his game was the extent of Harwell's culinary skill, and he was not sure how to proceed. Draško would know these things, surely, and so he laid out the various implements he had purchased in Cetinje and looked inquiringly at his companion.

Draško examined them one by one, making little clucking noises in his throat, and set them all aside in the grass, giving precedence to Lydia's kettle, which he placed on a rock in the middle, with a flower in its spout. The result looked like a shrine of some description, and when he was finished, Draško coughed and put his hand to his mouth to cover his smile. "You have salt?" he asked.

The fish was salted and set on a flat rock propped up near the fire, with the heads wrenched back over the top as a counterweight. The ducks, too, he seasoned, then showed Harwell how to make a spit from the thick green stems of the scarlet-flowering pomegranate, and how close the meat should be held to the flame. When the fat began to drip, he basted the fish with it, and went to the river to wash. The famished Harwell was left alone with his task, and the smell of the roasting meat set his mouth to watering. He distracted himself by holding the spit so that the drippings made fiery cascades, the droplets vaporizing and exploding even before they reached the live coals.

They ate in silence, first the fish, then the duck, burning their fingers on the hot meat and cracking the leg bones between their teeth when all else was consumed. Harwell made tea in Lydia's kettle, offering the mug to Draško and drinking his out of the pot. Then they smoked her other gift under the mantling of early stars.

The food, the tea, and the tobacco put Draško in an expansive mood that Harwell had not seen before, and they were talking of Draško's home in Herzegovina, that unhappy land, when Harwell shifted to put another branch on the embers of the fire. Draško stopped him with a little gesture of his cigarette. "There is enough light for us to see, and we want no guests."

"There is no danger here, surely."

"You would not think so, but this is a small country, so the enemy can never be far away. Everywhere you travel there is a story to be told of some great deed, or treachery, which happened in that place. Such things will happen again."

"Even here?"

"Did you see the automobile on your way here? They were German tourists, and their wheel was broken." Harwell had seen it, a vast cream-colored Daimler touring car in the ditch where the road branched off to Podgorica through a range of low hills. It was the only motor vehicle he had seen since he landed at Kotor, but he had not stopped, for he had no tools and knew nothing of the workings of such a machine. They, the Germans, had watched him ride by in the distance, and had made no sign, either of greeting or distress.

"I saw them, but . . ."

"Did you mark the thorn scrub on those hills?"

"I did not. Or I may have seen it and paid no notice."

"That place is called the Field of the Sultan's Felling, and two hundred years ago, when we fought side by side with the Russians against the Turks, the enemy ran away into those thorns and were caught there, so that we butchered them to the last man." Harwell could no longer see Draško's face, but from the tone of his voice it was clear that he was smiling at this memory, a scene which had come down to him through generations.

"It was a great victory."

"Yes, God was with us that day, and my grandfather's great-grandfather, along with his brothers, took twelve heads from the Turks in those thorns. Perhaps the victory was too great, for the sultan came back, in his wrath, with a greater army, and burned Cetinje."

"You are from a line of heroes, then. Have you fought against the Turks yourself?"

"Yes, I fought for my home and my people in the last war. We fought until we were told that the tsar of the Russias had made peace with the sultan. But my family had been killed, every one of them, and all the buildings burnt."

"And this is how you came to know Danilo Pekočević?"

"Yes, a hero among heroes."

"Will you tell me about him?"

Draško was so deliberate in the manufacture of another cigarette that Harwell wondered when or if his curiosity would be satisfied. He poured a little whiskey into the silver cap of his flask and passed it to his companion.

"To your journey," said Draško. "And to the confusion of your enemies."

"And to your safe return." Harwell took a pull from the flask. "And to the heroes of Herzegovina." He drank again.

"Danilo had no fear of any man, and wherever he went he was like the hand of God, slaying the Turks, driving them before him, even though we were few and they were many. They came to fear him, to know his name, because it seemed that he was everywhere, and could not be killed. And he wore the heads that he had taken into battle, tied by the hair or the beard to his belt, so that the Turkish soldiers would have to look on the faces of their slain comrades."

"There were many heads?"

"Yes, too many to count or remember. We were camped in the mountains, in a place that the Turks never discovered, at the mouth of an old salt mine. Danilo would cover the heads with the salt, like hams. He was very proud of them."

"And he was your leader?"

"He was. Even as a young man he had the cunning of his elders, and he seemed to know what was in the mind of the enemy. He was never mistaken about the Turks; only in his friends."

"He was captured?"

"No, never captured, they would never have taken him alive, but we thought they had killed him."

"And you were wrong?"

"We had surprised a Turkish column in a place of many rocks, and we had the advantage of the high ground. But the Austrians brought up their cannon in support of the Turks and rallied them. Their explosions brought the cliff down upon us and broke our bodies and our minds. We thought God had deserted us, and many of us fled that place. Danilo was wounded, not by the Turks or the Austrians, but by the mountain falling. I did not see it, and where he had been there were only the rocks, so I thought he was dead." Draško scratched at the ground with the tip of his knife, as if making a map that only he could read.

"When we recovered our wits—and I was no better than the rest, having turned my back to the Turks in that moment of terror—when we came to our senses and realized that we had left Danilo behind where the enemy might take his head, I knew I had to go back, whether the others would or no. And when I came near the rocky place I heard the sound of rifles, firing only occasionally, one of ours and one of theirs, for they had different sounds. Then the firing stopped altogether, and I asked myself how this could be, and thought perhaps the Turks were exulting in their victory, and perhaps defiling the bodies of our men with their own weapons."

"But Danilo was not dead."

"If not dead, as near as can be. A great rock had fallen and smashed his leg against another rock, so that he might have bled to death, but that he took his knife and cut himself free and bound up the stump with his sash. Then he drank some water and returned to fighting the Turks."

"I wonder that they were still there, if your men were all dead or . . . driven off."

"The rocks had come down on them as well, and on the Austrian gun crew. They were in shock, the ones that had not fled, and Danilo killed them all, one by one. I had heard the last of the battle as I drew near, and when I found Danilo, I thought he too might be dead, for the rocks were spattered with his blood, and he had fallen into a faint." Draško sighed at this memory, in which Danilo's heroism redeemed the honor of Montenegro.

"He must have been glad to see you. Surely he would have died without your help."

"Yes, and he came close enough as it was. Two days we stayed in that place, and I made him broth out of the flesh of a horse that had perished pulling the Austrian cannon. The Turks did not come back, though we knew they might at any moment. And Danilo made me promise him that if he died I would take his head and return it to his family, so to preserve it from the enemy."

"Take *his* head . . . ?"

"It is a point of honor among our people. Perhaps you take other things from the dead to celebrate your victories?"

"No. We take nothing, and we bury our dead."

"As do we, when it is possible. But we have a legend about the making of the world, and when God had made all the other countries he had only rocks left in his bag, and these he threw into a pile, which is Montenegro."

"So I have seen. But you did not have to bury Danilo, or take his head, and so he must be greatly in your debt."

"I think the debt is mine," said Draško softly. "In any case he was angry with me."

"I do not understand."

"It was almost a joke. I had to carry him, or bear his weight, as he had only the one leg, but he wanted to take the heads too, for he was proud of what he had done by the grace of God, as he should have been. And I said that I could not carry him and the heads, so we compromised on one head, that of an Austrian. Danilo liked to think that it was this man who had fired the cannon shot that brought down the rocks. It may be so." Draško yawned.

Harwell offered his companion another drop of whiskey and insisted that he take the second blanket. A warm wind was blowing from Lake Scutari to the south, and they would both be comfortable.

With his companion asleep, instantly and noisily asleep, Harwell made one more clumsy cigarette for himself and delighted in the endless succession of blue wraiths struggling in the smoke and disappearing. A metaphor for human existence, he thought sleepily, and when he inhaled on the cigarette the wraiths were banished altogether. He was very tired now, and he had just the presence of mind to check the fire and listen for the sound of bells against the background of river noises before he, too, fell asleep. The dew had already dampened his blanket, and thanks to the tobacco, which had put him in such an expansive and reflective mood, his last thoughts before sleep were of Lydia.

Chapter Six

THE DAWN DID NOT WAKE HIM, for in the middle of the night, when he pulled the sodden blanket closer around his shoulders, the fierce light of the stars had distracted him from sleep, and to blot out both the girdle of Orion there above his head and the crescent moon that hung over the Ottoman lands to the east, he had thrown his coat over his head. The sun was well up and beginning to dry the dew when he started at the clash of metal practically next to his head. The ass, with its hobbled feet planted in his collection of pots, stared back at him, chewing peacefully.

Draško was gone, and the blanket he had used lay neatly folded there in the grass. He looked around for the mare and had a moment's uneasiness until he caught the sound of her bell beyond the bushes towards the river. On the whole it had been a comfortable night, certainly in comparison with his ordeal on the Lovćen road, and he stretched now, letting the sun warm him where he lay. He surveyed the mountains to the northeast, trying to make out the course of this river, which he must follow for many miles.

He made his breakfast, using Lydia's kettle to boil water for a mug of tea, and in a small pot, somewhat damaged by the ass, he cooked maize meal with a piece of salt pork. He did not know, for he had never done this before, how much meal to use, or how much water, and the result was a porridge that hardened as it cooled into a rubbery brick, undercooked but not unpleasant in taste, that might last him for two days. He wondered, as he ate, what possible use those other utensils might be put to.

By midmorning the ass was packed and ready to travel. Harwell was satisfied that his arrangement of knots—a slight variation on the hostler's masterpiece—would hold pretty well, and at noon, when he reached a tributary stream where the main road bent northwest towards Spuž and Nikšić, he was pleased to find that only a minor adjustment was needed to silence the obnoxious clanking of his pots. The exertion of remounting the mare left him light-headed. The coarse porridge rumbled in his gut and the river water had a strange taste. He emptied his bottle into the stream and resolved to drink no more until he found a spring or could boil his water.

Across the ford, travelling nearly north now, he rode through a sullen little village and found himself surrounded by the ruins of what must have been a very noble town in antiquity. Duklé, his map told him, and in parenthesis Doclea, which he recognized, with a smile for the shade of his tutor at Oxford, as the birthplace of the Emperor Diocletian. There were signs here of excavations, none too recent, and Harwell rode in wonder past columns and the shell of a basilica with an inscribed architrave, saw paved streets leading right and left into thickets of coarse grass, and gave wide berth to a serpent basking on a mosaic pavement. He noted the thickness of the serpent, and the evil triangle of its head: a viper, no doubt.

A few miles farther on, the road, a much more primitive affair than the one he had left at the river crossing, rose up out of the plain over a series of low hills, and so into the gorge of the Morača. He had never in his life been afraid of heights, had delighted in scaling the modest peaks of the Cairngorms, and had accompanied Raymond on an expedition to the Swiss Alps. But never had he ridden a track such as this one, a narrow, sloping shelf nearly as steep as the wall of white rock that he could touch with his left hand. He thought at first that he must have missed a turning, but the dung on his path reassured him that horses had come this way before him. He would have dismounted to lead his animals, but he was so dizzy that he dared not.

He came to the mouth of a cavern where the road broadened out for a few yards in the darkness, and here he slipped from his saddle and sat with his back to a cold rock. He breathed deeply, to the mare's rhythm, trying to conquer the pervasive feeling of sickness that came on him in waves. A long swallow of whiskey cleared his head and made a fierce burning in his stomach. There, he muttered, hoping this was the end of it. But the hand twisting his bowels, for that is how he imagined it, would not release its grip on him, and so he sought out the darkest corner, where the stink of human urine was overpowering, and eased himself.

He felt better at once, though his own stench now filled the cave, and he made his way to a sunny rock and waited for a breeze. I am not the first to have so used this place, he thought, and it would be madness, and false modesty, to risk falling into the gorge. He smoked a cigarette, wishing that he had something to drink other than whiskey, and wondered how much farther it could be to the monastery. He was not ready to remount yet, or to face the narrow track, and so he sat and smoked, reflecting on his home, the life he had known in England, as if they were things half remembered from a dream, or parts of a story told to him in childhood. It was easier, in a way, to imagine what he had not yet seen, fantastic images fashioned out of what had been told to him by Lydia, or her pupil, or Draško. They were waiting for him up there, where the mountains, some of them capped with snow, reached up into that infinity of sunlight, and his life would not really have begun until he reached that place.

There was no one to greet him at the monastery other than a boy in a stained gray cassock and a peacock that the mare tried to kick. He thought the monks must be at their prayers, for the door to the church was shut. The boy would not answer any question, whether it was put to him in Serbian or German, but he did lead the mare and the ass away and brought tea in a badly cracked cup. Harwell waited there in the courtyard, gazing around at the rough-hewn archways and bell tower of yellow rock, conscious all the while of the boy's unwavering stare.

There was no place to sit. He was tired, tired and ill, and his thighs ached, for he had used his knees on the mare all the way up the gorge, keeping her every step of the way under his control, willing her away from the abyss. The ass, thank God, had followed sensibly, and he had never once turned in his saddle to check on it or the pack. But he had listened carefully, and held the lead lightly in his right hand, ready to drop it rather than be pulled off balance by a balk or a false step. He had not exactly prayed for his preservation, but had made the following bargain with some higher power: if the mare and the ass carried him up the gorge without event, he would reward them with as much grain as they could eat, and if none was to be found at the monastery, then he would let them eat his own maize meal.

At the sound of voices, singing voices, from the church, the boy inclined his head towards the closed door, and in a few moments the monks came forth, chatting to each other, some scratching themselves beneath their heavy black cloth, some looking off into that radiance in the west and sighing in satisfaction. Harwell remembered, through a haze of resentment at those enforced chapel services both at Winchester and at Oxford, how sweet this moment was, the issuing forth from church with the slate wiped clean for the moment, the benediction ringing in his ears, and there before him, waiting at the very door of the chapel, the bright sin and glory of the world. At such a moment as this, reading the stern, contented faces of these monks, he could wish that he still believed enough to go to church himself.

At length his presence was noted, or acknowledged, and a tall, black-bearded monk strode over to him and greeted him. In fact, they were all tall and black-bearded, but Harwell had his eye on this one, had perhaps been staring at him, because his bearing and the set of his features made him a brother or cousin to the brigand on the Lovćen road.

"*Dobro veče.*"

"*Dobro veče,*" replied Harwell. "I have come at an awkward time perhaps."

"There is no time that is better or worse than another, and because of the road, we are used to seeing travellers at all hours. Those who know it, however, will not travel in the dark, or in a storm." Amen to that, thought Harwell.

"And what is your country?" asked the monk. "You are perhaps German?"

"No. I am English, and my name . . ." At the mention of his nationality the silent boy muttered, "Ah!" and the monk slapped him hard across the face.

"*Dosta!*" The boy did not flinch at the blow, but lowered his eyes at the rebuke.

". . . my name is Harwell. I am glad to know that the child is not mute."

"He is not mute, but he is disobedient, and the abbot has ordered him to be silent until he learns our ways. His mother, my cousin, wishes him to devote his life to God." Here the monk crossed himself, then took the boy's face in his hand. "I am not sure if God wills it, or the boy either. He is Janko, and if he becomes a monk he will be named Sava. He may not speak, but he will be angry with you if you call him a child."

"And he thought I was German?"

"Yes. The Germans are great climbers of rocks, and they sometimes come through here on their way to the Tara or to the Rugovo Klisura. Montenegro has all the rocks that any German could want, but they are all spies in any case."

"I am not a spy."

"No, you are English, as you said, and the English come to dig up the past. You have come by Duklé? Then you have seen the work of your countrymen. We do not build as well as the Romans, but I will show you what we have, and in such a place as this, it is still pleasing to God."

Harwell wished greatly to sit down or, better still, to lie down and sleep, but he also wished not to offend his host, and so he followed the monk, Stefan, into the church, where there was just enough light from the western windows for him to make out the items that were shown to him: the fine fretwork of the choir stalls; the dark portraits on the iconostasis hiding the sanctuary; an old fresco of the prophet Elijah being nourished by a raven; and, in the narthex, where the peacock stood fanning his tail against the light of the open doorway, a more recent fresco of the Last Judgement and the Genealogy of Christ. It was here, looking into the blue eyes of the water-damaged Christ, that Harwell's strength gave out. He fainted, or at least began to fall, and was caught by the strong arm of Stefan, who helped him to his bed.

Harwell stayed three nights in the monastery, where he had intended to spend only one, and when he protested that he must get back on his road, Stefan laughed and pushed him gently back down onto the straw mattress, saying he would be a poor host to send a sick man out to fall off the mountain. From this Harwell guessed that the road ahead was perhaps as difficult as that which he had already travelled.

This was on the morning after his collapse in the church, and he admitted to himself that he felt worse rather than better after his long, troubled sleep. He now had a fever that made him sweat in the blankets that smelled so strongly of wood smoke. He dozed or slept most of the day, and when his bowels were seized again he was helped by the boy to a dank little shed over a hole, and the atmosphere there was so poisonous that he had kind thoughts for his cavern, with its breeze, and for that cigarette.

The boy stayed with him throughout the day, squatting with his back against the white wall, eyeing, but never touching, the rows of Harwell's possessions, which had been neatly laid out on the stone bench. When Harwell was woken by the fleas and began to scratch himself, the boy left to fetch straw and some wood, and set about lighting a fire in the corner with steel and flint. Harwell tossed him a box of matches and eventually, by signs, made him understand that the match must be struck on the side of the box. Because he held the match by its head, the boy's fingers were burnt when the match caught, but he made no sound and managed to light his fire. As there was no chimney in the cell, the smoke eddied slowly in the currents of air, almost suffocating him; but the fleas subsided, and he slept again.

When he woke, it was late in the afternoon, and he remembered his animals. "Janko," he said, and surprised the boy, who had just lit another match for his own delight and was absorbed in that task. At his feet were the stumps of a dozen spent matches, and he swept them quickly into the fire.

"Janko, is there any grain in the monastery?" The boy looked at him without understanding, then offered the box of matches. "You may keep the matches. A present. But have you any grain, any . . . corn, or . . ." He could not think of any other words, and the fever had thickened his tongue on those harsh consonants so that he barely understood his own speech.

When Janko made a tentative pantomime of eating, Harwell shook his head. He had no hunger, but the mare and the ass must be fed. Seeing the sack of meal against the wall, he gestured at it until Janko took it up. "I want you to take that to my animals and let them eat it, if they will."

With the sack held carefully in both hands, Janko backed out of the cell. Stefan came in a few moments later, with the sack in one hand and a bowl of tea in the other.

"You are hungry?"

"No, but my horse must be hungry."

"She has been fed, and the ass. Brother Petar has tightened one of the mare's shoes, which was coming loose. Did you not notice? In any case, there is nothing more to be done for them. Drink this."

Harwell did as he was told, and the strong, sweet tea made his stomach growl. Perhaps he could eat something after all. "I have food there. You are welcome to it."

Stefan looked in each sack, at the meal, and the rice, at the piece of salt pork, and at the dried *scoranze* from Lake Scutari. One of these he put in his mouth and chewed it, head, bones, and all. He lifted the lid of the pot that held the remains of breakfast from the day before and made a face. "These things would do you no good now. I will bring you soup. Tomorrow, when you are stronger, you will eat with us, for it is a feast day, and there will be meat. Fresh meat."

The monk stayed with him after he brought the soup, a strong broth of vegetables, and Harwell asked him about this place, how it came to be built of yellow rock in contrast to the white or gray rock that surrounded it. Stefan did not know why the yellow rock had been chosen, perhaps for its beauty, perhaps to mark this as a holy place in the karst. But he knew that the rock was found at Tuzine, which was a full day's journey away, and that the blocks had not been carried here, for there was no road, and not even a Montenegrin could travel the karst with such a burden. Each block had been passed from hand to hand, from hero to hero in a long chain of men that stretched from here to the quarry, in the days before the great defeat at Kosovo, when all this land was the kingdom of Zeta.

"The last Englishman we had here knew these things, had studied them in a book, and so I did not think to tell you before."

"Well, I have heard of Zeta, and the Nemanja kings, and Kosovo, of course . . ."

"Yes, but you are not a scholar of these things. You have no tools for digging up the old stones. And you are not a soldier, and you say you are not a spy. What then?"

Harwell drank the last of his soup, and pointed to the pile of books that had been unwrapped and laid on the stone shelf. "That is what I am, although I do not know your word for it. 'Botanist' we call it."

Stefan nodded, but did not touch the books. "I have seen them while you slept, but I can make nothing out of them. Perhaps we have no word for what you are, or what you do."

"You may call me a traveller, then. Tell me, have you heard of a man named Danilo Pekočević?"

"Who has not heard of Danilo? He is of the Vasojević."

"Can you tell me where to find him? I am hoping to be his guest. I have letters from his daughter in Cetinje." Stefan was silent for a moment, as if considering whether to give Harwell an answer to his question.

"It is not so far from here, a good day's journey at most. You would go by way of Kolašin, and then east through Berane or through the mountains."

"And how will I know his farm?"

"If you get that far, you cannot mistake it. There is a *stupa* there, and an old hermit's dwelling. His bell tower commands a view of the valley and the mountains for many miles, and there is nothing else like it. From there you can see much of the Sandžak, even to the mountains of Serbia, and to the south a good part of the lands still held by the Turk." Harwell could tell from the expression on Stefan's face, or the absence of expression, that this information was not given willingly.

"And you, Stefan, is your family of the Vasojević clan?"

"It is not, and I thank God for that." Here Stefan crossed himself.

"And why is that? Are they not heroes? Would not any Montenegrin be proud of their history?"

"Heroes, yes, and for hundreds of years, but they are unlucky. Their lands have been raided and their villages burnt by the Turks and by the Albanians, and some of what was theirs has been taken away by the Great Powers, including yours, in Berlin. Those who live in the mountains, like Danilo, are free, but those who live down on the plain, in the Sandžak where the soil is good, must answer to the Ottomans, and now to the Austrians. Some of them, I am told, have abandoned our faith and become Mahometans, for otherwise they could not live. That is a misfortune, and there are others besides. I do not think that any man in Montenegro envies the Vasojević."

"Well, I shall see all this for myself, and hear his side of the story."

"We will talk tomorrow about this journey of yours. If I decide it is good that you should go, I will send Janko to guide you. His family lives not far from Kolašin, and he knows the mountains there."

The soup in his stomach and the effort to understand what Stefan told him made Harwell's eyelids heavy. Stefan saw this and wished him good night. But before he slept, Harwell reached out and took his maps from their case. What he wanted was not on the big map that the Foreign Office had given him, but on a small, crude map that he had copied himself from Lady Mackenzie's *Travels in the Slavonic Provinces of Turkey-in-Europe*. Her route in 1863 had taken her south from the town of Novi Pazar along the eastern limit of the Sandžak to Ipek, or Peć, in the mouth of the Rugovo, which now lay in the territory of the Albanian Mahometans, though it had once been the seat of the patriarchate of the Serbian church. There, on the border of Montenegro as it existed before the wars of 1875–78, was the name Vasojević, as a kind of lettered shield between the mountains and the Sandžak. A shield, he thought, or perhaps an affirmation of Lady Mackenzie's belief that the land below the mountains, the Sandžak itself, belonged to these people.

From the time he woke and all through the morning, Harwell had heard the sound of voices from the courtyard, laughter and the stamping of feet as people passed back and forth before his closed door. The boy brought him tea and a cake of sweetened meal, and looked pleased when Harwell sat up and consumed them avidly. His cell was a pleasant place, and the light fell on the painting above his bed, where a sainted king, his gown hemmed with jewels and a golden halo around his head, spread his arms across the rough white wall. Had he been too ill to notice this yesterday? Or had the light not caught it so? Perhaps for the monks this was enough: to wake and pray, and at the far end of the day to pray and fall asleep, under this image that comprehended history and salvation. But for him, now, the sounds from beyond the door were irresistible, and so he put on a clean shirt and his boots and stepped out into the light, the noise, and the happy confusion of a courtyard filled with men and women and children gathered for the feast of Sveta Bogorodica.

He had not known what to expect, but it was certainly not what he saw. A celebration in a monastery, especially that of the Holy Mother, would surely be a solemn occasion: the blessing of food and wine; the local people eyeing the roasting meat hungrily, but careful of their speech and bearing in the presence of such learned and holy men; everyone looking slightly ill at ease in their clean, sober clothes. But this . . . this was overwhelming.

His first impression was that there was not a scrap of black cloth to be seen anywhere in that riot of color. Then he saw Stefan by the door of the church, and he was, indeed, dressed in black, but now with a wide sash of brilliant purple around his waist, and wedged in there the long silver handles of a pistol and a knife. A shrieking child, in pursuit of another, was seized by the monk and thrown high into the air, caught again as he fell, and set down with a blessing. Stefan laughed, the child's parents laughed, and the child, who had been astonished by this adventure, managed a tearful smile.

The men were dressed more or less as in Cetinje, in long tunics of coarse white cloth, or of finer stuff in pale colors, dark baggy breeches stuffed into boots or white leggings, scarlet waistcoats under the tunic, and the short sleeveless jacket, scarlet as well and trimmed with gold or fur, as the outermost garment. And guns, guns everywhere: pistols jammed into the bright silken girdle, and the long rifle, chased in silver, slung over the shoulder on a leather strap twined with a colored cord. When a new guest appeared at the gate, his fellows cried out to him, "Živeo! Živeo, Marko! Živeo, Branko!" and pistols were fired into the air to celebrate his arrival.

The women were scarcely recognizable from the creatures Harwell had seen in the town or in the pastures along his way. Instead of black they wore white, with bright aprons and headdresses that fell to the waist behind. Even the cloth of the poorest among them was worked and hemmed with embroideries. He stared, and they gazed frankly back at him, no doubt curious about this stranger who was so drably attired.

Stefan came to him through the throng and greeted him, offering him the blessing of Sveta Bogorodica. Harwell apologized for his clothes, and hoped that this plain white shirt and buff breeches would not be taken as a lack of respect. "Even the children playing there are better dressed than I."

Stefan put his hand on Harwell's shoulder. "It is true that you will find no bride in Montenegro today, dressed like a mud hen. Miliceva," he spoke to a striking young woman who stood with her mother near the wall, "would you take a man who wears no sash, and has no pistol to put in it?" Miliceva smiled and cast her eyes down, shaking her head. "But look here, Miliceva, this man is as tall as anyone here, and these hands." Here he held his own hand up to be measured against Harwell's. The monk's was broad and strong, but Harwell's was greater still, and the fingers thicker. "Truly, the hand of a hero. Will you not have him?" Miliceva blushed and shook her head, laughing now.

"I have a pistol of my own," said Harwell, not knowing how far this game was to be continued.

"Bring it, then, and we will see what can be done. Marko! Our guest has need of a piece of cloth."

When Harwell returned with his revolver, Stefan was waiting with a length of striped material that had lately adorned Marko's cap. This he wound around Harwell's waist, and then he took the revolver and tucked it into the folds.

"There, an English *capetan*, perhaps even a *sirdar*. What do you think of him now, Miliceva?" Miliceva looked at him, and he felt that he was being measured by those fine dark eyes against the monk who stood beside him. He wondered what she would look like without her cap and the covering on her hair.

"Better," said Miliceva, and then whispered something to her mother.

"She says she will not have him," crowed the older woman, "because she does not want her children to be born with pale hair." This put an end to Stefan's bride-market, and the two women walked away arm in arm. But Miliceva cast a look at Harwell over her shoulder and made peace between them with her eyes.

"You do not mind my joking with you?" asked the monk.

"Why should I mind? I am not married, and I would have stood by her decision, either way."

"It was a joke, but not a joke. She was promised to another man, who is now dead, and she must marry soon."

"Can you not take a wife?"

"Our priests may marry; we may not," replied Stefan. "But the man who takes Miliceva will have to be like a lion on his wedding night. The old way here is for the bride to wrap herself tightly in the wedding clothes and her mantle and make her husband fight for what is his. If he does not do that, she may send him away, for a man who will not fight for such a prize is worth nothing."

"Lucky devil, whoever he turns out to be."

"Perhaps she will not marry. She has said that she will not, but she is young, and, as you can see, she is no longer in mourning."

Stefan led Harwell away then, around the side of the church to a spot where several sheep fretted in a pen of wattles and stakes. Down the valley, at the point where the steep descent of the gorge began, Harwell saw the arches of an old bridge across the Morača, a Roman bridge, he guessed. It was peaceful here after the din of the courtyard, and at least he could hear himself think. He counted five sheep in the pen.

Stefan unwound his sash and laid the knife and the pistol upon it, then pulled his cassock over his head. Underneath he was wearing plain breeches and a homespun woolen shirt that reached only to his elbows. From the shoulders and the thick, veined forearms on this fellow, thought Harwell, he has done many things in his life besides praying.

"If we would eat meat," said Stefan, lifting a sheep effortlessly over the wattles by the scruff and the tail, "then we must kill it first." He held the animal down under his knee and bound its feet with a length of rope. The animal, once bound, did not struggle further, and Stefan reached into the pen to catch another.

"All of them?" asked Harwell.

"All," replied Stefan. "And even then I am afraid we may not have enough. You have seen how many have come to honor the saint, and if we do not feed them well, they will drink all the more, and then God knows what might happen. Listen, it has started."

Harwell listened to the singing, in which he caught the oft-repeated words *"Tamo je Serbija,"* and when the song ended there was a rolling volley of pistol shots and much cheering. "I do not understand," he said, "why they are singing about Serbia: 'Yonder is my Serbia' indeed, but we are in Montenegro, no?"

Stefan looked up at him from his work. "Wherever Serbs live, that is Serbia, according to our way of thinking. Where you wish to go is very near the Sandžak of Novi Pazar, which is but a finger of land between Montenegro and the kingdom of Serbia, where the other free Serbs live, and the Sandžak is Serbia. Also there"—he pointed north—"is Bosnia, and there to the west and north is Herzegovina, where the princely family of Njegoš comes from, and behind us are Peć and Kosovo and Prizren, the heart of Stefan Dusan's kingdom of old."

Harwell had never slaughtered a sheep, but he had certainly dipped his hundreds, and shorn them too, and so he caught one now and handed it, kicking and bleating, to the monk. "But is Montenegro, then, Serbia as well? It is tiny compared to those lands you have named."

"We are all one, and Montenegro is the heart of Serbia, for here the sultan has never had his way, even after the defeat at Kosovo, and Serbs everywhere know this is true. Look," and he knelt to scratch a map in a patch bare of grass. "Here is Montenegro, and Serbia, and the Sandžak lying between them. And what we call the Idea, the Idea of Great Serbia, is that the lands I have named should all come together, along with Dalmatia and Bulgaria, and be one nation again, as they were before Kosovo, in the time of King Stefan Dusan. Who then could stand in our way?"

This famous Kosovo, reflected Harwell, though he did not dare voice his thought, *was a good five hundred years ago, and then some.* "An ambitious plan," was what he said aloud, "and who would lead such a coalition, or empire?"

"Some say our Prince Nikola should be given pride of place, some say the king of free Serbia. It does not matter to me as long as Serbs, wherever they are found, are allowed to have their schools, in their own language, and follow their God, as they cannot do now."

"And would you fight for this Idea of Great Serbia?"

Stefan did not answer at once, for he was crossing himself and then closed his eyes briefly in prayer before taking the bound sheep, one by one, and slitting their throats with his great curved knife. Harwell looked at the heavy blade, the whorls of Damascus steel bright beneath the blood. Such a weapon, if swung rather than drawn across the neck, might sever a man's head in one stroke. When the sheep were finished thrashing, he cut the thongs and hung them by the back feet to a rack against the wall of the church to bleed. The final sheep, having struggled free of the knot, got to its knees, spraying blood in every direction.

"Knock him down!" cried Stefan. "He is past hurting now." Harwell kicked the legs out from under the ram and held it down with his boot until it stopped moving altogether. When he looked down at his shirt he saw that he wore a badge of blood on his left sleeve, near the shoulder.

Stefan grunted as he worked the knife under the skin of a ram, flaying it from head to tail and leaving the naked, gleaming corpse. Harwell would have helped, but it was a messy business, and his offer was acknowledged, and refused.

"I do not like this work," said Stefan when he had finished gutting the last one, "and I do not think I would be much good at killing men. But my friends there who have not taken holy vows, they will fight for Great Serbia, and kill gladly for her."

"And when will that be?"

"No one can say. Our prince tells us it will be when all is in readiness, but we have been waiting for that moment for thirty years, since the rising in Herzegovina, or even since he came to the throne. We must have the blessing of the Great Powers, he tells us, and he works ever towards that end. But it seems to me that the Great Powers showed themselves to be fools when they drew lines on a map and told us where we must live. The Devil himself could not have made a worse job of it, and if you ask the Vasojević where the border runs they say that it floats on blood. And so there are those who say that the Great Powers will never see the truth of this matter, and we must act on our own. They say our prince has waited too long."

"The Turkish Empire," began Harwell, with no clear idea of how he would finish his thought, "is still . . ."

"The Turkish Empire cannot stop the Serbs. It is as dead as that sheep whose head you were standing on, or would be, without Austria to patrol the Sandžak, and without the guns and money and even great ships that your queen sends to the sultan."

"The queen is dead, has been for seven years now."

"It is true, she is dead, but what has changed? It is said among us that in order to buy an English rifle you must kill a Turk."

"I cannot explain this to you. I do not understand it myself, and can only hope that such policies will change." Harwell thought then of Sir Percy Foote, and knew that his words were empty.

"The young men will not wait for this change, or until Nikola tells them the time is right. Some of them, indeed, say that our prince is paid by Austria, and Russia, and will never act. They say he is now the enemy and cannot be trusted."

Seeing Harwell's look of polite disbelief, the monk squatted where the sheep's blood had pooled and dipped his hand into it. Then he crushed a dark clod of dirt in his fist and spread his fingers before Harwell's face. "Do you know what this is?"

"A hand," said Harwell, then thought: *No, it is a black hand.* "I know what it is."

Stefan pressed his palm to the flayed hide of the last ram, leaving a distinct mark on the fleece which he then smudged away. "I did not say it, and you did not say it. The words are never spoken, but this is the sign of a brotherhood united in desperation and sacrifice. Above all, this thing must never be mentioned where you are going, for it is the woe of the Vasojević, and in particular of Danilo, who had three sons, and now has but one." He wiped his hands on the grass and stood to put on his cassock. "I must clean my hands now, and you should put some water on your shirt. Will you carry my sash for me, and my pistol?"

The feast began towards the end of the afternoon, when the sheep were basted to a steaming, sputtering crispness, and Harwell, who had not eaten solid food for forty-eight hours, had paced back and forth by the row of spitted carcasses, driven half mad by the smell. All through the afternoon the English *sirdar* had been offered plum brandy, and strong red wine from goatskin flasks, and he had not dared refuse a single drop. He paced by the spits because when he sat down, and especially when he closed his eyes, everything began to spin.

The bells were rung at last, somewhat erratically, it seemed to Harwell, and the abbot blessed the food. The meat was borne by the monks from table to table on the roasting spits, and each man hacked off what he thought he and his family might eat. Harwell's neighbor helped him to most of a leg, and a piece of the rack for good measure.

When he had wolfed the meat, he further gorged himself on *cicvara*, the maize meal and cheese stewed in goat's butter, until he thought he would burst. Several toasts were offered to Queen Victoria, and after the second or third one, Harwell abandoned his explanation of the English succession. In return, he drank to the glorious future of Montenegro, which seemed a safe enough gambit. Towards sunset those families that lived nearby made ready to leave, while there was still light to see the way, but the greater part of the host, having come from the farther slopes of the Brda, settled in for the night.

Darkness fell, and torches were lit, a holiday extravagance, explained Stefan, and by that time, some of the heroes of Montenegro were already paralyzed by drink. A while later, when Harwell's head was beginning to swim again, he found Stefan seated alone at one of the long tables. He sat, and the monk poured him some wine in a bowl which he first emptied of its contents. The wine was from a bottle, one of the few Harwell had seen in the course of the feast.

"If you want to know whether the Sandžak is worth fighting for, you must taste this. It is Vranac, and if there is a better wine to be had in all the Balkans, I do not know of it." Harwell tasted it, then drank, wishing he had not already drunk so much lesser stuff.

"I must go in the morning. Will you lend me Janko?"

"Yes. It will be good for him to get away from us for a while. And you have already met some of the Vasojević here today, and drunk their wine."

"Which were they?"

"Miliceva, her mother, and Marko are all cousins of Danilo Pekočević, though they do not live near him. He will probably have heard of you when you get there. Do not forget what I have told you."

"I have not forgotten. But I will ask you one more favor, which is to explain this thing to me." Here he held up his hand before the monk's face. "I do not want to blunder onto dangerous ground by some back door." The monk nodded and poured them both more wine, and when he spoke, it was in a whisper that only Harwell could hear.

They wished each other good night not long afterwards, and Harwell asked for a candle, so that he could pack. When he had finished, he sat on the edge of his bed and wrote down everything he could remember. It was late when he blew out his candle, but he had not missed much sleep, because the celebration continued outside, and the night was punctuated by shots and snatches of song. The last thing Harwell heard when he finally lay down was several choruses of "Onward! Onward! Let me see Prizren!" and this was in honor of Prince Nikola and his father, the Grand Vojvode Mirko, whose fondest dream had been the recapture of that ancient city of the Serbian kings. *Onamo! Onamo!* It was shouted, not sung. It was, thought Harwell, a battle cry.

The boy knocked on his door before six o'clock and said it was time to pray. In the courtyard Harwell stepped carefully, for there were people sleeping everywhere, and some of the women were already making fires outside the gate. There was Marko against the wall, on his back, snoring majestically, and a good deal of last night's dinner now decorated his chest. A little distance away Miliceva lay with her head on her bent arm. The headdress had been put aside, and so the dark, unbraided mass of her hair spilled down onto her neck and bosom and onto the dusty grass below. Her eyes were open and she saw him, but did not move. He touched his own hair, as if to say, *There is nothing to be done,* and so made her smile.

The prayers themselves meant little to him, for he had set his mind against such things, as had Raymond, but he was glad to see the inside of the church in this strong light, and he counted the unnamed Nemanja kings attending the Sleeping Virgin, Bogorodica herself, while the monks chanted their responses to the abbot. One of the kings, he was pleased to note, had a mane of bright yellow hair that outshone his halo.

Janko already had the mare and the ass out by the gate, had transported Harwell's belongings from the cell, and, in his excitement, was trying to fit the pack harness to the mare, whose ears lay flat against her head. When Stefan came, Harwell strapped on his revolver and handed the striped sash to the monk, who refused it.

"You remind me of the Austrian officers, who have leather pouches to hold every last article of their equipment. Keep the sash, and wear it, for it is more becoming to a guest in our mountains."

"But it belongs to Marko . . ."

"He will not remember how he lost it. But if you wish, you can give his wife something in return."

"Yes," said Harwell, with enthusiasm, "a gift for his wife." He took a metal pot from the top of his pack and handed it to the woman.

"Ye . . . ye," she approved, and passed the article to Miliceva. Harwell whispered in the monk's ear.

"I have others . . ."

"No, this is a fair trade for the sash. The others you can give to Janko, whose mother will be especially glad to see him."

Then Janko, emboldened by this mark of favor, touched the pistol butt in Harwell's sash.

"Guns are for men, not for children," said Stefan, and quickly corrected himself, "not even for boys who will be men all too soon. It should be enough that the abbot has released you for now from the penalty of silence."

"And the road?" asked Harwell.

"The broad way is to Berane and then back up into the mountains, but you must pass through the border, where there are Turkish officials and Austrian guards."

"Well . . ." said Harwell, remembering the unpleasantness in Cattaro, and also the pages he had written last night, now folded carefully into his books.

"The other way is through the mountains, and you will not find it on your map. Janko will show you."

Harwell mounted and rode through the gate, with Janko ahead of him leading the ass and fairly strutting with pride. He waved. Stefan cried after him, "*Živeo*, Harwell," and Miliceva lifted the pot in a farewell gesture. Around the first turning of the road Harwell asked what this expression *Živeo* might mean, and was told that the monk wished him to live for a long time.

All day they rode and marched, higher and higher into the mountains, through beech forests and evergreens, for they had left the karst behind, and there was now enough earth for the ass to kick up a little plume of pleasant dust. There were farms as well, and from the shoulder of one broad hill he could look across at a two-story farmhouse perched on another, with the dark forest behind and a vista of grassland flowing down to the road. There was plenty of water here, and Janko said it was good to drink.

They stopped once to eat the cold leavings of the feast, and when Janko's jaunty pace began to slacken, Harwell put him on the mare for a while, which revived his spirits. Though he did not use the stirrups, there was an easy grace in the way the boy sat on the mare, and he made her run on the flat ground before Harwell called him back. The mare looked as if she would prefer running to walking.

At Kolašin they turned east, and entered a forest of evergreens that rose to meet the snow. Janko showed him a road that would take them to his parents' house. Over a pass they went, where the cold wind encouraged Harwell to think that there were weeks of spring left, with mats of bloom following the retreating snow higher and higher into the bare rock above the tree line. The road began its descent towards the border, and Berane, and the Sandžak beyond. From time to time the forest opened out to show them the land below, where stark limestone needles rose like islands out of that dark green sea.

Janko stopped on the track when they saw the rough white tower in a sward of brilliant grass. They were on a steep face of rock that made Harwell nervous, and if he had thrown a stone, he might have been able to hit the tower. The land dropped away again beyond the meadow and Harwell thought he must be looking north towards Serbia.

"That is the home of Danilo Pekočević," said Janko. "Have I done well?"

"You have done very well," replied Harwell, "but I think we should go down. My mare does not like these high places."

"May I be allowed to carry this?" asked the boy, laying his hand lightly on the fowling piece bound in the ropes of the ass's pack. "I do not ask to shoot it."

Harwell let him take the gun, and he wore it slung across his back, so that the stock nearly dragged on the ground. "Now I am ready to meet him," said Janko, without a flicker of humor.

They got down to the flat land and it was like being held in a bowl between the mountain and the plain. A one-legged man came out of the house and watched with folded arms as they made their way across the meadow, past grazing oxen and horses. One of these, a dark, shaggy stallion, made circles around them in a kind of procession step, whinnying, and the mare answered him. When Harwell looked back across the meadow, the man had been joined by a tall woman, and a youth who seemed a few years older than Janko. No greeting was offered, and Harwell dismounted in silence.

"My name is Harwell, and I carry letters from your daughter in Cetinje. This is Janko, who has led me here." Now Janko knelt before Danilo and muttered his patronymic. Danilo laid his hand on Janko's bowed head and smiled, creating new lines in that scarred face.

"*Ne . . . ne. Crnogorac digne glavu,*" by which he meant that the Montenegrin always raises his head. It seemed to Harwell as if the mountain itself had spoken. "I am Danilo. This is my wife, Sofia, and my son, Toma." It was a grudging sort of welcome. Harwell looked at Sofia, who said nothing. Was there, he wondered, an ugly woman to be found anywhere in these mountains? Her eyes met his, but lingered on his sash.

"What is your country?" asked Danilo.

"I am from England."

"*Englez,*" said Sofia, with a brief smile whose meaning he did not understand. Perhaps she, too, had expected a German? Danilo had no comment, and Harwell could not tell if that scowl was meant for him.

The youth, Toma, inspected Janko without approval, and Janko fidgeted under his gaze. "Do you know how to fire that thing?" Toma asked, and got no answer. "I thought as much," he said, and led the mare and the ass away. As he passed Harwell he said, in English, "It is a good horse."

It had been a long day, and it was nearly dark. Harwell and Janko sat on a bench beside the door of the house with the pot of cold, viscous stew between them and they ate it all; but the true luxury, at least for Harwell, was having one flat, stationary surface to sit on, and another at his back. He would go straight to sleep tonight and not even try to read or write, but he must relieve himself first, and so he walked off in the direction of the tower, where he would be screened from view of the house. There, next to the road that must lead down out of the meadow to the Sandžak below, he found a low stone enclosure with a little roof set upon poles. It might, from a distance, and in this light, have seemed like a shrine or a cemetery plot, but it was neither of these. Instead, there were orderly rows of heads, twenty-two in all, set upon stakes, and one of them, wearing a tattered military cap that he did not recognize, had hair as bright as his own.

Chapter Seven

THE NIGHT WAS COLD, even in the low shed that abutted the kitchen wall. Harwell woke once to wrap himself in his coat, and had a passing thought of Janko making do with the spare blanket outside in the pasture, where he had insisted on sleeping. He is young, thought Harwell, it will be no hardship to him. He rolled over and slept.

The next thing he knew, Janko was shaking his shoulder and trying to tell him something about the mare: she had broken the fence, and he should come quickly to see. There was just enough light coming through the small, unglazed window for him to find his boots.

The mare had indeed broken the fence, for though the stallion was now in the enclosure with her, the rails lay scattered out into the wider pasture where she had broken through, only to be chased back into the pen, and she stood there now, her hind legs spread and her tail held high and to the side. Janko and Toma hung on the fence, watching carefully as the stallion, his neck arched, circled the mare nervously, now sniffing her, now touching his nose to hers, now biting her on the shoulder. His swollen verge, the size at least of that viper in the ruins, thought Harwell, swung awkwardly beneath his belly. The mare stamped her foot. She was ready.

Harwell was no stranger to barnyard matters, though at Newton

Court such pens and stables where the mating took place were carefully sited away from the house, so that one could not even hear this strangely pitched whinny that the mare now made, and the eleven-year-old Bron Harwell might have continued in his ignorance had not a stable hand with a split lip and drink on his breath taken him down there to see.

"Watch, now," he commanded, in a voice rendered nearly unintelligible by his ruined face, and by whiskey. "Watch close, and ye'll learn a thing or two."

And Harwell had watched, much as these boys now watched, but without comprehension at all until the man actually put his hand on that monstrous thing, mottled pink and black, and guided it home into the mare. "Easy now! You don't need to kill her to get it done!" And that was it: the thing he had heard about, and yet could scarcely believe. The thought of his parents in such a posture made him close his eyes in embarrassment.

"Open yer eyes, for Christ's sake, boy! Did ye see that? Ye'll be getting yer own soon enough, and yer man enough." He put his hand roughly between the stallion's legs and stepped quickly back as the horse made an awkward effort to kick him. "Ha! There's more than one load in him, I don't doubt. Ye might think she don't like it, for all her carryin' on. But she'll be back for more, I can tell ye that."

Janko talked excitedly to Toma, or to himself, a muttered monologue punctuated by the admiring exclamation: "*Eh!*" Toma said nothing in return, but watched carefully and impassively, wrapped in self-conscious dignity. He looked back once at Harwell and asked if he should stop them. Harwell shrugged and shook his head, for now the stallion had mounted the mare, thrusting savagely at her, and the great muscles of his hindquarters rippled and shimmered there beneath the tawny highlights of his rough winter coat. He held the mare's withers with his teeth, drawing blood.

Though the sun was rising behind them, this scene was bathed in the reflection from the abrupt walls and turrets of limestone on the far side of the pasture. Harwell was admiring the light, and the formations of the rock, trying to ignore the stirring of his own desire, when the door opened behind him and Sofia came out to throw a basin of water onto the bare, trodden ground.

"Toma!" she called. "When he is finished, you must put the rails back in place and tie her on the far side of that pen." To Harwell she said: "The food will be ready soon. The boy must eat before he goes."

The night before, at her insistence, Harwell had entrusted all his stores to her, as there were mice in his shed that might spoil them. She had looked in each of his bags and commented on the fineness of the maize meal, and on the rice, which could not be had in the poor markets nearby. The *scoranze* also pleased her, for while there were rivers and lakes here with trout in them, this little fish had a flavor all its own, and was to be found only in Lake Scutari, so many miles away. He kept for himself a packet of tea, which the mice would not eat. He did not know if mice would eat sugar, and so he placed that packet inside Lydia's kettle.

Harwell had planned to make a pot of tea for himself when he rose, but he had not had time to light a fire, and now the smell of strong coffee wafted from the open door of the house. "I must wash first," he said.

"And that sash?" Harwell looked down at his shirt, and his own leather belt. "Where did that sash come from that you were wearing when you came here?"

"That? It was given to me by a man at Morača, a monk there told him that I needed it for the feast day."

"The girl that my son was to marry wore a cloth such as that one," said Sofia. "Perhaps it is the same family."

Harwell struggled to keep the expression on his face from changing and thought, *Oh, Christ.*

"Wear it," she said. "It does not matter now."

When Janko departed he carried away the treasure of Harwell's enthusiastic purchase in the bazaar in Cetinje: a toasting fork, a grill, and a kettle not unlike Lydia's. Janko eyed a large covered pot, but Harwell did not offer it, as he must keep something back as a present for Sofia. Janko admired each item in turn and several times repeated the phrase "from England." When Harwell asked him to carry his greetings and thanks to Stefan, the boy lowered his eyes. So much for life in the monastery, thought Harwell. He was pleased to see that Toma was at least civil to Janko, and wished him a safe journey.

Harwell had taken his breakfast with his hosts in a long, low room that comprised the first floor of the dwelling. One end was the kitchen: an open hearth with no chimney, where a metal stanchion set into a stone in the floor held a blackened pot. The other end of the room, though bare, bore unmistakable traces of animal occupancy. Perhaps in the winter, when the wolves came down from the mountains, Danilo Pekočević sheltered his livestock in here. There was no other stable that he could see. Opposite the door where he entered, in the center of the room, was a worn table basking in the extravagant light of two glazed windows. He was surprised to note, over those windows, a shelf with several books on it.

The boys had eaten in a matter of minutes, or seconds, sitting still only while Danilo blessed the food, which consisted of meal cakes. Then they left to repair the fence. Harwell ate the cakes—he could not determine what sort of grain had been used—with a helping of the coarse plum jam that Sofia put on the table after the boys had gone, and drank his coffee and goat's milk out of a bowl. Silence reigned over the meal, benevolent on Sofia's part, guarded on Danilo's, and Harwell was left to wonder if conversation might be the guest's prerogative or obligation. He produced his packet of letters and offered it to Danilo, who inspected it gravely, front and back, then handed it to his wife. "He can read," said Sofia softly. "But he thinks the spectacles will make his eyes weak."

In the packet were several separate letters, two for Toma, one each for Sofia and Danilo, and yet another one, in a separate envelope which bore Lydia's handwriting. Sofia first read Lydia's letter aloud, and when the chronicle of Natalia's achievements was done, Harwell was surprised to hear his own name. "Mr. Brown Horvelle." Sofia repeated it slowly and looked at him to see if she had gotten it right. He did not correct her, as it had such a pleasing sound on her tongue.

Mr. Brown Horvelle was warmly recommended to their hospitality and described as one of the leading experts in England on flowers, who hoped to study the native species in their mountains. This information produced on Danilo's face an expression not of curiosity but of disbelief. "Flowers," he said. "Can this be?"

"Miss Wadham is too kind. In fact I am not such a great expert, certainly not in the kinds that may grow here, but I have been sent to study them and collect the seeds."

Sofia came to his rescue: "It is true that people study such things. In America they have experts who have used this knowledge to make corn and wheat that bears more seed, and cannot be ruined by disease."

"It is too early for the seeds," said Danilo. "Even below this place, down in the valley where it is warmer, we are just ploughing and planting the seed from last year. There are many flowers, but up in the high places they have not yet come, and it will be weeks before they set seed. Will you stay here for that long?"

"That is my hope," replied Harwell, trying to read Danilo's face. The scar that ran from the left cheek across the mouth to the point of the chin made his task more difficult.

"You are welcome here. We do not turn travellers away."

"Perhaps I can be useful to you in some way."

"Perhaps." Danilo contemplated the remaining cakes gloomily, and took another onto his plate.

The next statement about Mr. Brown Horvelle contained a further surprise. He had been to a great university in his own country, and would know how to help Toma study the books she had sent. Harwell's eye went to the shelf above the table, but he could not see what those books were. Then he noted the radiance, the triumphant radiance, that had transformed the severe lines of Sofia's face. He wondered what this woman must have looked like when she was young, when she was Miliceva's age, or even Lydia's. A blush spread from her cheek to the fine white skin of her neck. "Yes," she said. "Will you do this?"

"It would be a small enough thing to repay such hospitality. I will do whatever I can." He felt he could not look at her any longer without blushing himself.

"You are a scientist, then?"

"No, no, I am certainly not . . ."

"English is the same language that they speak in America, is it not?" asked Danilo, who stared at his plate.

"Yes . . . well, more or less."

"So." Danilo pushed himself upright and lurched towards the door, where he paused, all but blotting out that rectangle of light. "I must take Toma with me today. He must learn to plough as well as he speaks English. It will be almost dark when we return."

"You must take food, then. It will be ready when the oxen are harnessed."

When Danilo had gone, Harwell experienced a release of tension, as if his body were a bow that had just been unstrung. It was exhausting to be in the presence of his host. He sat back against the rough-hewn pillar behind him, with his cooling bowl of coffee still warmer than his hands. There was no reason now that he could not return the gaze of Sofia, whose eyes had scarcely left his face.

Women in England, he thought, do not behave thus. Lydia's eyes had never engaged his for more than a moment . . . or was it he who had looked away? Daphne had scarcely ever sought his eyes, especially after the pleasant embarrassment of their first kiss. And his mother, he was almost certain, had not made eye contact with him since he had become a man, perhaps not since she was furious with him for being so rude to Lady Merion, for saying, not quite *sotto voce*, that she bored for the universe, for which offense he had been beaten with a hairbrush. That was it: a woman might gaze into the eyes of the child, but not the man, unless . . . and here he had to expand his theory to accommodate the frank, unnerving stare of that girl, or woman, in Shepherd Market.

When he looked at Sofia now, her head turned in a moment of beautiful distraction to the song of a finch at the window, he saw the streaking of pure white hairs in the deep, rich brown of the rest. How old was she? If Toma had two elder brothers, then she must be nearly of an age to be his own mother. But not quite so old, he thought with relief; not old at all, but caught in some limbo between youth and age, both of which could be seen there, or imagined vividly. He was not her son, and yet he was more than a stranger, for he had brought into her life some joy, whose nature he would presently discover, and it enveloped them both, held them, like music, a scent, or light.

"I am surprised that your husband can manage the plough."

"It is a wonder that he can walk, or that he can do any of the things that he has done. Everything you see here was built by him, except for the tower, which was the hermit's work."

"But you helped him."

Sofia rose to clear the plates, and from the rafters above the hearth took a long, blackened strap of what he thought was leather, but it must have been meat, for she cut it into pieces and wrapped it with the cold meal cakes.

"I helped him, and he had his two elder sons to help him while they were alive. And now he has Toma."

"But Toma is to be a scholar?"

"Not a scholar, but a scientist, yes, or an engineer."

"He will have to go away, even farther than Cetinje."

"Yes." The answer was a long time in coming, perhaps not willingly given.

"And how will your husband manage then?"

"That is a question Danilo himself has yet to ask, and the answer is that I have done such work before, and I can do it again." She laid her hand flat on the dark, worn surface of the table, and they both considered it.

"May I see the books there?"

Sofia handed down three of the volumes on the shelf: a dictionary, a much used English grammar for foreign readers, and a text on modern hydrostatics, by Armistead Drinker, O.B.E., of the University of Edinburgh, filled with charts and statistical tables that inspired a cold dread in Harwell. Drinker's book bore a blue stamp on the flyleaf: *Property of the British Legation, Cetinje. Not to be removed from the premises.*

"I have promised Gospodja Wadham that I will send them back to her, but only after Toma has read them and knows them by heart. If he knows both these books, could he be a scientist?"

"Yes," said Harwell, reaching up to replace the books. "I suppose so. I mean it would be a good start. And does he read them now?"

"He reads the blue one to me, so that he will have the sound of your language in his head and on his tongue, even if I do not understand the words. The red one, not so much. I think it must be very difficult. But with your help . . ."

Harwell was contemplating a reply that would convey polite reservations about the enterprise when Sofia spoke again, almost fiercely: "You have promised this thing, have you not?"

He looked at her and saw how the expression of trusting anticipation might become a frown, how the features might rearrange themselves to accommodate disappointment, and darker moods. "I have promised. I will do what I can." He heard Janko calling from the yard, and he went out to say goodbye to him.

He had watched Toma and his father harness the oxen to the plough, had been on the point of offering his help, when he saw that it would slow them down to explain what needed to be done. Down the road and past the tower he followed the oxen on their stately, clamorous procession, and when they came to the edge of the meadow, where the land dropped steeply away, he saw the rickety little guard's shack, now empty. Danilo halted the plough while Toma leaned on the counterweight of the sapling that barred the road.

"What is this?"

"This is the border," answered Danilo, "and there is the guard's station. He will be here when we come back, to see if we will give him *baksheesh*." Almost below their feet, beyond the blue-green girdle of the forest, another valley opened out, marked with broad bands of cultivation and dotted with a few houses. Off to the northeast, the terrain broke away again to a wider and gentler plain below.

"You come and go as you please?"

"Nobody troubles us." There was a dangerous look to Danilo as he spoke these words. "That is our land down there, and neither the Turks nor the Austrians can dispute that."

"They cannot dispute it," said Toma in a tone of sarcastic amusement, "and yet if we would plough that land, and take the grain and potatoes to market, we must pay *harac* to the Turk, because it is within their border, or so they say."

"And is the tax a great sum of money?"

"You must ask my father," replied Toma. Harwell would have dropped the subject there, but as the plough began to move again, Danilo spoke over the clanking of metal wheels on the stone.

"It is whatever they decide it will be, however much the sultan needs to fight his wars, and if the Albanian, the Arnaout, must pay one piastre, the Christian must pay ten, or twelve. It is a blasphemy."

"And yet you pay it?" Harwell was walking beside Danilo but was not certain he had been heard.

"If the *harac* is not paid, they say they can take my son and make a soldier out of him, a Janissary, to fight for the sultan against Christian nations. Is this not madness?" Danilo's voice drowned the noise of the plough, would have prevailed against a dozen ploughs, and as he passed the gatepost of the frontier he struck it a savage blow with his ox-goad.

"They must catch me before they can make a soldier of me, and I will lead them on such a chase through the mountains . . ." crowed Toma.

"Perhaps they cannot catch you," said Danilo with something like a smile for the boy's bravado, "but they will know where to find me, or your mother. What good will your running do you then?"

"Any man who lifts his hand against my family is a dead man."

"This is as my father taught me, and his father before him. You will remember this." Turning to Harwell, Danilo said: "You must go back. If they find you down below the border without your papers, they will make trouble for us. Now that the Austrians have their garrison at Bijelo Polje, the Turks are suddenly brave, and even the *mudir* of Berane, a coward from the womb, is not afraid to ride out with his *zapties* to study how the tax shall be levied on our people and on the Arnaouts."

They left him there in the middle of the steep road, and Harwell watched until they entered the line of trees. Below, in the valley where they would plough, he saw distant, diminished figures: a herdsman against the green of a gentle hill, a ploughman already at his furrow in the field, unfurling a slow brown ribbon of earth in his wake. Over the rim of the valley he noted a haze of smoke, and he guessed that Berane must lie in that direction.

Since he had first set foot on the quay at Cattaro, Harwell had been possessed by an obscure sense of urgency that had colored all his waking hours. Urgency and anxiety combined, for most of that time, though the degree to which this was true only became clear to him now in the sunlight of the meadow, when both the urgency and the anxiety had evaporated, like the half-remembered chill of the morning. What is the name of this place? he wondered: Lydia would surely want to know, and Lord Polgrove too, naturally.

For the first time since he had left Oxford four years earlier, he knew exactly what the next few weeks, or even months, held for him: the perils of his journey were past; he would encounter no brigands on these mountain paths; and he would not need to be careful of his speech in the society of Cetinje. He had arrived at his destination, and now he had only to wait for the seed to ripen, and for the story of this place and the Sandžak beyond to unfold to him.

He sat in the bare yard before the house, working a piece of borrowed leather, which he had split along most of its length and bound with lashings of strong waxed thread into a crude martingale to be attached to the mare's bit and cinch, and if this did not curb the impatient tossing of her head, then nothing would.

When he was finished, he held it up to the sunlight at arm's length and admired it. It would have been straighter if he had had a proper table to work on, but it was straight enough, and when he had oiled the leather it would be better still.

"Thank you," he said to Sofia, who sat a few feet down the bench from him, peeling potatoes. She smiled, but did not look at him. They had been sitting there in a comfortable silence for half an hour at least. "What is this place called?"

"It is called Stupa Vasiljeva," she replied, and indicated the tower of whitened stones. "There is the *stupa*, and Vasili was the hermit who built it."

"It seems such a peaceful place. There is water, and grass, and enough soil to grow vegetables. If I lived here I think I would never go anyplace else."

"Perhaps. But Vasili, who lived here for many years, was not a peaceful man, nor is Danilo at peace with himself, so I wonder if you are right after all. Look there, on the wall, near the top," and she pointed with her knife to a blooming shrub and a trickle of water on the steep limestone near the meadow's mouth, over the road. "That is where Vasili cast out his demon and threw him over the cliff, and a spring came out of the rock at his feet. That is where he lived." Harwell saw fissures in the limestone that might be caves, and just to the right of the bush the remains of a broken stone arch.

"And the tower?"

"He built the tower later, it is said, and for the glory of God. He could not live with other men, not even with the monks at Decani, where many hermits lived in chambers such as that one. Here he could live by himself, but he missed the sound of the bells, and so he built the tower, and rang the bells, even though they deafened him over the years. In the end, it is said, he could hear only the words of God."

"And the bells are there still?"

"They are there, and Danilo may ring them on feast days. But I have told him I do not want to live with a deaf man."

"When did the hermit live here?"

"It was after the Turks came, but still long ago, perhaps two hundred years."

"And in all that time no one has harmed the tower, or taken the bells?"

"To the Christian this is hallowed land, and the Mahometans are afraid of this place. They say that the spirit of Vasili lives on in the *stupa*."

"And they are afraid of Danilo as well?" Harwell thought of the heads.

"Yes. Perhaps they fear him more than Vasili. So if you find peace in this place, it is because you have brought it with you."

Harwell walked up into the mountains instead of riding because he did not want to take the mare through the pasture, where the stallion paraded himself back and forth along the repaired fence. He did not plan to go very far anyway, which was just as well, because his pack was ridiculously heavy. At the last minute, in addition to the food that Sofia had given him, and the bottle of water, and his drawing materials, he added his three reference volumes, wrapped in their protective chamois cloths. His courage had failed him when he imagined Lord Polgrove reading his halting description of some alpine plant growing in its native rocks and his tentative connection of that specimen with genus and species.

He had seen the curling, contemptuous smile on those features in his interview with his lordship, and knew how readily it came, almost in gratitude for further proof of human folly and the incompetence of subordinates. Here was a man who might have risen even beyond the influence of his enormous fortune had he not been so eaten with disdain. And although the real business at hand had nothing to do with flowers—flowers having been proposed almost in jest as his excuse—Harwell knew quite certainly that accuracy and dependable good sense in the matter of botany would be the foundation of Polgrove's opinion of him. For the time being he would happily carry the sage Linnaeus and those other authorities on his back wherever he went.

He followed the track that he and Janko had used until he came to the first faint pathway leading high into the forested crags, and before long, puffing like the Great Northern express, he emerged onto a steep slope where the trees diminished in size and alternated with tussocks of coarse grass. Above him lay the snowfields and the high, barren peaks, but here, where the broken rocks from a cliff face filled half a gully in a treacherous slide, mats of wildflowers grew in such profusion that he was afraid he would not be able to catalog them all before the blooms faded into obscure deadheads and seed pods. Start with what you know, he thought. That mass of narrow, reddish-purple flowers must be a penstemon, surely?

All afternoon he worked in the shadow of a pillar of rock which shielded his head and neck from the strong sun, and still he was warmed by the updraft of air from the talus slope, which carried the scents of all these yet-to-be-named plants, a mixture of spices and strong resins released when he had unavoidably trod on this carpet. His hands, too, reeked as if dipped in some exotic perfume, for his method was to cut a spray or shoot of the plant and place it in a little cup of water, first to sketch the pattern of leaf and blossom, then to render in watercolor, as faithfully as he could, the hues, which sometimes faded even as he worked. Then he would make some effort with the books to narrow the range of possible identifications.

It was slow work: the Latin of Linnaeus was a trial to him, and the color plates in Haworth were almost comically inaccurate, even as to the color of the foliage, let alone the blossom of *Saxifraga grisebachii*, which was the only plant he had identified to his complete satisfaction. Perhaps at home, in his shed, without the distraction of such infinite possibility, he would be able to make more sense out of his field descriptions and that vast index in Waldstein, working from one to the other in the tedious process of eliminating alternatives.

What if he could not identify these plants with any degree of certainty? Well, he had presented himself to Polgrove with no pretense of expertise, with such modest credentials that Polgrove ignored them. Careful descriptions and careful sketches would be an honest substitute for what experience could not supply. And yet the work would drive him mad if he were nothing more than a blind conduit for seeds, for information, all served up for his patron to accept or dismiss out of hand. However frustrating and time-consuming the task, he would have to learn whatever he could, even if this was not something he himself had chosen. Had Raymond not said something to this effect about the study of Greek? a defense of his passion for mastery? Had he not had some inkling of this in his own study of the law? Well, in Raymond's case the reward had been a shelf full of prize books, won at Eton and Balliol. In his own case, it might be too late for prizes.

There was another possibility that took hold in his mind during this long afternoon of baffling work: the plants he found in this place, some of them at any rate, might be nowhere found in these books, and not in any of the hundreds of books in Lord Polgrove's library. Would such an original and picturesque setting as this not be provided with a flora as distinct, as individual, as the mountaineers who peopled it? Was it not Polgrove's secret hope that his Matterhorn, in the spring following, would be dotted with fantastic variants that would be reported by the honest secretary of the International Alpine Society, which reports would in turn plant a seed of envy in the breast of his mortal rival, Graf von Eisenberg? Finally, might he, Auberon Harwell, not be allowed to name a plant that he had discovered in this place? He smiled at this presumptuous thought. It was a ridiculous idea, and yet it was possible.

When his brain was thoroughly muddled with new information, and his hand had begun to cramp with the exercise of pen and brush, he decided to climb the pillar that had been his sunshade for the day. The rock was so eccentric that he had little difficulty in finding holds, though his boots were certainly not designed for this exercise, and at one point he had almost committed himself to a ledge when it broke away entirely and crashed down, narrowly missing his pack.

The top of the pillar was a bare, flat space of about twenty feet in diameter, and it commanded a fine view in all directions, except where the last spur of the mountain to the southwest blocked it off. He was alone in the sky, as close as he would ever come to the sense of command that an eagle must feel, or to the ecstasy of the ascetic saint, and to his great pleasure he found that he could see not only for great distances—there was the whole of the Sandžak laid out before him—but also almost straight down into the meadow, where Vasili's tower gleamed white against the green pasture. At this distance that patch of green was just about the right size to fit into his cupped hands.

He had never owned a piece of land in his life, and never had any desire to do so, though he supposed that Newton Court and its few hundred acres of sheep and tenant farmers must one day become his responsibility. But his connection with Newton Court, time-honored and fully explicable, was different and not as deep as the mysterious pull that the rock-walled meadow exercised on him, and for the second time this afternoon the word "home" occurred to him in this unlikely context.

He lay at the edge of his eminence and brought the tower into focus with his binoculars. That hint of motion near the house must be the stallion, still hoping to get at the mare. A figure emerged from the house to set something down in the yard, and then made several more trips back and forth. Surely that was Sofia. Harwell had excellent eyesight, and yet even with his binoculars he could make no sense of the repeated pattern, from the house to the yard and back, until the figure stopped there, and, like a moth struggling free of its chrysalis, metamorphosed from black to white. That was it: she was bathing, and with every trip from the house she had been filling her tub with warm water.

His first instinct was to look away, but after a sweep of the horizon with his binoculars—he must check his map later to identify that distant town to the northwest—he came back to the meadow, to the white tower, to that now-reclining figure luxuriating in the warm water and in the last heat of the spring sun. At this remove there was really nothing personal about the scene below, nothing that identified that figure as Sofia, as opposed to Woman Bathing. The abstraction of it removed any taint of embarrassment, any consideration of modesty. A valley as beautiful as this must necessarily be inhabited, and the inhabitants must necessarily bathe. What better occasion than a warm spring day with the men off at their work and the guest conveniently away sketching? What harm if the guest, through some accident of topography, became a witness to this scene of domestic tranquillity? At last she rose from the tub and, lifting a vessel high above her head, let the clean water flow down on her. What strength was in those arms, thought Harwell, in the long moment when Sofia stood as still as a statue, and he shivered once, as if he could feel the play of water and air on his own back.

He reached the meadow just as the harsh music of the oxen dragging the plough frame could be heard beyond the crest of the road. Danilo and Toma might be a half hour or more getting the oxen home and unharnessed, and so Harwell had time to clean his brushes, wash, and make tea.

He took his tin mug and the sketches he had made into the house and laid them on the table. Sofia stirred a blackened pot hanging over the fire and looked blankly at him when he asked if there was anything he could do to help her. "Later," she said, smiling now, "you will read to Toma."

She wanted to know what was in his mug, and he encouraged her to taste it. Tea she knew, but not Indian tea, and while she drank it he showed her what work he had done that day on the mountain. "This one," she said, pointing to a white-flowering shrubby plant that Harwell could put no name to, not even a family. "We take the leaves of this one, and also the little twigs, and we put it in the water when we bathe. There is an oil in it, and it is pleasing. Do your women do that in England?" Harwell shrugged his shoulders, for he really had no idea what women in England did in their baths, but his attention was fixed on a particular scent, familiar because he had just scrubbed it from his hands, which emanated from her still damp hair.

Dinner consisted of potatoes cooked with goat cheese in that cauldron, and over the top of it Sofia had laid a blanket of chopped wild onion grass and a bitter herb that grew among the clouds of crocuses in the meadow. Harwell ate as if he had been walking behind the plough all day, and when he was offered the last portion he refused it, as he knew he must, even though he could have eaten more, for in this country the guest's capacity must never exceed or even equal what his host has provided.

It had been a silent meal. Danilo and Toma projected an absolute weariness and gave themselves almost grimly to the task of eating. Perhaps they had been arguing about something. And so when Harwell pushed back his plate he said, in a tone of bantering good fellowship, "I could not eat anything more, for I have not worked today as you have, and yet you would think that I had been pulling the plough."

Danilo raised his eyes from his plate and settled himself in his chair with a look of satisfaction on his face. "I have done that myself. When my sons were small, and the wolves had taken an ox in the spring after a hard winter, I had to pull the plough with the other ox, and my wife drove us both as if she did not know the difference between us." He laughed and tore a fist-sized piece from the round of bread. Harwell did not know how to react to this information, but the expression on Sofia's face—pride mixed with a tender melancholy—told him that the story must be true.

"But how . . . ?"

"God took my leg from me, and God gave me the strength to do this thing. It was not the greatest of his works, nor the last. If we believe in God, all things are possible."

"Yes," said Harwell, with as much conviction as he could manage.

"Have you seen the hermit's tower?" asked Danilo. "How could one man build such a thing, an old man, if not by the grace of God? Look at the rocks tomorrow and tell me how a man could accomplish such work, unless he believed in God, and God heard his prayer."

Sofia took away the dishes and put a lamp and the blue book on the table. Harwell thumbed through the grammar section to the readings and muttered under his breath *Jesus wept*, for here were fusty old passages on King Alfred burning his cakes, Dick Whittington and his cat, and an account of the great fire of London in 1666, all dressed up with perfectly ludicrous questions and answers. It could be worse, he thought. It could be the other book.

"We begin with King Alfred," he said in English. "I will read the page, then you read it. Do you know who King Alfred was?"

Toma shook his head. "Was he a great man?"

"Yes. I will explain to you later."

To Harwell's astonishment, the boy read perfectly well, though some of the words meant nothing to him, and could answer a good many of the questions. How had he managed it with such a book, and in such a place?

The reading put an end to Danilo's good humor. He sat there just at the edge of the lamplight and took no notice of the lesson. From time to time he filled or relit his pipe, and once he spat on the floor, which drew a sharp stare from his wife, and caused Harwell to lose his place in the text.

Sofia, by contrast, hung on every spoken word, her arms folded on the table, her eyes keeping Harwell at his task well beyond the point where he and his pupil had tired of the ancient Briton. He did not think she had understood anything of the story, but the lamplight and the sound of these foreign words worked a kind of magic on her, took years from her face, and left her, it seemed to him, with an expression of wonder that seldom survives childhood.

When he was in bed, and the many events of the day circled lazily in his mind, his thoughts returned to the scent of that white-flowering shrub that was also the scent of her hair, for it lingered still on the back of his hand. At last he allowed himself to imagine that this is how his hand might smell if he had touched her hair.

Chapter Eight

LYDIA DID HER BEST not to look at the envelope that lay cater-cornered on her lap, dropped there in apparent indifference, but so substantial that the weight of it alone distracted her, and by the slightest pressure she could catch those corners in the black nap of her skirt and receive in the flesh of her thighs a sensation that she likened to a jolt of pure and dangerous electricity, causing her to lose track of what Mlle Petrovna was saying.

The assembly proceeded from the mail call to general announce-ments about the coming week, to a recitation of yesterday's demerits for disciplinary and academic shortcomings—certain heads were bowed in shame here—to a reading from Corneille, and finally to prayer, at which point Lydia, being exempt from kneeling by virtue of her Protestantism, lowered her gaze to her envelope and viewed it through half-closed eyes. He was alive. He had written to her. Mlle Petrovna could pray for as long as she liked, and Lydia would float languorously on this river of anticipation.

And yet her mind would not be still. It was unfortunate that the instructors were called before the pupils, as that focused all the more attention on her, for she rarely received letters, and she imagined a smirk on every face in the hall as she went up to receive the envelope, the very large envelope with no foreign stamps on it, from Mlle Petrovna. But she could perfectly well deal with that: let Zara Petrović so much as raise her eyes from her text this afternoon and she would be crushed under an avalanche of demerits both academic and disciplinary.

Lydia was more concerned with the notice taken by the director of the Girls' Institute. Mlle Petrovna's expression of stern good cheer had not wavered, but as she extended the envelope there was a slight motion of her hand that could only mean she was recording and storing away the weight of this correspondence. She had a reputation for knowing everything—that restless energy scoured every dark corner of the building—and she was very well connected in the diplomatic circles of Cetinje, particularly to the Russian minister, for she was his distant relative. And had she not, along with virtually every other foreigner in Cetinje, come under general suspicion only last year when the bombs intended for the prince's palace had been intercepted at Kotor, and on the border of the Sandžak? The Sandžak . . . why had Lydia not made this connection before?

Mlle Petrovna labored under no cloud of suspicion now, for the prince had inaugurated the new gymnasium since Lydia's arrival, and the hand behind the conspirators was more likely to have been Serbian or Austrian than Russian. Still, Draško's account of these events had been quite dramatic, and it seemed entirely plausible to Lydia that the director's connections and influence extended into affairs of state. Much more plausible, in fact, than the idea of Bron Harwell having anything to do with such things. Furthermore, Bron's letter had been in the director's possession since the arrival of the post yesterday afternoon, which was doubly aggravating to Lydia. She would make a careful inspection of the seal on this letter. She would instruct Draško, beg a favor on the strength of their secret connection, to intercept any mail for her from this quarter. (Could he read? Could he at least be trained to recognize this handwriting?) And as for the letter itself, she would put it away until this evening, when she would have time to herself, when she could smoke her cigarette, when she could imagine that Bron Harwell himself was there with her.

The Hermit's Tower (Stupa Vasiljeva)
Kolašin District
Montenegro
12.iv.1908

Dear Lydia:

   Would you believe that there is a postman who calls in such a fantastic place? and that I must hurry to complete my letter to you while he is
consoled with coffee in the kitchen for the rigors of his journey? I had
imagined that I must make my way back to Kolašin, or at least to Andrijevica, and there negotiate the mysteries of the postal system. But this
morning—and it is my luck that the rain kept me housebound today,
when I would otherwise have been off inspecting the ripening seeds in
some alpine pasture, or the flowering specimens at the edge of the snowfields—the postman rode across our meadow, out of nowhere, as if he
knew I had a letter waiting for you. He will be back, he says, in about
two weeks' time.

   In my ignorance of the postal system, and not knowing when I would
be able to get away—I imagine whole mountainsides blooming and
shrivelling unseen—I have resorted to a kind of serial letter (enclosed)
comprising a general description of this place and a sketch of the family,
which in some ways seems to share the characteristics of the landscape,
to have grown out of the rocks themselves, and in other ways is utterly
individual, to the point of striking the visitor as bizarre. I am mindful of
what Count Tolstoy has written about the difference between a happy
family and an unhappy one, and the universal qualities of the former.
My difficulty is that I have yet to decide in which category la famille
Pekočević belongs. In any case, not knowing that I should have this opportunity to address you almost directly—are you sitting in your parlor,
and is that luminous dusk falling from the shoulder of the mountain?—I
wrote all of this up in a general way, and enclose it with this letter. I
hope you will look upon this as information, the sort of particulars you
yourself would have noted, and not hold me to any higher literary
standards.

   Life in these mountains is different and more complex than what I
had expected. You, perhaps, with your understanding of the history, and
your access to the excellent Draško, might have been less surprised.
There is still so much that I do not understand, and which I hope will
become clear to me when I manage to breach the guarded silence of the

master of the house, who seems, for some reason, to resent my presence. Until then, I have the confidence, or at least the good will, of the mistress, who seems an angel out of place in the cruel and strenuous beauty of Montenegro. What young woman—and I do not blush to tell you how beautiful she must have been at the time—deserves a life of near isolation with a maimed and disfigured man, however great a national hero, or, later, to have her two eldest sons taken from her, one in a brawl in the marketplace of Berane, the other mortally involved in some foolish local politics? This background, of course, attaches her all the more to the remaining son, hence her approval of me, as I am to be his salvation, his passport to the world beyond the Hermit's Meadow.

There are few requests or favors that I could deny to Sofia Pekočević, as I stand to such a degree in her debt, as I do to you for the many kindnesses you have shown me, most particularly for the gift of the teakettle, which restores a corner of England to me at sunrise each morning, and the gift of tobacco, which in the evening soothes my mind and invites all manner of pleasant reflections. You may wonder, then, how I can reproach you with anything: but there is this matter of Mr. Drinker's text, which you have supplied, and which the lady of this house wills me to communicate to her son. Was there no other book of a scientific nature that you could have filched from Sir Percy's library? What earthly use can the boy make of the study of water in a land where it is so scarce and where it behaves so erratically, vanishing here, reappearing there? I feel as if I were training a de Lesseps to build his canals in the Sahara, or a Darwin to practice his arts in the barren lunar wastes.

Here is the proposition we wrestled with only yesterday, properly credited by Drinker to Mechanics by O. Lodge:

> A solid has both size and shape.
> A liquid has size but not shape.
> A gas has neither size nor shape.

This is all well and good, but I tell you that by such apparent simplicities we are soon led into pages of the most bewildering material, abstruse theorems and one equation after another in the Hospitalier notation (damn him to Hell whoever he may be). And all of this misery pertains to hydrostatics alone, which is to say the study of liquids at rest; a glance at the later chapters on hydrodynamics makes plain that the difficulties are compounded when your liquid is allowed or encouraged to move.

Still, though I understand almost nothing of this wretched book, it cannot be denied that the boy somehow grasps the ideas through the barrier of language. "Do you understand this?" he says to me, as if I were the pupil, or even a child, and the fact is that I understand the words alone, and in the shallowest sense. What can you tell me of his sister's ability as a student? I am no teacher, and yet the qualities of mind in this boy seem extraordinary to me. He learns English on the strength of your grammar, and glimpses the workings of the universe through the opaque prose of Mr. Drinker. It may be that his mother has chosen well for him. Whether Danilo will allow it remains to be seen.

Of the Sandžak I can give you no real report, as I have only just grazed the edge of it, and peered at those fields and vineyards through my binoculars from the picturesque rim of our meadow. Perhaps its gentleness and fertility—the Sandžak, I mean—are qualities to be appreciated only in relation to the austere magnificence of the surrounding mountains from which I write. But surely the mountaineer, accustomed as he is to the fine air and the strenuous freedom of his life, must gaze down on such a scene and yearn for the relative ease and abundance of lowland agriculture. Danilo, it seems, would have his cake and eat it too, would possess both the mountains and the plain, and everything else that stands between this meadow and the kingdom of Serbia. For the Sandžak, as we discussed, is but a scrap of land lying northwest to southeast between the Serbs of these mountains and those in the kingdom, and from my few conversations with Danilo neither the Turks nor the Austrians have any right to that territory, and will be driven from it when the two halves of his people are reunited. He spoke of this quite vehemently yesterday when I, perhaps unwisely, showed him the purple mountains of Serbia through the binoculars, looking northeast directly across the Sandžak. The image that came to my mind as he spoke was of the waters of the Red Sea, parted for five hundred years rather than a moment, closing again over Pharaoh's army. God help them, I thought.

I have run on at great length in what was supposed to be but a hasty postscript, and perhaps bored you with so many details. God knows what the valiant postman has found to do in the kitchen. It is possible that he too is of the Vasojević clan, in which case the conversational possibilities are endless. It is pleasing to think that this letter will reach you by following my route, more or less, in reverse. Please do not delay in sending

on the other enclosure, as discussed. Any news you can send me of yourself, or of England, would be greatly appreciated.

Faithfully yours,
Auberon Harwell

P.S. Laughter and the clink of glasses from the kitchen, so I have a few
moments' reprieve, which I will use to tell you what I have observed in
the way of social intercourse here, the postman apart. Two days ago, towards the end of the afternoon, we received a call, a ceremonial visit,
from the local Mahometan beg or bey named Esad, who is a principal
landowner in the valley below us, the closest neighbor to this meadow,
and a man of standing in his community, as Danilo is in his. He was
accompanied by his daughter, a girl of fourteen or so, and as the local
people of the other faith do not take the veil until marriage (some influence, perhaps, of the common Serb heritage, or their remoteness from the
centers of Ottoman influence) I was able to view her face, very pleasing,
and remarkably similar to some of the young women I saw at the monastery. In fact, Esad Bey himself, dressed differently and seated like a
Christian in a chair instead of lounging on the ground, would be a
plausible cousin to Danilo, or to Sofia. A vigorous, intelligent man,
whose every motion projects an absolute indolence, which is seen as the
perfection of Ottoman civilization. And whether he knows it or not—and
I would bet that he does not—young Toma has made a conquest, for at
every pause in the conversation the daughter's eyes stole to his face,
though he never addressed a word or a glance to her.

It was certainly not an informal visit. He rode a magnificent white-
stockinged Arab horse and the girl walked, leading an ass, which carried
cushions and a large, gaily striped cloth on which the bey might recline,
and some small gifts. The subject that they had come to discuss was the
fencing of some pasture that abuts Danilo's field, and the diversion of a
little stream through that pasture so that his cows may drink.

Esad Bey is very careful and ceremonial in raising this matter with
Danilo, who has something of a reputation in his dealings with his
neighbors. (Father and daughter would have had to pass by that grisly
collection of heads which I described to you in the serial letter.) Danilo
listens carefully and impassively—they speak exactly the same language—and after several puffs on his pipe, says that it is a reasonable
request, and that he will send Toma to accomplish this work.

There were smiles all around, and a general sigh of relief when Danilo had delivered his judgement, and you were, unwittingly, the agent of a higher diplomacy that saved what might have been a complete rupture of decorum. Danilo, in an expansive and magnanimous mood, offers Esad, seated on his cushions and cloth like the sultan himself, a glass of šljivovica. This is pure carelessness—he cannot have entertained many of his Mahometan neighbors—and even I know that the bey can neither refuse the honor, nor brazenly defile his religion with liquor. As it happened, the visit had interrupted my own preparations for tea, and your kettle was full and just off the boil. I was able to intervene, therefore, with a tin mug of Fortnum and Mason's best Darjeeling tea, which our guest pronounced excellent. Such a look of affectionate gratitude I received from Sofia, and even the maiden bowed her head prettily in my direction. The day was saved, and the victory was yours.

P.P.S. I saw a curious bird yesterday, and I wonder if you know it. It inhabited a high place in the mountains, and it clung to the nearly vertical walls with its feet, the wings spread wide to show its red rump. It must be a kind of creeper, but I have no books with me to consult. Perhaps Draško will know, or you yourself may have seen it.

I enclose a sketch of what I believe is Ramonda serbica, and it is not spoilt or in any way inferior to what I will eventually send to Lord P. I had already sketched this flower in another location, but while I was admiring the creeper I saw a tuft growing so prettily out of a cloven rock that I could not resist. This green is the exact color of the rosettes in that high, clear light, and note the tiny golden hairs. You must think me a foolish fellow to be so caught up in the fancies of spring.

Lydia indulged herself in another cigarette and tried to imagine the textures of life in that remote place, building on the images in the very pleasing letter that lay in her lap, now covered in a careless dusting of tobacco shreds. She had read the "serial letter" first, and was surprised at such an outburst of information where she had steeled herself to silence or to an occasional reticent note. Had she misjudged him? She felt that she had extracted an unwilling promise of a "real letter," and its arrival both embarrassed and delighted her. But for all his careful descriptions of people and place, the parts of the letter that resonated for her, were most real, were those passages in which he described himself: how he made his tea in the morning, how he had cut his hand on one of his forays, how he had made such a botch of washing his clothes that Sofia had taken them away from him and done them all over again. This last item caused her a pang, for she would so gladly have done that service for him, would have knelt by the stream and taken the shirt with the precious dirt on the collar and . . . The idea of the shirt was very distracting to her. She wished that she had the shirt to remember him by, would rather have had the shirt than the letter, if it came to that, for it would evoke, with no effort of her own will, that starry evening with the cold wind on her back and her face pressed to his chest. Well, she thought, I must be grateful that he writes to me, and thinks of me, and that he is alive. It should be enough for me that he is in good hands.

Without thinking of it, she picked up the other letter, as weighty as her own, that had been enclosed and which she must send straightaway to Lord Polgrove via Mr. Baxter. The seal on this letter was broken, which presented a problem. The seal on the outer envelope was intact when she received it—her suspicions of Mlle Petrovna notwithstanding—and she recognized the mark there of Bron's signet ring. But this inner envelope for his patron had the merest skim of sealing wax, and somehow it had broken in transit. Should she explain? Should she reseal the letter? Would not Lord Polgrove assume, in any case, that she had taken this liberty? Believing herself to have been unfairly judged in advance, she opened the letter in a spirit of vindication.

> *c/o Miss Lydia Wadham*
> *The Girls' Institute*
> *Cetinje, Montenegro*
> *10.iv.1908*

Your Lordship:

I am arrived at a spot in the mountains of southeastern Montenegro which must be almost exactly 20° east and twenty miles or so south of 43° north, and here I intend to stay for as long as the Pekočević family will have me, making such excursions as reason and caution dictate to inform myself on conditions in the Sandžak of Novi Pazar and the relations between the population, the beleaguered Turkish administration, and the Austrian garrison. I hope that the rough map I have enclosed will clarify this difficult geography.

The valley, or hanging meadow, in which I am lodged seems particularly propitious from this point of view: I am near enough to the Sandžak itself that I can literally look down upon it from the sheer limestone crenellations rimming the meadow, can see not only the ploughmen at their tasks in those fields, but also the shells of houses and abandoned hamlets belonging to Christian families who were burnt out in the fighting along this desperate and wholly whimsical border, or who simply gave up their livelihoods in the face of a firmly established (or reestablished) Mahometan oppression and retreated once more to these forbidding heights.

The meadow is so placed that I am only a few miles west and on the same latitude as the border between the Sandžak and the vilayet of Kosovo to the south, of which the Sandžak used to be an administrative district before being garrisoned by Austria according to the terms of the Treaty of Berlin. (More on this heading later.) Although the Austrians have been gradually establishing their control over the Sandžak—their most recent garrison is installed in Bijelo Polje, a few miles northwest of me—they do not influence the Kosovo region south of the Ibar, which is as loosely held as any Turkish province ever was, and is overrun by the ethnic Albanians, or Arnaouts, as they are called by the other races and religions in these parts. These Arnaouts are a capricious and ungovernable bunch, and they will shoot a tax collector or even a governor as soon as look at him, and in any calculation you make of the political and military future of this place they must be taken into account. There are more than a few of them in the Sandžak as well—they are for the most part, and for the sake of convenience, co-religionists of the Turk—but their lawlessness is held in check there by the strenuous presence of the Austrian garrison, which takes a firm hand in local matters affecting the stability of the Turkish civil administration, as they do in Bosnia and Herzegovina.

To the north of this spot, then, is the Sandžak, and I can see diagonally up through it as far as those mountains of Serbia proper; the Sandžak bends around our mountainous promontory to the east, where it meets Kosovo province, and that land continues on around me to the south, into the mouth of the Rugovo Klisura, a steep defile ending in the wall of Montenegro, which can be negotiated by a narrow and

18°
Sarajevo
BOSNIA
SERBIA
R. Drina
SANDŽAK OF NOVI PAZAR
Prijepolje
R. Lim
HERZEGOVINA
R. Tara
R. Piva
Bijelo Polje
R. Tara
Nikšić
Morača
Kolašin
Berane
Stupe Vasiljeva
MONTENEGRO
Andrijevica
DALMATIA
Ragusa
Spuž
R. Morača
ADRIATIC SEA
Kotor
Cetinje
Podgorica
ALBANIA
L. Scutari
42°
20°

dreadful road to Andrijevica. Were there not rugged mountains at my back I could look south from my eyrie into the vale of Peć, seat of the ancient patriarchate of the Serbian church, which is embraced by the mountains of Rugovo. It is said that the Christians in that place have suffered terribly from the combination of misrule by the Turk and lawless depredations by the Arnaout.

Although I do not set much store in Divine Providence, it is the most amazing and fortunate coincidence that has landed me in this exact location, and the position of this family in Montenegro proper and in the context of the disputed border only became clear to me in conversation with a monk on my journey here.

You will remember, no doubt, the noise made over the discovery of those bombs in Cattaro (Kotor) last year, how everyone from the tsar to the pope to Prince Michael of the royal house of Serbia was suspected of having a hand in this effort to blow up Prince Nikola. It turns out that the conspiracy was wider than was suspected at the time of the discovery in Cattaro, and that some of the conspirators came directly overland from Serbia, through the Sandžak, and were apprehended here in these mountains on their journey west to Cetinje. More astonishing still, some of those conspirators were local people, of the Vasojević clan, long counted the staunchest patriots among the mountaineers.

My host is of the Vasojević, and counted as one of the greatest heroes in the wars in Herzegovina thirty years ago, where he collected the heads of many of his enemies, which trophies he has placed here, in a state of almost miraculous preservation, as a warning to every Mahometan who sets foot in this meadow. Imagine, then, the anguish of Danilo Pekočević, to learn that his son Vuk has taken part in this conspiracy organized by what they call the Black Hand, has been taken into custody as an enemy of the state with a bomb from the Serbian royal arsenal in his baggage. Imagine also the anguish of his mother, and the other children, when Vuk Pekočević is summarily condemned to death with two other plotters, and the entire family is made to witness this execution, which is carried out at a lonely crossroads in the Montenegrin style, by which I mean a firing squad comprising one member from each of the several clans, so that the death cannot be avenged via the interminable blood feud that would otherwise pertain. The boy was hastily buried on the spot, and the family was not allowed even to touch the corpse. I have not spoken of this matter with my host or his wife, but the monk's testimony is, I believe, quite reliable. The son's name has never been mentioned here.

From this incident you can infer a good deal about the relations among various parties in this region. The bombs quite certainly were manufactured in Serbia, and so it may be that King Peter of Serbia has sanctioned this attempt against his father-in-law, Nikola, in an effort to establish his preeminence in the Serb world. That the explosives should have arrived in Montenegro via the Sandžak must indicate some Austrian compliance, perhaps even encouragement. (The Turks would always be happy to spit in the Montenegrin's eye, needless to say, but I doubt they are capable of organizing anything.) But the willingness of any Montenegrin to be involved in this Black Hand business, to be a pawn of Serbia—and, perhaps, ultimately of Austria—and a mortal enemy to his own sovereign, is quite baffling, and shows to what an extent this Idea of Great Serbia, as the monk put it, has inflamed the imaginations of at least the younger set of "patriots," who grow restless and resentful of Prince Nikola. He has been promising his people for almost fifty years now, ever since his accession, that the time will soon be ripe to sweep the Turks and the Arnaouts from the Sandžak and join with their brothers in free Serbia.

I cannot help feeling that it all comes back, in the end, to the Treaty of Berlin, that mischief devised in the name of diplomacy by the Great Powers. A blind and drunken man could not have made a greater mess of the job done in these mountains, where the commissioners dared not venture to see how the land lay, how their line would divide brother from brother, and, in the case of the Pekočevićs, cut right through the holding of one family.

But if the Sandžak had been divided between Serbia and Montenegro as originally envisioned after Russia and the South Slavs humbled Turkey, and if some guarantees had been given for the safety of the non-Christian population, then the Turk could have retreated to more easily defensible regions, and the Austrians would have been out of it altogether. And, by granting the Serbs at least a portion of their Great Serbia, this deadly squabbling would have been avoided. But Austria would not be denied her corridor of influence towards Salonika and the Aegean, and she had Germany to back her and, finally, England, because we feared Russia as the greater evil.

My host has as yet had nothing to say on politics either local or inter-

national, but he labors under the twin burdens of a sense of wrong (the border affair, now thirty years old) and a sense of guilt (the bomb plot). He makes no threats, but his own exploits speak for themselves, and he has written a letter, so the monk told me, reaffirming his loyalty to Prince Nikola and pledging himself and his family to the prince's service. The merest word from Cetinje would unleash him on the Turks, or the Austrians, or the Arnaouts, or whoever stands between him and the mountains of Serbia proper. He is in himself a bomb of sorts.

Although I have not yet found a pretext for visiting the Sandžak, the Sandžak has come to me, in a manner of speaking. Just this afternoon we received a visit from one of the closest neighbors to the Pekočevićs, one Esad Bey, a man of substance. The discussion, quite stiff and formal, was of no great interest to you—a matter of a fence and a ditch of some sort—but the bearing and breeding of this man brought home to me the complexity of the land below us.

It would be a mistake to think of the situation in terms of two teams in a tug-of-war: the Montenegrins on this side and the Mahometans across the border (with a sprinkling of Christian rayahs, or serfs). In fact this man Esad Bey is more like Danilo than either would care to admit, and in their small talk they referred most slightingly to the Arnaouts, who are a plague to them both. Esad is what Lady Mackenzie refers to as the Bosniac, which is to say one of the defeated Serb lords who accepted the religion of the Turk in order to preserve their estates. Several hundred years ago these two men would have been brothers. Today they are cautious neighbors, but they can never be friends, and I do not know how far Danilo would be willing to observe the distinction between his guest this afternoon and the Arnaout rabble. I do not know if there are any true Turks, or Osmanlees, among the population of the Sandžak— other than the tax collectors and local governors—now that the Turkish troops have been replaced by the Austrian garrisons.

Finally, while I hesitate to put myself forward as anything other than a collector of seeds, I have enclosed several sketches of plants that have seemed particularly striking or noteworthy, along with a list of what I have been able to identify (quite tentatively) among the alpines here. Do please let me know which among these seem interesting, and I shall concentrate upon the seed of those species. There are two saxifrages that particularly intrigue me, and of which I can find no mention in your reference volumes: one a shade-loving white with a delicate flower spike

that trembles in any breeze, and the other a pink kabschia, I would
guess, with veining of red in the throat of each tiny flower that I could
study for hours with my glass. Please see my sketches for a more objective
rendering of these two species, which may perhaps have escaped the notice of previous travellers in these parts.

Your servant,
Auberon Harwell

Chapter Nine

IT WAS ON THE NIGHT of the full moon that Harwell thought he heard the earth speaking to him. The weather was warmer now, so that he slept with just the one blanket, and through the open door came, unmuted, many sounds of the night: the little stream swollen by snowmelt, tree frogs, the soft stamping of horses, and, every now and again, the call of some nightjar. But the sound that he conceived as the voice of the earth itself came not from the pasture but from somewhere in this very room, a kind of rattle with an eerie undertone to it, something halfway between music and a friction of the rocks from which God had made Montenegro. He smiled to think that such a notion had stuck in his head, then rose to close the door so that he might hear the noise more clearly.

Had he been fast asleep he would probably have heard nothing at all, but the moon shining through his window cast uneasy shadows about the walls, and there, through the black rectangle of the door frame that was like a window onto a dream, the pasture was invested with a brilliant colorless light, redoubled by the brightness of the limestone crags. He had known when he lay down that sleep would not come early, even though he had ridden many miles that day to a snowfield—one of the last remaining—on a northern slope of the mountains. His body was tired enough, and he had eaten a dinner of meat that made him drowsy even at the table. But afterwards, Danilo had offered him a glass of *šljivovica* and had asked him if he would not consider moving into the house with them, now that Toma had taken himself off up the side of the cliff to live in the hermit's cave. It was a most curious conversation, aside from the fact that it drew Danilo into more energetic intercourse than Harwell expected from him in a whole day: Toma stared fixedly at his empty plate, unwilling to enter any discussion of his removal from the house, and, if Harwell was not mistaken, Danilo's offer was prompted by a gesture from Sofia, who stood near the hearth, drying dishes on her apron.

Harwell had refused the offer with effusive thanks that strained the limits of his vocabulary, but he was definite on this point. The shed he occupied was quite sufficient for his needs, more than he expected or deserved, and he would not impose further on their hospitality. And besides, he said, he could keep an eye on all his belongings there, and he liked being able to make a fire for his tea without disturbing the order and the routines of their kitchen. And besides, he thought, raising his eyes to measure the ceiling above him, there would be only a few feet and a thin wooden partition between his bed and theirs.

There had been no lesson that evening, and after a second glass of the brandy and some desultory conversation about methods of planting, Harwell excused himself. As he was now fully awake, his head bursting with confused thoughts, he began a letter to Lydia, and filled two sides of the sheet with a description of his travels in the mountains, which, upon rereading, he found somewhat wanting in tenderness. He put the letter aside, to be finished when he received some word from her, which might come as early as tomorrow. And because he was still not drowsy, because Lydia and Sofia were both with him somewhere in the bright shadows, he undressed and lay down on his bed with the little dictionary that Princess Zorana had given him as a parting gift in Paris, saying that if he would read it every night, he might someday come to a mastery of the Serbian language, though her eyes told him that she was in grave doubt of his success.

She was no more a princess than his mother was, he suspected, though certain artifacts on her desk and shelves did suggest a distant splendor that contrasted oddly with the shabby present. Her manners were faultless, and she disdained vulgarity in any form, but how her eyes did light on that little envelope of crisp banknotes that he slid onto the corner of her desk each Friday afternoon. Well, she probably meant no harm, and he had learned the rudiments of the language, and more, in the course of his six weeks with her. And if he had not followed her advice to the letter, he did spend a good deal of time thumbing through the dictionary in pursuit of words and phrases too common to have been used by the princess. He had just encountered the word for "diamond" and connected it with the hostler's phrase to describe that unorthodox knot, when his eyes closed at last and he drowsed fitfully, flinching from time to time at the bite of insects drawn to his candle.

The noise had roused him, and now, with the door closed, he heard it again, more distinctly, from somewhere over near his pack and the rude hearth that consisted of three rocks arranged in a triangle. Lydia's kettle rested on another rock that was really part of the floor, though it rose several inches above the packed earth like the flattened top of an iceberg, something too big to have been moved during the construction of the shed. Harwell laid his hand on the kettle and felt a tingling against his dry palm, as if an electrical charge ran through the metal. He took his hand away, and there was the sound again, the metal vibrating to the rock, never loud, but occasionally much fainter, a kind of antiphony, one region of the earth speaking to another. He took the kettle away, laid his ear to the cold, rough rock, and heard, or felt, more distinctly the thrum of that tuning fork so vast and deep, for all he knew, that it touched the center of the earth.

He searched his mind for rational explanations, scientific explanations, and found none. Well, that was not surprising, for he really knew nothing about such matters, and there might well be some perfectly simple key to the phenomenon. When he stopped worrying at it and merely listened, he could almost discern a kind of rhythm or pattern to it, almost as if . . . And then it stopped altogether. He lay down again, resolving to write down this incident for Lydia tomorrow, and took up his dictionary. It was a relatively modern book, printed in Paris, and yet it offered nothing at all on the heading of Electricity or Magnetic Field. He yawned. Well, such a handicap would render Princess Zorana's explanation of the mystery all the more colorful: the singing of whales, perhaps, or the Nemanja kings forging new weapons in a volcano, preparing for that second coming in which every true Serb secretly believed. He blew out his candle and was soon asleep. One of the last sounds he heard was a rock falling. That would be Toma.

There, thought Toma, who had been watching the window of Harwell's shed for some time, *he is asleep at last.* They had left the house together in a friendly silence, each going his separate way, presumably to sleep. But the moon which troubled Harwell had a special meaning for Toma, for on this night he had an appointment to keep.

He climbed the rock face out of the valley floor easily, for he was strong and agile, and he had found through trial and error, and mostly with his eyes closed in concentration, the all but invisible hand and foot holds that the monk had used before him, and which his brother, too, must have discovered for himself. Vuk had lived in the cave for the last two years of his life, and now he, Toma, had decided that it was his time. He needed only some fresh straw to make a bed out of the old piece of canvas that Vuk had brought up here, for he was determined to be no less ascetic than those who had gone before him. His mother had stared at him when he announced where he would go, but said nothing, and his father, silent as well, had seemed almost pleased.

He had at least an hour to wait, and he sat on a roughly squared stone, right at the edge of the steep access, with his back to Vasili's ruined arch. Weeds grew rank in the little courtyard, or what was now a courtyard after the collapse of the roof and the cave mouth. Vuk must have cleared the debris when he came to live here, for Toma had found, at the base of the cliff, a rock with a fragment of the monk's painting on it: an angel's wing, and that was all. There in the moonlight, when he turned his head away from the valley, was the rest of the painting, the grand celebration of death fading into true darkness at the top of the cave. Vasili was no more accomplished at painting than he was at building, and yet his works remained, in spite of everything: time, earthquakes, and the violent frustration of the Turks, who had not found their way to this place, though they could see it from below, and had contented themselves with shooting the eyes out of Vasili's saints and damned souls. Below was the tower, another of his works, which the Turks had not dared to touch in all these hundreds of years. Toma wondered if he should have put fresh straw in there this afternoon.

To the right of the tower, a short space across the ghostly meadow, was the shed with Harwell's guttering light in the window. He would be reading now, or dozing and wasting his candle. Or perhaps writing his letters, which he often did when he had his books and his journal spread out before him on the table in the kitchen. Toma had found one tucked between the pages of the large flower book, the edge of it just showing. It was a letter to a woman, he was sure, for while he was hindered both by the English words and by the unfamiliar cursive script, he recognized it as a love letter by its tone, a letter such as a man might write to a woman he longs for, such as he might write to Aliye if there were any means to send it to her, or if she could read it. And in the diary itself, filled with Harwell's botanical notations and record of the temperature, weather, rainfall, et cetera, there were other passages, writing of the sort found in that letter, but addressed to no one, a kind of dream sequence in which the only clear message was the wretchedness of the dreamer. Toma had no intention of prying into Harwell's affairs, but it sounded very much to him as if this man was sick for love, just as it was described in the ballads.

And was he himself sick for love, as it was described in the ballads? He thought not, in spite of the hot flush he felt in his face and the inexorable excitement of his flesh when he dwelled on the image of Aliye rising from the water at his command, endowed with grace, and beauty, and modesty that flooded his mind even in recollection. This memory disturbed him because he had no power over it, was in fact its slave, and he held it against Aliye sometimes that because of her he could not be as pure in his thoughts, as single-minded as the monk who had made this place, or his brother who had followed after him. And she was weak, where he wanted to be strong, and when her father had come to ask a favor of his father she had made no attempt to keep her eyes from him, and he knew that the English had seen this.

He was a curious man, the English, like a child in the things that he did not know, or at least asked about. How could a grown man not know which way the wind blows during the winter, or how the barley is made into bread, and who could not tell time by the stars? And yet, although he was like a child, and as friendly as a child, there was something in him, something about the people from which he sprang, and Toma had respect for this . . . he did not know quite what to call it, except that it was like a power that must be answered or acknowledged. Toma recognized this in the very articles and implements that the English carried: his silver-capped pen; his pocket-knife with a blade as sharp as any razor and cunning brass rivets that shone like true gold in the shell handle; even the little compass with its leather case and oil-filled crystal, without which the English had not the faintest idea where north lay, or east. Harwell had offered him the compass one day in the mountains, giving him to understand that it was his to keep, as he had a spare. Toma refused, partly because he had no need of the thing, but also because he hoped that the knife might one day be his. The only disappointment to Toma was that Harwell did not carry a real English rifle, but that curious weapon which was useful only against birds. He had seen a real one once, belonging to a kinsman on his mother's side: it was not new, having been taken from a Turkish soldier years ago in Herzegovina, but it was so carefully preserved that it seemed better than new, and when he touched the bolt mechanism it slid open like a hungry mouth. "English," his kinsman had said, snapping the bolt to. "English."

English. The word had stuck in his mind before he knew anything about that place and that people other than that they made this beautiful, lethal thing that he would have given his arm to possess. English. And when Harwell appeared in the meadow and came to live with them, that is what Toma called him, behind his back at first, now as a familiarity that Harwell seemed not to resent. But the real power of this man, the English, lay not in what he carried, but what he knew, or had studied.

As a child Toma had been given a knife purchased for him by his father in the bazaar at Berane, and he played with it, sometimes cutting himself, but never seriously, until it became almost a part of him, something that he could use without thinking. And his sister had been given balls of wool or of flax when she sat in the sun before the door, tied by a ribbon to the bench so that she could not wander away into the animal enclosures, and by the time she was eight she was able to make a fine thread, just with her fingers, and again without thinking of it. The English was like that too, but his toys must have been books, for he could call up whole passages of what he had read, or had been read to him, with no more effort than Danilo, with the *gusle* in his hands, could recite for hours the ballads and the heroic poems that were the unwritten books of Montenegro.

Harwell's books, those he carried and those he had in his head, were from many countries, apparently, and they did not consist solely of songs of war and valor. He told Toma about these books and the men who had written them, sometimes reciting whole passages in languages that Toma did not understand, although one of these poets, Harwell's favorite, spoke a tongue that reminded him of the Phanariotes, or Greeks, who were sometimes to be found selling oil and dried fruits in the market at Berane.

That poem, Harwell's favorite, had indeed been a story of war, and both he and his mother listened in satisfaction to the words they did not understand, knowing that Harwell, afterwards, would tell them what it all had meant, and why this Homer had been the greatest of poets. He had lived many hundreds of years before even the battle of Kosovo, which was on the farthest horizon in Toma's mind, and he was said to have been blind, which perhaps accounted for . . . Blind? Yes, according to the legend. And Toma smiled, for even in these mountains, among the bards of his own people, this ancient blind singer was known and honored.

When Harwell tired of the books that Natalia's teacher had sent—how soon he tired of these!—he might read to Toma from a little book of writings, essays, he called them, about the great men and the government of England, which Harwell insisted was the best in the world. Toma did not begin to understand Harwell's government, which sounded improbably complex, but there was a power in the words that even he could appreciate when he was made to read aloud: ". . . but in the House of Commons, not a single one of the malcontents durst lift his eyes above the buckle of Pitt's shoe."

"But this is not science," his mother had said in a tone of gentle reproof.

"Ah," said the English, wrapped in the happiness that these words brought him, "it is better than any science." And Sofia smiled and bowed her head, unwilling to contradict him, for anyone could see that when he was reading or remembering these books Harwell was thinking of his country and his family, and missing them.

Would he miss his family if he went away to study, as his mother and Harwell said he must? He could not imagine it, though if Natalia, who was two years younger than he, could survive in Cetinje, he would be ashamed to fail. Would he miss Aliye? He glanced at the heavens and knew it must be nearly time.

He took his knife, the big one, and with its tip explored the unforgiving ground at his feet. When he found a spot where he could get it down half a hand's breadth, he took a stone and tapped the handle to lodge it deeper still, then plucked the handle once, felt the thrill of it in the rock he sat on, and sat back to wait.

Minutes passed, and the moon shadows of the broken arch above him touched the toe of his shoe. He plucked the knife once, and again, and held his breath to listen. Nothing. She was late, perhaps had encountered one of her sisters on her way to the privy. Maybe she slept. And yet he knew that was not so, for she burned as he did, and had told him that she often woke from a sound sleep at just this hour, even on nights when the moon was not full, and when she knew he would not be calling to her. And sometimes, she told him, looking away from his face, sometimes on those nights when she woke she went to the dark slope behind the privy and stabbed her knife into the ground as he had shown her. And she waited, knowing he would not send for her. She would rather be there than in her bed.

And so he waited for her now, but not without hope, and in fact it was as if he could see her in his mind's eye making herself ready for her journey. Everything must be placed where she could find it without a sound and without thinking: an extra shawl, a stout pair of slippers. She would already have hidden the knife in the rocks, so that she would not drop it on the floorboards, would have stolen, early in the day, a drop of her mother's perfume for herself, so that the smell of it would be no surprise in the darkened house. And when they lay together her body would be as sweet as the melon that has been picked in the morning and set in the well against the heat of the day, to be drawn forth in the evening.

He saw these things now as if they occurred before his eyes, and he did not know if this was what happened to others, or something special to him. His mother had told him about the saints and kings who had lived before the battle of Kosovo, and who saw visions, sometimes of the Lord or the Holy Mother, sometimes of their own fate in battle. The bones of these holy men were revered by the true Serbs, and carried away into the mountains from such places as Peć or Decani when it seemed as if harm might come to them. The hermit who had lived in this cell or cave, and who had been a monk before that at Decani, must have had a kind of vision of the end of the world, for he had painted it there on the ceiling. He would find a way to ask his mother about this. Perhaps this was a place of visions.

He had known, from the first time he laid eyes on Aliye in the market at Berane, that something must come of it. That was a year, more than a year ago, and he smiled now to think what a child he had been, how he had known nothing of what might pass between a man and a woman, only that there was this fate that they recognized in each other's eyes before a word was spoken. Aliye had said that this was what she felt as well, and that no words were necessary, or possible. Perhaps later she said to her sister, or to herself, "I have seen a boy . . ."

He may have seen her before, for their families were known to each other, and there was a kind of mutual respect in the prickly formality that governed such encounters. But if so he had paid no attention to her, and it was at this moment that he saw her truly, saw himself in her eyes. A couple of times afterwards, in the next few weeks, he had glimpsed her again, because he was always looking for her, and it was the same each time. There was no way for them to speak, but he had learned her name from an Arnaout candlemaker at a stall in the bazaar. He had seen Aliye's mother with the old woman, bargaining comfortably and conversationally to arrive at the same price as the month before, while he watched from a carpenter's stall, for he followed them through the marketplace without any hope beyond a glance of those eyes back over her shoulder. *Aliye*, the old woman had told him, looking hard at him. *She is a good girl, the light of her mother's eyes. If you buy that candle there, the scented one, I will give it to her when she returns.* And he bought the candle, telling a lie to his father about how he had come to lose that coin in a drain.

He had seen her next in the field, when he had been sent down to pull the weeds that sprang up between the young shoots of corn, and he knew that from that day on she would be looking for him as well, for the candlemaker had been as good as her word. She had offered him water and a piece of dried fruit, and he had told her his name.

In the time between the ploughing and the harvest, there was nothing for the oxen to do other than rest and eat, and as Danilo must make hay for the winter from the rich grass of the meadow, he sent the animals away for the summer months to be tended with the considerable herd that gathered in the pastures to the northwest, a gentle, unfenced grassland that stretched from the flat country near Berane up into the higher elevations, and these pastures, a day's journey from one end to the other, had been used by Serb and Turk alike for generations, wherever the border might be drawn. Toma was now old enough to share the work of tending the herd—one hundred oxen and more—and there he met other boys his own age, many of them his cousins, and slept under the stars, moving with the herd, turning them sometimes in the middle of the night if they wandered too far in the direction of the Mahometan herd, which was kept by boys very much like himself, perhaps Aliye's kinsmen.

It was here that he learned to catch a trout with his hand, and how to take the musk glands out of a boar or a deer if they were lucky enough to shoot one. And here also he learned how one herder might signal to another, far away, that the animals were moving, and in which direction. This was done by a knife driven into the ground, like the one now at his feet, and a knife in the ground a league away would vibrate in sympathy to the one that was struck or plucked, catching exactly the rhythm and the force of it. He had never been happier in his life than during the time he spent in the high pasture.

Food was sent up to them from time to time, oil and bread and fruit, and often it was the women of the family who walked out together, turning the journey into a holiday excursion, just to make sure that sons and brothers had not turned too far towards savagery. From the top of one low hill, on a hot midday, he had seen several girls, driving an ass before them, entering the camp of the Mahometans across a little wooded creek, and there had been laughter and shouts as the baskets were lifted down. He had wondered if perhaps Aliye was among them, and thought how they could walk for a whole day in the grasslands or sit on this hill under the stars all night and be seen by nobody.

The weather grew hotter, and sometimes Toma would walk up that creek that skirted the camp of the Turkish boys to its source not far upstream, a spring and a pool in a rocky cleft where the land grew steep again. One afternoon he was lying in the cool water, in the shadow of a rock, when he heard voices above the flow of the water, and yet he was not afraid. He moved behind the rock so that he might not be seen.

The voices belonged to women, and one of them, he was certain, was Aliye. They had come to sit in the shade of the trees, or perhaps to wash their legs and their arms where the boys could not see them, but they would not bathe.

"You must not go in the water, Aliye."

"But I will," she said, "for I can swim as well as my brother. Are you afraid of the water? Think how it will feel on your neck."

"And on your . . ." There was a word that Toma did not catch, and which was drowned anyway in nervous laughter. He thought there might be three girls. He held his breath.

"Yes," said Aliye, "there too, and why not? Think how far we have walked this morning, and how far we must walk to get home."

"Aliye, do you not know what this place is called?" asked another voice. Apparently Aliye did not care, for there was the sound of great splashing—she must already be in the water—and the laughing protests from the others grew faint as they retreated down the path. Except for the trickle of water over the lip of the pool, there was no sound at all.

Toma put his hand over his mouth so that his voice would be thrown against the rock at his back. "Aliye." The name echoed around the pool and he could taste it on his tongue. "Aliye," he called again, and then edged out from behind the rock so she would not be frightened anymore.

They faced each other across the pool, a distance of a few paces, and except that she had her lip caught between her teeth she showed no sign of being afraid. It was he, now, who was afraid, in spite of the new strength in his brown arms and shoulders, in spite of the brave, coarse jesting in camp about what they would do if they found the Turkish girls alone. And since he did not know what to say, or what to do, he swam closer until he felt the rocky shelf rising under his feet and crouched there, an arm's length away, his ears full of the sound of his own breathing. She had not moved a muscle at his approach, had not blinked, and the little ripples lapped just at the points of her collarbones.

"Stand up, Aliye." He did not know what else to say, thought that something must be said. And perhaps because she was accustomed to obeying when a man told her what to do, she stood up out of the water and showed herself to him without trying to cover herself with her hands. The first motion she made was to touch her hand to the skin of her forearm, to the prickled skin there.

"Goose bumps," she said softly, trying to rub them away. He would have looked at her all day, or longer if the sun would stand still, and would have asked no more. Even the crease in her elbow was perfect and beautiful. But she grew anxious under his gaze, and would not meet his eyes, but bowed to the task of smoothing away the chill from her arm.

"And you, Toma?" The sound of her voice—she had spoken to him only once before—caught his heart in his throat, and because he could not speak he rose out of the water, stumbling slightly when a rock shifted under his foot. She made a little noise, perhaps the beginning of a laugh, and he did not know what to think, for the cool water and the fear—fear of what?—had taken all desire from him, and that part of him lay shrivelled against his leg. Should he cover himself with his hand? Should he be angry with her? He stood there, mute, waiting for what must happen next, glad for the heat of the sun beating down on his body.

She reached up behind her head, her breasts lifting to him as she did so, and took the comb from her hair. It was this gesture that made her seem a woman and not a frightened child, and the coiled plait fell so thickly about her when she shook her head that she could have hidden herself from him if she had wanted to. And because she was a woman in his eyes, and not a child, he must be a man. Desire was restored to him, and a certainty of how to proceed. He took her hand and led her out of the pool to the cool shade.

Later that same evening he put his bed near the fire—there in the distance was the fire of the Mahometan camp—and asked one of the older boys what that place was called where the water came out of the ground and fed the pool under a cliff. The boy replied that it was called Our Lady's Fountain by the Christians, and something else by the Turks, but the legend about it was the same for both: that women who could not conceive might do so if they came to that pool to pray and to bathe in its waters.

There: the sound that he had been waiting for, and yet he had been so rapt in memory that he almost missed the faint, humming vibration of his knife, a sound like the wings of the small hovering bird. Perhaps he had not heard her first signal, for he had been thinking of that afternoon by the spring, how the stubble of grass had pricked them and how a fine, sweet dust lay on them when they were spent. His hand had been damp with the sweat of her, and when he touched the curve of her hip he left a muddy mark in that dust. They went back to the water, she leading him, and they washed each other, then sat in the shallows, their hands entwined, listening to the birds above them, knowing that everything was changed.

He struck his knife now and got her response—it was a poor little knife that she had, and yet it worked just well enough—and then began his message in the code that they had devised, that all was well, and that she was to meet him in half an hour's time in the hermit's tower. He paused to give her a chance to signal back that she understood: once for Yes; long and short, which would mean that she did not understand, or please repeat; and three rapid strokes, a signal that she had never yet used, to mean No.

Half an hour—which suddenly seemed a long time to wait— should be just long enough for her to climb to the meadow, as the road was clear and the moon would show her the way. Last month there had been a week of rain and heavy clouds and he had told her not to come, and the month before that, the first occasion after the forced abstinence of the winter, it had been so cold that even the heat of his body could not warm her fully, and the hermit's tower had been a dank, unwelcoming place. From the high window that night he had watched her make her way across the moonlit meadow, and saw how she left the road to give wide berth to the heads, and so had to wade through the puddles of snowmelt. And the first time she had seen them, which had been in the autumn, she had uttered a shriek, which, though she had strangled it in her shawl, might have woken his parents.

Well, he thought, trying to dismiss the awkward subject from his mind, there is nothing for it: she must pass by the heads to come to him, and he would show her what it meant to be alive. There was a kind of desperation to their trysts in the tower, because it was so cold there and because they must make no noise. He longed for the warmth and the light that might be theirs in summer.

Harwell's light was extinguished at last, and Toma looked about him to see where he had left the skin of water, the fruit, and the sweet cake. He might have brought her here, and it would have been a welcome change from where he was bound, where he had to stoop in the darkness that smelled of mice in order not to smash his head on the hermit's bells. But even with his help she would never have found her way safely to this view and to the comparative luxury of his bed. And even though he had gotten used to it, had turned his mind away from it as a test of his will, there was the smell of death in this place.

Toma was thinking of his brother Vuk as he descended the cliff, and that was how he missed his footing and would have fallen but for the strength in his hands.

Auberon Harwell had a passion for sharpening knives, and it was one thing that he thought he did better, because he cared more about it, than most men he knew. He would test his pocketknife every time he used it, and if he could not fell a hair with the merest pressure, out came the tiny whetstone: the finest black Arkansas stone on one side, leather on the other for the final pass. The mark of this obsession was a permanent stubble of stunted hairs on the back of his left wrist.

Sofia's knives were already quite satisfactorily sharp, a labor which had rewarded him with several hours of conversation, and now he turned his hand to the sharpening of those tools of Danilo's which he had found stacked in corners and hanging from pegs in his shed. He did not know whether Danilo wanted him to do this, and did not ask, but saw it as one small thing he could do to repay his host's hospitality.

He had found a piece of coarse whetstone, broken off at about six inches, which was too short to do the job properly, and with this he had put an edge to a scythe and a kind of sickle, both of which had light blades of soft steel. But when it came to the ax he despaired, for it had nicks and gouges as if it had been used on rocks, not wood, and there was an implacable roundness to the edge that would not yield to the stone. He needed a proper grindstone for this, or at least a file. He sat in the sun before the door of his shed and fretted.

"Sir," he called to Danilo, who sat on the bench by the kitchen door, inspecting a piece of harness. "Have you a . . . the tool for making the ax sharp?" What a cursed language this was, and what a fool he.

"You have that thing, the stone, in your hand. Does it not work for you?" Danilo had made no comment this morning on Harwell's project, had not even seemed to notice.

"No. Well, yes . . . but for the ax I need that metal thing, with little teeth on it, the . . ."

Danilo stared at him. "The saw?"

Harwell got up to fetch his dictionary, and returned, blinking in the strong light. "The file," he said triumphantly. "I need the file."

Danilo had exactly such a thing. He produced, from some corner of the house, a wooden box with various woodworking tools, many of them carefully wrapped in leather, and from these he offered Harwell both a rasp and a file. Harwell took the latter and was pleased to find the diagonal ridges only moderately worn. He could work with this.

"I had forgotten I had these things," said Danilo, staring at the rasp. "I built a bed for my wife once, and then a cradle, which served for each child. But that was years ago, and I have turned my mind to other things. Perhaps I should have given these to my sons. Perhaps . . . Well, you have the one you need?"

"Yes," said Harwell cheerfully, hoping to lead the conversation away from Danilo's memories. "At home we would use a large stone wheel, turning it with the foot to sharpen an ax or a hoe, but this will work just as well. We call it a bastard file, because . . . well, I'm not sure exactly why we call it that."

"What name do you give it?"

"I suppose there are several names, really . . ."

" 'Bastard' you say?"

"Yes." Harwell sighed. "A bastard file." And at this point Danilo broke into a huge smile and clapped Harwell on the shoulder. He repeated the word several times and chuckled to himself.

"You speak our language well. Do you like it?"

"Yes indeed. I'm very . . . fond of it."

"And you speak our language in your country?"

"Sometimes, yes, I suppose we must."

"And your family speaks it?" Harwell was not sure he had ever actually seen Danilo smile before, or if so it had been only a fleeting expression. His host stood before him now, a few inches closer than would be customary in England, and positively sweated with pleasure.

"No." Harwell spoke very carefully. "I don't believe I have ever heard my parents speaking your language." Danilo's smile diminished. "But they will be very pleased to hear me speak it when I return. They will be most interested to learn the story of your people."

"Yes," Danilo agreed, "it is a marvelous story, though it has certainly not yet ended, not so long as there is breath and strength of arm among the Vasojević, and there are many miracles in it. It is best told in our songs. Do you know them?"

"Some, I have heard some. I am told that you yourself are a singer of these songs."

"Sometimes, yes."

"Well, I should very much like to hear them. I will be able to give my parents a more accurate report of your people."

"We shall find a time. And you must send a particular greeting from me to your parents when you write to them. Are they important people?"

"Important? No, I suppose not. But they are important to me."

"A good answer. That is a good answer."

This exchange put Danilo in such a good humor that he stumped off into the house to find Sofia, and Harwell, standing in the yard with the file still clutched in one hand, heard that rumbling voice compressing everything, including his gaffe, into a few sentences. Danilo emerged again into the light.

"She says the boy has forgotten to take his food with him. Shall we bring it to him? He is moving the water for Esad Bey."

"I would be honored to go with you. Only . . ."

"There is no difficulty for you. You will take your pieces of paper, and in all likelihood you will not be noticed by any man. The guard will certainly not be at his post until after he has eaten his dinner and slept it off."

Harwell found his passport and they set off past the tower and the heads and followed the road down into the valley, into the Sandžak of Novi Pazar. It was a clear, bright day, with a warm wind blowing in their faces, and owing to Danilo's mood, their outing had the feeling of a holiday. Danilo pointed to some considerable boulders of broken limestone that lined the road on one side and said that in the days when he had first come here those stones lay on the road itself, having been brought down by an earthquake in years past, and it had been Esad Bey, and his cousin, and of course Sofia, who had helped him remove them so that the oxen might pass, and the plough.

"He is a good neighbor, then?" asked Harwell, thinking to himself that Esad Bey's gesture had not prevented Danilo from erecting his grisly little monument of flesh and bone.

"Good enough. I did not ask him to help me, and yet he put his back to the stones with a good will. It would have been very difficult work without him."

"And he is a man of great influence among the Mahometans who live down there?"

"He has his cattle, and his fields, his vineyards and orchards, and he has a large family. He is not a Turk, though we often refer to his people as if they were true Turks, and he has refused any office that the sultan has offered."

They walked on for a while, admiring the view through gaps in the trees, for they had now entered a wooded zone, and the road twisted back and forth. Harwell worried the question in his mind, and finally found the courage to ask it.

"What would happen to these people if the Sandžak were to be . . . turned over to the Serbs, I mean to Montenegro and Serbia?"

"It is a good question, and I have given much thought to it. The Turks themselves—they are not many—would leave of their own accord. Even now they all long for Constantinople and its lewd pleasures. The Arnaouts we would drive back to their own country, to the south."

"And Esad Bey? His family and those like them?"

"They might stay, if they chose our religion. They were Christians once, and Christ might forgive them for their error."

"But if they do not? And if the Arnaouts do not go away as you have said they must?"

"Well, if they will do neither then they must all be killed, as our people were killed when our king fell to the sultan at Kosovo. You will understand these things when you have heard our songs. It is all explained there, and what has been once shall be again." Danilo crossed himself and fell silent. Harwell could not think of a single thing to say.

The fine smell of spring and the pleasant heat—it was nearly summer down here—had distracted Harwell from these thoughts by the time they reached the brook, which followed a different course down from the meadow above.

A few paces farther on and they emerged from the woods within sight of that point where the stream and Danilo's ploughed land and Esad Bey's pasture all came together, and there was Toma, knee-deep in the water, straining to lift a flat rock out of the streambed. He was not alone: the girl, Esad Bey's daughter, sat on the stream bank behind him with her skirts hitched up around her thighs and her legs dangling in the water. Toma, intent on his work, paid no attention to her, and in the long moment before Danilo spoke, Harwell had time to take in the spectacle of the girl's near-nakedness, the clean lines of her legs disappearing into the rushing water, and to think to himself: *This is no child.*

"Toma!" It was the girl who heard him over the sound of the stream, and her involuntary reflex made Toma aware of his father's presence. Danilo made his way awkwardly off the road and down to his son, who stood up to face him, wearing only a cloth wrapped around his hips, and sweating mightily. The girl looked in alarm from Danilo to Harwell, who did not move from the road, and it was Toma who dismissed her with a wave of his hand. She ran to the bend in the road and looked back, then vanished.

Danilo spoke to Toma without looking at him, and while Harwell could not make out what was said, there was no mistaking the cold anger in his voice. Toma clambered out of the water and knelt before his father, whereupon Danilo struck him a blow with the flat of his hand that knocked him down. Toma clung to his father's one leg, expecting another blow, and when it did not come he raised himself slowly and kissed his father's hand. An unequal contest in every respect, thought Harwell, marvelling at how the boy, who moments earlier had pitted the graceful strength in that back, those legs, against the slab of rock, was so reduced by a few sharp words. And yet was he not careful, even gentle, in his embrace of the father's leg? as if he were playing a part, and wary of any sudden motion that might threaten Danilo's balance?

Danilo turned to go, and did not look back or break his stride when Toma called after him, "Will you not see what I have done?" Danilo reached the road, nearly falling on the bank, and Harwell wished for invisibility, which might have been granted, for his host neither spoke nor glanced at him as he passed.

The work that Danilo did not deign to see was very nearly finished, and it took Toma only a few minutes, with Harwell's help, to horse that big flat rock up onto the bank, where he set upon it with hammer and chisel. While he did this, and the blows attracted a few curious cows to the fence line, Harwell inspected the construction already completed.

Toma had built a dam across the stream that wanted only the one flat rock, stood on its side, to close the spillway. The level of water in the pool would rise then, if the dam held, to a point a few feet upstream where it would escape through a fissure in the rocks— marks of a pick there—and flow away along a shallow ditch lined with fitted rock, and the cows would have their water. It was all very neatly conceived and executed.

"Over there," called Toma, resting from his work with the hammer, "you see how the water will follow the land and find its stream again."

"Yes," said Harwell, "I see how it will be. This is the work of an engineer, I think."

"Perhaps. But I could have done this without your book."

My book? thought Harwell, but he said nothing.

Together they lifted the last rock into its place against the flow of the stream, and the water began to rise on the little dam. Some found its way through, but not so much, and in time debris and silt would make the dam more efficient. Soon they heard the hiss of water through the escape fissure, and a gurgling in the ditch. A cow, now standing in a few inches of muddy water, made a sound of approval and drank. Toma stood astride his ditch and exulted in his success.

"Look," he said in English, pointing down at the line of turbulence marking the surface of the water after its violent passage through the crack in the rock, "that is the vortex, a hole in the water. Will you see?"

Harwell went and stood next to Toma, put his arm on the boy's shoulder to steady himself on those now-glistening rocks, and marked the heat and the quick strength under his hand. He saw how the water boiled in the narrow place and resolved itself into little whirlpools a few feet beyond, each one drifting off in an arc at the edge of the current with the unhurried grace of so many smoke rings.

"With your book, would it not be possible to determine the necessary path of every vortex, and the force of the current at each point in the hole?" Toma dropped a leaf into the current to emphasize his query.

"I am quite sure it would be, provided we had the mathematics at our command." Harwell's memory served up for his consideration the awful phrase "coefficient of viscosity," and the series of ostensibly enlightening equations that followed.

"I studied mathematics in our school here. It was not so difficult."

"But you no longer go to this school?"

"The schoolmaster said there was nothing more he could teach me, and besides, we had not the necessary books. Perhaps Gospodja Wadham will help us?"

Harwell made a noncommittal noise in his throat. With any luck he would be gone before Lydia found such a book.

Before they ate they went to wash, Harwell squatting on the bank while Toma cast off his cloth and scooped handfuls of water over his back, sluicing away the stone chips and dust. "Will you not join me in this new lake?" he cried out, and kicked some water in Harwell's direction.

Harwell's boots were already sodden from his labor on the dam, and his shirt half soaked and otherwise damp with sweat. So he laid his clothes out in the sun to dry and entered the pool awkwardly, for he was a tall, heavy-boned man and the sharp rocks on the soles of his feet made him flinch and go cautiously. Toma played in the water like an otter, ducking beneath the surface or blocking the flow of water through the fissure with his body. Harwell's familiar mythology supplied the comparison: *Achilles*, he thought, *the young Achilles.*

Harwell himself lay full-length in the water, chilled and invigorated by this first immersion since the Grand Hotel, and wished for a bar of soap. He was distracted by the thought he had when Toma had raised the subject of mathematics: that he might be gone before such a book arrived. How would he leave? and when? Would he ever return? How would he know what became of these people? He raised himself up and sat on a rock to let the sun dry him.

Toma approached from behind and startled him unwittingly, for his mind was elsewhere, a vortex following its own trajectory from the Hermit's Meadow to England.

"English," said Toma, at his shoulder, "what do you call this?" Harwell turned and saw that the boy held his member cupped in his hand.

"Cock," said Harwell, turning an astonishing shade of red, "that's your cock, but it is not altogether a polite word."

There followed an awkward silence, as if Harwell had explained to the boy the concept of shame, and in that moment both their thoughts were for Aliye. Harwell glanced around him at the streambed and the road and the edge of the trees, for he thought the girl might still be there, somewhere, watching them. Toma, on the other hand, was absorbed in contemplation of this thing, his cock, and remembering that the night before, Aliye, using the only advantage she had in that cold and inhospitable tower, had joked with him as he lay there with her, in her, saying that if her father discovered them it would be this part of him that would be cut away.

Chapter Ten

THE ARRIVAL OF THE POST from Cetinje was delayed by two full days beyond Harwell's expectations, and when he asked what might be the matter—he would have asked more than once, but did not want to betray his eagerness—Danilo cocked his head at the line of clouds that made a darkness high above the mountains in the west and delivered occasional squalls of rain to the meadow. There would be a storm on the western flank of the mountains, with strong winds and perhaps hail, Danilo guessed, leaving Harwell to imagine the perils of the Morača gorge under such conditions, and to fear for the safety of his correspondence.

So certain was he of the imminence of these letters, Lydia's and Lord Polgrove's, that he spent the two days following his foray down the mountainside in restless work with his books and his notes, using the mildly inclement weather as an excuse for not undertaking a journey to one of those far snowfields. Toma had offered to guide him there, saying that when he tired of the flowers he, Toma, would show him where the goats dwelled in the highest part of the mountain range. From Toma's description of these creatures, Harwell guessed that they must be chamois, or some closely related species. They might go, Harwell thought, when the weather cleared.

He spent his time in the kitchen now. The books and notes were laid out before him, for both the space and the light here were suited to his purposes, though he was ever wary of Danilo's tread, for the man clearly did not approve of books, or trust them. Sofia was a constant presence, but unless he asked her to look at a plate in one of the references—had she ever seen such a flower?—she maintained a respectful distance and silence. He now had his letters ready for the arrival of the postman: one for Lydia, which included the incident of his interrupted sleep, and one for Lord Polgrove, which reported his first tentative exploration—perhaps an overstatement—of the Sandžak of Novi Pazar.

He cleared his books and papers from the table when he heard Toma hallooing to the postman across the soaking meadow, for he knew that the little man must come in out of the damp while Toma tethered the horse in a patch of heavy grass. And because the post was entirely his—a clumsy envelope containing at least two smaller packets—he felt an obligation of courtesy to the carrier, and instead of withdrawing to the privacy of his shed, he drank a cup of coffee that sat badly on his stomach and followed it with a glass of burning brandy, listening all the while to the postman's enthusiastic gossip of doings at Kolašin and Andrijevica. With the others so obviously engrossed in this conversation, he eased his chair back from the table and opened his mail, choosing Lord Polgrove's elegant and pristine buff over the plain white of Lydia's letter.

The salutation was in order and the first few paragraphs were perfunctorily polite. But when his patron got down to the business at hand, it was evident that he expected much more and much sooner than the information Harwell had provided in his two dispatches to date: the information on Cetinje was no more enlightening than what he might pick up from the Foreign Office, or in casual gossip at the Travellers' Club, and he could not understand what prevented Harwell from simply saddling his horse and making his way into the Sandžak to see for himself how things were, rather than lurking on the edges of it and getting information at second or third hand.

Had he, Harwell, failed to understand that both England's policy regarding the Balkans and the disposition or redistribution of national interests and strengths there were of the utmost importance to the peace of Europe, not to mention Lord Polgrove's personal ambitions? And did he not realize that at the present time this policy, owing to the blindness of Whitehall, was based on an absolute vacuum of information? For example — Lord Polgrove's handwriting at this point mirrored the hasty and angry process of his mind — the Treasury had recently informed the Foreign Office that it no longer wished to receive any economic information whatsoever pertaining to the Balkan states. No information at all! But he, Polgrove, was nobody's fool, and in fact this paralysis of government at the highest levels was the principal motivation in his own political aspirations. He, and perhaps he alone, understood what must follow from such complacent ignorance, and what rewards might be reaped for England and the Empire by bringing cunning pressure to bear on the turbulent nationalisms at work in those provinces lately or imminently independent of Turkey-in-Europe.

But without Harwell's active and intelligent cooperation Polgrove could achieve nothing. In order to formulate a policy that might serve as an effective counterweight to the naked ambitions of Austria with respect to the territory lying between her and the Aegean, in order to gauge the strength and possible duration of Turkish influence on the Balkan populations, he would need to know everything that Harwell could supply in respect to tax data, agricultural practice, commercial developments, troop movements, railway construction, et cetera, et cetera.

Embedded in this complaint — or encouragement, as its author may have conceived it — were some specific items of information which Polgrove found reliable enough to disclose to his agent. They might be useful in shaping Harwell's inquiries into developments in the Sandžak. For example, had Harwell any inkling of the trouble brewing in Turkey proper? It appeared, from Polgrove's other sources, that the reform party was very active, and very frustrated with the sultan's resistance to administrative reform, to progressive ideas of any sort. Should this crisis come to a head, there must be the gravest repercussions in those far-flung parts of the Ottoman Empire where the central authority exercised only a tenuous and erratic influence.

Secondly, through his underground connections to the Foreign Office in Vienna, Polgrove had two extraordinary pieces of information directly related to the matter of Ottoman instability. He had heard, without any supporting documents, that an Austro-Hungarian annexation of Bosnia and Herzegovina was being openly discussed in the Ballhausplatz, and even in the court itself. Furthermore, and here he had a draft document, without which he would never have given credit to the report, it appeared that Field Marshal Conrad von Hötzendorf, the Austrian chief of staff, was mobilizing for war the following year. "Foundations for Concrete Preparations for War in the Year 1909" was the blunt title of this draft document, and there could be no other possible enemy than Montenegro itself. Five and a half divisions, some 68,000 troops, were to be deployed within striking distance of Montenegro's borders in what was familiarly referred to as the "Yellow Mobilization."

Harwell was to use this information as he saw fit, and see if conditions and the mood in the Sandžak tended to confirm or contradict anything that Polgrove had conveyed. They both knew that any reports coming from Cetinje were worse than useless, as Sir Percy Foote was not only foolish but monumentally complacent, to the point of laziness, which made him the perfect tool for the policy of Sir Edward Grey, which was to do, precisely, nothing. And yet William O'Reilly, chargé d'affaires in Montenegro during Sir Percy's recent leave, had told Polgrove confidentially that the Sandžak, so strategically located with respect to Montenegro, Serbia, and Austria, must be the key to any military or political crisis in the region. And that was why Polgrove depended so heavily on what Harwell told him—or might tell him—for on the basis of direct, current information in any proximate crisis, Whitehall's deliberate ignorance might be used as a weapon in Polgrove's hands, a vote of no-confidence might be forced in the Commons and the government brought down.

It was not what was said so much as the manner of stating it that distressed Harwell. This was a letter such as one might send to a marginally competent and insufficiently energetic subordinate, operating at an inconvenient distance, who might be roused to one useful action before he was discarded. Lord Polgrove asked if he needed funds to carry out his work properly, that is to say, promptly, and the question of how this was to be done through the awkward banking connections between London and Cetinje—let alone the eastern frontier—led Polgrove to offer a word of advice about the security of their channels of communication. Did he understand that the information on Austrian preparations for a putative crisis in Turkey was of the utmost sensitivity? A word breathed carelessly, the merest hint, could ignite the tinder and entail serious, perhaps mortal, consequences for Harwell personally. At this point, well after the fact, Harwell inspected the seal on the letter, which he had broken in such innocent haste.

As a postscript to his instructions, Lord Polgrove scribbled his thanks for the drawings, the notes, and the first batch of seeds that Harwell had so kindly sent. He had not really had the opportunity to attend carefully to the botanical information, he said, but the seed had been given to Hatchard, the curator of the glasshouse, and a very competent man, and we would just have to wait and see what came up next spring.

Lydia's letter might have redeemed Harwell's spirits, and it did indeed contain much that was pleasing to him, and flattering, though her continued anxiety for his safety—in spite of the assurances he thought he had included in his last letter—seemed to overshadow her pleasure in the correspondence. The mood in Cetinje was quite grim. The Petrović family had not yet recovered from the shock and sadness of the deaths of the two young princes, grandsons of Prince Nikola, who had been carried off by a fever within hours of each other. The prince himself was preparing for a state visit to Vienna and St. Petersburg in order to assert his long-standing claims to territorial compensation. It was a long journey for an old man, and some said he would never return alive. Did the gloom of Cetinje reach so far as the Hermit's Meadow? Would he take care to behave prudently in those wild surroundings? She could not bear the thought that her care, her worrying about him, was of no practical value whatever. Was his work not almost finished?

On a more cheerful note, she had, with the aid of Sir Percy's excellent library, found the bird he had mentioned at the end of his letter, *Tichodroma murana*, indeed a kind of creeper, and a very curious creature, as it was said to prefer skulls as its nesting site, and human skulls in particular. Although she was not given to superstition or omens, she could not be completely comfortable with the instincts of this bird, and would he make an effort to avoid that place in which he had seen it?

Finally, and most tenderly, she thanked him for the washed sketches of the flowers, which were in fulfillment of his promise to her. She was particularly fond of his rendering of a white-flowering shrub—Draško had recognized it—because it had on the back some pencilled lines, erased, but still legible, of what seemed to be poetry. He must have cut up a larger sheet of paper to fit the drawings into his envelope, and so part of the poem was missing, but what she had read, about this flower and scented hair, seemed very accomplished, and made her remember and miss him in a way that was wonderful and heartbreaking at the same time. Would he, when he saw fit, send her more of his poetry? She closed the letter with her most affectionate wishes for his health and well-being.

Harwell sat in stunned and oppressed silence at the edge of the lively conversation around the table. He forced himself to smile from time to time, and nodded in sympathetic understanding at the anecdote of the man in Andrijevica who got so drunk that he missed his path and drove all his goats over the side of the mountain. This put Danilo in mind of an incident in the war in Herzegovina when he ran a patrol of Turks off a mountainside in the mist. "I was a bad shepherd to them" was his comment. Sofia had put a piece of brightly printed cloth around her neck for this occasion, and her animation was wonderful to see. Harwell tried not to look too long or too often in her direction.

The postman's original, stated intention was to drink just the cup of coffee and be off, as the storm had so delayed him. But after the second cup of coffee he came to consider his dampness, past and future, and with this in mind he accepted a glass of brandy. He was now on the second glass. Harwell sat with his notebook on his knee and scribbled a few leaden lines in response to Lydia's letter, so that she would know he had received it. About Lord Polgrove's letter, or rather his own in the light of this new imperative, he could do nothing at all. It would be better to send no letter than the one he had written. The worst interpretation Polgrove could put on his silence was that he had come to an unfortunate end.

Sofia rose and made her way around the table to Harwell, her kerchief the one bright thing in the room, and spoke into his ear.

"You are not yourself. Leave your letter with me, and go for a walk. You do not need to stay."

"It is raining still."

"You will not melt. It will do you good."

The walk succeeded in distracting him from his thoughts by offering an array of physical discomforts. He had the presence of mind to take his waterproof from the peg by the door, but he was halfway through the meadow, going in the direction of the mountains, before he realized that he was still wearing the pointed shoes, slippers of a kind, that Sofia had given him without explanation. Property of a dead son, had been his assumption. His feet were soaking wet now, and when he paused, thinking there might be time to go fetch his boots, the heavens opened in earnest, and the defenses of his waxed coat were overwhelmed. He knew a moment of blinding anger—at the rain, at Lord Polgrove, at himself—and kicked clumsily at a stone in the road, and then it was over.

He was thoroughly wet now, and the thought that nothing worse could happen to him, that there was no further stage of discomfort, lifted his spirits. Was the rain not abating? Did that lighter patch of sky over the rim of the wall not mean that the weather might clear soon? He was not cold, and would not be as long as he kept walking. And as for Lord Polgrove, that old man, a semi-invalid, was many hundreds of miles away, and the truth was that he would have given a great deal to trade places with Auberon Harwell. As for Harwell's indiscretion in the matter of his correspondence, well, so far it was only apparent to himself.

He walked, or splashed, past the house, and past the tower, carrying on towards the break in the rim where the road descended to the Sandžak. He gave a glance to the heads, noting how, in this diffuse and ambient light, there was a great deal more bone to be seen, how the remaining flesh, dry and papery, hung here and there in tatters. These objects were a great barrier between him and the inhabitants of this place, even . . . even Sofia, who had lived with them, slept in their shadow, for twenty-five years and more. English people, he reflected sadly, do not do these things, would not tolerate such barbarism.

Before he knew it he had climbed the little rise, and there below him, mocking him, was the object of Lord Polgrove's desire and fascination. He tried to imagine how that sodden landscape would look to his patron's eye, how political ambition, and perhaps avarice, might clothe it in brighter colors, endow it with a promise to which he was blind. From this point—he leaned now against the flimsy barrier rail—the stream where he and Toma had labored was hidden from view, and a good part of Danilo's holding as well. There in a grove of fine trees, just at the margin of the gentler land, were the orderly red tiles of Esad Bey's roofs, and in the distance, on the crest of a bare hill, a mean hamlet of half a dozen whitewashed houses. There were a few cows in the corner of that field, and one, two barns or sheds to be seen. But in all that sweep of country, the only likely improvement to the land, dwellings aside, was the dam that Toma had built.

He thought of Raymond now, and was saddened by the fact that he had not heard from his friend in all the time since he had left England. No, there had been a letter to his hotel in Paris, a letter about the niceties of the fisheries litigation that would have been tedious if not enlivened by his friend's ironic observations. Perhaps his own letter had been . . . dull? Had he perhaps neglected to give his friend instructions on how to reach him on this wild edge of Europe? When he thought about writing to Raymond, his joy at the prospect was checked by reflecting how different his life here was from the brave scenes he had invented in the club, in the flush of that excellent claret, and also by the fact that there were several subjects that would be awkward to raise, even with this oldest and most intimate friend. Could he put into words what he felt for Sofia? He could not. He sighed, then found a bright thought to hold on to: his journey into the Sandžak would be bearable because its true purpose would be to report to Raymond, as much as was appropriate for him to know, and not simply to gather information at the bidding of the odious Polgrove.

In his emphatic and impotent fury at the thought of his patron, Harwell struck the barrier pole a blow with his fist, and the whole contraption shivered. A man dressed in what may have been a uniform materialized out of the tiny guard shack and stared fiercely at Harwell. Had he been watching the entire time?

"Doz volite da izrazim koliko mi je žao," said Harwell, trying to sound properly contrite in this expression of his regrets. The man nodded his red fez and wiped his mustache with the back of his hand, but the expression on his face did not change. He coughed. Harwell remarked on the weather, and the man coughed again. Remembering his conversation with Danilo, Harwell fished a coin from his pocket, offered it, and was rewarded with something just short of a smile. As he retreated from the barrier, Harwell wished the guard good health, and the guard, in reply, asked that Allah should bless him.

On his way back to the house Harwell spied the lonely figure of the postman, slouched in his saddle, already halfway up the trail on the far wall of the meadow. Then a low cloud overtook him, and he was gone. Though the warmth of Sofia's kitchen beckoned, Harwell stopped first in his shed, where he changed his shoes and his shirt, and made a careful inspection of his drying seeds, which were ranged in little scraps of cloth and bits of broken pottery on the beams around the room.

He lit his lamp in order to see properly, because he was afraid that the days of damp weather would rot his specimens before they dried. So with his light hung from a nail above his head he rearranged the feathery whorls of the dryas on the broken plate, giving each one a quarter turn as if they were so many bottles of champagne. He marvelled at the tight umbels of the androsace seed heads, their long arching stems now dried to the color of ripe strawberries. But when he came to his handkerchief, where the seed of the two specimens of saxifrage, yet to be identified, were spread out, he uttered an oath, for most of the seed was gone, and there remained a haphazard waste of chewed husks and mouse turds.

Mice were his familiar enemy, not just here, where he had heard them scampering along the beams and nosing at his belongings, but in an earlier time, and, as he recollected with a smile, in a room not so different from this one—low-ceilinged, crudely constructed, and badly lit—a storeroom in an outbuilding at Newton Court where his mother had grudgingly allowed him to house his collection of soldiers. Tompkins, the gardener, had helped him to erect some shelves along two walls—how that friendly, inept old fellow had sweated in his heavy tweeds as he sawed away at the planks—and when it was done, after young Bron himself had driven a few nails, the heroes of Rorke's Drift and Isandhlwana were transferred from their pasteboard boxes and cotton wool to this new home, where they could be ranged defiantly within sight of the Zulu. The lower shelf was for the cavalry, and here the brilliant yellow tunics of the dusky lancers, Skinner's

Horse, took pride of place, even above the Life Guards of the Household Cavalry in their familiar red capes. And it was on this lower shelf that the mice did the greatest damage, for a mounted lead figure is no match for a mouse, and Bron would find, each morning, whole ranks of his cavalry laid down as if by Kitchener's Maxim guns, and sometimes tumbled off the shelf altogether, at the expense of a sword here, a horse's leg there. The answer then, as now, had been a cat: had he not heard one up in the loft where Danilo and Sofia slept? and seen it skulking in the bushes on his trips to the privy? He would borrow this cat for a day or two, and his seeds would be safe.

But while he tidied up after the mice, and transferred the most edible seeds to the lidded shelter of his cooking utensils, his mind drifted back again to the shed where his soldiers were kept—was it possible that they were still there?—and to the powerful influence that those bright figures had exercised on his imagination. The Mahdi's dervishes were always defeated by Kitchener's Cameron Highlanders: the memory of Gordon's martyrdom at Khartoum, rather than Maxim guns and dumdum bullets, was the factor that stemmed the dark tide and saved the day at Omdurman. Those faithful sepoys of the 4th Punjab Infantry always prevailed at the gates of Lucknow against their brothers who had succumbed to the Mutiny: through the narrow gap in the wall of the Sikander Bagh they poured, following the kilts of the Sutherland Highlanders, and there, to the music of bagpipes, they slew the unrighteous. Even now, years away in memory, and farther still from the actual event, the sound, the imagined sound of those bagpipes could start tears in his eyes. All of this lore and passion had connected quite seamlessly with Bron's idea of the Empire as a vast, benevolent association of heroes, and to his conception of time itself, which he thought must resemble a ladder, or a series of ladders, on which he occupied a particular rung, which was his place in history.

Was it possible, any longer, to think of things in that way, with himself now an actor on the great canvas of the Empire? Would a chapter of that story be written in these mountains, on the basis of what he might write to Lord Polgrove? And would the enemy, in the game of some child a generation hence, be the Turk? And not just any Turk, but, for the sake of argument, the sniffling little man he had just encountered, reduced to a figurine and inadvertently buried in the soil of the flower bed after the battle was over?

In the kitchen, Sofia hummed to herself, perhaps still wrapped in the pleasure of that second glass of plum brandy, and she greeted Harwell with warmth, and took his coat to dry near her oven. From the loft came the sounds of Danilo sleeping, and as Harwell had once been told by his tutor that snoring marked dreams of a violent nature, he wondered what the nature of his host's dreams might be.

He wiped the table with his sleeve and set his books and notebooks down on it, leaving a space on the far side for Sofia to work, for she had her knife there and was rummaging in the sacks that held potatoes and onions. He intended to complete his identifications of the plants seen and collected almost out of spite for Lord Polgrove, who apparently regarded this effort as no more than a necessary ruse. There was a moment of awkwardness in the thought that these were, after all, Polgrove's books, that those cold hands had leafed through these pages, but he was soon immersed in the identification of a saxifrage, one he had seen most recently on a high and desolate ridge of rock, and he found a keener pleasure in this work because he knew that it was now truly his own enterprise, that this was scholarship of a purer kind.

Polgrove's letter, in some sense that was difficult to articulate, had set him free, free to love the flowers for themselves. And as he turned the pages of Haworth's *Saxifragëarum Enumeratio*, he had another recognition, which was that in the several weeks that he had been poring over these volumes, trying to connect what he had observed growing on windblown slopes and in shaded clefts with the dry descriptions on these pages, he had, without intending to do so, committed the books to memory. He no longer had to work through the tedious index, eliminating possibilities one by one, but could go straight to the genus and sometimes the species itself, because the whorl of this leaf pattern or the singular ribbing of the stem recalled a line that he had read, even if there had been no illustration of the plant.

"Madame," he spoke softly to Sofia, "may I trouble you for another glass of the brandy?"

She brought him the glass, and at his urging took the first sip from it. "The rain has washed your soul clean. You have forgotten those letters, yes?"

"Yes. The walk did me good, as you said. And my work is going well. And this brandy does me good. Really, though, I think it is you yourself that does me the most good." She laid her hand on his head in a gesture of neutral affection, and might have tousled his hair, but stopped, as if suddenly conscious of some propriety. He took her hand and kissed it with exaggerated courtesy. "Thank you for the hospitality of your house."

He then showed her a plate in the book which was very nearly the same species as the tiny aquilegia he had just identified. She touched the curving horns of the flower on the page and remembered that she had seen such flowers, or ones like them, when she went out to the pasturelands where her brothers tended the herds. But that was years ago. She leaned across him to get a better look at the engraving, and as she did so there emanated from her blouse the odor of the onions she had been cutting and of damp, unwashed wool, a combination which had almost a narcotic effect on Harwell. Her breast practically touched his shoulder. He could not move.

"It is like science, what you do?"

"We call it a natural science."

"And are there not other sorts of science?"

"Of course . . . physics, chemistry, and so forth, but for them one needs an understanding of mathematics, and there I am altogether deficient. Your son, though, would seem to have a natural aptitude, a gift for such studies."

"Yes," said Sofia distractedly, "a gift, if only he would use it."

"I am not sure what you mean. He has certainly impressed me, and I think even his father would have to admire Toma's solution to the problem of Esad Bey's cows and the watercourse."

"These things, the books he reads with you, are no challenge for him anymore. Do you not notice how his attention wanders, even as he reads?" Harwell had in fact noticed this very thing, but kept his silence. "And do you not notice how, since he has removed himself to that cave I showed you, the hermit's cave, how he comes and goes at all hours of the night? I have heard him return closer to dawn than midnight, and make his way up the rock clumsily, as if he were drunk, or carrying something."

Harwell said that he had heard nothing other than a falling rock on the night of the full moon. "Has he not said that he goes out to hunt the chamois? the wild goat that lives in the highest part of the mountains? He has offered to take me with him, but I have been too busy with my work here."

"So he says. But where is this famous goat? Has he cooked and eaten the whole thing up in his cave?"

"That I cannot say. Perhaps he missed his mark. And if he seems different to you than before he moved out of this house, perhaps that is just the age he is at now, when boys will do anything just to get away from their parents. I remember when I was his age . . ."

"Yes." Sofia cut off Harwell's anecdote before he could begin. "But this is not England, and it is exactly because he feels as you say that I worry for him. I know all too well the trouble that boys can get up to. Do you know the history of this family?" Harwell wondered if it was prudent to admit to such knowledge, but nodded anyway. "Well then. How can I not notice when my son begins to act like his brothers before him? And how can I not worry about it?"

"But if you are worried about your son when he is only a few hundred yards up the hill, what will you do when he goes off to study in Vienna, or Budapest, or Oxford?"

"He will not go to these places," said Sofia quite simply.

"Where then?"

"He will go to America. Only to America."

Harwell pondered this statement while listening to Danilo's deep, sonorous snoring, and saw that just at this moment the sun had finally escaped from the clouds and poured light onto the meadow, into this room, where it resonated with the joyful expectation in Sofia's voice. He spoke carefully, watching her face all the while, ready to stop at any moment, afraid that the radiance investing those features might vanish.

"I have been thinking about Toma, in the course of our lessons, and what would be best for him. Perhaps not just at this moment, but quite soon, provided he had the right sort of help and tutoring, he might apply for admission to one of our great universities. As I have told you, my own university was Oxford, where I have many useful connections. And if that were not suitable, given his interests and aptitudes, there is another university, where greater emphasis is placed on science, and that is called . . ."

The expression on her face did not alter, the same that he had noted when they had their first conversation, when she showed him the books, but now she shook her head, gently dismissing his idea. "No. You are very kind to have given thought to this, but I will not be happy unless he goes to America. That is truly the new world."

"But if he went to England, aside from the benefit of the education there, I might be able to keep an eye on him myself, and could write you of his progress."

Here Sofia reached across the table and took his hand. "You are a good man. You . . . What is this?" He saw that she was staring at the patch of razed hairs on the back of his wrist. She touched it with the point of her knife, the knife that he had recently sharpened, and gently cut two of the blond hairs. She laughed, and Harwell covered his wrist with his sleeve.

"You have never been to America, I think." She spoke with her back to him, having risen to reach for a book on the shelf, one that Harwell had not seen before, as it was both large and thin, a kind of bound magazine, and it lay flat in the darkness above the window. "Here," she said, turning the book on the table so that he could read, "now you will understand me."

Auberon Harwell had only the vaguest ideas about the United States of America in general, although he possessed a fair knowledge of its particular form of government, having once written an essay to suggest that the American Revolution had resulted from defective political philosophy in London and Philadelphia. But of its great cities, its various populations, its extravagant geography, and its manufacturing base, he knew only what he read in *The Times* or what had been related to him by an American lawyer, an acquaintance of Raymond's, also involved in the fisheries dispute, and more than half the information from this source seemed to him frankly incredible.

Had he ever heard of the World's Columbian Exposition in Chicago, in 1893? He supposed he had, though the details ran together in his mind with the world's fair in Paris shortly before or afterwards. But now, here in his hands, was this official handbook and guide to that event, with its cover of imitation leather flaking away as he held it, and the pages quite yellowed and brittle. He could see that the book had been well read, and he turned the folios carefully.

Every right-hand page had a photograph. Even at such a distance in space and time from these artifacts and inventions, and further removed by the faintness of the reproduction, he was impressed by the rude energy and sheer immensity of it all. Here were acres of buildings—whole acres contained in single buildings!—and everything was so astonishingly white: a White City indeed, enthusiastically decorated with lagoons and fountains, rotundas and spires, a victory column, a classical peristyle, and an arch worthy of Hadrian. A photograph of a burly young man in a round-brimmed hat standing by a hoisting engine, all heavy ropes, cogged gears, pulleys, and great brass spools for the winding of the cable; a scene from the Garbage Crematory, which had its own Sewage Laboratory with shelf upon shelf of glistening beakers, retorts, and stoppered bottles; a display of windmills, tall and short, on fantastic steel towers; a gallery in the Department of Ethnology with rows of cases containing skulls; the California exhibit in the Horticultural Building, featuring a tower of citrus fruits some thirty feet high; the Broom Brigade of the Children's Building: twenty-five little girls dressed in white, each one holding her implement in the manner of a shouldered rifle.

Towards the back of the book he came upon photographs of the industrial displays themselves, and was sobered by the Krupp gun, so long—forty-eight feet—that it required a foldout photograph to do it justice, and so massive at the breech that the man standing there was a good foot shorter than the steel of its diameter. In the Machinery Hall, a milky vista of strange devices stretched away beneath fretted steel vaults that were all but obliterated by light pouring through the glass roof. ("We are now in Machinery Hall. Just think of it! Seventeen acres of palpitating iron and steel lie before us, and each machine is performing some wonderful task, as if possessed of its own intelligence . . .")

When he came to the Electricity Building he laid the book down on the table, for it was no longer convenient to hold it in one hand. The single wheel of the vast Allis-Corliss generating machine dominated all else, oppressed him, fascinated him.

"Read to me," said Sofia, and he read.

" 'All that electricity has done is shown in this display; the secret means of transmitting power lies before us. We see inductive coils, and converters of the latest types, with direct and alternating dynamos, fitted for railroads or stationary machinery. Here, coiled up like a great serpent, lies the cable through which electric whispers circle round the world!' "

He paused, wondering if she wished him to translate, but she muttered, in her own language, "Ah, the serpent . . ." as if she had understood every word he had read.

"Where does this book come from?"

"It was sent to me by my cousin, who now lives in America, even in Chicago, and he saw these things with his own eyes. Is this not one of God's greatest works?" Harwell cleared his throat and nodded reluctantly. "And do you see now why my son must go there? He has read everything in this book, and now even I know what these machines are."

"And your husband?"

"He does not like the book. And he does not wish his son to go to America. He says that there are lies written here, or at least things that only a child would believe; but I do not think that is truly his thought."

"What then?"

"I think he is afraid that he will lose his son, his only son, and that then his life and everything he has dreamed will be over, finished."

"And are you not afraid? He will be lost to you as well."

"If he stays I will lose him, and I could not bear that, not again. Anyway, he will write to me, but always in English, never in Serbian, and I will have Natalia here to tell me what he says." Her face was sad now, in spite of these brave words.

"Look," she said, reaching across the table and turning pages in clumps until she reached the front of the book. "Here is poetry for you."

Harwell's eye skimmed over Miss Harriet Monroe's "Columbian Ode," stanza after stanza celebrating dewy flowers, expressions of the democratic spirit plucked from those mighty hills and wide prairies, and he allowed as how, yes, this was poetry of a kind. He was tired now, and he drained the rest of his brandy.

"Is there nothing I can do for you, then, no way that I can help?"

"You have done much simply by being here. You are the world beyond, about which we know so little, and so Toma can see that fighting over the lost empire of King Lazar is not the only future he can choose. And whether you know it or not, you are my ally in this matter, my ally against him." She cast her eyes upwards, and no smile softened her words.

"And who will decide? Toma?"

"Yes. He must stand up to his father, which is not an easy thing. And you can help him to do this. I feel less certain now that I know his mind, or that he knows his own mind."

"Is there anything more I can do?"

"Yes." She was silent for a moment, as if she weighed him against the task. "You can climb to that cave and tell me what he does there."

Harwell saw first that she was embarrassed by her request, then that she had hardened her mind to this difficult discussion because she knew it was right. They watched each other.

"If I could go myself I would not ask you to do this for me," she said.

"Of course I will do it, as I would do anything you ask. But there is a price." He paused for effect. "You must lend me your cat." She smiled again, as he had hoped she would.

Harwell stood at the base of the wall and called out to Toma, even though he was certain the boy was not in the cave above him, nor even in earshot: he had seen him going over the crest of the road with a hoe on his shoulder shortly after the rain had stopped. Under other circumstances, he was quite sure, Toma would have welcomed such a visit. He tried to think of it that way.

The face of rock was dry beneath his hand, and the strong afternoon sun lifted a gentle steam from the few remaining patches of dampness. The trickle of water that sprang from the spot where Vasili had conquered his devil was swollen now into a true waterfall, and it battered the shrub roses marking its nearly vertical course down from the cave. If all else fails, he thought, I could climb straight up the waterfall holding on to those stems.

He had often watched Toma making his way up or down the face, and admired the grace with which this was done. But he had also, without any conscious effort, recorded the route taken, so that he had confidence that he, too, would find the foot and hand holds. He was not afraid of heights, and although the mountains had left cruel scars on his boots, they now fit him perfectly, would take him anywhere.

About halfway to the top, with some fifteen feet above and below him, he paused and cautiously turned his head to scan the rock, for a gust of wind had brought the stink of rotten flesh to him. He saw nothing but rock and sky, and there over his shoulder were the tower, the house, and the meadow, its vivid greens altered by his few feet of elevation. The monk, he thought, had a good idea: to live not in the meadow, but somewhat apart, so that he might hold it in perfect contemplation. His hand found the next hold, a diagonal crevice that would be invisible from the base of the cliff, and he wondered if it was possible to conclude from such slender evidence that Vasili had been a very short man.

When he reached the top, his mind still fixed on the riddles of his diminutive predecessor, the full force of that stench struck him like a blow, so that he could not draw breath, and he sat on a block of roughly shaped stone. When he put his head down between his knees, he caught a draft of fresher air that smelled only like the watercourse. In a minute or two he found he was able to sit up without his gorge rising: either the wind had shifted or he was growing accustomed to whatever foulness the cave held.

The block on which he sat seemed once to have been part of an arch, perhaps the entrance and support to the roof of the cave, much of which had collapsed, leaving a little space open to the elements and roughly paved with weed-rimmed slabs of whitish stone, a kind of courtyard to what remained of the cave. A pinkish stucco or plaster lined the roof and inner walls, beginning at about waist level, and the vault itself was elaborately and energetically painted with figures involved in some cataclysmic struggle: bright angels wielding instruments of terrible destruction upon a multitude of the living and the dead—there the ax of an angel severed a skeletal forearm—and the wretches were driven down, down towards a pit ringed with fire where, like their brothers before them, they were to be impaled on those stakes of sharpened wood. Every one of the damned, noted Harwell, wore a turban, whether he was alive or risen from the grave to meet this judgement, for that is what the painting must signify: Vasili's vision of the end of all things, as promised in the Book of Revelation. And there above him, just where the roof of the cave had faulted and collapsed, was the left arm of the avenging deity, palm and fingers spread in a gesture of denial, of divine wrath, that sealed the fate of the Mahometan damned. There was no face to be seen, but Harwell was certain that it must have been turned away from the horrors that the monk had painted in such furious and fanatical detail. Turned towards what? Surely towards some vision of salvation, a vaulted, beatific paradise that now lay as dust beneath his feet.

He stood, appalled and moved by this crude artwork—this exorcism—as he had never been by any painting or statue. He was angry as well, though he could not identify the object of this wrath until he thought of Sir Percy, of those fluttering, dismissive gestures of the soft hands, and wished that he could summon him by force of will to this place to see this terrible thing, to breathe this foul air. *Here is a work of art for you, sir. Laugh if you will, but at your peril.*

Harwell might almost have believed that the stench of death proceeded from his own overactive imagination; but once he was inside the cavern proper, and his eyes grew accustomed to that light, he saw that there was a rectangular block of stone at the far end—an altar or a sarcophagus—and on the stone lay pieces of what had once been a man.

The body was lying in state, or in as much stateliness as could be allowed to a near-skeleton lacking an entire arm and the better part of a leg. The one hand lay on the breast, and there was a clean, folded cloth beneath the head. The features were mostly gone, but from the abundant dark, lustrous hair, he guessed that this was the body of a young man, the body of . . . it came to him quite suddenly, and with absolute certainty: the body of the brother, Vuk, whose story had been conveyed to him in whispers by Stefan over that bottle of excellent wine.

Harwell heard the hiss of his own breath between his teeth. How many trips to the lonely crossroads had been required to retrieve these remains? And how long was the boy prepared to live with this smell before the worms and flies had cleaned the bones altogether? Like the monk before him, and perhaps like the being who had once inhabited this body, the boy simply did what some voice, some instinct, told him must be done, and there was then no reckoning of hardship or danger. Whatever needed to be done: it was an absolute imperative. Was Harwell surprised? Had he not seen this, heard it in every conversation with Danilo, or even with Sofia? Was this not what the monk Stefan had told him about these people, the Vasojević, about the true Serbs wherever they were found?

At the foot of the bier lay three heavy and irregular metal objects, and Harwell carried one of these to the light at the cave mouth. Although he had never seen such a thing before, he recognized it as a bomb, and so his hand trembled slightly as he turned it over to discover the place of manufacture, Kragujevac, along with the arms of the kingdom of Serbia. There was no timing device that he could see, only a lever that might be cocked. And then what? Was it thrown? Or did the bearer, assured of his place in paradise, lock his victim in a final, fatal embrace? He put the bomb back where he had found it, and thought without pleasure that he would have to lie twice over about what he had seen: first to Sofia, and then to Lord Polgrove.

He was contemplating this falsehood on his way down the cliff, wondering whether a simple sin of omission would suffice, or whether something more elaborate would be required to put Sofia's mind to rest. Why could the boy not have had a simpler and less dangerous secret, something that would not have destroyed his mother and put all of them at terrible risk? He hoped that his lie would be convincing to Sofia.

His right foot grazed the rock, feeling for that lip that seemed to have vanished, and his left foot would not hold without the fierce grip of his fingers, which might fail unless he could plant that right foot. He had wandered from the course in his distraction, and must go back and up if he could manage it. There was a good twenty feet left below him, more than enough to break an ankle if he landed wrong.

"To the left, and down a hand's breadth." Toma spoke to him from the base of the cliff. "Put your feet there and rest for a moment. I have made the same mistake often enough myself."

With his feet planted at last on the flat, welcoming soil of the meadow, Harwell breathed deeply of that soft, clean air and mopped his sweating face with his handkerchief. Toma looked at him, looked into his eyes, with what might have been a trace of amusement.

"And what did you find on your perilous journey?" he asked.

"Nothing," replied Harwell. "Nothing that would justify such a risk."

Chapter Eleven

HE SHOULD HAVE KNOWN it would be no ordinary day when he was torn from his sleep by a pealing of bells so loud that it might have been inside his head. Sunlight streamed into his shed through the open door to dazzle him, and a soft spring day lay on the meadow, mocking him with its beauty.

Toma appeared in his doorway and told him, without ceremony, that unless he was up and washed and dressed by the time Danilo had finished saluting the archangel, he would have to travel to Rožaj on his own. Harwell was having trouble bringing Toma into focus; the boy was standing there against the strong light, but there was something different about him, perhaps in the pose, perhaps . . . Harwell's mind was not yet working clearly and his head ached.

"Here," said Toma, stepping forward to thrust a bundle at him.

"What are these?" asked Harwell, though they were plainly his own clothes.

"My mother has taken pity on you and cleaned these things, in honor of Sveti Arhandjel Mihajlo and his feast day. You will see a great market today in Rožaj, and you must dress for it. She says to wear the sash." Harwell saw now that Toma himself was dressed for such an occasion, that his breeches were a deep blue instead of the colorless homespun, that instead of the *opanki* he wore a pair of old black boots which glistened even in this dim light, and that the vest against his white shirt was a deep purple silk piped with green and scarlet. This was a man, not a boy. Or perhaps, he thought, a soldier.

"Well, Toma. You will flutter all the hearts in the marketplace today. Are you shopping for a bride?"

"I am not thinking of marriage. This is how we dress, that is all. You will see finer than this." He plucked at his sleeve as if his mind were on other matters. "Hurry now, or my mother will be truly angry with you."

The clamor of the bells persisted, the two notes over and over in no discernible order or rhythm. Harwell doused his head in cold water and cleared the cobwebs left by last night's whiskey. He had forgotten about that bottle—a gift from Sir Percy delivered to the Grand Hotel with a gently condescending farewell note—until he was repacking his belongings yesterday afternoon to accommodate the dried seeds. He brought it with him to supper, and after he and Toma read a long section in Professor Drinker's text on the development of the modern water turbine, he plied his host with this unfamiliar liquor.

Danilo had been pleased by the whiskey—as well he should, it being a fine single malt that came close to revising Harwell's own view of Sir Percy—and even before that he had been so buoyed by anticipation of the feast and the market on the morrow that he actually stayed in the room while Toma and Harwell conducted their halting dialogue on the relative merits of the undershot versus the overshot waterwheel.

What were these things drawn on the page? demanded Danilo. They were devices for using the power of the running water to grind corn, to run machinery, even to forge iron and steel. And this information set Danilo to reflecting on the water mills he had once seen on a river in Herzegovina, a whole brood of them, funny little houses set on stilts over the water, where the miller sat all day grinding whatever was brought to him. And on the day he had seen this, he and his fellows who were hunting the Turks, all the inhabitants of that place had fled in fear except for one man, and his waterwheel turned not a millstone but a wooden device of cogs and great hammers that beat upon a trough filled with soap and water and garments. The heroes of Montenegro that day had burnt the grinding mills, and the heated stones—when they fell at last into the river—made the water boil and spit forth geysers of steam. But they had not harmed this man with his garment-beating machine, because they knew he must be mad.

At this point Sofia, who never spoke against Danilo, observed that at the great exposition in Chicago they had such a machine that would wash the clothes, and that instead of water to turn the machinery there was a kind of fire that came from a hole in the wall. Such a machine, she said, was not madness at all, but . . .

"Well," said Danilo, laying his hand on hers in a gesture of patronizing good humor, "that is what your book says, but I can only tell you what I have seen with my own eyes."

"But it is not just what the book says." She pulled her hand impatiently from his grasp. "Sava Bogdanović himself has seen these things. I have his letter still."

"I knew him well, and he would not lie. But I do not understand why he would leave his family to live where only God can find him, even if they have this fire that comes from the walls." Danilo sighed in contemplation of things beyond his imagination, and Harwell, who had been avoiding Sofia's eye all evening, thought this might be the moment to produce his bottle.

They drank, which is to say that Harwell sipped while Danilo threw back his tumbler as if it were nothing more than weak tea. Harwell poured another measure into his glass, and offered the bottle to Sofia, who declined.

As always in the presence of Danilo, it was difficult to know how any conversation should begin, for it was more like lighting a fire than anything else Harwell could think of. If the wood and tinder were dry, one match would do the trick; at other times, no exertion would induce the flame to catch. When Danilo spoke, it was to articulate his thought or to refresh his memory of sorrow and joy, and the result was not, generally, what would pass for conversation in England.

Now he picked up the thread suggested by Danilo, which was the war in Herzegovina thirty years earlier, when the Christian *rayahs* had at last risen in revolt against the intolerable oppression and outrages of their Mahometan lords, and had called upon their kinsmen in Montenegro in that hour of need. "I have met a man who may have been with you when the mills were burnt. His name is Draško, and he has asked to be remembered to you."

"Draško Stepanović. One of our heroes. Did he tell you how we defeated the Turkish *nizam* that day, and even the Austrians who had come to impose their peace on the Herzegovina? And did he tell you that I had only so many bullets as there were Turks after the rocks had crushed us all? One of the best of our heroes, Draško was, and I drink to him." Danilo touched his glass to Harwell's and they both drank.

"It was he who carried me back to my family in these mountains, for I could not walk. Many were the Vasojević who did not return from that war."

"Why did you fight? It is very far from your home."

"The Vasojević have not always been free of the Turk, and some of us"—here he gestured in the direction of the Sandžak—"some of us are not free now. These mountains, which we call the Brda, are separated from the old Montenegro of the prince-bishops by a broad plain, where the Morača joins the Zeta and flows down towards Podgorica and the great lake below. When the Turks were strong, and exulted in their empire, we were cut off from Cetinje, and we had to pay tribute to the sultan who used our people so cruelly. But when we could, we cast off the sultan to stand with our brothers in Cetinje, and this was our freedom. Still, before that war, there was just this narrow space that connected the two halves of Montenegro, mountains to mountains, and on the plain, from Podgorica north to Ostrog, there was only the distance of four leagues, a morning's walk for a strong man, with Turks to the north and Turks and Arnaouts to the south. How could we not answer this call?" As Danilo spoke, warming to his task of instruction, Harwell noted that Sofia stared off into some middle distance, as if the tale had cast a spell on her.

"So it was the danger to yourselves and to your freedom that caused you to fight in Herzegovina?"

"That, certainly, and also to save our kinsmen. Do you not know that the family of the princes of Montenegro, and of the prince-bishops before them, comes from the Herzegovina? And when we heard how these people had been used, how the pasha had impaled them for his pleasure and taken the bread from their mouths in the years of famine, we rejoiced that they had risen. I myself wept tears of joy. We left, many of us, even before the call to arms came out of Cetinje. Would you not have done the same?"

"In the circumstances you describe . . . the sufferings . . . I suppose . . ."

"Sufferings, yes, that is a well-chosen word. I will tell you about suffering." Here Sofia closed her eyes. "We came upon a church one day, a little church such as our people built in that country, and half underground, so as to cause no offense to the Turk. And inside we found women and children slaughtered as if they were animals to be eaten, their limbs scattered so we could not tell which parts went together, and shoes with the bloody feet still inside them. They had been sent there for protection, because the Mahometans were killing every Christian they could find. There were no men there to guard them, though, only the priest, and the Turks had found them. The priest sat with his back to the altar, as if asleep in a pool of his own blood, for they had cut the bowels out of him, and these were lying in a silver plate on the altar. I tell you that the Serbs have never done such things."

An awful silence followed this revelation, and Harwell was aware only of the pounding of blood in his ears, which gave way in a few moments to the ticking of the watch in his pocket. He glanced at Sofia without moving his head, and the lines on her face—not quite a frown, more the settling of age on her features—made it clear that Danilo's story twisted that same knife in her bowels, and that she could not bear this sorry history that might also be the future of her children. And he, Harwell, was to blame for the turn the conversation had taken. She held him in her gaze, but did not seem to take note of him.

He closed the book—for Toma too stared away at some invisible horizon—and made some show of rising to put it away on the shelf, a signal, however tentative, that the evening might now be concluded with honor. But there remained the awkward matter of the open bottle, and when Harwell's eye fell on it, his host made a good-natured gesture with his empty glass, tapping it on the table, and Harwell had no choice but to fill it. To his surprise, Sofia nodded her head when he queried her and accepted a glass nearly as full as Danilo's. What scruple or custom, he wondered, prevented her from simply excusing herself and going to bed?

The rest of the evening was measured by the annihilation, inexorable and deliberate, of Sir Percy's excellent bottle. Nothing Harwell could do would hasten this end, other than to drink more himself, and even his conversational gambits backfired on him. When he asked why the market tomorrow would be held in Rožaj and not Berane, Danilo told him that this was no ordinary market, but a great feast day as well, perhaps the greatest feast day of the year for the Vasojević, for this was their *Slava*, or Glory, which celebrated the anniversary of the first baptism of the clan, when they had taken as their patron the Archangel Michael, and the feast must be held, as always, on the site of the ruined church, just by Rožaj, dedicated to the archangel. He, Harwell, would see for himself the spirit and the greatness of the Vasojević.

The thought of tomorrow's solemn festivities put Danilo in a mood that Harwell had never seen before, a kind of charismatic euphoria that brooked no interference; such a man would exert a powerful influence on all who came near him. The feast to come connected with the stories he had been telling about the past, and it was as if an electrical circuit had been completed. The celebration of the archangel was proof that the sacrifices in Herzegovina—here he struck his wooden leg with the heel of his hand—had not been in vain; it would be an affirmation of the Vasojević and, by extension, of all Montenegrins and all Serbs. And it was also a sign of things to come, for some of the Vasojević still lived under the Turk, and even he, Danilo, had to pay the *harac*. There would come a time when all of these wrongs would be righted, and the *Slava* was a seal on the determination of his people. He would give his other leg to see such a day, he said, but another generation must carry this thing forward. Here his eye fell on Toma, whose head was now bowed.

The evening ended, quite surprisingly, with a song. When Danilo enumerated the next day's festivities, he mentioned first the *kolo*, which would be danced by young people, such as his son or his wife. He laid his hand on her arm to emphasize this gallantry, and Sofia made a brief effort to smile at him. "If it will give you pleasure," she murmured.

Then Danilo said that there would be singing as well, and did Harwell understand that these songs were the true books of the Serb people? He gestured dismissively at the shelf above the window, and

Toma, who had not uttered a single word since the discussion of waterwheels, rose and fetched an odd bundle which hung from a nail on the wall. He unwrapped the cloths to reveal a simple stringed instrument which Harwell recognized as the *gusle*. "You must remember to take this tomorrow," said Toma in a low voice to his father.

After Danilo had tuned the one string and tossed off the remaining whiskey in his glass—at last! thought Harwell—he sang a song which so mirrored the course of the evening's conversation that Harwell thought at first his host must be extemporizing. But as the ballad continued, and Harwell grew accustomed to the flow of words in that deep, resonant tone, he realized that the song was not about the war in Herzegovina, but about an earlier time, and a valiant defense of the mountains against a vizier's army. And when the men fell, having slain their dozens and scores of Turks, it was the women, some with babies at their breasts, who took up their husbands' rifles and slew yet more of the enemy.

Harwell was quite drunk when the song ended, but not so drunk that he was unaware of the peculiar tension in the room. For Toma, having provoked the recital, sat in rapt concentration while his father sang and never took his eyes from his face. Sofia, all this while, gazed at Toma as if her heart would break, or had already broken, and she seemed to be willing him, without the slightest success, to turn away from that song.

"What is the name of that mountain?" asked Harwell as their road, now thronged with brightly clad peasants, both Christian and Mahometan, wound towards that astonishing limestone eminence which he had glimpsed only from his high excursions from the meadow. Seven thousand feet, and more, he estimated. His head had cleared sufficiently in the course of their two-hour ride for him to enjoy the sights and smells of this fine day, this new land.

"That is Haila," said Sofia above the rumble of the wagon. She sat in the back, cradling a basket of eggs in her lap. "It lies beyond Rožaj, on the other bank of the Ibar, in what we call Arnaoutluk."

"Nay," called Danilo from his perch on the driver's seat, "that land is Stara Serbia, the land of our kings. A half a day beyond Rožaj is

Peć, where they are buried, and where the Patriarch had his seat. And a day beyond Peć, to the east, is Kosovo, where our kingdom was lost to the cunning of the Turkish dogs, and to the treachery of our own people."

Danilo spoke in a loud, deep voice, and if Harwell, riding behind the wagon, could hear so clearly, then those on the road ahead must have received it as the trumpet of judgement, and they fell away right and left, Christian and Turk alike, to stand in awed silence as the wagon passed.

Their procession, even without Danilo's apocalyptic utterance, would have presented quite a spectacle to the other travellers. They had encountered few wagons of any sort on the road, though occasionally they overtook even slower vehicles which were no more than great tree trunks, crudely shaped, set upon axles and rounds of solid wood for wheels. Children and women sat upon the tree, which was the bed of the wagon, and tied to it were crates of chickens, bundles of market goods, slaughtered game, and soon-to-be-slaughtered sheep and pigs, with their legs trussed.

Danilo's wagon, elegant by comparison, carried only his wife, with her basket of eggs, and a great load of manure, swept from the house after the winter, to be sold in the market. The smell of this cargo, though not unpleasant, was nonetheless strong and ammoniac, and so Harwell rode his mare just to the side of the wagon, and not behind it. He was dressed in his best clothes, such as they were, but both Danilo and Sofia seemed plainly dressed for such a great day. Behind them, or in front, as the fancy took him, rode Toma, on the black horse, and he had taken it upon himself to herd the heifer all the way to Rožaj rather than simply tie her to the back of the wagon. Whenever the heifer was distracted by the other travellers, or took it in mind to turn back, there was the stallion behind her, tossing his head and flecking foam, to urge her forward.

Toma rode without the slightest evidence of care or effort, as if he had only to will the heifer towards the market, and the stallion would make it so. Every now and again, when the stallion fretted at this slow task, Toma would give him his head where the road ran through some meadow or grazing land, and they would cut a bold arc in the bright green grass. The boy would return with a grave face that betrayed none of the vicarious joy that Harwell felt: Harwell himself was no natural horseman. "See him now," said Sofia in a tone of wondering approval during one of these dashes, when the horse sprang suddenly over some hidden ditch or obstacle in the grass. At that very moment Harwell's heart leapt with the horse, and he noted how the rich purple of the boy's vest was very nearly the color of those sweating flanks, making them one creature that might have ridden out of or into some myth.

They parted company at the edge of town. Harwell wished to wander through the marketplace on his own, to see it with Lord Polgrove's eye, and Danilo had specific matters of sale and purchase to attend to: he had promised to buy for Sofia two long-fleeced sheep, a ram and a ewe, for her weaving. They would meet, if not in the market, then later in the afternoon for the celebration of the Feast of the Christian Name at the archangel's church. Toma pretended not to hear when his mother asked him where he would be in the market.

Harwell left his horse at a tumbledown *khan* near the entrance to the market, where the inner courtyard was already crowded with local men—Arnaouts, they must be—sipping coffee out of little cups and smoking their long pipes. The proprietor, a fat man in a gown of grimy cotton, came out to greet him and asked if he would need a room for the night. No, said Harwell, just some water for his mare, and some hay or oats if they were to be found. Certainly, by the will of Allah, certainly, said the proprietor, wiping his hands on his garment.

The town itself was a disappointment to Harwell, not because it was lacking in novelty or color—most certainly not in color—but because he could not imagine what, in all this welter of leather goods and copperware and fruits and livestock, would be of the slightest interest to Lord Polgrove. On his ride to Rožaj, once his head had cleared of last night's cobwebs, he had taken everything in, asked questions of Sofia about the crops in the fields, noted the relative numbers of Christians and Mahometans on the road, even made rough estimates of the flocks of sheep and cattle in the grazing land. All this he had stored away in his memory, for he carried no papers with him other than his passport and the precious document signed by Aehrenthal.

But he had seen nothing that signified, at least not in what he imagined to be Lord Polgrove's frame of reference. There were no towns at all, not even villages, no evidence of construction, and no machinery whatever, except for one lonely mill on a tiny stream. This had been pointed out to him by Toma, for otherwise he would never have guessed its function, and Toma observed that while the mill must have existed on this site for many years, to judge by its dilapidation, the wheel turned horizontally in the water, very much in accord with Professor Drinker's recently discovered principles. In a field beyond that mill Harwell had seen a row of stakes, widely spaced, with scraps of colored cloth tied to the tips.

The *čaršija* of Rožaj was laid out as a maze of lanes between white plastered shops with steep roofs of wooden slats. Each shop or building had a covered porch that extended into the street, so that Harwell, walking down that narrow space, might reach out with one hand to take a beaten copper vessel, and simultaneously, with the other, an embroidered apron, or a mousetrap, or a measure of crude nails. Several times he turned to tell the children who followed him that he had nothing for them; he even turned his trouser pockets inside out to show he had no coins. They stared at him round-eyed, in their gaily striped Turkish trousers that gathered at the ankle, and because they all had painted fingernails and hennaed hair, he could not tell which were boys and which girls. In any case, they did not believe him.

He ducked into a short side-alley, swung the gate shut behind him, and latched it. He was now behind the shops, and when he peered over the chest-high fence of wattles he saw a thin, unhealthy woman who was naked to the waist, washing herself. She must have been a Mahometan, he reasoned, for when she recovered from the shock of seeing his blond head above the paling she grabbed a handful of straw and buried her face in it. *This is ridiculous,* he said aloud in his embarrassment, and thought bitterly that nothing he had seen so far could justify his getting out of bed, much less the waste of Lord Polgrove's money.

At the far end of his escape route he found himself in what must be the main square of the market, an open space surrounding an elegantly housed fountain. He was glad to be quit of the dusty lanes and the importunate vendors in their little cubicles, but there was still much to see, and to hear. An old man, a coffee pounder, thumped away at his trade in a hollowed tree trunk, and from the unseen mosque came the cry of the *muezzin*. A garter maker, his embroidered scraps piled around him, sat in the dust, using his bare feet as a loom for his work. Bread sellers were gathered around the fountain, their wares laid out on low tables, and the women—Serbs in their gaudy finery and Mahometans in veils and dark, shapeless gowns—jostled each other in their eagerness to test the weight of each loaf. Across this throng a figure on the far side of the square caught his eye. It was Sofia, and he must have recognized her from her posture or some characteristic gesture, for in no other particulars did she resemble the woman who had ridden in the manure pile this morning. Silver coins glinted in her hair, and there was more silver on her fingers, at her throat, and at her waist. Like many of the Christian women in the marketplace she was dressed in white, but over her blouse she wore a long crimson jacket, sleeveless and trimmed with fur. How like a queen, he thought. A shouting at his elbow distracted him for a moment, and when he looked back he could no longer see her.

The altercation proved to be two tradesmen engaged in a tug-of-war over a steelyard. He could understand nothing of what they said, but deduced from the comment of a bystanding Serb that these were the only scales in the entire market, and if there was to be blood shed this day it might as well be over possession of this object.

There was no actual violence performed, but much seemed to have been offered, and both men clasped in desperation to the slender metal beam as they hurled oaths and insults at each other from a distance of inches. The crowd, which had been very vocal in refereeing the dispute, fell silent at the approach of the soldiers in blue tunics, two enlisted men and a captain with a roll of fat or muscle bulging over his tight collar. The latter seized the scales and handed them to one of the disputants, who fled with his prize. When the other Arnaout complained meekly of his loss, the captain took the bag of grain, lifted it high in one hand, and proclaimed it to be exactly twenty kilos, no more and no less.

"And that," he said, rounding on Harwell, "that is how you must deal with these people. Do you speak German?"

"A little."

"What then?" The captain eyed Harwell's dress, with particular attention to the sash. "Surely you are not from these parts?"

"I am English. My name is Harwell, Auberon Harwell, and I have papers if you . . ." He touched his breast pocket.

"Papers? We need no papers here among Europeans," said the captain in English, with emphasis on the last word. "I have been in London, you know. It is my favorite city, after Vienna, of course. Captain Schellendorf, at your service." He bowed and they shook hands. Captain Schellendorf asked Harwell if he smoked. Yes, Harwell replied, sometimes.

"Come then. Surely you have seen enough local color for one day. We shall sit and smoke, and drink a bottle of beer, and you will tell me how you come to honor us with your presence in this place at the end of the world."

"Do you believe in coincidence, Mr. Harwell, or perhaps I should say providence?" The captain's tone was correct, perhaps even cordial, and yet the expression on his face, some fleeting hint of irony or mockery, was not lost on Harwell.

They sat in the courtyard of the *khan* where Harwell had left his mare, and the proprietor had made a place for them in what he called his garden, a cheerless little space separated by a row of dusty shrubbery from the general press of market-day customers. At the captain's suggestion, two tables had been cleared, the former occupants made to gulp their coffee under the landlord's stern eye, and so they sat now at their ease, the two privates at one table, Harwell and his host at the other, and the captain had smoked, with elaborate pleasure, half a dozen gold-tipped Bosnian cigarettes.

Before the Austrian occupation, he explained, lighting another for Harwell, the local people consumed what they grew, arguably the world's best tobacco, and what they could not smoke up they sent in bales to Egypt, where the authorities were glad enough to claim it as their own and make into "Egyptian cigarettes." But now there was a factory at Marienhof, near Sarajevo, where hundreds of people were employed, putting the tobacco into these tubes, and sixty, sometimes eighty, thousand cigarettes a day were exported to Europe or to the United States. Our gain, your loss, he said, smiling at his guest. Here was an example of the benefits conferred by the resources, the organization, of the Austro-Hungarian Empire, wherever it was given a free hand. Was that not an excellent cigarette?

Harwell had never in his life smoked three cigarettes at a sitting, and so his head spun even as he agreed with this proposition. The captain called for more beer, and when it came, he raised his glass and intoned loudly, *"Nach Salonik!"* which the enlisted men echoed with enthusiasm, though they had no more beer in their glasses. Harwell had already decided that he did not care for Captain Schellendorf's company, however pleasant it might be to sit here where no urchins could get at him, and to converse with a man who had probably read books, even been to the opera.

His first response to Schellendorf's curiosity had been a vague statement about travelling in the highlands, with the possible object of writing a book. That had seemed to do the trick, and their conversation had passed on to other matters, chiefly the backwardness of this region where the ambiguity of a dual administration—meaning Turkey and Austria-Hungary—prevented any true progress of the sort that had been achieved in Bosnia and Herzegovina in just a few years. But of course the people here were the problem, for the Albanians, whatever one wished to call them, were a mongrel, lawless people who took pleasure in murdering the representatives of any central authority, and the so-called Christians were a sorry lot.

Still, much would be possible, even here, if only Austria had a free hand: tobacco, mining, a railway . . . Was there to be a railway, then? Those colored stakes Harwell had seen? Well, perhaps in time, and that was in fact Schellendorf's very mission in this godforsaken place, to survey a possible route to Salonika, and . . . alternatives. Had he, Harwell, any training in engineering or surveying?

No such training, Harwell said with a wry smile, but perhaps his time would have been better spent that way than in the study of literature.

"Literature!" exclaimed Schellendorf. "That is excellent. I have read your Byron and your Wordsworth, as you have no doubt read Goethe and Schiller. But what does a literary man find to occupy his mind among such persons as you have seen hawking their wares this afternoon? Do they not excite your contempt rather than your interest?"

Harwell thought about the brown curve of Toma's neck as he bent over the diagrams of the waterwheels, and of Sofia's features when she was distracted by the sound of a bird outside her window. There was a vein beating in the captain's forehead, like a fat worm descending into the line of his brows. He expected an answer.

"I do not believe I have ever encountered such civility, such openhandedness, among any people as I have found among my hosts in Montenegro. As for the local people here, I hardly have an opinion, as we have only just come down for the market and the feast today."

"Well, I should have known from your sash. A proud people, your Montenegrins, too proud, and always meddling in our affairs here, always complaining about the border and the Treaty of Berlin. We shall deal with them soon enough. This feast of theirs, you know, is no more than an excuse for troublemaking, and I would advise you to have no part of it. And what is at stake in all this? Why, a few miserable farms and towns such as you see here, and these filthy people. Do you see that fellow there?" Harwell followed the captain's glance to a figure squatting in the line of meager bushes. The man watched them closely. "That is a Jew or a Gypsy, and when he thinks I have drunk enough beer he will come and offer to sell me his virgin daughter. And if I decline, why, he will offer me his equally virgin son. Can you imagine it? Will you put such things in your novel, Mr. Harwell?"

It was at this point that Harwell retreated to the defensive perimeter of botany, and spoke of seed gathering on behalf of an ardent English collector, a very great expert, who was unfortunately prevented by circumstances from making such a journey himself. And that was when the telltale smile had shadowed Schellendorf's face, and he posed the question about coincidence.

"Shall I tell you why I ask?" the captain continued, for Harwell had not chosen to answer, knowing that Schellendorf held some advantage. "You must bear with me for a moment while I tell you a story." He refilled Harwell's glass, then his own, and lit yet another cigarette. He had one of those unfortunate faces, thought Harwell, where the smile is less appealing than the frown.

"When I was a young man, a very junior officer, I had the honor of being seconded, through family connections, to the guard unit accompanying Graf von Eisenberg—a count, you would call him in English—on his expedition into the Rhodope Mountains, in the land of the Bulgars. It was a detachment of Prussians, of course, very decent men, on the whole, and excellent soldiers, and perhaps I was there because even then, in the days before the year '01, the lands between the Danube and the Aegean were recognized by the Germans as being the fiefdom, in a moral sense, of the Austrian crown. In any case, it was a very great distinction for such a junior officer, and an important step in my career.

"We travelled for several months in the mountains, starting in Salonika, of course, and we reached Sofia at the end, which is perhaps two hundred kilometers east of here, as the bird flies. A very colorful city, though primitive. And all the while, we were collecting specimens and seeds, as you are, and the count, who is a very great amateur of botany, would stay up half the night in his tent reading his books and making his notes. We were caught more than once in blizzards, for it is very cold in those mountains, even in the springtime, and the wolves would come down into our camp. I remember one night when the watch was under my command, and we saw three wolves gathered round his tent, which glowed like a lantern in the falling snow. We chased them off, of course, and in the morning the count said he had heard nothing at all, even though the wolves were digging at the corner of his tent where he kept his supply of chocolate, and you could see where they had chewed the canvas."

Harwell was watching the captain's face as he spoke, hoping that his own presented a polite blank, and wondering how old this man was, and what the point of his tale might be.

"You have heard of my patron, so to speak, Count von Eisenberg? I know nothing of these matters, but he was particularly interested in the alpines, those little plants that grow in the high places."

"I know his reputation. I believe there are several species named in his honor."

"Exactly so! I am glad to hear you confirm my impression that his work is of international importance. He was in touch with experts in other countries, men who shared his passion for these matters, members of some society, the International Association of Alpine Fanciers, I believe, and he would correspond with them, even from the Rhodope Mountains. Once I had to escort the mailbag thirty kilometers overland to the nearest town, and we rode through the country of brigands who would slit the throat of any traveller, rich or poor.

"But my point is this: there was an English gentleman, a peer, as you say, whose name came up often enough in the count's conversation, but with whom he did not correspond, for they were not fond of each other, not even friendly. And this Englishman had a withered leg, or a clubfoot, and I know this because the count mentioned it often, and without charity, I am sorry to say. Do you see what my thought is here?" Captain Schellendorf leaned forward slightly, and Harwell made an effort not to recoil from the stale breath.

"I'm afraid I do not. In 1901 I had not yet gone up to Oxford, and I knew nothing of these matters, and I do not believe that I have ever heard of the association you mentioned."

"Yes, it has been several years, and much has changed in the world. But tell me, is your patron's name not Lord Polgrove?"

"That is certainly his name. But whether he was ever . . . Forgive me, but I am not used to drinking in the middle of the day, and this beer . . ." Harwell put his hand to his forehead and rubbed his temples.

"You are quite correct. It is disgusting, this Greek stuff, but there is nothing to be done. Waiter! Some bottled water for the English gentleman. *Schnell!* When you visit us in the *Kaserne*, and it is just beside the town, we will have some proper German beer, or indeed a Mosel if you would join us for dinner. What is it? Friday? *Stein Forellen*, which is nearly the equal of your English trout, or perhaps the *solo Krebsen*—how do you call them?—that live beneath the rocks in the river."

Harwell drank two glasses of water in quick succession, and during this time the dark man, colorfully but shabbily dressed, approached from the shrubbery to whisper a few words to Schellendorf. Harwell rose, thinking his host was distracted, but the captain took him by the wrist in a grasp that was too strong to be friendly. "We have not finished." The dark man, the Gypsy, was waved away, and he squatted again in the shade of the shrubs.

"I am so sorry," said Harwell, reaching for the notes of the new Montenegrin currency that were folded into the papers in his breast pocket. "You must allow me to pay, as you were so generous with your cigarettes."

"Sit, I pray you," said Schellendorf, who had not released his grip. Harwell was astonished at the strength there, and at the boldness of the gesture, for the man was considerably smaller than he. "I would not allow you to pay for donkey's piss that makes your head ache.

What I wish to say, to ask, is whether this Lord Polgrove does not take a very lively interest in foreign affairs, because his name is known to me in another context altogether, and . . ."

"I am sorry that I cannot enlighten you there. His lordship's interests are his own, and it would be the greatest presumption for me to . . ."

"Yes, of course, you are a literary man, as you told me. It is a pity that the subject does not interest you, for I myself have a great curiosity to know Lord Polgrove's mind. He and I would have much to discuss."

"Well, as you have observed yourself, it is difficult for him to travel, and so . . ."

"And so he sends others in his place to do the work for him. That is exactly my point, Mr. Harwell. We were quite aware of his efforts when I was in this region with the count, and that was seven years ago. He must have a very extensive collection by now."

"So I am told, though I have not seen everything for myself. I am not, you see, an intimate of Lord Polgrove's."

"But that is an awkward position, Mr. Harwell, if I may offer you a word of advice. You should strive to know everything you can, especially in such unstable regions, where life is governed by so many uncertainties. I must tell you that some of your patron's expeditions have ended very unhappily, and they were young men not unlike yourself, who may not have asked the right questions when they could have, and then they asked the wrong questions." Captain Schellendorf smiled complacently at this turn of phrase.

"You will allow me to observe, Captain Schellendorf, that I have asked no questions whatsoever, though I thank you for your concern. And now, if you will excuse me, I must ask the innkeeper for the use of his facilities. All this damned beer . . ."

"But I am a very poor host indeed. Come with me, for the landlord graciously allows me to use his own rooms, where there is even a basin of water. We will piss this Greek poison out of our systems and then . . ."

"Let me speak plainly, Captain. I am afraid I shall be sick. Perhaps if I could lie down for a few minutes it will pass."

"You shall have the landlord's rooms to yourself then, and I wish you a speedy recovery. If it does not pass, you must send for me at the *Kaserne*, for we have just completed the infirmary there. And my invitation to dinner stands, depending on your health. I have just remembered the story, from the count's own lips, concerning the falling-out between himself and Lord Polgrove. It is very amusing. As a collector or fancier yourself, you should know where such passions may lead. Until we meet again." Schellendorf bowed, made a little click with his heels in the dust, and turned away to give instructions to the landlord.

Harwell lay upon the odorous and probably verminous cushions of the divan with his eyes closed, and while the sickness he had complained of had been a ruse, his fatigue was genuine, so that after a few moments he fell into a shallow, troubled sleep.

In his dream he was with Lord Polgrove in a railway carriage inching towards Calais through the stifling heat of Belgium. Ahead lay the Channel, sea air, safety, home; behind, like a shadow in the east, was the humiliation of Bad Lauterberg, where Polgrove's jealousy and mania had overpowered all common sense, where Count von Eisenberg had made an ironic parting gift to Polgrove of the very plant that he had tried to steal, the prize of the Bad Lauterberg collection, the Blue Elf saxifrage, which the count had found and named, and which had never, until now, left his estate. The count had pressed their hands warmly, and even wished them a safe journey, as if nothing whatever had happened, as if James Curran had never existed, or had no connection with Polgrove whatever. "Perhaps you will succeed in forcing its flower" were the count's parting words, for the blossom of the Blue Elf was known only from one description on a steep scree somewhere in the heights of the Rhodope where the von Eisenberg expedition had encountered it.

Between them on the floor of the compartment sat the travelling Wardian case, its glass dome hidden and protected by leather, and the specially constructed ice drawer leaked slowly onto the carpet. Polgrove was forever sending Harwell to beg more ice from the dining car, to demand an explanation of these delays, for the train moved backwards and forwards as if to the rhythm of some idle hand. He was to speak to the conductor, cried Polgrove, beating his stick on the upholstery, to the engineer, offer them money, threaten them, if only they would bring him instantly to the Channel. Polgrove's fury was terrible to endure: they both knew the Blue Elf was rotting in its case, as the count must have foreseen. They had slept in their clothes for two nights, and Polgrove's bad leg, no longer under his control, twitched violently when he dozed. There was a smell in this claustrophobic space that permeated Harwell's clothes, the upholstery, his hair, and it was the smell of death. He must get out, or he would go mad along with Polgrove, rot with the plant. At the next station, or even now, with the train halted in the middle of the poppy fields, Harwell would simply walk away into that shimmering distance until he no longer heard anything behind him.

Harwell woke with a start and felt his heart beating too insistently. He was safe, for now, though this was not the first time he had dreamed of that journey which he knew only in Reg Farrer's telling, and even Farrer could only guess at the details, for Polgrove had fled from Bad Lauterberg alone, leaving James Curran to recover from his terrible beating and make his way back to England, a broken man who could scarcely put two words together or walk a straight line. Curran had been Farrer's cousin, much younger, but a promising botanist, and he would have gone on to great things had he not been seduced into Polgrove's mad scheme. Farrer had offered this to Harwell as a cautionary tale about his prospective employer. He, Farrer, had once been on very good terms with Polgrove, for the man's learning was immense, and his vital energy, but after the incident at Bad Lauterberg they had scarcely spoken, for he knew Polgrove had put young Curran up to it. Harwell should know what he was getting into. And the irony of it all, as Farrer explained without any trace of a smile, was that the plant Polgrove succeeded in saving from the hairy mildew was not, after all, the fabulous Blue Elf, if that plant even existed, but a very common *Saxifraga paniculata*, which grew and thrived and eventually spread its cheerful white flowers up and down Polgrove's private Matterhorn, where he had placed it with his own hands. As common as a weed it grew, and Polgrove's gardeners had weeks of work in destroying every last seedling.

There was a sound, distinct from the voices and clatter of crockery that filtered through the latticework of the window, and Harwell raised his head to look towards the door, where a child stood, shuffling her feet. When she saw that he was awake, she approached the

bed and wished him good day in German, though he scarcely recognized the sound of it. He could not tell how old she was: older,
perhaps, than he would have guessed at first glance, but certainly not
old enough to wear that painted face. She looked steadily upon him,
without blinking or glancing away, and after a long moment she
pulled the shift over her head in a gesture that lacked all art and
grace and understanding. She stood naked before him. "It is all paid
for," she said.

"What?" asked Harwell, and she repeated the phrase.

As he struggled to put his boot on, the girl stood closer to him so
that his knee was caught between her legs, and her breast pressed
against his face.

"No!" he said, wiping his mouth with the back of his hand, and
looked up to see the expression of despair on her face. "Put your
clothes on." He tried the phrase first in Serbo-Croatian, then in
German, but it was not until he held the garment up to cover her
body that she understood, and then she turned her back on him to
dress.

He stumbled out into the light, then remembered his watch and
his knife that he had left by the bed. She was sitting there, with her
head in her hands, and did not even look up at him. "It is all right,"
he said in English. "You have done no wrong."

Harwell tied his mare to a post at one side of the silent and emptying square. The marketplace seemed a weak imitation of itself: the
bread sellers were still clustered around the fountain, but they sat on
their heels and smoked now, for their tables were empty save for a
few loaves either undersized or broken by too eager a customer; the
crowd of children that had harassed him was nowhere to be seen;
and the figures walking through the narrow lanes, or bent over some
pile of merchandise, were all somberly dressed, all . . . That was it,
there was no color, for the Christians, in their finery, had vanished,
leaving these veiled women and leather-faced, turbaned men to close
up the shops. Harwell looked at his watch, then at the sun, and saw
that he had missed the time he said he would meet Danilo and Sofia.
He was hungry. The dusty loaves of bread drew his attention: what
difference could it make if they were broken?

"How much is this?" he asked, pointing politely and speaking very slowly, not sure what language would be understood.

"It is yours if you wish it," said the man, ignoring Harwell's twenty-*perper* note. "No one has bought it, and perhaps Allah desires me to make a gift of it. And no one here will take the Montenegrin currency."

"Thank you." Harwell wolfed the bread, and the dry crumbs in his throat reduced his voice to a whisper, or a croak. "And can you tell me where I might find the church where the Christians gather? It is called after Saint Michael."

"It is no church, sire, but a ruin which they say is a holy place. Walk towards the sun, beyond the town and the Austrian barracks, and you will find the Serbs at their feast. Listen. Do you not hear it?" Harwell listened, and heard the sound of what might be distant gunfire. He nodded.

"That is how they celebrate their holy days. Do you know what my wife says to me when she hears that? 'They are coming. If not now, then soon.' Every year she says it, and asks how a man can let this happen, why he will not protect his own children. I tell her I can do nothing." The bread seller spat in the dust. Harwell thanked him again and mounted the mare. He rode west, away from the market and towards the sound of the shooting.

There were no other travellers on the road, which was a relief to him, for his time in the mountains had accustomed him to silence, to long stretches of time spent in his own solitary company, and while he treasured true companionship now more than ever before—what would he not give for an hour with Raymond? or a letter from him?—he acknowledged also that loneliness and the willing withdrawal into his own thoughts was now a habit of mind.

It was not yet the hour of sunset, but the temperature was falling, and as he rode, on a course roughly parallel to the steep and rushing Ibar, there arose a cold haze from the water and the whole glen of the river and the great limestone tooth to the south were veiled in a pinkish light, and he was filled with wonder.

Had he not been late, and had the shooting not made him anxious, he would have stopped there on the track to lose himself in this scene, for he felt he needed time for clearheaded reflection on all that Captain Schellendorf had said, and also on what he had not said. He had not sought this man's company, or his conversation, and would willingly have satisfied Schellendorf's curiosity by showing his papers, even the *laissez-passer* signed by Aehrenthal, if only he could have avoided all that insinuating talk with its forced and false good fellowship. Well, he had put his foot in it, no doubt of that, though just where he had gone wrong he could not remember. But in order to avoid the objectionable intimacy of this fellow, and the even more dangerous ground that lay beyond, he had several times denied any meaningful relationship between himself and Lord Polgrove, and that shallow evasion, he now saw, merely fixed and confirmed him as Polgrove's servant, even in his own mind, and there was no honor in that.

At one point in the conversation, Schellendorf had touched his glass to Harwell's in a private toast and murmured, "God for us," which may have been a literal translation of some thought in his own language. It made no sense, for Schellendorf could not have been so naive as to believe their interests or destinies to be intertwined in God's favor. But those same words were engraved on every piece of flatware at Newton Court, along with the curious device of a half fish, the tail alone visible above a scrolled ribbon in the silver. Even his mother, from whose family the service had come down, could offer no explanation of the words or the device. Did he, Harwell, believe in coincidence? The answer must be yes, though he could imagine no possible connection between Schellendorf and that silver.

These thoughts were interrupted by a bugle call, and away to his right, where the forest gave way, he saw the Austrian encampment, a parade ground surrounded by crisp new buildings and rows of tents hemmed in between the dark wooded hills. The sentry at the gate eyed Harwell as he rode past, but in no way acknowledged him. On the parade ground soldiers in the dusty blue uniforms of the engineers formed themselves into ranks. Harwell counted them out of the corner of his eye, and saw that the roadways in the camp were paved with stone. Whatever they were doing here, they apparently intended to stay.

The road crested a wooded ridge, and there in a wide grassland beyond and below him he saw the colorful multitude of Serbs that had graced the market in the morning and then deserted it. They were gathered near a low, irregular hill in the center of the meadow, and in a hollow rimmed with carts and tethered horses lay the white oblongs, half swallowed by the turf, of a ruined building.

He did not know how he should take it all in, keep his eye on all that was happening at once, for if he fastened on the dance on the lawn by the ruin, where two lavishly brilliant circles revolved in slow opposition, then he would miss the preparations for the horse race away on the flat land by the streambed, where another crowd was gathered. And without these distractions he would gladly have watched the man on the steep side of the hill above the dancers, for he would climb up to the rim with a shrieking child under either arm, then slide on his back all the way down that smooth green throat to the bottom.

A gun sounded the beginning of the race, and the horses soon disappeared behind the hill. From the course of the spectators who surged towards him, some firing pistols as they ran, Harwell understood that the race would end at that pole stuck into the ground, which he himself must pass to reach the church. He reined in the mare and waited.

The riders came around the flank of the hill, heading directly at him, and so he had no perspective at all, could see only that tight ball of color, the flailing whips and flying manes, as they tore through the grass like some terrible mowing machine. It was only at the last moment, as the great arc of their course bent past him, that he saw the black horse surging free of the others, and Toma leaning from his saddle to wrest the piece of silk from the pole. The other horses thundered past, slowing now, the pack breaking apart to describe solitary loops in the fresh grass, until again they faced the boy on the black horse and the riders saluted him with cries of "*Živeo*, Toma!"

"*Živeo*, Toma!" bellowed Harwell, as loud as any man there, and Toma heard him. He held up the piece of silk, which glowed green in the last light of the day.

"Now do I have a fine thing to wear," he called to Harwell. Then he dismounted and was carried away by a band of boys, confounded in their joy, uncertain whether the greater honor was to stand next to the victor or hold the rein of his horse. Looking at the other riders, Harwell thought that Toma must have been the youngest of them, and perhaps the favorite of the crowd.

The sun was now below the line of the shouldered mountains to the west, and the twilight was perfumed by the smell of roasting meat, and of the torches, not yet lighted. Harwell, wiser now after his experience at the monastery, knew that he must be careful before he had eaten, and so he pretended to drink deeply from the wineskins that were pressed upon him or from the bottles of brandy. He found Danilo enthroned like a patriarch on a block of white stone, and complimented him on the prowess of his son.

"Did you see how Jovo, on the bay horse, whipped him in the face? Hah! Even that could not stop him." Someone offered a bottle to Danilo, and he drank. "This is a great day for Toma, and a great day for the Vasojević. The archangel smiles upon his chosen people who are gathered here. Look. Have you ever seen anything like this?"

Indeed he had not. And when he found Sofia, he asked her teasingly if she had danced the *kolo*, which he had seen from a distance, and she blushed, saying she had done so at her husband's insistence. "I am no longer a girl," she said, looking at his eyes.

He said nothing in answer to this, but smiled. The costume he had seen in the marketplace, but what he had not noted was the skein of dyed blue horsehair braided into the black of her own, which, with those silver coins, confirmed a barbaric splendor and made him remember a tale, read to him as a child, about the queen of some land, far away and long ago, an imaginary land, he had assumed. But now this thought came full circle back to the present, with Sofia standing before him, and his own tale, should he ever write it, would it not seem to some other child in England, yet to be born, like a dream, or an invention?

When the meat was ready they ate together, she as ravenously as he, and she introduced him to her kin, to neighbors he had not met until now, but would see again if he stayed for the harvest, and finally to Miliceva and her mother, and it was Harwell's turn to blush. He thought he should find something to say, some lighthearted observation connecting the cloth he wore as a sash to the identical material Miliceva wore as a headdress. But he could not find the right words, and perhaps there were none, for after the greeting the four of them stood there in a melancholy silence that contrasted oddly with the laughter and the spirited conversation surrounding them. At first he was preoccupied with his own awkwardness, but Miliceva and Sofia stood there face-to-face as if there were no feast, no audience at all, as if they needed no words to evoke the son and husband who should have connected them. Sofia glanced once at the white and scarlet garments of the younger woman, noting the extravagance of this costume for a girl who said she would never marry. Before they parted she embraced Miliceva and whispered something in her ear. The girl turned and smiled at him, making him blush again.

"Tell me what I have missed of the celebration by being late," he said, when they were alone again. And Sofia told him that there had been prayers and speeches and much drinking and the horse race . . . "The horse race I saw," he said, "and the *kolo.*"

"Well then, you have missed only the prayers, for the speeches will come again and the drinking has never stopped." She laughed at this, and Harwell realized that she had probably refused no wineskins herself.

On the far side of the church, in the light of the torches, the younger men, Toma among them, engaged in a display of horsemanship to the delight and terror of a group of women seated in a tight circle on the grass. Straight at them each man rode, from a distance of fifty yards or so, and at the last minute pulled his horse up short, so that it churned the air above their heads with its hooves, held there on its hind legs as long as balance and skill would allow. It was a trick of the Turks, whispered Sofia, and much practiced among the Bosniacs, who were great heroes with their horses. This was something that the boys learned from the Mahometans when they went up to spend the summer with the oxen in the high pasturelands.

And who was the girl, Harwell inquired, who sat in the very front there, and looked up so fearlessly with Toma and the stallion towering over her? Marjeva, said Sofia, and the prize that Toma had taken from the pole had been hers.

And would she be a fitting bride for Toma? "Yes," said Sofia, "a fitting bride. Not unlike Miliceva, though perhaps more forward. If Toma were to be a man like his father, I would be pleased to have Marjeva as my daughter. But that is not his fate, do you not see? That is why I have asked your help."

Harwell was not certain what he was being asked to agree to, or if he believed at all in the concept of destiny, much less in his power to intervene or shape it. What he remembered is that he had promised Sofia his help, and this was a bond as sacred as any he could think of. He took a long drink from a bottle of violent *rakija* that was offered to him, and found that it did nothing to alleviate the weight in his chest that he felt whenever he thought of this vow he had made to Sofia. It was not so much that he doubted of his success—he had already written to Lydia to make discreet inquiries at the British Legation and at various ministries in the capital—but once this thing was arranged, when Toma was on his way to America, or when Danilo had at least given his blessing, then his own time among these people would have ended. And yet he felt now, more strongly if no more rationally, what he had felt when he looked down on the meadow of Stupa Vasiljeva from that high place just under the roof of sky: that he belonged here, and that it would be as desperate a wrench for him to leave as it would be to send Toma away to an unknown land.

The speeches began again when the multitude had been fed, and the bottles were passed, and when the name of some legendary Vasojević was invoked, or a battle which had shaped the history of the clan, the crowd cried out their approval, and pistols were fired into the air. Harwell was dumbfounded to see the speed with which his neighbors could reload those quaint old pieces in the uncertain light of the torches, ramming the charge home with scarcely a glance, and certainly without setting the precious bottle down. These outbursts of oratory were not so much speeches, it seemed to him, as religious toasts, for as often as the history and heroism of the common ancestry was cited, so often was the will of God mentioned, and the protection of the Archangel Michael, and at every possible opportunity the listeners rechristened themselves with drink.

Danilo himself did not speak, but he sat on his block of stone as if presiding over this occasion, and many of those who addressed the crowd stood beside him, or even laid a hand on his shoulder, and when Danilo raised his bottle in approval of some phrase, the crowd roared. Harwell wondered where all this might end.

This question, which he had been turning over for some time, was answered by the arrival of the Austrian garrison, a long double file of those well-fed and well-armed engineers that Harwell had glimpsed on the parade ground, and at their head, like the point of the arrow, Captain Schellendorf rode straight into the heart of the gathered Serbs.

He dismounted before Danilo, who did not rise to acknowledge this intrusion, and at a single barked command the soldiers fanned out, facing the crowd. Harwell could see, across the ruin and beyond Danilo, that a second column had taken up a position along the bank of the creek. He tried to match those numbers with what he had seen earlier in the afternoon, and thought there might be yet a third column somewhere in the rear. The crowd, after an initial stunned silence, now sent up a murmur of complaint like a vast hive in the hollow of a tree.

Harwell made his way towards Schellendorf with difficulty, for everyone in front of him was pressing forward or standing on tiptoe for a better view. He jostled shoulders and made his excuses, pushing when no gentler tactic would work, and more than one man turned on him. The fierce expressions softened then, for Harwell was recognized, but did some doubt remain? Was this tall, fair man Danilo's guest, or the Austrian officer's ally? The tension rose in him and around him, an almost palpable current of violence that might coalesce around a single gesture or even a word.

"Captain Schellendorf!" Harwell was nearly out of breath. Perhaps he spoke too loud.

"Mr. Harwell. I am sorry you did not take my advice." Schellendorf had no smile for him now. "Do you know this fellow? Can you get him to talk to me? He looks to be the chief of these drunken fools."

"I know him, he is my host, Danilo Pekočević. You must show him respect."

"Indeed? Respect for what, exactly? This is an illegal political gathering, even without these firearms. I could turn everyone here over to the Turkish authorities, including yourself, my friend. But there is no time for this: tell him to send his people home, and then I will respect him. It would be foolish to disobey this order." He called out again, and the command was repeated by an officer near the creek, and another out in the darkness behind; but it was the clicking of bolts, a sound that reminded Harwell of beetles, that silenced the murmur of the crowd.

"Many people could die here, Mr. Harwell. Tell him to be sensible."

"Danilo . . ." Harwell began. The name sounded awkward on his tongue.

"Do you know this man?" asked Danilo, looking up at last.

"I met him in the marketplace today."

"Tell him that I am not afraid of him, that no man here is afraid of him. Tell him also that we did not come to fight. When that time comes, we will not bring our women and children."

In English Harwell said to Schellendorf: "You hear what he says. He understands you perfectly when you speak his language. Will you leave this matter in my hands?"

"I am responsible only for my own soldiers, Mr. Harwell, not for the well-being or happiness of these people, not even yours. But you may use your influence if you will."

Harwell spoke slowly to Danilo, hoping his voice would carry. "He says that we must leave now. The Austrian captain . . . apologizes for interrupting the feast of the archangel, who is a saint among his people as well. He is himself acting under orders." Harwell held his breath, hoping that Schellendorf would have the wit to say nothing.

"If he honors this occasion, and the archangel, tell him to have his men put aside their rifles, for a Serb will obey no man who points a gun at him."

Schellendorf called out in German, the order was repeated by his subordinates, and the soldiers uncocked their rifles. Then he spoke to the people in their own language, telling them to go home.

"Hear him!" cried Danilo, and the soldiers, their rifles slung to their shoulders, began to move through the crowd, breaking up the knots of angry men, urging everyone towards the wagons and horses.

A sudden movement on the far side of the church disturbed the rhythm of the soldiers' progress, and a dark shape rose up to blot the torch from Harwell's view. A soldier had seized the bridle of the black horse with Toma still mounted, and when the animal reared, the soldier lost his footing and went down to his knees. His comrades would have caught the horse, perhaps pulled the rider to the ground, but Toma was too quick for them. The stallion sprang free before his front feet even grazed the earth, making a prodigious leap with the hindquarters alone, and then away through the crowd at an impossible pace.

Harwell watched in admiration and in panic as Toma rode directly at the church as the shortest way to his freedom, cleared the one wall, scattered the soldiers standing in the grassy nave, and then sailed over Danilo's stone as if it had been a pebble in his way, and so close to Schellendorf that he could have spat on him. The captain had drawn his pistol, and when the horse had passed him, he leveled it at the retreating figure.

"Captain Schellendorf!" Harwell bellowed these words so loud and so close to the Austrian's head that he flinched, as he had not from the horse. He did not fire, but brought his weapon around to bear on Harwell.

"Mr. Harwell, I grow tired of your company."

"Forgive me, the boy is my pupil. I should be sorry to lose him. I am sure he is on his way home even now."

"Ah, a teacher as well. So many talents, my friend. The boy is your responsibility, then, and I shall hold you accountable for his good conduct. My advice to you is not to concern yourself too closely with these people, any of them. Neither their history nor their God will save them when the time comes." Schellendorf put away his pistol. "I trust we shall not meet again."

Danilo's voice surprised Harwell with its hushed but urgent tone: "Ride with her," he said. Harwell pulled in the mare, dismounted, and tied the reins to the rear stake of the wagon. Behind them the torches ringing the church of the Archangel Michael were being extinguished one by one, and at last the darkness was complete. Night as God created it, thought Harwell, surprising himself. It sounded very much as if Sofia were praying: that mumbled monotone could have no other meaning.

"May I ride with you?" He hopped up easily onto the bed, for the wagon's pace was no more than his own, and settled himself against a fat trussed sheep that bucked once against its ropes and then accepted his weight. She was silent now, but the rhythm of her breathing betrayed her agitation.

"He will come to no harm. He has the horse, and he knows the way."

"What did you find in the cave?" Her voice was a sharp whisper for his ear alone, her breath hot and ripe with liquor. She thrust the bottle into his lap, and he drank, thinking: *I am become the keeper of secrets.*

"There is nothing in the cave for you to worry about. And as for his comings and goings, perhaps he has a girl. You saw for yourself today how it could happen."

"So I did. Perhaps the time is shorter than I thought. I will speak to Danilo tomorrow."

They were not alone on the road, for many of those who had gathered for the *Slava* went their way, walking and riding, and the night was full of murmured conversations. When they passed the camp of the Austrians, its lights burning fiercely, Harwell could see how large this band of pilgrims was. A man called out to Danilo, saying that their *Slava* was not complete until he sang the *Gorski Vijenac*, that now more than ever they needed to remember this lesson, and the Austrians must hear it.

And so Danilo began to sing, with no accompaniment other than the creak of harness and the rough bass of wheels upon the stony road, and Harwell understood most of the words, could glimpse the power in those dreadful images of war and destruction, could feel his soul adrift on that mighty stream and surrendered to its current the way he had to Macaulay, or to Homer, and at last, in spite of himself, he thrilled to the triumph of this deed of blood.

> *Strike these blasphemers of Christ's holy Name!*
> *Baptiz'd be they, with water or with blood!*
> *Hunt we the leper now from out our fold;*
> *Let chanted be some terror-bringing song;*
> *Let the true altar rise on blood-stained stone!*

On and on the song went, long after many of the other travellers had branched off the road towards their own houses. And Sofia had listened to none of it, but wrapped her shawl tight around her head and laid herself down to sleep on Harwell's lap.

Chapter Twelve

"IS CHICAGO BY THE SEA?"

Harwell was concentrating to such a great degree on the translation of Sofia's prior sentence into presentable written English—a task that brought to mind the anguish of the schoolroom and caused him now to perspire—that he did not hear her question, and he asked her to repeat it.

"Is Chicago by the sea? Will Toma find a ship in Kotor that will take him directly to my cousin's city?"

Harwell reflected on this and wondered why he could not summon a single fact from all those years of his education at this critical moment. He had not the faintest notion of where Chicago might be. Had he been asleep when the geography of America was being discussed? He had certainly never heard of anyone in England sailing for Chicago.

He half rose from his chair and took down the guidebook, that repository of extravagant information, and was relieved to find a map of Chicago and its environs. That blank space to the right must be a prodigious body of water—he estimated its partial breadth against the scale of distance—but it was a lake. Could it be a lake? He did not see how it was possible.

"It is as I thought," he said to Sofia, and pointed to the map. "Here is a body of water several times as large as the Bay of Kotor, and yet it is not the sea but a great lake, which means fresh water. I think Toma must find his way to Chicago by railway from New York." Sofia nodded, pleased with this information.

"Then we must tell Jovo to watch the railway station, and not the docks on this lake. But we will come to that later. What did you write last?"

"I wrote what you told me to write: 'He is a good son, and he can ride a horse the way you once did in the pasturelands, when I used to watch you and pretend that I did not. But his true strength is in his mind, and that is why I must send him to you.'" She smiled at these words, a shy and fleeting expression, as if the words and the thought behind them now belonged to someone other than herself.

"Now write, if you will: 'You must teach him the ways of America, so that he will uphold the honor of the Vasojević in this new country.' Danilo would be pleased with that, do you not think so?"

"Yes, but surely you will not . . ."

"He will not see this letter, and your part in it will remain hidden also."

"Thank you," he murmured, not daring to look at her.

"Write also this: 'Danilo sends his blessings to you, and remembers still the days of your youth, when the world was such a different place, and we did not know what paths our lives would take. I might wish now that I did not, could not, see what lies ahead as if it were written: that a war shall come which will swallow us in its sorrows, and it will be this rather than Kosovo that will be called the grave of our people. I wish with all my heart that I could see you again, that we could walk again in those same pastures, but it is not to be. We must try to see God's wisdom in all things, and for myself I ask only that you receive Toma and treat him with kindness. Watch for him to come by train, from New York, and if there is anything that you can do to help him with the officials or the police, do it for my sake. And if you have any kind feeling for me, let that be your gift to him also.' There. I have finished."

Her face, to Harwell's furtive glance, reflected not only exhaustion, but something deeper and more lasting: defeat, perhaps. As he blotted the paper, a cloud that might have been the hand of God covered the sun and took away the light, so that he could hardly read his own words. He blinked impatiently to stay some tidal pull of grief and love.

"What salutation, what ending shall I put?"

"I do not know. I have only ever written to my daughter, and once to the prince, on Danilo's behalf. You must help me in this."

"Everything depends on the degree of your acquaintance. If he is not well known to you, you might put *Yours most humbly*, or *Very truly yours*. To a close friend, or a family member, you could write *With kindest regards*, or even *Affectionately*, or even—again, depending on the circumstances—*With love*. Sometimes, simply *Love*, just the one word."

"But do you not think that Jovo may have to show my letter to the officials there?"

"That may be."

"Well then, we must put the middle one."

Harwell sighed and wrote *With kindest regards*, then pushed the paper towards Sofia. "You must sign it." She made energetic strokes with the pen, producing a large, bold, childlike emblem in the Cyrillic alphabet. A fleck of ink landed on the back of his hand. "I shall make a copy later for Toma to carry with him." He wrote the cousin's name on the envelope. "Do you think he will still be there after all these years?"

"Yes, and there are many Serbs where he is living, so that the letter will reach him, even if he is not in the same house. I feel much easier in my mind now that we have done this thing." The light had returned to the meadow, and it was again a glorious midday, but his own melancholy had not lifted.

"How hard this letter must be for you, and all that goes with it." He took her hand in his, and kissed it, and, because she did not draw back, held it there against his cheek, against the stubble of his beard. He was afraid his heart would overflow with these emotions, that he would make a fool of himself. How could she bear to contemplate the end of so many things?

"Are you so sure of this darkness? Is there no other way for you, for all of you?" And for me, he thought, and her face swam in his vision now, for he had not been able to hold back his tears.

"I cannot know what God's will is, but if it is left to our doing then there must be war. In years past, the *Slava* celebrating our baptism in the archangel's name was a secret mass, and even the ruin of that church was proof of the Turkish power over us. It was forbidden to fire a gun, or even to light a torch, and still we were not safe from them. And now you see what the Austrians have done: they keep the Serb and the Turk like two chained dogs, ready to kill each other, and when we have done that, the Austrians can pick and choose and take what they want. They have come to keep the peace, so it is said, but I think this peace is as dangerous as any war, like a wound that cannot drain, and will not heal."

"How do you know this?" Their hands now lay on the table, gently entwined. *There, that is peace,* he thought.

"I hear it in the voices of our young men when they are drunk with wine and the spirit of the archangel. I feel it in the marketplace where the Arnaouts, who are unruly servants of the Turk, will not look at us when they sell bread to us. I see it sometimes in the eyes of my son."

"And Danilo, too?"

"That, of course. Nothing will change him. But this letter will break his heart."

"And has he a heart, then?" asked Harwell, giving in to his despair.

Now Sofia took her hand away, and looked at him as if he stood naked before her. She saw the spot of ink on the back of his hand and rubbed it away with the corner of her shawl, which she had first touched to her tongue. "Oh, yes," she said at last. "Danilo has a heart, as I do, as you do, and that heart wants the things it cannot have. That is the way of this world."

Even under the best of circumstances, packing or organization of any sort was not Harwell's strong suit, and he approached the task now at hand with an agitation of mind that made it impossible to think clearly.

He was being sent away. Well, not so much sent away, not permanently, but asked if he could occupy himself elsewhere for a day, perhaps two, while she, Sofia, took up the matter of Toma and his future with Danilo. He expected there would be a terrible row, and he wondered if he should try to stay near in case . . . in case what? No, she was surely right about that: his presence could only complicate matters, provide a distraction for Danilo from the cruel choice she would force upon him. Was there a choice? What argument or weapon could she bring to bear if Danilo simply refused? He could not imagine how it would go, what she could say, but the thought of Sofia's displeasure was as unnerving as any rage of Danilo's.

He did not know how much time he would have on the other end of his excursion before he and Toma must set off for . . . he had not even thought ahead to where they must go. Cetinje, of course, and then Kotor for the steamship, or perhaps Bar or Ulcinj farther south along the coast. And so he must make sure that all his seed containers and those cunning bulbs were safe in his absence and ready to go, and that his journals . . . Christ! the journals: he had meant to finish writing up his notes when he returned from Rožaj, from the *Slava*, but Sofia's agitation had been so great that they sat down at once to write the letter to her cousin. And he had letters of his own he must write, to Lydia, preparing her for their arrival, to Polgrove, of course. And where in all this would he find even a quarter of an hour to talk with Sofia, whose cool hand, or the memory of it, still burned on his cheek?

Perhaps she would come with him, just to show him the way, the forks and crossings to the high, hanging valley that Toma had described, where the snowmelt fed a little stream all through the summer, and where the chamois came to graze, so that their scent haunted the place, even when they could not be seen. And he would find a little grassy place and tether his horse, crushing violets and the flexed stars of dwarf tulips however careful he tried to be, and by the time he had made a fire and boiled up the tea for Sofia, who was sitting there on a rock, lost in contemplation of the glorious quilt of flowers climbing the scree under the forked peak, by that time it would be too late for her to get back. Harwell sighed, and sat on his bed, and put his head in his hands.

He finished his packing with a grim set to his mouth, annoyed at himself, at his weakness, annoyed at Sofia for banishing him, annoyed at Toma, who, in spite of all his earlier offers to guide him to this place where the chamois were to be found, had surprisingly, and rather curtly, declined to accompany him. Well, if the boy was acting strangely, was it any wonder? There was no argument about that, really: the sooner Toma could be gotten away from this place, the better. He must focus his thoughts on that, on this great task that Sofia had set for him. He could not think of it as happiness, but it was a purpose, and he would cling to it.

He left without ceremony. The mare stood ready to go, and he stuck his head through the door to ask when Sofia expected the postman, but found Danilo there ranting about the absence of his son, who had been sent by Sofia on some errand to Berane. Did she not realize that there was work to be done in those fields down below? Must he do everything by himself? Harwell could not bring himself to meet Danilo's eye: under other circumstances he would have offered his own services, as he had several times accompanied Toma or Danilo to those plantings. Sofia gazed on him from the shadows near the hearth—almost a glare—and it was all he could do to mutter a hasty farewell.

The directions he had been given were not difficult, and Harwell had not thought to write them down. In any case, he knew that his journey tended towards a particular peak, visible from many paths in the high country, and so he had no anxiety about getting lost: he had only to make his way towards that mountain.

He rode in a kind of trance, his mind occupied with untangling and reweaving the strands of his own small history and destiny from those of Sofia, and Toma, and Lydia, and when he surfaced again to an awareness of his surroundings he realized that in a technical sense he was lost. He had encountered no landmarks, remembered or promised, for some time now; the stream no longer sounded down to the left of his trail, and instead of climbing, as he knew he must do, the way now seemed to bend north, descending somewhat, so that little patches of agricultural land could be seen between the gaps in the trees. The mountain was still away to the west: he would take the next left-hand fork in the trail, and hope for the best.

Now the trail bent again to the right, and he found himself on a rim of bare rock overlooking a *polje*, one of those curious sinkholes so common in the karst surrounding Cetinje, but less often encountered in these mountains, and there in the shade of a tall rock lay two figures, one of which was undoubtedly Toma, and the other quite certainly a girl dressed in black . . . the bey's daughter, he would have guessed. They lay on the grassy verge of a vineyard, close to one another but not touching, and so still that they might be dead, or simply inanimate, like costumed dolls dropped from the height of rock.

The path ahead followed the rim of the sinkhole, and Harwell could see that if he continued he would end up heading exactly in the wrong direction, doubly so, since he would be descending as well as travelling east. He pulled the mare in when he came to a place where there was room to turn her, and felt his face flush with embarrassment that this maneuver must be performed in full view of his audience. Would they think—how could they not think—that he had come to spy on them? What other reason could there be for the boy's studied indifference to his presence? He rode until he reached the safety of the trees, and did not look back.

There was, contrary to his expectations, plenty of light left when he reached his destination, for the valley, if he could call it that, was held high in the sky by the misshapen hand of cloven limestone that had yielded up flakes, and pebbles, and boulders enough to make a flat, an alpine lawn, carved by the meandering stream. There were no tulips to be seen—perhaps this site was too high and exposed—but he smiled to acknowledge that his imagination was confirmed in so many other details, as if he had actually seen himself and Sofia in this place. He made a slow circuit with his eyes of the broken cliffs and talus slopes, hoping to glimpse the chamois, and was disappointed, but when he took little sniffs of the crisp air through his nose, as Toma had told him to do, he could almost taste the musk of the goat. Once he lit his fire this trace would be lost to him.

It would not be much of a fire, for he was well above the line of the last stunted spruce trees, but he gathered enough sticks from those tenacious, half-dead shrubs to see him through a mug of tea and the gruel he would make for his supper. Then he sat down to write, for his baggage consisted mostly of books, his paper, and his journal, and when he had spread them all around his boulder, within easy reach, he looked at the sky again, to make sure there was no danger of rain. Start with the difficult one, he said to himself, then smiled to think that he had not really narrowed the field much.

above Berane
1.vi.1908

My Lord:

I am pleased to be able to report some progress along the lines suggested in your letter, that is to say I have made an excursion into the
Sandžak itself, and from where I write much of that territory to the
north and east is spread out below me.

It is a sorry, backward place. I travelled the road between Berane and
Rožaj, which is on the Ibar at the southernmost limit of the Sandžak,
and of the Austrian occupation. There is a considerable Austrian garrison just outside the town, comprising a detachment of engineers, part of
a Bosnian regiment, and some cavalry—uhlans, I think—though I can
give you no firm numbers on any of these units. It was an impressive
show of force—more on this heading later—and my first reaction was
one of surprise that so many troops were necessary for any conceivable
peacekeeping effort. This may tend to confirm your intelligence about
impending developments in the Ottoman Empire and the eagerness of
the Austro-Hungarian Empire to expand into the void and teach their
neighbors the Serbs a lesson or two.

The railroad project continues: I saw surveying stakes in a pasture
near the road and the town itself is full of Austrian engineers, including
an officer with whom I had a conversation. They talk of nothing so
much as Salonika, and perhaps this goal of completing the rail link between Vienna and the Aegean gives some purpose to what must otherwise be a monotonous and featureless garrison existence.

It is my impression from speaking with Captain Schellendorf—he was
so kind as to invite me to drink with him, and I might even have dined
with him at the Kaserne had I not been otherwise engaged—that Austria has no interest in the Sandžak other than as a conduit towards the
Aegean and, seeing little opportunity in these parts for mineral, industrial, or agricultural exploitation, that she has adopted a hostile, even a
provocative attitudes towards the neighboring Montenegrins.

I did attempt, with no particular success, to draw him out on the
route of the railroad, for although his engineers may indeed be surveying
alternate routes for the main trunk towards Salonika, and I have no reason to doubt the intended terminus, still this is unpromising country for
a north-south line, which set me to speculating. Perhaps the engineers
are here to ponder other problems, such as fortifications of some sort, or

perhaps the eventual construction of an east-west spur off the Salonika trunk, rather like the one Captain de Windt described in his book on Bosnia last year. You may remember that he came across such a spur, in the neighborhood of Višegrad, and that it came to a dead end at the Serbian frontier. His inference was that the only possible purpose of such a line was to thrust Austrian troops and supplies into Serbia at a moment's notice. Any strong Austrian presence here, whether fortified or rail-connected, within a few miles of Peć and the road into the Albanian highlands, gives the dual monarchy a commanding presence on three sides of the principality of Montenegro. The fourth side, of course, is the Albanian frontier, and there is no comfort to the Montenegrins there.

Certainly they, the Austrians, are cocks of the walk in Rožaj, and they treat the local folk, the Arnaouts or Albanian Mahometans, with a contempt that exceeds even their disdain for the Serbs. Still, he was an interesting man, this Schellendorf, and had travelled widely in these regions several years ago under the auspices of Count von Eisenberg, who may be known to you as a fellow botanist, a specialist in the alpine species. What a small place the world is after all.

Harwell broke off here, though he knew he must provide an account of his further encounter with Schellendorf and some words, perhaps borrowed from Sofia, on the relations between the Christian Serbs and their Mahometan neighbors in the Sandžak, and on the role of Austria in maintaining the balance of hostilities. He knew he must do this, and he would do it, and yet just now his thoughts were clouded and his palms were sweating in spite of the advancing chill of the cloudless early evening. He was remembering, at the moment his pen ceased, how deep a chord his experience with Schellendorf had struck, and how his loathing was more pronounced now in reflection than it had been at any earlier moment: loathing for the Austrian captain, for Lord Polgrove, and even, most uncomfortably, for himself. The act of writing something down, as so often in the past, clarified—perhaps even precipitated—his own inchoate thoughts and feelings, and he now saw, in the words he had written, and in those he had yet to write, the grinding of empires and his own dishonor. Was he not preparing to retail Sofia's wisdom to Lord Polgrove as his own? Would she ever know that an observation she had made on the bread vendors of Rožaj would add its delicate weight to one side of the scale or the other, hasten the arrival of the cataclysm she foresaw, or put it off for a year, a month, a week? What had blinded him, until this very moment, to the essential character of his patron, in spite of all that Farrer had told him, and to the true nature of this "adventure" of his? He was a spy: it should make no difference to him whether the bread seller was killed in his bed by a rabble of ascendant Serbs; no difference if Captain Schellendorf's head were to grace one of Danilo's sharpened poles; no difference if the Hermit's Meadow and those who lived there were swallowed by that war that lay just beyond his horizon. His heart turned in his breast. He could scarcely breathe.

He thought he might brew up some tea, but when he stood he found he was stiff from his ride and from sitting on this boulder. There was enough light left to climb around a bit on that scree, where plants clumped up thickly along the course of snowmelt hidden beneath the gravel.

Near the top of the steep bank, having noted the dense pincushions of *Saxifraga sempervivum* dotted with bloom, and mats of *Aubrieta gracilis* strewn like pink silk on the lower slope, he came upon a most pleasing plant, a species he had not yet encountered, not very different from *Diapensia lapponica*, which, even on the page of the book, had so captivated him, though *lapponica* was never found in these latitudes. Cheered by this pleasant mystery, he broke a sprig from the plant and descended in great bounds, taking a childish delight in the avalanches that surged beneath his feet.

It had been a very long time since Harwell had felt, or allowed himself to feel, anything like the uncomplicated, thoughtless, physical joy of that descent. When he reached the level ground his legs were trembling slightly and he felt almost drunk with those few moments of pleasure. He looked back up the slope, following his craters through the bright clumps, pink, purple, and white, that gathered the last light into themselves, beacons now against the ragged stone. Should he do it again? No, he decided not to, but the euphoria he felt, this sudden fullness of heart, made it impossible to continue his account to Lord Polgrove.

Montenegro

Dearest Lydia:

It is my fond—and futile—wish that you could be here with me at this very moment: evening gathers in this cleft above the tree line, and I can just make out the flowers on the slope which moments ago were so sharply defined for me; soon I shall have to light a candle to see the words on this page, and I shall be writing from memory, recovering from the darkness a scene that has so impressed itself upon me.

I have done my best in these letters to convey a sense of this place and the people I have found here, and yet I know how far short I have fallen. I remember now, and have on several previous occasions, how you proposed that you should come with me on this trip, a suggestion that so took me by surprise that I reacted quite abruptly, and I may have given offense in my eagerness to cut off that line of conversation. Of course there was the danger of the expedition and the perceived unorthodoxy of my travelling with a female person who was neither my wife nor a blood relative. I was still too close to England and everything that had formed me. In our campfire at night I would have seen the ghostly presence of Dr. Jowett in the smoke, humming his disapproval of such an arrangement.

I have often thought, in one or another situation that has arisen, that you would be an abler observer of events, a shrewder judge of character, because you know so much of the language and the history of Montenegro. But I confess that I had not thought of sharing this experience with you, except by my letters, probably because I never had brothers and sisters with whom I had to share things, and because I conceived of this as a gloriously lonely undertaking.

Lonely it has been, but in ways I would never have been able to imagine beforehand. In England, all isolation seems deliberate, in a sense artificial, and limited in that when one stops striving towards it, the natural order of things, the press of affairs and humanity, reasserts itself to engulf the would-be romantic. Perhaps that is not the case with those desperate islanders in the Orkneys, or for disordered personalities who can find no place in the common intercourse and associations of mankind. But I think I have described my own situation adequately. Imagine then my surprise to find that not only is isolation a physical fact in this country, but a habit of mind, and perhaps even the meaning of history.

I do not know what got me off on this tangent. Perhaps a certain mel-

ancholy at the thought that I must soon leave this place and bring
Toma with me through Cetinje—I hope you will be looking for us—en
route to some coastal town, probably Kotor. Certain matters coming to a
head—and I will try to be more explicit when we see each other—have
advanced the timetable of Toma's departure for the United States: his
mother will hear nothing of England, and so I beg that you will make
inquiries as to the likeliest port of embarkation for New York. Also, if it
is within your power to urge forward the authorities—in my ignorance I
do not know what they might be named—in the matter of any necessary
identity papers for Toma, please do so. I do not relish the idea of playing guardian to him in the capital while waiting for some ministry to
process his papers.

The prospects of the Pekočević family seem bleak to me, and not only
with respect to this imminent departure, perhaps forever, of the remaining son. From the moment I arrived, armed with what I had learned
from you, and from Draško, and from the monk at Morača, I understood
that the deepest wish, the truest happiness that Danilo could conceive,
would be to begin again the war of his ancestors against their enemies,
and also that he would not blink at the cost to himself or his family.
The agony for him in the death of the son who died recently—Natalia
must have spoken to you of him?—was not the fact of his death, but the
dishonor of it. On the other hand, Sofia would prevent this waste of her
family, of her son in particular, with the last breath in her body.

Only recently have I come to understand two things: first, that the war
may very well come whatever Danilo does or does not do, and whether
Toma stays or goes, and in spite of everything Sofia might do. All I have
seen and learned here points only in that direction, though I am hardly
an expert in political predictions. And the second realization is how ab-
solutely marginal I am in these affairs. This is the rock upon which the
romantic illusion founders, at least the version I brought with me. For if
one imagines an adventure in such a place—and what landscape more
suited to that than these wilds?—one imagines oneself at the center of it,
rising above one's limitations to heroic actions worthy of Rider Haggard
or Kipling. That is the model on which I was reared, implicit in books
and bedtime stories and even sermons, and it now fails me. I can see no
course of action, no heroic sacrifice, that would put things right. It is
true that I am somewhat uncomfortably placed between Danilo and Sofia, a kind of fulcrum in their struggle for the soul of Toma. But there is
no glory in this, and I am simply waiting to be told what I must do.

Would it not have been better, then, had I been wise enough to see over that horizon in Cetinje, to have agreed to your proposal? What have I gained by disappointing you, as I know I have? I do not think that you would have found any answer to the predicament of the Peko-čevićs, but a great deal of loneliness might have been avoided. (You see that I am in full retreat from that romantic ideal.)

I hope that you will forgive the wanderings in this letter, which began as a quite uncomplicated desire to communicate the evanescent beauty of this scene. I have already cut you a sprig of the diapensia, and in the morning shall take some florets of the draba, bright yellow and standing out boldly from their cushion on stems the thickness of a hair. And by the time I reach you in Cetinje, they will be pressed between leaves of my journal, almost dry, and yet they will carry still some faint suggestion of this wild setting.

> *Most faithfully and affectionately yours,*
> *Auberon Harwell*

Harwell was pleased with his letter, or, more accurately, relieved to have so unburdened himself from the cares that had been feeding on his mind, even though he could not, of course, be quite explicit about certain matters. He hoped she would understand it well enough, even though it had all come out in a great torrent, and almost in spite of his original conception of the letter as simple relief from the odious letter to Polgrove. But it was, now, all connected in his mind: his information on the Sandžak, his reaction to Schellendorf, to Polgrove, his nameless, bitter distress at leaving Sofia, and this reaching out towards Lydia. But perhaps he had made a hash of it?

He could not read his own words on the page any longer, for the sunset was no more than an afterthought, a gray dappling of clouds, marked with violet, behind the dark mass of the mountains, and the first stars were pricking out in the infinite sky above him, and the moon had not risen. He felt in his breast pocket for his matches and found there the paper packet that Sofia had given him the day before, forgotten until this moment. Because he could not see he took it gently between thumb and fingertips, trying to imagine what that faint bulk beneath the smooth paper might be.

He lit his lantern and collected his various papers before the damp should get to them, then staked his mare by the rill in a patch of pungent, silvery stemmed flowers and gave her a couple of handfuls of his cornmeal to eat out of his hat. Listening to her little mutterings of satisfaction, musing on those flowers, he wondered why he himself was not hungry. And then the thought was gone, for his mind still turned upon what he had written, puzzling at this realization as if it had been a rotted thing turned up in a shovelful of earth.

He took his blanket from the saddle and removed a couple of fist-sized rocks from the gravel near his boulder. With the candle now smoking and guttering in the lantern, there was just enough light for him to see the object enclosed in Sofia's note: a cross cunningly made of woven silk ribbon in many colors and attached to a length of ribbon beaded with mother-of-pearl, so that it could be worn like a necklace, or a rosary. The note enclosing it was a few words in that unpracticed hand, and some of the Cyrillic letters baffled him, but he got the sense of it, and in many rereadings it would no doubt all come clear. This cross had been given to her many years ago, and it had come, so her cousin told her, from Bulgaria, from the monastery at Rilo. She did not know what he believed in, but she hoped that this cross would protect him now, and that it would remind him always of her gratitude, her infinite gratitude. She signed it *Sofia, with love.*

He took the cross to his lips, committing to memory the texture of it, the odor of wood smoke, the faint scent of her, and then he put the loop of ribbon round his neck and let the cross fall down inside his shirt. What was the phrase she had used? *The heart wants the things it cannot have.* With his hand he moved the cross as near to his own heart as the ribbon would allow, and held it there.

The evening was growing cold, but he did not mind. He had gathered wood enough for a fire, for his tea, but he did not want the bother of it, or the smoke. When his candle went out he was glad to be alone in the dark with nothing to distract him from this object, this gesture, and all that it might mean. He thought also about what it did not mean, for her gift was an act of the purest charity, a cool hand to the brow, a salve to those racking emotions that he had declared to her in everything except plain language. But it was no more than that, and he must put those thoughts away or go mad. He would have taken one good strong swallow of whiskey if he had had any. In the end, almost with regret, he rolled a cigarette for himself and smoked it slowly until the stub burned his fingers. Then he lay down to sleep, wondering if it were possible, by an act of will, and out of the ruins that lay scattered in his mind, to reestablish his belief in God.

He awoke at first light when the mare snorted explosively, just the one time, but a sound so freighted with suspicion that his eyes were open and staring wildly before he could move hand or foot. He had been dreaming of the kings of Serbia, a dream as full of violence as any of Danilo's songs, and the horse's sound of alarm might well have been part of that procession of images. It was by looking at her, by following her gaze and the set of her ears to the cliff that he saw the goats, the chamois, poised on some invisible ledge cutting across the shadowed rock. There were three of them, and the two small ones could not be more than weeks old. One by one they knelt, so that their legs disappeared into the coarse tangle of fur, and now even more than before they seemed to be suspended over that sheer drop. He stared back at them, yawned, and thought that he would close his eyes just for a moment. When he opened them again, the rock was awash in sunlight and the goats were gone.

The first thing he did when he was fully awake was to check his store of food in the saddlebags. The very sight of one of those nasty dried fishes caused his mouth to water, and he rather regretted his largesse in the matter of the cornmeal. Still, the mare must eat too, and he could see that she held the vegetation at her feet in contempt. That was a yarrow, was it not? Something about it tickled his memory. He put another handful of the meal in his hat and carried it to her. He would boil up some tea for himself, then . . . then he would simply throw everything else into the pot and see what happened.

With a full belly, and the prospect of more tea, Harwell unpacked his journals, books, papers from the bag that had served as his pillow and went straight for his unfinished business, which is to say his account of the Sandžak of Novi Pazar for the benefit of Lord Polgrove. He read what he had written and thought that his obligation was very nearly satisfied. A few lines sufficed to describe the colorfully sullen market at Rožaj, a couple of paragraphs to convey the feast of the Vasojević and its abrupt termination by the Austrian garrison. He would write no more about the Pekočević family because . . . because it was none of Lord Polgrove's business, and he wished now that he had seen this sooner, had never mentioned their name or divulged their sad history.

I am sorry to have to inform you that an urgent personal matter has arisen which requires me to cut short my efforts on your behalf. I hope that I have been of some use to you here, but I do not think that anything I have seen or heard supports what I understand to be the premise of your own interest: that England can usefully intervene in the affairs of these people as a counterweight to the influence, pernicious as it is, of Austria or of Turkey. It is too late for that now, and I doubt there was ever an opportunity. The Serbs, in Montenegro and in Serbia proper, would certainly accept English arms, but only on their own terms, and in support of their own agenda, which I think must remain inscrutable even to the wisest heads in Whitehall. You would come, in the end, to many of the same conclusions as the current representative of His Majesty's government in Cetinje, Sir Percy Foote. In short, the Serbs will do what they want, or what they can, with your help or without it, and no glory will accrue to your efforts, only blood.

If I have presumed too far upon our relationship in offering these observations, I ask your pardon. My advice, unsought, would be identical to that of M. Voltaire: il faut cultiver son propre jardin. And on the heading of gardens, I shall return your valuable books at the earliest opportunity, and I shall make arrangements to turn over to you the balance of the money you have advanced on my behalf.

Most sincerely,
Auberon Harwell

He folded the letter into an envelope, but did not seal it, and several times in the course of the morning, when he felt the ripples or aftershocks of that fine cathartic anger, he would put down his journal and read again what he had written to Lord Polgrove, wondering at the curt tone of the letter, curbing the impulse to add or take away any thought, experiencing anew the liberation of this swift and surprising ending.

He had kept two journals during his time in the Hermit's Meadow, one strictly botanical, where he had made his sketches of various alpine species and kept notes on those he was unable to identify, and the other a more general record of what he had seen and thought. He had intended originally that both of these journals should be turned over to his patron, the two slender volumes corresponding to Polgrove's dual interests in this part of the world. But his experience had deepened and broadened far beyond anything he could have imagined when he was in London, or even Cetinje, or later still at Morača, so the second journal grew quickly into something that could never be shared with anyone, and Polgrove would have only those passages of it to which his funding entitled him.

The morning grew warm, and Harwell interrupted his work on the journals in order to search out the yarrow in his books and satisfy his mind. There it was: *Achillea serbica.* Achillea. Achill . . . Harwell shook his head, tried not to smile. "Auberon Harwell, you are no scholar at all."

He found his letter to Lydia among his papers and, all but laughing aloud, added this postscript:

> *You will have noted that this letter contains, or is contained in, its own great bundle of aromatic vegetable matter, and this is a yarrow,* Achillea serbica. *May we not believe that this is so called in honor of Achilles himself? Might this not be the "bitter root" of which Homer wrote in the* Iliad, *that was used to bind and staunch the wounds of the Greek heroes? Draško will know the medicinal properties of this plant.*

He rose then, first to take a handful of the yarrow, from which he knocked the dirt, then to take the more delicate cuttings of diapensia, draba, and that fragrant alyssum before the sun in any way discouraged them. When they were safe between the last pages of the journal, he wrote a brief account of the species in this valley below the horned peaks and placed the book under a stone so that the leaves and flowers would dry before the colors faded. And of this botanical journal, now complete insofar as was in his power, Lord Polgrove would have nothing whatsoever.

"But surely, Bron," he could almost swear to hearing Raymond's voice in his ear, "this is ungenerous of you, even, though I hesitate to say it, somewhat childish. I have no idea what your financial ar-

rangements were, but a crumb from that table would keep such
church mice as ourselves happy for a very considerable time, and
what was he buying but access to this part of the world through your
eyes? Would you not think a few flowers cheap at the price? A sweet-
ening of the bargain?"

"He showed no great interest in the drawings and identifications I
sent him." It was usual for Harwell to lose arguments to Raymond's
cool and dispassionate analysis, perhaps even this one, this borrowed
brief.

"Yes, but his impatience there simply reflected the ordering of his
priorities. First things first, he might have been saying, though I will
not defend the tone."

"The tone indeed: he mocked me. And he used me. If you and I
turn out to be wrong about the mysteries of the Christian faith, if
there is to be a Last Judgement after all, then do not be surprised if
from shallow, rocky graves in these mountains, and from similar sites
in Bulgaria, and Macedonia, or from the plains north of the Danube,
there arise several young fellows who resemble Auberon Harwell in
many particulars, and who owe their early ends to the carelessness
of this man to whom you would have me send posies and seed packets. I think I have given him more than his due. He certainly did
not buy *me*."

"Ah, Bron," Raymond would have said, "how you have changed.
What a sorry end to your grand adventure. Much better that you
should be holding the pass against the swarming tribesmen, a latter-
day Leonidas, though I wish you no martyrdom. This bitterness is
hardly becoming to you."

Harwell found this imaginary exchange with his friend upsetting
and liberating in equal measure: there was much that remained un-
said, even after he had written to Polgrove and to Lydia, after he had
entered so many thoughts and reflections on the Sandžak in his journal, after he had spoken with Sofia . . . especially after speaking with
Sofia and after receiving this benediction from her. There was nothing like the conversation of a friend, particularly so wise and knowing
a friend as Raymond, for putting one's own thoughts in order, for
making sense out of these thoughts and feelings which pulled
him in every direction. He took his pen and began: "My dear Raymond . . ."

He wrote happily through the rest of the morning, or at least with an ease and freedom of expression that eluded him even in his journal. And there was, too, an occasional playfulness of tone, a spontaneous gaiety that had been missing from his written words, his conversation, even his thoughts since . . . well, since that long afternoon in Lydia Wadham's sitting room. He did not now care a fig for the sanctity or secrecy of Lord Polgrove's enterprise, and so Harwell allowed himself, on top of everything else, the delightful, the sinful, pleasure of indiscretion. Was there not, after all, something comic as well as dangerous in the coincidence of meeting Schellendorf, this man who was clearly more than a mere engineer, and who had extensive and compromising knowledge of Polgrove's machinations, of his own poorly excused presence in these parts?

But when he came to describe his conversation with Schellendorf, the parry and thrust cloaked in politesse, his mood changed, for he remembered the incident of the Gypsy girl, connected the sound of Schellendorf's knowing, mocking laughter with the pale contours of the girl's body as she undressed to his speechless and appalled fascination. There was something about that scene that he had not understood or even noticed at the time, a connection that made sense of the change in him that Raymond had observed.

She was a pretty girl. He remembered that now, though at the time he had been too disoriented by drink and sleep and anxiety to register that impression. Pretty enough to be used by a man, a man who might come back to her time after time to lose himself in that body, who would pay good money for the privilege until . . . until she was no longer pretty, no longer young. He hoped that she had not paid a price for her failure to do her master's bidding. It would not have surprised him in the least to learn that Schellendorf, for all his contemptuous disclaimers, had known the girl, had beaten her in his displeasure, or, worse, in his pleasure. As indeed he, Harwell, might have beaten Ariana had he had any inclination.

. . . It may seem to you, my dear fellow, that I have lost whatever feeble powers of sequential reasoning were granted to me, for I must break off here to ask a favor of you which has no apparent connection with blood feuds, national interests, or even the Balkans, and yet it is more urgent to have this done now, and done right, than anything else I can think

of. And if it does not make sense to you, still I invoke our long friend-
ship and pray you will do exactly as I ask. There is a certain house in
Shepherd Market with a red door, and may this be the first and last
time you will ever have heard of it . . .

As quickly as he could, and yet with enough detail to give his account
the force of a confession, he described to Raymond the events that
had taken place behind that red door, his deep shame at the weakness
of his own flesh, a shame compounded by his subsequent stalking of
the occupants of the house and his discovery of Ariana's mutilation.

He stopped to read over what he had written, and was shocked, as
he knew Raymond must be, by the carnality of it. And here was a
point worth reflecting on, though it could not affect what he had
written, nor could it possibly come up in this or any correspondence:
he had not the slightest idea if Raymond had ever so much as gazed
upon the naked form of a woman, much less known her, much less
. . . Well, he was engaged to Cynthia, and this would become a moot
point soon enough, would it not? But still, the correspondent's own
experience of such matters must necessarily determine the sympathy
with which such a confession would be received. He remembered
now the ascetic elegance of Raymond's body as he stepped from the
bath after a long summer's day of climbing in the Alps, or after the
more energetic encounters on the fives court, and thought that it was
very nearly as familiar to him as his own. And yet it was also a mystery
to him. Flinders, their first-year tutor in Greek, had on one occasion
made a perfectly transparent allusion to the highest expression of
friendship between males in classical Greece, even Socrates and Al-
cibiades, in a certain reading of Plato . . . They had known perfectly
well what Flinders meant, and hoped, as he had something of a
reputation among his students, and both Raymond and Harwell had
returned blank stares of apparent incomprehension, though of course
there had been several rather coarse jokes passed between them at
the expense of this unfortunate young man. Harwell sighed, and took
up his pen.

Find this house and the young woman I have described to you, and
find also whoever employs her there. You are to strike a bargain with
that employer, in effect purchasing the freedom of Ariana, and with

*whatever money remains in the account at Lloyds, I beg you to find
some suitable position for her, where she will come to no further harm,
and make it plain to her that the money will only be paid out to her if
she does as she is told. You will be, in effect, her trustee.*

*I am sorry if my "adventure" seems to have dwindled to this small and
difficult matter, but having travelled in this world and seen how the
game of empires is played, I find I am interested, obsessed, if you will,
only by the personal connections and consequences that together make
up any large view of national interest, or historical imperative. Sir Percy
Foote, that clown of Cetinje, was my introduction to the way one is supposed to think about relations between states, and although I may dismiss him as a comic figure, still he signified. But this fellow Schellendorf
is the real article, a man who will do the dirty work of empire, and he
will be humming Wagner, not Gilbert and Sullivan. If I had not met
him, I doubt I should ever have asked this favor of you, for it is only
through the example of his words and actions that I recognize my own
complicity, however awkwardly I may have expressed the thread of my
thoughts.*

There, it was done, and he felt indeed as if the weight of sin had
been lifted from his shoulders. He touched Sofia's cross through the
material of his shirt, and wondered if he should write to Raymond
about her. No, there had been no sin there, he had done no harm.
All the thoughts he had of Sofia were for him alone: they would light
his way.

The letter carrier was halfway up the trail out of the meadow when
Harwell came upon him: another ten minutes spent in his camp, or
a wrong turning on the way home, and he would have missed this
chance to send his letters to Lydia. The little fellow looked more
dour than usual, even allowing for the fine drizzle of rain now falling.

Harwell had nothing to seal his letters, had not even a proper
envelope, and so he crouched down to shield his paper from the rain
and wrote a hurried note to Lydia, asking her to post these letters to
the proper addresses. Then he wrapped the whole packet, yarrow and
all, in a large sheet from his watercolor block, and folded the ends
in. Had the letter carrier any string? He had not, and so Harwell

reluctantly cut a piece of his leather martingale from the mare's bridle and secured the packet, addressed it to Lydia Wadham.

The letter carrier brightened at last: he would himself place it in Gospodja Wadham's hands, if God was willing, and if his donkey did not injure himself, for he was bound directly for Cetinje. Harwell apologized for having no money in his pocket. It was nothing, replied the letter carrier. He would look forward to seeing him on the return trip. And was everything well down there? Harwell cocked his head in the direction of the tower and the dwelling beside it. He got no answer, only a deliberately vague shrug of the shoulders.

When he was on the flat, and within hailing distance of the house, he started to call out, but the sound died in his throat, for just at that moment he noticed that there was no smoke rising from the chimney, even though it was dinnertime. When he drew nearer still, he saw that the door to the house was open, with no light or sound from the kitchen, and beside the door was a carpet, rolled, tied, and stood on end. Even from looking at the backing he could tell that it was an old and valuable carpet, beautifully figured. How had such an object come to this place?

Chapter Thirteen

"IT IS AS YOU SAID." Sofia's eyes, always the first thing Harwell noticed about her, were like smudges against the pallor of her face, and he wondered if she had slept at all since his departure. He himself had spent a restless night in the shed on an almost empty stomach, as he would not venture into the empty kitchen. For all he knew as he went to bed, the inhabitants of the house could have died or been murdered in their sleep.

But there was more to be read in her face than mere fatigue. The eyes, especially in profile, were slightly protuberant, which accounted for their command of the features, and except for those rare moments—he kept a mental inventory of each one—when she smiled or laughed, one could say she wore a frown, or at least a quizzical expression, which lent itself to a whole range of emotions. Now he saw reserve or even, though he could not bring himself to believe it, hostility. He waited for her to speak again, not daring to ask what she meant, or what he had done.

"Did you not tell me that he had a girl? that this was the explanation for his comings and goings late at night? Did you not tell me this?" Harwell nodded. He could scarcely disavow his lie, or his half-truth, which had seemed innocent enough at the time, certainly in comparison with what he might have told her about his visit to the cave. He could, with a small effort of will, conjure up still the smell of that place.

"Well, then," and here she made a dismissive gesture towards the doorway, where the bottom of the rolled carpet sagged out into view beyond the frame.

"I am sorry to say that I do not understand a word of all this. Where is Toma?"

"He is up in the cave, where he fled at the approach of Esad Bey, for he knew what mission he was bent on, though he may have thought the girl's father would come in anger rather than peace."

"Peace?"

"What he wants is that Toma should marry his daughter, now that she is with child. You have seen her. She is little more than a child herself." Harwell remembered that glimpse of the girl's legs: at the edge of the brook, she had jumped back from the water as if it burned her. He could not agree with Sofia, but neither would he contradict her now.

"And Esad Bey brought the carpet? Did the girl come too?"

"No, only Esad Bey. He says she is mad with grief because Toma will not have her. He hoped that this gift would win us to the thought of such a union. He is a proud man. He does not want our pity."

"It would seem that you have not been moved, or that Danilo has not." Above his head Harwell heard a sound, the shifting of the bedstead, and the groan of one who is sick or drunk. In a lowered voice he asked, "Will you step outside with me?"

He followed her, carrying the bowl of coffee and milk she had made for him, and stepped carefully around the roll of carpet. They stood in the shade of the house with the meadow spreading green before them, and drafts of cool air, still fragrant of the night, fought an unequal contest with the coming heat of the day. She took the bowl when he offered it to her, drank absently from it, and wiped away the mustache of foam with the back of her hand.

"And how did it go with Danilo? I mean the conversation you intended to have after I left. So much has happened . . . I feel as if I had been away for a month."

"Yes. The world has been turned upside down twice in as many days. I did what I had to do, and it was easier than I thought. Danilo will let him go, or would have done so. I made him see that he had to choose between us: he could not keep us both. And then I took him to my bed to show him that he would not regret his decision." Harwell felt his face coloring, but would not look away.

"And now?"

"Now he has seized on this offer by Esad Bey like a drowning man. He has convinced himself that the child, his grandchild, will be a boy, and he has tried to make me see this as a way to go forward. It has happened before, he says, that a Serb has taken a Turkish woman. He does not care about her one way or the other, so long as he has Toma and the child, his grandson."

"Well, it is only a matter of religion, and if they love each other . . ."

"Toma will not have her. I would not let him do it."

Harwell was silent for a moment, then spoke carefully: "Can you be so hard? What will the girl do?"

"I have nothing against her, but I owe her nothing, and no one made her do this thing. She has a family, a good family."

"But if the Serb marries the Turk will there not be peace? If Danilo can live with this, how can you refuse?"

"With the help of his *šljivovica* he has fooled himself into believing what he wants to believe, and he says it does not matter. He is wrong, and when he wakes up he will know it." What a stern look she had on her face as she stood in profile to him, staring out over the meadow, frowning upon it. "Being married to a Mahometan will not save any Serb from their wrath, nor would it soften his heart towards them. Perhaps . . . perhaps if all the Serbs married all the Turks. But one marriage will not change the world, and I have only the one son."

She turned to face him now, and her eyes—was he imagining this?—fluttered once to the ribbon at his neck. "Are you still with me?"

"Always," he replied. "I have put myself in your hands." And now it was his turn to look away, to gaze out over the windblown grass, past the valley wall, beyond and away until his eyes found the far column of rock he had climbed to see the Sandžak, to see Sofia bathing practically where he now stood. He tried to put himself back into that moment, tried, without success, to imagine how events might have followed another course had he thought or acted differently.

He had forgotten that time could pass so slowly. It was like being back in school with one hundred lines of Virgil to translate on a summer afternoon, with the excited cries of his fellows and the *choc* of the cricket ball filtering through the half-opened window. But this was worse: no cries, no cricket ball, not even the lines of Virgil, as if the master had simply said, "Sit here," and closed the door.

He repacked his belongings so that he would be ready to depart on a moment's notice. He swept out his shed and repaired the mare's martingale. There was a knock at his door, and Sofia stood there, her eyes cast down as if she knew he was upset with her. Did he not want the letter that had come from Cetinje?

She sat on his bed while he opened the envelope and scanned Lydia's covering note, so full of concern, knowing concern for the delicacy and danger of his situation. And here, in answer to the urging she had not yet received, was the paper, sealed with maroon wax and green ribbon, identifying Toma Pekočević as a citizen of the Principality of Montenegro.

He handed the paper to Sofia, who wiped her hands carefully on her apron before touching it, and she turned that smile upon him which was to be all his reward. It was a curious expression, for while it conferred upon him the light of her gratitude and approval, still she did not lose herself in any momentary happiness: the thoughtful frown lurked at the corners of her eyes and mouth like the shadowed underlayer in a painting. A young woman, he thought, is more extravagant, more a changeling in the grip of her emotions. This expression of hers, now, was an emblem of something beyond beauty. Wisdom, perhaps, or goodness.

"Who sent this to you?"

"It was Miss Wadham, Natalia's teacher. I told her what was needed."

"I am all the more indebted to her. Does she please you?"

"Does she what?"

"You are a young man, and she is a young woman. I have met her."

"Ah. Yes, she pleases me more and more, though it is only through letters that I have come to know her."

"And how do you sign these letters?"

Harwell was saved from having to answer this question by the approach of Danilo, on his way to the privy. He seemed to have aged ten years since Harwell had last seen him.

"What will happen now?"

"I think I must feed him, and then we shall talk. I will keep this paper safe." She rose to go. Had Danilo seen her there as he stumped past the door? She laid her hand on his arm. "I will miss you when you are gone."

Harwell endured an afternoon, and a night, and another whole day of waiting, and during this time when all useful tasks were either completed or denied to him—there was something in Sofia's manner that reinforced his own inclination to keep to his shed—even the solace of reading failed him, as it seldom had before. He glanced at his Homer to see if, as he had suggested to Raymond, there might be some thread of continuity between the spirit of classical Greece and the lays of the Montenegrins. He got through most of Macaulay's essay on Hastings, but although the prose was as sonorous and energetic as he had ever found it, he could not force his mind to focus on the doings of the moghul princelings. In desperation he began a letter to his parents. Several times he walked the length of the meadow. He drank quantities of tea.

He kept his ear cocked for any sound from the house, where, for the most part, silence reigned. Occasionally he would hear Sofia talking in a perfectly normal tone, and sometimes she would get a few words in response from Danilo. At one point during the day Sofia and Danilo walked out together past the tower to the crest of the road overlooking the Sandžak, and Danilo, to Harwell's amazement, had his arm around his wife's shoulder. There was no sign of Toma.

On the second night after his return Harwell was awakened by a sound that he did not recognize at first as a human voice, caught as it was in the repetition of one word, a hoarse keening that may have been intended as a whisper. The one word was the boy's name, and when he could stand it no longer he lit his candle and pulled on his shoes and clothes.

He came, candle in hand, to the steep rock face below Toma's cave, the hermit's cave, and Harwell would have walked right past her had he not stumbled over her crouched or kneeling form. She had been silent for some time, perhaps dazed or exhausted, and he caught just the white flash of her face in the instant before he dropped the candle into the weeds, an expression there of terror and incomprehension.

"Aliye." He spoke to her gently in the same tone he had used to the horse that had broken its leg. He pulled her gently to her feet, feeling the listless weight of her, and the chill of her flesh through the dank, almost sodden wool of her shawl. There had been a shower of rain shortly after he went to bed, and the sound of it on his roof had put him to sleep at once.

"Listen to me, Aliye. He will not come down to you. He will not answer you, and you must go home now, or you will catch your death out here. Do you understand what I say?" She raised her face to him, a pale shadow now that his eyes had grown used to the dark, and she began to tremble. He put his arms around her, felt the damp chill seeping through his own shirt, and then the faintest warmth growing between them, for they were pressed together like lovers.

"He must marry me." This she said with her face pressed to his breast so he could not hear it at first. He took her face in his hands and made her repeat the words. "He must marry me, or I cannot live."

"Of course you will live." He shook her gently by the shoulders now. "You must think of your child and forget Toma, for he will not marry you. He cannot marry you." Harwell thought that she might have stopped breathing when he spoke these words, so profound was the silence which followed. Then, in a slow and deliberate gesture that had almost an air of ceremony to it, she raised her hands to his face and sank her nails into his cheeks.

His reaction was involuntary, and he knew from the gasp she made that he had hurt her when he brought his hands up so suddenly, but the pain had taken him by surprise. After a moment he felt the slow trickle of blood on his face. "I am very sorry. I did not mean to hurt you."

She made no sound, but was bent over, holding her wrist, he thought. She let him put his arms around her again.

"Will you show me your arm? Is it broken?"

She shook her head. "It is nothing . . . It does not matter. I must go." He found her left arm with his hand. There was a swelling, just above the wrist, and her whole body stiffened against the impulse to cry out.

"Can you find the way?"

"Yes. But you will . . . Will you walk with me a little? I do not know what spirits there are in this place. I think there must be many."

He stooped to retrieve his candle, and with his arm around her shoulder he guided her away from the cliff, through the damp grass and broken stones, until they found the road. Not once did she glance back in the direction of the cave, where Toma, for all Harwell knew, might have been watching as well as listening. He wondered if Sofia had been awakened, as he had been, and what her thoughts might be. He struggled against the realization that for Toma and for Sofia the girl no longer existed.

They passed the tower and she looked up at it briefly, then cast her eyes down to the road again, and he knew what had happened there. And when they passed the staked heads she drew closer to him, pressing her face to his breast, making herself small so that she could not be seen.

"There is nothing to be afraid of," he whispered into her hair, summoning a conviction to his voice that tasted very much like a lie.

"These are the bones of my people. My father told me that, and Toma."

"That is true, but they are only bones, and nothing more. See, they are behind us now, and no harm has come to you. Ahead of you is your home, and a warm bed."

"I can feel that there are spirits here, and when I am alone they may come upon me." They had reached the crest of the road, and in all the land below them there was not a single pinprick of light.

"In my country it is said by people who fear spirits, or ghosts, that light will keep them away, even so much as a candle. Will you take my candle with you?"

"*Da,*" she said, almost before he had phrased the offer; then, as an afterthought, "Thank you." He lit the candle for her and placed it in her good hand. The other she hid in the folds of her shawl. He hoped she had not far to go, for her face in the light seemed ravaged by exhaustion.

"There is no wind, and if you walk slowly the flame will not go out, though the wax may drop onto your fingers. It will keep you safe all the way home. Good night."

"Thank you," she said again, and with her injured hand she touched her breast, mouth, and forehead.

He watched her for a few moments, saw the light dip suddenly as if she had dropped the candle, but it was only that she must scramble under the gate at the frontier. The frontier. She was back now among her own people.

On his own way home he made himself stop in the road next to the enclosure of staked heads. There was a crescent of moon, veiled by clouds, that silvered the wooden shingles of the roof, but he could see nothing inside beyond the paling that kept the wild animals away. He listened for sounds, and heard none, closed his eyes and knew that he was the only creature awake and abroad in the meadow. The dead were simply dead, and the living were asleep. The sleep of the just. Following this vein of bitter thought, he reflected that he himself had played his part, done his duty, without even having to be told what to do.

Sleep was a quarry that must be hunted in the dark. He tried to imagine the sound of the rain on his roof that had been so soothing, but then thought of the girl on the road with her poor candle and her mortal fear of the night. Let it not fail, he thought, which was as close to a prayer as he could bring himself. And still the marks on his face burned him.

When he opened his eyes it was broad daylight, and he felt a sluggishness in his limbs, a leaden weight on his brain that only coffee would cure. On his way to the house he noted the peculiar aspect of the sky, where a pale sun was hunted by clouds whose like he had never seen before. Danilo and Toma were crouched in a corner of the pasture, the boy, whom Harwell had not seen for several days, holding one of the long-haired sheep from Rožaj while Danilo chopped away at the fleece. He called out a greeting to them, but the sheep lunged at the same time and his words were lost.

Sofia greeted him with a sound in her throat that could only have been amusement, and he was baffled for a moment until he saw that her gaze touched twice on his cheek. She took a cloth, dipped it in a basin, and held it out to him. Had he not packed his mirror away, this embarrassment might have been avoided. He was furious with himself, with . . . everything.

"Do you know how I came to have these marks?" She nodded, still smiling at him, and took the cloth from him to do the job herself. He was confused by her touch, efficient as it was.

"I can guess well enough. But now it is done, like a fever that has broken. You do not need to think on it again. Will you have coffee?"

He sighed. "Without it I am a dead man." She smiled still: there must be more to this mood of hers than his comical face.

"I have heard people say that they would die for many things, or for the lack of them, but this I have not heard. Country. Honor. Love . . . And now coffee." It was his turn to smile.

"And did you never feel that you would die for love?"

"Oh." It was a soft, almost musical exclamation that she made. "Once, perhaps, long ago, but even then I knew I was being foolish, and after a few days I did not feel that way at all."

"And now? What is worth dying for now?" He watched her, waited as she dried her hands very deliberately.

"My children. That is all." She continued to work the stuff of her skirt between her hands. He regretted his question, wanted that other side of her back.

"Something has happened. I see Toma in the pasture as if he had never shut himself away up there with . . . the hermit. And here you are pounding coffee beans for my breakfast. By the way . . ."

"The coffee, yes. To preserve you. As for the other, it is as I said: the fever has broken. Toma will go with you, and I have made my peace with Danilo."

Harwell drank his coffee slowly, gratefully, heard the whinny of the mare, and was thinking that he would go out to help with the shearing when Danilo called out, "*Dobro jutro.* You are welcome." There was a tone in that deep voice that belied the words. Now he heard the stamp of the horses' feet, the musical jangling of harness, and the sharp, ugly sound of a rifle bolt, and a second one.

"We have come for the boy." Harwell knew that voice. He knocked over his chair in getting to the door, and there was Schellendorf, smiling at him, seated comfortably astride his horse with his hands resting on the pommel. "Mr. Harwell," he said in English. "We meet in the most unfortunate circumstances. You will remember that I warned you against associating with these people." Harwell counted three of the engineers mounted behind him, and two other men, not in uniform, who held the rifles.

"By what right do you come here with your weapons drawn?" Danilo stood by the fence, one arm on the rails, the shears dangling from his other wrist. Toma sat on the ground behind him, his legs embracing a half-naked sheep, which struggled against his grip.

"I have not drawn my weapon," replied Schellendorf, smiling as if engaged in a duel of wits. "I am here because the local authorities in Berane have asked my assistance in a very grave matter." Without taking his eyes from Danilo he indicated by a jerk of his head the two ill-kempt and turbaned *bashi-bazouks* behind him. "They are very distressed. I think you are lucky that I am here." Harwell noted the expression on those faces, the expectant sheen to the eyes. He held his breath. There was Sofia beside him. Her hand went to his shoulder just as he was about to speak.

"The girl is dead," Schellendorf continued, "the daughter of Esad Bey, and her connection to this boy is the talk of all Berane. It is said by some that he came in the night and killed her with his own hand."

At this recitation the two Mahometans muttered harshly to each other, and one of them called out: "Stand before us, dog, or I will shoot you on the ground." Toma released the sheep and rose to his feet.

"What reason have you to suppose that the boy had anything to do with the girl's death? Has a witness come forward?" Harwell spoke carefully, as much for the benefit of the rifleman as for Schellendorf.

"A witness may be found. But for now the circumstances are compelling enough. She was found on a bed with her belly slit open, as one would gut a sheep, and it was right in her parents' home, with all the household asleep in the adjoining chambers. I saw it myself, and will not soon forget it, for she had taken the cushions to the floor and arranged them as a marriage bed with the most admirable silks, all worked with the embroideries her mother had taught her, for this is how these women spend much of their childhood, preparing for the bridal night. Everything was as it should be for the entrance of the groom, even the graven brass tray with rose water and fruit upon it, and she lay there on the striped green silk in a bath of her own blood. It was like a painting, an allegory, but I have never seen anything like it."

"An allegory of love, perhaps, but no murder. She took her own life."

"Perhaps, Mr. Harwell. We shall see when we question the boy. But there are two curious facts, or three, which require explanation. Her feet were filthy and soaking wet; her left wrist was broken, which is a curious mutilation, even for a distraught girl; and there was a candle in her room, the stump of a candle which no one in the household recognized. Can you deny my curiosity about the boy? or the agitation of these men?"

In English now, Harwell addressed Schellendorf, stepping out into the sun so that he would not have to raise his voice. "Captain, this is not plausible. The boy wanted nothing to do with her, had cast her aside and had no reason to kill her. He could not possibly have stolen into that house to perform such an act. Furthermore, you have no jurisdiction, no . . ."

"Forgive me for interrupting you, Mr. Harwell." Schellendorf held up his palm, looked at Harwell's face, and smiled as if at some private joke. "If we were in England, or Austria, I might agree with you, but I must be governed by other rules here. It was only by luck that I was passing through Berane, otherwise these fellows would have brought their friends and performed a ruder, swifter justice. If the boy did not cut her open himself, he might as well have, at least in their view, and so we are debating a rather fine point of the law. He will have to come with us."

"And you will answer for his safety? I repeat that you have no jurisdiction here."

"English," Danilo called out, as if on cue, "tell him that they will have to go. This is Montenegro, and we are all free Serbs here." He began to walk towards the pasture gate, which lay directly between him and Schellendorf. The shears clashed in his hand as he walked, and his good leg knocked the half-shorn sheep head over heels.

"Tell him" — Schellendorf did not deign to address this threat — "tell him that if he crosses the gate I will have his son shot, perhaps in the stomach, so that he can watch him die."

"Danilo!" It was Sofia who spoke, and Danilo paused with his hand on the gate.

"As for jurisdiction, these people are criminals, as I told you, and that is all the jurisdiction I need. *Kaporal!*" and Schellendorf barked an order in German that made no sense to Harwell.

The corporal, a heavy, unhappy-looking man, rode forward and began to unwrap the bundled cloak which he held on the pommel. As he did so, Schellendorf's horse shied to the side, smashing with his hindquarters the trellis at the corner of the house that Harwell had made for Sofia. The horse stood now in the splintered frame, with a flowering vine draped on his flank, and it stared wildly at the corporal's burden, the head with yellow hair. Except for that hair and the curious dignity of the hat, it was little more than a skull. Danilo made a sound in his throat, angry or approving: it was hard for Harwell to know which.

"Do you see the hat, Mr. Harwell? and the remains of the feathered cockade? The weather has not been kind to the officer, but that is what he was: an Austrian, a lieutenant of the *Jaegertruppe*, in the earlier version of that uniform. As I said, these people are criminals. Only barbarians behave in such a manner. You may wrap it up again, Corporal."

"For God's sake, Captain, the boy had no hand in that. Will you start a war over this girl's death?"

"The boy must submit to my authority. He is brave enough when he thinks he is beyond our reach; now we will see what other virtues he has. If he answers the questions and proves his innocence, we may let him go. But unless I bring him back, there will be a situation that I cannot control. Then you may indeed have your war."

"This is a coward's solution." Harwell put his hand to the bridle of Schellendorf's horse.

"You forget yourself, Mr. Harwell. I could have you shot by any one of these men. And I will tell you something else." He bent over his saddle so that his face was only inches from Harwell's. "The girl's fingernails were broken as if she fought with a man, though I could find no evidence that she had been . . . violated. You should take care for your own safety. In fact, you should have accepted my earlier generosity." He sat back and smiled to see Harwell's blush. "Corporal. Take the boy and bind his hands. You will stay here to guard these people and see that no harm comes to them."

The corporal dismounted awkwardly, and then handed the bundled head to one of his men, a boy who seemed hardly older than

Toma. He took the lead rope from one of the *bashi-bazouks'* horses and advanced to the gate where Danilo stood with his shears, and the terrible expression on that face cowed him.

"With your permission . . ."

Danilo looked from Schellendorf to Sofia and then back to the muzzles of the levelled rifles. "What guarantees do you give of his safety?"

"None whatsoever. The local people must be satisfied of his innocence. But if he does not come he dies right here. The choice is yours." Danilo stood aside to let the corporal pass.

Toma, agile as the chamois and strong as the stallion, was unable to mount the corporal's horse with his hands and elbows bound tightly behind his back. The corporal saw the difficulty and gave a good push at just the wrong moment, driving Toma forward onto a bright stud projecting from the pommel and splitting his lip. The corporal apologized. The boy's face, which was ordinarily so expressive, registered nothing except mild curiosity at the taste of blood.

Sofia had played no part in this drama other than the single word she had spoken to Danilo, and the hand that had lain briefly on Harwell's shoulder. Now she went to her son and pulled his face down towards hers, but did not touch his bloodied lip. She spoke urgently to him in a whisper, staring straight into his eyes like a lover, and the boy nodded once. Captain Schellendorf grew impatient.

"Come, mother, enough of all this. He is mine now, and has no need of your good advice." She looked at him then, willing him to silence, to some sort of submission, and at last Schellendorf lowered his eyes. The expression on that face, the absence of the customary smile, told Harwell that Sofia had done Toma no favor.

As the cavalcade wheeled and raised the dust of the yard, Sofia came to stand beside Harwell, and when they rode off she reached behind her to find his hand, drew it partly around her waist, and held it in a fierce grip with both of her own, as if she did not care what might break. Toma, bound as he was, could not look back; but Schellendorf did, his mocking humor now restored, and he could not have failed to note and approve the wordless desperation in that embrace.

When they were gone over the crest of the road she released him. The corporal had drawn his pistol at a signal from Schellendorf, but

seemed embarrassed by it. He asked Harwell and Danilo, very politely, if they would sit there on the bench under the eaves of the
house where he could see them both. And he asked Sofia if she
would be kind enough to bring him a chair and a cup of her excellent
coffee, as he had left Berane without his breakfast.

Chapter Fourteen

"STAND, ZARA PETROVIĆ, and give me that knife!"

Lydia did not raise her voice, for of course a scene, a little drama of some sort was exactly what the wretched girl wanted, and would be denied. Lydia sometimes wondered what it was about her that set the Petrović girl off, triggered this insolence, for it did not seem that the other instructors had the same experience. They all walked on eggshells with respect to this pupil who was distantly related to the prince, and it could not be otherwise; for during the bomb plot of the previous year, when suspicion and wild surmise had gripped the capital, it was rumored that the prince's portrait had been taken from the wall of the Girls' Institute and trampled upon.

Lydia thought it might have something to do with her being English—though that made no particular sense to her—or, in moments of self-doubt, with class. She had tried to be friendly, particularly and perhaps unprofessionally friendly, towards the girl, to see if that would smooth over this awkwardness that had begun, now that she came to reflect on it, the day of Auberon Harwell's arrival in Cetinje. But her overtures were in vain: Zara Petrović clung to her provocative sullenness, answering only when it pleased her to answer, and using her idle but undeniable wit to interject phrases into the English conversation class that were either comically stupid or even suggestive of barnyard matters. Only recently she had taken to carving her initials into the fine wooden tables that had come all the way from Russia as part of the empress's gift.

The knife was passed from hand to hand along the row of girls at the refectory table, and this took a little longer than it should have, as each girl inspected the instrument with shy admiration: another small triumph for the offender.

"Eat, Natalia, you must eat," said Lydia to her favorite pupil, whose place in the dining hall was at her right hand. She gave Natalia's arm a little tap, and the child, staring solemnly at the plate of mush before her, essayed another bite, a small one. Well, who could blame her? The food was frankly disgusting. She must do what she could to encourage poor Draško, who had been pressed into kitchen duty following the cook's epileptic seizure.

"Thank you." Lydia took the knife from the girl on her left and closed the blade, admiring the fine mechanism of the spring and the filigree of gold upon the case. This object was worth a month's wages, her wages, at least, and this perception brought spots of dangerous color to her cheeks. "Stand back away from the table, Zara Petrović, and do not rest your hands upon it. You are forbidden to touch it." The girl, of course, could buy another knife, a pocketful of them, the next time she was allowed to go to the market, if they sold such elegant things there. In the meantime, however, she would not be able to sharpen her pen, or would have to borrow an inferior knife from a classmate, and the fine quality of her penmanship would suffer, and she would receive lower marks, perhaps even a demerit. Lydia hoped that the other instructors would become her unwitting accomplices in this exercise of discipline, of revenge.

Turning her attention back to her food, now colder and less edible for the interruption of the meal, Lydia steeled herself and took an ostentatious forkful of the substance on her plate—what in God's name was it?—and made a show of enjoying it. She encountered a large and only partly cooked root of some sort that nearly choked her, evidence of Draško's misguided enthusiasm. "The fork in the left hand, Katerina, and the knife in the right." They were poor enough things, these stamped metal forks, and yet some of the girls could never get the hang of them, handled them as if they were dangerous weapons, and made a mess at every attempt. The real forks, dozen upon dozen of heavy silver forks with Maria Alexandrovna's crest, were now in the safekeeping of the director, Mlle Petrovna, and reserved for her private dinners. How Lydia wished she might use that service every day: perhaps even these girls would learn something from a proper piece of silver. It was a waste to keep it all shut away.

Her own life, of course, might be considered a waste: this thought had occurred to her more than once since the night when she had made her bid to throw it all away, to start over, rushing headlong into whatever fate might arrange for her, for them. And she had even said it once, if only by accident, if only to that dull child who could not be made to understand the idea of the conditional clause. "Why should I waste my time on you," she had intended to say, but it came out "life" instead. And as dearly as she had loved receiving Harwell's letters, keeping them all by her bedside to read over and over just before she went to sleep, she positively hated the idea, the image of his dried flowers. But it did not matter. She would see him soon enough if all went well—here she closed her eyes and drew a deep breath to collect herself—and this silly feeling about dried flowers would pass from her like a headache. He would make a joke about it as he . . . as he kissed her.

The Petrović girl was looking at her out of the corner of her eye, with the faintest smile on her face as if she could read these thoughts. She had a nose for trouble, the vixen, and when Lydia put her letters away under the mattress each morning, it was always Zara Petrović whom she imagined finding them. She was of an age now when she seemed conscious of nothing so much as her physical appearance, which was striking enough, and of her dramatic effect. Lydia had remarked the shameless flirtation with Antonelli, that poor vain fool of a gymnastics instructor, and she almost wished that the girl would push matters too far, miscalculate the delicate balance of desire and taboo, and become truly the tragic heroine of her own romantic script. Antonelli, with those many white teeth, might well be the man for the job, though she did not dislike him to the point where she could wish such consequences on him. Still, uncharitable and unchaste as this thought was, Lydia would welcome anything that broke the tension, the antagonism between herself and Zara Petrović.

The students were excused—the offender casting a long look at

Lydia and at the penknife lying by her hand—and Lydia was left alone at the table with her coffee. The servants were slow in clearing the dishes, and Draško himself came out of the kitchen to shake his head over so much uneaten food. "More salt, perhaps?" he inquired hopefully.

"Perhaps not," said Lydia. "I will come this afternoon and we will discuss the menus. You are doing your best, and we all know that. Look: there is nothing left on my plate." Draško departed, unconsoled, and as he passed the tired arrangement of cut flowers on the serving table, he made a little gesture with his hand and muttered that he was only one man and could not be . . . The rest was lost as the door swung shut.

The pile of uneaten food on Natalia's plate was a reproach to Lydia, and somewhat spoiled her appreciation of the coffee, which was excellent. How she wanted a cigarette right now. That would be the greatest luxury in the world: to drink this strong black coffee, smoke her cigarette, and read again the letter that had arrived last night in the great packet of correspondence that the postman, with a conspiratorial smile, had placed directly in her hands, having first asked Draško to summon her. What a strange object it was, with those bits of weed hanging out of it.

But while the letter had lifted her spirits, there was other information in the packet that oppressed her, the more so because she knew she ought not to have read further than the one meant for her. She was neither surprised nor shocked: he was a man, after all, and even she knew something of the world. She did blush when she reread certain passages which baffled her, blushed not for his sake but for herself, because she realized that she wanted to know precisely what was at stake in this halting confession. More than that, she wanted to know exactly how it had felt. Could words convey such feeling, an apprehension of realms unknown? Yes, she thought with a shiver. Yes.

It was the letter to Lord Polgrove, in particular, that accounted for her present heaviness of mood, and for her anxiety about Natalia, that serious child who hardly ate anymore, who seemed to share Lydia's worries about what might be happening or about to happen beyond the mountains, beyond their control, their slightest influence. Perhaps Natalia too had received a letter from her home? If so, Lydia did not remember it, though the postman might have made a special delivery of that one as well. What would the child make of such news as had come to her, or through her? It was difficult to imagine Natalia focusing her attention on anything less immediate than her preparations for tomorrow's classes, or whatever book she was reading. How she loved to read, and what pleasure Lydia took in that fact. Next year she might be at the point where she could try, with help, some of the novels that had shaped Lydia's own coming of age.

Next year. What a burden of irony attached to that phrase. If Harwell's forebodings held any grain of truth, next year might as well not come at all. Surely the child, with her grave face and downcast eyes, understood this? And if these clouds, these rumors of Armageddon, should pass, did she not hope with all her heart and body that she would be borne away, lifted up, her life turned upside down by the man who had written these things? Lydia took a deep breath and tried to steady her mind against the foolishness of hope.

What had preserved her sanity in the long months of Auberon Harwell's absence was exactly this hope that now shook her being, and he *was* coming, had assured her it was only a matter of days. She had dared to hope, and her imagination was fueled by the details in his letters, and by scraps of history gleaned from Draško, and even by what she learned from Natalia, and here she blushed to remember the artifice of those conversations wherein her pupil was encouraged to recount everything she could possibly remember about the meadow where she lived, her family, the feast days, even the weather. The narrative made a halting kind of sense, and through it, and through the other sources of her information, she felt closer to Bron than could ever otherwise have been possible: in fact, it sometimes seemed that he described to her situations which she had already experienced, so thoroughly had her imagination transported her. She remembered that when she had parted from Bron in March — in the moments before she formulated that rash idea that they not be parted — she had slipped her arms around him under his coat and felt his flesh against hers separated only by those two layers of insubstantial cloth. And there had been this moment of confusion, a very sweet confusion, in which she tried to determine, from the sensations that flooded her, whether her arms were cold and his back warm, or vice versa. It did not matter at all, and of course it was his back that was warm, but what remained in her mind was this idea that they had, even then, become one flesh.

It was a particular burden on Lydia, therefore, to sit in this dining room, drinking coffee, and realize that Bron, who was only a few days and not really so many miles away, felt such anxiety. She knew, certainly she knew, that he had chosen a dangerous and unpredictable place, and that he was the bearer of secrets that made his presence there even more hazardous. Anything could happen at any time. But *now*, when he was almost back, almost safe . . . she did not know if she could bear it. This man Polgrove was an utterly odious creature, and if she met him she would not hesitate to slap his face. And yet she must send off this letter to him, for all the joy it would bring him. In that sense Bron's letter was very nearly the equal of a good slap in the face. But there must be something more than waiting, and watching the road. She closed her eyes. She did not pray, but thought: *I must preserve him.*

Ludmilla's cough caused her to open her eyes. The old serving woman was so bent with arthritis that practically the only function left to her was carrying messages, and she shuffled slowly up and down the corridors throughout the day. She placed the white envelope on the table. "The Englishman's servant says he will wait for an answer."

Lydia tore at the paper in disbelief, but it was only Sir Percy Foote's card, and an invitation to drive out with him in his phaeton at half past three this afternoon. Her pulse slowed, and she tried to think clearly. She would not go out in the carriage again with Sir Percy: the last time, a month or so ago, she had been left with actual bruises from the aggressive pressure of his leg under the lap robe. But last night she had been awakened by the sound of a galloping horse on the road, which might have been the aftermath of some forgotten dream, or even a sign.

She scribbled a few words on the back of the card in case her reply was not clearly understood: "Tell him, ask him, to convey to Sir Percy my thanks and my wish to ride rather than drive, provided he has a lady's saddle. Tell him that I am particularly interested in the eastern road, and would dearly love to see the summit of the pass, and what lies beyond."

On her way out of the dining hall she noted that Zara Petrović had managed the initials "LW & AH" very nicely, but that the heart which would surround them was only half completed.

Toma did not think that they would kill him, unless it was by accident. That was the way he thought about what was happening to him, and for a while it had worked to calm his terror, to dull the pain. Now, kneeling naked on the floor of the room or cell, he could not think clearly about anything except the pain. He rested his cheek on the cold stone, tasted the blood inside his mouth, noted the swelling discoloration of his right forearm, which might be broken. Aliye's arm had been broken, that white and perfect thing, and he could hear the sound of it in his head, feel her pain just there where their arms had once touched.

He closed his eyes and saw the pool of blood as the captain had described it. He must listen carefully, for if they came upon him like this they would again kick him between the legs, and his gorge rose at the thought of it.

They were resting in the outer room where there was a desk and some chairs, tired, perhaps drunk. The Austrians had sent out for a bottle of *rakija* with their midday meal, cursing the man who said there was no cold beer to be had, and at one point the captain had tried to pour some down his throat when he fainted from the beating, then spattered it on the fresh wounds on his back. The captain's voice, which he heard more often than the others', sounded both tired and drunk.

As for the others, the *bashi-bazouks*, though he doubted that they had dishonored their prophet by drinking the *rakija*, they seemed drunk as well, but on the strong wine of their own rage, rage and the savage pleasure of this work. Outside the building, the jail, a crowd had gathered when he was brought there, and the rabble of Berane, hearing the sounds of his ordeal through the window, called out, "Kill him!" or "Give him to us." The captain had gone out to speak to them, told them that the boy was his prisoner, that justice was being done, and that they should all return to their homes.

He had told them nothing, for there really was nothing to tell, even though there had been the excuse of the pointless questions to justify, to punctuate, the blows of the fists or the cane. He had told them that he knew nothing of the death of the girl, and would not use her name, which seemed to infuriate the Austrian captain. "Can you not put a name to this corpse, out of decency?" he had hissed, seizing Toma by the throat. "Do you deny that you knew her, that you have taken your pleasure from her? Have you no pity on her?" *Pity.* It was the very word his mother had used: he must do nothing out of pity. Tears came to his eyes. He bit into the ragged flesh of his lip so that he could say nothing. It was at this point, before they had taken his clothes away, that the youthful Austrian soldier, at the captain's signal, had kicked him in the testicles. That was the first time.

When it was clear that he had no answers for their questions, they took turns beating him, practicing their techniques, and for a while he was bound to two rings on the wall, then cut free and his hands tied behind him again, perhaps so that he could collapse unimpeded to the floor from a cunning blow or kick. But his mind was elsewhere, deliberately so, and it was in this way that he coped with the pain, which came from every direction, and even by accident, as when one of the Austrian soldiers lurched off balance and brought a heavy boot down on the instep of his foot. Toma did not cry out, because he was in the monk's cave with his brother Vuk, now risen from the dead as he had so often prayed might happen, and together they were rebuilding the arch and the collapsed ceiling of the outer chamber so that the vision of paradise was made whole again, and Vuk had only to touch the cracked stones and painted plaster with his finger and they were healed.

He thought also of the songs which he had heard so often, mostly in his father's voice, and those words came to him now as easily as if he read them from a page. There were songs of victory, as when Marko Kraljevic came to deliver his people, and songs of defeat, wherein the spirit of the Serbs rose from disaster, even from death, just as his brother Vuk had been raised from death in his vision of the cave. And now on the Field of Kosovo, which he had seen so often in his mind's eye that he knew it as familiarly as his meadow, the poppies stretching to the horizon were about to bloom over the bones of King Lazar's army, which had been slaughtered by the Turks. On the cap of every Montenegrin man, on his own cap now, there was bright red cloth on the crown in remembrance of the poppies of Kosovo and the blood shed there, so that day might never be forgotten and would in time be avenged. Might that army, too, not rise above death? Were not all things possible to those who believed?

In the middle of the afternoon, after they had finished with their meal in the outer room, the captain had come in to him with a cloth full of the scraps and set it on the floor with a mug of water. Toma's hands were untied so that he could eat: he was apparently no danger to his captors now. The captain stood between him and the food, very close to him, and with the tip of his stick forced his chin up so he must look into that face.

"When it is dark, the door will be left open for you, and you may find your way home. I will put out the word that you have been questioned, thoroughly questioned, and released. In the meantime, you may expect some further unpleasantness. But you should remember this as a favor, out of pity for your mother." There was a silence. The captain's face swam in and out of focus in Toma's eyes. "Have you nothing to say? Have you no gratitude? You owe me your life . . . or do you perhaps think that you are immortal? But look at all this blood." Toma felt the other hand trace a slow course, slick and stinging down his chest and belly until it came to rest on the bruised flesh between his legs. This was not the touch of a tormentor, but a doctor, or a woman. And still the metal-shod point of the stick under his chin immobilized him, so that he must look at the captain, smell the *rakija* on his breath. "This also you owe to me, for they would have taken it from you. That is their practice."

"What is your name?" His voice was a dry croak.

"What do you say?"

"What is your name?"

"Schellendorf. Hauptmann Gerhard Schellendorf." The captain did not smile now.

"Thank you. I must remember that. For the favor you have done me." Trusting to his strength that had never yet failed him, Toma lunged for the throat, but the captain stepped easily aside, then caught his foot in the cloth full of scraps, and fell backwards, cursing. Toma went down clumsily onto his hands and knees, was still in that vulnerable position when the others rushed in upon him from the outer room and took up their work with a vengeance.

He sang his songs while they beat him, at the top of his voice, such as it was, and did not even hear the blows that rained upon him. The beating was probably the more savage for the songs. They wanted no music from him, but other sounds, and got none, even when a kick snapped his rib. They grew tired of their work, for the captain would not let them finish the job, and this thing on the floor provided no further satisfaction.

He was resting now, cheek upon the cool stones, and humming to himself a prayer to Saint Sava, which took all his strength, and so he did not hear the voice that provoked the captain's response: "Well, I thought you would turn up sooner or later. Please sit down. Will you have something to drink?" He thought that the English had come for him.

"Do you see? I have brought a paper." It was his mother's voice, there could be no mistake about that. "This is the paper that will take him to America, so he will never trouble you again, I swear it. Only let me take him now."

Schellendorf laughed. "And what else would you give for this favor?"

"I have nothing else. Nothing . . ."

"Nothing? But I will not give you the boy for nothing, nor for a scrap of paper. He struck me, or tried to, and his life is forfeit for that alone."

The silence that followed was broken by the scraping of a chair. When he spoke again it was in a softer tone; he might be standing right next to her, touching her perhaps. "Will you not have something to drink? You please me, and you should be glad of that: otherwise I would never give you the boy. I could have his throat slit before your eyes. Hmm? The *bashi-bazouks* would do that, and more."

"Let me see Toma."

In his officer's voice Schellendorf cleared the room, told them all to wait outside, to send the people of Berane back to their homes, and to close the door. Then, in a more intimate tone, "Drink, and I may grant your wish. To your health, and the boy's long life. Let me fill the glass again. Good. Again. How you perspire: you must have run all the way to Berane."

"Where is he?" She called out: "Toma, do you live? Answer me!"

He made a sound in his throat loud enough to be heard, but he could not move.

"He is here, and he is going nowhere, so there is no hurry. But first let me show you something else. There, is that not an excellent thing? Did I not tell you that you please me? Let us take off this shawl now, and the rest, or you really will be too hot." There was a pause, and the quick rustling of some material, but she did not speak. "Come, mother, you have done this before. There can be no harm in it."

There was then a scream, a high-pitched exhalation of disbelief, of fear, of pain—not his mother's voice, he was sure—and then the loud clatter of boots on the stone floor.

"Hold her! Make her . . ."

"I'm trying! Jesus Christ, but the bitch is strong. Drop it! Help me, or she will cut us all!" There was then a thud, the sound of splintering wood on bone, and the shouting stopped.

"Sir, sir, let me help you. Will you sit here?"

"Ah, how it bleeds, and I have no idea how deep it is. Tell me, is there a hospital in this town? and a doctor?"

"Yes, sire," said another voice, "a most excellent hospital, and two physicians. But shall we not send to Rožaj for your own doctors?"

"We shall have to see if the gut has been touched. Otherwise it is just a scratch . . . but see how it bleeds still. Give me that cloth. It was my stupidity not to have her stripped first, but I thought . . . I did not think she would be so brave or so stupid. There, that is better."

"Will you have something to drink, sire, some water?"

"Thank you, no. If the gut is pierced I must not drink. We shall see when we get to the hospital. But in the meantime you will finish this job for me, yes? It is my order. Put her on the desk there, and hold the chair leg over her throat, for sooner or later she will wake up."

When she woke Toma did not know: the chair leg clamped on her neck may have choked off all power of speech, or the blow to the head may have kept her mercifully unconscious. But what was happening there was evident enough from the other sounds: exertion, pleasure, sniggering laughter, encouragements, mock admiration, and feigned ferocity.

"Finish, boy, finish," said Schellendorf brusquely, "or the Turk behind you will have you instead."

Several times he had tried to stand, and each time his strength failed. He prayed again to Saint Sava, as the heroes in legend and song had prayed for strength, prayed for deliverance from evil. His concentration on this task was so complete, so consuming, that he did not hear the captain depart, supported by the others because of the numbness in his legs. And if the evening light flared strangely through the window, it was only the reflection from the drawn sword of the saint. And when the earth shuddered, then lurched sideways so that part of the wall was rent, stone from stone, he was neither surprised nor afraid, for this was the thunder of Saint Sava's horse as he drew nigh.

The saint, mounted on that great white horse, came to Toma, stepped through the ruins of the wall, and he touched him on the shoulder with his sword, which restored his strength. From that moment on, he did not have to wonder or question what he must do, for he was in the hands of the saint.

The central beam in the outer room had fallen, breaking the neck of the Austrian, the young one, who had been left on guard, and in its final descent had pinned and crushed his mother to the desk, so that he could not move her. Her eyes opened and she knew him. She spoke that one word, *America*, and that was all. He could not tell if she still breathed. He found the paper on the floor, the one she had brought with her, and put it in her hand, but he could not make it stay there, and he knew she was dead. He took the paper and smoothed it as best he could. How would he carry this thing?

The Austrian boy was close enough to his size, and his own garments were buried somewhere in the rubble anyway, so he took the tunic, and the boots, and last the trousers, the flies of which were not even buttoned. He felt a surge of rage then, not for this poor broken thing whose flesh, still warm to the touch, revolted him, but for Schellendorf. He must find Schellendorf. The saint would lead him where he must go.

He touched his mother's hand, assured himself that she was now dead. His knee hurt him—he had been kicked there—and the saint pointed with his sword to a long splinter of wood which had broken from the beam. Leaning on this like an old man upon his staff, he followed that dazzling light through the broken wall and then through the darkened streets of the town, until he came to the place where Schellendorf lay.

The building, which must once have been a palace, was familiar enough to him, though he had not known it as the hospital. It sat adjacent to the market, on the rising ground, and he had often looked across into the invalids' garden where the white-robed figures sat for hours by the fountain without moving.

"They have all run away, the cowards!" said the porter, holding his candle up to see the caller's face and uniform. Toma noted how those eyes were ringed with white, the wild stare contrasting with the perfect calm of his own mind.

"I have come for Captain Schellendorf," said Toma, and the old man led him down a long corridor past empty rooms, past a pile of rubble where a ceiling had collapsed, until they came to a doorway that spilled weak light into the desolation of the passage. "Thank you," said Toma, and the porter hobbled away.

Schellendorf lay in a fetal position on the bed, apparently asleep. Standing beside him was a nurse, a young nurse, he thought, but because of the veil he could not be sure. He could see only the uncertainty of her eyes. A fire had caught somewhere in the market-place, and its light filled the room with lurid shadows. The next tremor might bring down the rest of the hospital. She had reason enough to be frightened. Schellendorf stirred.

"You may leave him to me," said Toma, and for a moment the nurse looked puzzled: Did she wonder at the bloody swelling of his face? Did he speak her language too well? Did she recognize him from the marketplace? If she did not leave he would have to kill her as well.

They glared at each other. The shouting and cries of distress from the market were louder, and the light brighter still. She handed him the damp cloth that she had been using to wipe the captain's face, and he knew now that she would leave them alone.

"Take the light with you," he said, "and be careful of your footing in the corridor." When she was gone, and when he had closed the door, he took the staff that the saint had put into his hand, and struck the captain with all his strength on the temple.

The shock of that blow made his forearm ache intolerably, sent a sword through his broken rib, and because he had no knife he had to rip the sheets into strips with his hands, which required those same muscles. The sweat poured from him, and he could actually feel the heat of the burning market on his back as he worked to tie the captain, hand and foot, to the frame of the bed. When he had finished he rested. Listening to the anguished confusion without, and lulled by the play of red light on the naked man awaiting his final ordeal, he imagined himself once again back in the hermit's cave, where this light and this moment of judgement were prefigured.

Much of his strength was gone. Had it not been so, his blow to the head might have killed the captain, and that did not accord with his vision of what must be done. It was God's will that the captain be impaled: he had known that from the moment that the saint told him to take the splinter as a staff, and yet now he could not summon his beaten and broken body to the task. He set the tip of the wooden stake between the buttocks and shoved, straining so that the ragged edges of the wood drove home into the flesh of his own arms, and drew from the captain a sonorous groan that could only be the true music of the damned.

In the corridor he found a piece of broken masonry that seemed heavy enough, if he could carry it, and wield it. In the monk's painting, the tips of the stakes on which the Turks were impaled could be seen there in each mouth opened in blasphemy or futile entreaty. This is what he must strive for.

Six times he swung the rough stone against the base of the stake, driving it home like a tether pin, and then he could do no more. The captain, who had shrieked once and bitten the sound off, lay in silence, panting for breath. "Water," he said, and the whispered word echoed in the boy's ears. He did not hate this man after all, or not enough to refuse such a request.

The bottle of water stood on the table by the bed, and the captain had just enough strength to turn his head. Although most of the water spilled down onto the pillow and bedding, he swallowed once, twice. "Who are you?"

"I am the angel of death," said Toma, supporting himself on the mattress with his good arm, afraid that he might otherwise fall down. He did not know how long the captain would live. There was a song that told of the martyrdom of a warrior, the king's son Dragutin, who survived on the vizier's stake for three days and three nights, and tormented his captors by the singing of hymns until they killed him with stones.

He did not see that the captain's left hand had come free of its binding: either the knot or the fabric of the sheet must have failed. Now in one motion that might have been practiced a thousand times to achieve that unerring, dextrous grace, he seized the bottle, smashed it on the table in passing, and drove it home into the thigh of his angel of death.

Toma staggered away from the bed, fell, and thought he might not be able to rise again. He crawled to the bed, and found that the captain breathed no more. The body lay frozen in the contortion of that final effort, which may have ruptured some vital part against the splinter.

After a few minutes Toma was able to stand, and although he could not see exactly what damage the shards of glass had done, he bound his thigh with the remains of the sheet so that he would be able to walk home.

The corporal was not a bad man—certainly he lacked cunning and any instinct for evil—and yet the longer they sat like this, staring at each other over the fire and listening for the fall of rocks from the mountain, the less sanguine Harwell could be about the outcome of this peculiar standoff. It had been, what, almost twelve hours since the soldiers had taken Toma?

In one sense time was on their side, Harwell's and Danilo's. The corporal had his pistol, which he had drawn from the holster when he realized that Sofia had fled from the privy; but he was also tired, and Harwell thought he had injured his hip or his back when he fell down during the earthquake, the aftershocks of which were even now strong enough to dislodge a burning log and send a plume of sparks flying up towards those other stars. In hindsight that might have been their chance, when the corporal was down. The hermit's bell had tolled once, and Harwell thought he might be sick to his stomach. Had the pistol fallen free? Could he have put that moment to good use? And in that other moment that he turned over and over in his mind, could he not have found the right words to answer Schellendorf's outrageous insinuation, to disarm that cunning lie? His face burned anew at this insult, at his own indecision, his cowardice.

The corporal's fatigue must now be mixed with the realization that the earthquake made any communication from Berane less likely, and it would be morning before he could hope to be relieved of this duty. They had eaten nothing since Sofia's departure—Harwell had caught a glimpse of her black dress when she crested the lip of the meadow—because the corporal did not trust either of them alone in the house. And Danilo, in spite of Harwell's discouraging signals, was talking to himself, which was clearly acting on the corporal's nerves. *If I were in his shoes*, thought Harwell, *I might well shoot these two fellows and say they attacked me, if anyone bothered to ask.* That, at any rate, might be the solution of a more imaginative fellow.

So they waited, for a patrol or a messenger they knew would not come, and Harwell found himself making cheerful and improbable conversation in an effort to distract the corporal from his need for sleep. For a while they discussed food, which was very much on both their minds, and Harwell hit upon the happy accident of the *Blutwurst*, the making of which had apparently occupied much of the corporal's adolescence in the family butcher's shop on the outskirts of Vienna. It was while he talked enthusiastically about the draining of the carcasses, and Danilo half hummed the refrain of some song, that Harwell saw the figure at the edge of their circle of light.

"Excuse me, Corporal," said Danilo, interrupting the soldier, "but shall I put more wood on the fire?"

"No, no," said the corporal in mock sternness, holding up a warning finger. He bent forward awkwardly—he was a heavy man, and the fall had stiffened his back—and with the pistol clutched in his right hand he heaved another length of the spruce into the embers. He regained his seat on the stump, and as he was expelling a great lungful of air to mark his effort, Toma brought the rock down on his head, in the soft center of his cap.

Harwell could not imagine anything more hideous than the sight of the corporal's head shattered like an eggshell, with part of the cap driven down into the skull and stuck there. The body had sagged sideways so that he could see only part of the wound, but there was no question that the man was dead, and he tried not to notice the galvanic twitching of the limbs. He put more wood on the fire, not that it would be any help to the corporal, and in the now-flaring light saw the boy's uniform, the dark seep of blood on his thigh, and the swollen contusions of the face. So distracted was he by this fresh evidence of catastrophe, by the reappearance of one he had assumed to be dead, who looked to be literally raised from the dead, that he did not hear clearly the more awful news that Toma whispered to Danilo.

"What? What do you say?" He approached them, then cried out in disgust, for he was standing on the dead man's fingers. "Where is your mother? Why have you not brought her?"

"She is dead." Toma's face did not move as he spoke, and he looked neither at Harwell nor at Danilo. "The saint has taken her, perhaps, after guiding me to the captain's bed." Harwell could make no sense of it. Why would they release the boy and keep Sofia?

"And the captain?"

"Captain Schellendorf. He too is dead, by my hand."

Danilo muttered his approval, kissed his son's bloody face. "You are certain, certain about her? Perhaps she . . ."

"She is dead. I was with her when she died. The roof fell on them both, my mother and the soldier, when the saint came and called me. But it was I who judged the captain, and I who killed him, according to the instructions of the saint. If I had the strength, and a knife, I would have brought his head."

"Yes," murmured Danilo, almost gently, and he clasped the boy's face in his hands. "And is your mother dead, then?" It was as if he had not heard or understood the prior conversation.

Toma nodded, and looked at Harwell's eyes.

"If you have killed the captain, and this corporal, then we must leave now, tonight. Can you ride?"

Toma looked at Danilo, and then back at Harwell. He said nothing.

"It was her wish. Think only of that. Can you ride?"

"I can do that, but I cannot walk anymore."

"And you, Danilo?"

"I will not go. I must wait here for her."

"But they will come for Toma, and they will find . . ." Here he indicated the body of the corporal. The right arm, closest to the leaping fire, gave up the odor of singed wool.

"Him." Danilo spat on the ground. "I shall bury him in the rubble over there." Here he jerked his head to the side, and the firelight was just strong enough to catch the whitened stones of the hermit's bell tower, one wall of which had partially collapsed. "Help me drag him over there, Toma, then go catch the horses. I will do the rest myself later."

As luck would have it, Harwell had nothing left to pack, and when he had rolled his blankets he dragged everything outside into the firelight and set the long rope on top of the pile. He heard Toma, out in the meadow, calling to the stallion. Danilo made his way slowly back towards the fire and stopped to glare at Harwell's belongings.

"And how will you carry this?"

"The way I brought it: some on the mare, most of it on the ass. We will take the trail slowly."

"There will be no trail through these mountains, not for a strong man on foot under the noon sun. Have you not heard the rocks falling?"

"Then there is no way out of here?"

"There is the road through the Sandžak, but you must ride west around Berane then follow it north to Bijelo Polje where it branches west again into the mountains, towards Kolašin, towards Morača. You must ride fast, and the ass will never keep pace with you." Danilo threw more wood on the fire to light their tasks.

"There is no shorter road to Morača?"

"No, unless you would pass directly through Berane itself. Wherever you go you may meet the Austrian soldiers, unless God has killed them all when he made the earth move. There is a nest of them in Bijelo Polje, just as you saw at Rožaj."

"And the border crossing?"

"Beyond the Lim as you travel west towards the Tara, there where they have drawn their line. The Austrians are great experts in papers and duties and taxes, and the more baggage you have, the longer they will take. If they are not too many, perhaps you can shoot them, and any Turks that are with them." He bent and seized the corporal's fallen revolver, blew the dust from it, and fired three shots into the air.

If I wanted to fight the Austrians, Harwell almost said aloud, *I would stay right where I am. They will come to me.* He glanced at

Danilo's face to see if he had the same thought, but he could read nothing there: Danilo stared open-mouthed at the fire. Out in the pasture the ass brayed anxiously, as if it knew it would be left behind. Time was collapsing on itself, and as Harwell tried to think about what must be done, a weight blossomed in his chest, making it difficult to draw breath. There would not even be time to say goodbye with any proper ceremony.

"Toma! Hurry!" he called into the darkness beyond the fence, and just then the boy led the two horses around the end of the house. Christ, what an awful sight he was. The mare flung herself back against the rope, her nostrils flaring at the smell of blood, and Harwell too recoiled, but with a prickling sense of complicity. He spoke very carefully to Danilo. "We need your help. Will you hold the horses." He took the pistol from Danilo's hand and stuck it in his belt, next to his own.

There was no light in the house, but he knew where the tub of water was and plunged his bottle in to fill it. She was everywhere in here. Her hand had been the last to touch this metal rim, had worn smooth this counter along the wall. He leaned his head against that wood and listened to the little music of bubbles escaping from his bottle. She could not be dead. He felt a stirring of anger that boiled in his thoughts and was as suddenly gone. *It is not his fault*, he said to himself. *It is not his fault that he is alive.*

He steadied himself against the counter to rise and his hand brushed against a clammy, glutinous thing: a loaf of some sort. By gentle groping along the counter he found also a knife and a cloth. He cut the loaf in two. Half for Danilo, half for himself and Toma. It was what she would have done herself. He dipped the cloth in the tub and held it against his face. Was this the last object she had touched in this house? He wrapped the bread in it.

On his way out the door, dazzled now by the light of the fire, he stumbled over the roll of carpet. It was woven of fine silk, and he could balance it on his shoulder with his free hand. He swung it up onto the stallion, thrust the bread and the bottle under the edge, and tied it there behind the saddle. Onto the mare he put his saddlebags, blanket, and the fowling piece, then shouldered his pack. There was no time to sort through the rest.

"Say goodbye to him." Toma embraced his father, who stood like a hitching post, one rope in either hand, still staring at the fire.

"Will you not stay?" asked Danilo. "She will be sorry not to find you here." Harwell, with a motion of his hand, signalled Toma to mount his horse.

"Danilo, perhaps you should put more wood on the fire, for it is dark tonight, very dark. And you must bury the corporal. Can you remember to do that?"

Danilo smiled, and nodded once. Harwell clapped him on the shoulder and mounted his own horse.

"Will you be back?"

"I am going to Cetinje."

"Then you must tell them what happened here. Tell them in Morača, in Cetinje. Tell the prince that war has been declared upon us, and the Vasojević stand ready to rise at his signal, to lead his people into the battle. Tell him that I shall look for him on the Day of the Field of the Blackbirds, in remembrance of Kosovo."

"Farewell, Danilo."

When they were beyond the circle of firelight he knew the truth in Danilo's advice, for the night was indeed dark, and even at a walk they would have to trust the horses to find the way. Leading the ass was out of the question. They did not look back when they reached the crest of land, but rode straight on, down into the blackness that yawned like a tomb before them. When they were past the frontier and halfway down to the dam, they heard a sound that carried over the braying of the ass, and it was the terrible clash of a bell, one of the hermit's bells, falling and sounding against the rocks in its descent until it struck and shattered in one tremendous, discordant note that echoed and was gone. Toma said nothing, and the stallion's pace did not slacken. Had it fallen of its own accord? Or had Danilo dislodged the one rock that held everything in crazy equilibrium and brought the ruin down on himself? Harwell did not know what he ought to hope.

Chapter Fifteen

HOUR AFTER HOUR THEY RODE, and Harwell did not know exactly what time it was, for his watch had stopped during the earthquake, and his conception of how far they must travel to cross back into Montenegro was a feeble guess based on what he remembered of the map. But it could not be less than forty miles, probably farther than that, and every step of the way, until they passed back over the border at the Tara, was through the moonless Sandžak, and he could not even guess who else might be on this road. He looked to the east, and assured himself of the absolute darkness there, for they were running a race against the unrisen sun, pushing the horses as hard and as fast as they dared, and they must cross over into safety by dawn. A boulder in the road, or a fissure, let a horse so much as stumble, and they were lost. He must not think on these things.

When they were safely past Berane and its pall of smoke—the light of some conflagration could be seen in the distance—Harwell stopped at a river crossing, a shallow ford, and rested the horses for just a few minutes. He made Toma dismount to drink, and to bathe his face in the cold water, for he could tell from the boy's voice, that monotone slurring of the words, that he was barely conscious. He risked a match to look at the wound on the leg. The trousers were sodden with blood, but it did not seem to be fresh blood. The bandage was holding.

"Is it too tight? If it is we must loosen it, or you may lose the leg."

"No," said Toma, "it is nothing. I can feel my foot. I can move it."

Harwell stole a look at the face, swollen now to twice its size, the left eye lost in the purple flesh. He would not have recognized that face, changed as it was, and he made himself look at it until the match burned his fingers.

He remembered the bread and drew it from the fold of the carpet. Lighting another precious, dangerous match, he showed Toma what he held, and offered it to him. Toma took the bread in a clumsy, hasty motion that left only the crumbled corner in Harwell's hand. The match went out. They ate in silence, then remounted and splashed through the ford. The water came to the belly of the mare, and where it was deepest, Harwell flung the corporal's pistol into the current upstream.

They walked their horses through the few darkened villages they came to, and even the dogs let them pass in peace. "Bioče," whispered Toma as they entered the first of these, soon after the second fording. "I was here once with my father and my brother. My mother did not come because she . . ."

"Hush," said Harwell.

After Bioče they heard the sound of the river, the Lim, growing louder and gathering strength whenever they stopped or slackened their pace, and for all Harwell's anxious anticipation of unseen obstacles in the road, it was the simple wooden bridge at Ribarevina that was nearly their undoing. He remembered this town from the newspaper he had read in Cetinje—how long ago all that seemed now!—because it was here that the railway line from Belgrade, the putative line from Belgrade, must turn up into the mountains of Montenegro.

The bridge was no doubt a temporary affair, for the road was barricaded at the main crossing, and it was the horses, in the dark and on their own initiative, who followed the detour down to the bank of the rushing stream and this perilous arrangement of planks and pontoons. While Toma held the mare, Harwell walked out onto the bridge and felt the current surging beneath his feet. The planking, he estimated, was three feet wide.

The mare sidestepped when he remounted, and balked so violently when he kicked her forward that the weight of his pack nearly threw him. Toma urged the stallion out onto the bridge, and after the first few steps the river swallowed those hollow sounds. Harwell could not know if they had reached safety, but at least the stallion had shown no fear. He dismounted again, but the mare would not be led. He tied the reins up on her neck, then pointed her more or less in the direction that the stallion had taken and slapped her as hard as he could on her rump. To his surprise, she did not bolt or shy, but walked straight out onto the bridge. After a few moments of listening for the vanished sounds of her hooves, he followed her, shuffling so that the grooves between the rough planks guided his feet. There must have been falls or a dam just upstream, for the sound of the water was not below him but all around him, as if a wave gathered in the darkness, waited for him there.

The land rose away from the river on the far bank—how meekly the mare stood for him—and Harwell felt his spirits, his hope, lifting within him at every step, for they were now headed west into the mountains, and still there was no sign of light behind them. But the road here was not as broad and as well-travelled as the one they had left at the Lim, and though they trotted when they could, the horses occasionally stumbled on rocks, or sent them clattering away into the night.

When the horses stopped, unbidden, breathing hard after a long ascent, Harwell listened for the sound of water, but heard nothing. Now the mare snorted, once, twice, and Harwell too caught the smell of raw earth, like a garden when it was turned in the spring, or a grave. He guessed that there must be a slide in the road just ahead. He let the reins fall slack and waited to see what the mare would do: if there was a way, she would find it. After several more sharp exhalations she stepped forward, tossing her head so that flecks of foam bathed his face. He sat as still as he might, felt the soft dirt yielding under her as she chose her footing on the steep angle of the slide. A boulder crashed away down the slope from them, and just as the mare began to struggle against the slow flowing of the gravel in the boulder's wake, they were through, and onto firm ground again. Toma pulled up beside him, and they let the horses blow for a minute, the slide grinding on past them with the sound of pebbles and shells on the shore of an invisible ocean.

When they had ridden less than a mile beyond the slide Harwell saw a light ahead and below, as the road turned the shoulder of a hill and began to descend towards the Tara. He looked over his shoulder and there was the dawn, or the beginning of it, not so much a light or a color on the horizon as a milky gradation in the haze of dust that had risen with the earthquake to obliterate the sunset and the night sky. He waited. In a matter of minutes there would be light enough for what he needed to do.

Toma was slumped forward in his saddle, holding himself there so that Harwell had to pry the fingers loose from the mane and the reins before helping him down. "Lie down there on the road," he said. "Rest while you can." Toma said nothing, did as he was told.

Harwell untied the carpet from the stallion's saddle and placed it on the ground alongside the boy, who might have been asleep, or only half conscious. Now the parallel shapes in the road could just be distinguished. He cut the mare's lead rope in two. *This will never work*, he muttered to himself.

When he had rolled that dead weight into the carpet and made a knot below the feet, he spoke into the open top of his silk chimney. "Can you breathe? Toma, answer me."

"Yes."

"Whatever happens, make no sound, and do not move. I will tell you when you are safe." He tied the top of the carpet, and when he had the thing in his arms, he spoke soothingly to the stallion, who stood perfectly still and accepted this strange burden, which was then secured fore and aft with the saddle strings. Finally, Harwell took his long pack rope and passed it twice under the belly and over the top, finishing it off with a knot that would have made the hostler wince. *It is not perfect*, thought Harwell, *but it is good enough.*

Though the sky above was brindled gray on gray, it was still dark in the hollow where the frontier post lay. The untrimmed lantern burned and smoked on its spike by the door, and when the guard came out to answer Harwell's hail he carried a candle.

"Where are you going?" The words were slurred, and at first Harwell thought the man had a defect in his speech. But as he handed over his passport he noticed that the buttons of the tunic were in the wrong holes.

"Cetinje. I am bound for Cetinje by way of Morača."

"I would advise you to wait. All night we have heard the rocks coming down like the judgement of God. It is a wonder that we were not all killed."

"I will take my chances. I have urgent business."

"You are English?"

"I am English."

"And what is this business?"

"I have been collecting flowers and seeds in the mountains near . . . near Rožaj. Now I am taking them back to England with me." The guard began to laugh. Harwell heard the scraping of chairs inside the guard post. All his specimens, all his seeds were miles behind. His fingers found Sofia's talisman under his shirt.

"You will not believe this, Ernst. All night we thought we would die, and now God sends us an Englishman who hunts flowers in the mountains. What do you think of that?" Ernst, absorbed in the task of buttoning his tunic, said nothing until he had belched.

"Are his papers in order?" Behind him the candle showed Harwell two men in turbans, the Turkish contingent at the border point. Four. He was wondering how Danilo would have done it. Now the man holding the candle spoke.

"Here is the stamp of Cattaro, but nothing further. How do you come to the Sandžak?"

"I came down from the mountains because of the earthquake. I have lost almost everything."

"Almost," said Ernst. One of the local guards spoke to the other, who giggled. They have all been drinking, thought Harwell. Ernst spoke a flat word of command without even bothering to look in the direction of the Mahometans. "You must excuse them. It has been a difficult night, and under the circumstances they thought Allah would be understanding of their weakness. Have you, by any chance, any coffee with you?"

"No, my baggage is gone, as I told you."

"Yes, as you said. And yet you have saved this carpet. A very fine carpet indeed. Will you look, Ibrahim?" One of the turbaned guards stepped forward to touch the corner of the carpet. He took the candle and inspected the stitching.

"He must be a thief. There is blood on the saddle."

"A thief, perhaps," said Ernst, "or something else. Will you step down Mr. Harwell?"

"No, I will not. I have urgent business in Cetinje, and I have ridden all night to get here. I ask you to let me pass."

"In time . . ."

"I have no time. Here. Read this. It is a *laissez-passer* signed by your foreign minister, Baron Aehrenthal." Ernst and his comrade together inspected Harwell's document.

"It is so," said the man with the candle, "for here is the seal of the Ballhausplatz. I know that one. I do not understand this." He handed the paper back to Harwell.

"He is a spy." It was Ibrahim who spoke, and his companion echoed the word, then uttered a screech of drunken wonder.

"You may pass, Mr. Harwell, but I would be very curious to know how you came by such a fine carpet, and what might be inside it. Stand back, Ibrahim. He must pass."

Harwell said nothing, let the mare step forward as Ibrahim raised the gate. Out of the corner of his eye he caught a soundless motion in the dusky half-light, a swirl of cloth as the other guard stooped and strode forward brandishing a heavy stake or sapling. The mare shied sideways, almost unseating Harwell, but the stallion stood firm and the splintering blow fell squarely on the carpet.

"Spy! Devil!" screamed the guard, now sprawled in the road. He struggled to rise, but the stallion cut him short with a vicious kick, then wheeled and struck the body with his forefeet before Ernst could grab the fallen lead.

"Jesu! Carry the fool inside, Ibrahim!" He turned to Harwell, who fumbled with the buckle of his holster. "My apologies. This land breeds lunatics. You may pass, and I hope for your sake that the road ahead is clear."

The first guard set his candle down carefully in the road and put his belly to the end of the gate. With the stallion following calmly, Harwell crossed over into Montenegro and did not look back.

His only thought was to get off the road, for he did not know if the boy had survived that blow, the sound of which circled in his head like a rat in an empty room, and although he was past the frontier and the Tara itself, the Austrians had no respect for that line, and still he feared the rising day as an enemy.

The light grew around him, a sickly caricature of the dawn, and when he saw a flat grassy way with a wall beyond, a hundred yards or so away to his left, he turned off the road, letting the mare find the easiest path, holding his breath lest the stallion should stumble in the rocks. *If the worst happens,* he thought, *I can dig a grave with my knife, with my hands. But she will not let him die. I must not let him die.*

The opening in the wall had the form of a gate, though he noticed that only later, for the wood had all rotted away, and his concern was to get the carpet off the stallion without further injury to Toma, who neither moved nor uttered a word, though Harwell spoke to him as he undid the ropes, calling his name softly, reassuring him, against reason, that all would be well.

He eased the awkward bundle off the saddle, amazed at the weight of it, and laid it on the grass next to the wall. Everything smelled of dust, even the crushed grass, except for the carpet with its reek of blood. He untied the top, listened to hear the boy's shallow breath, and when he made to shift the roll so that the patient lay on his back, he was frozen by the muffled scream from within, an agony that wiped his mind perfectly blank. The carpet, of its own momentum, completed its half revolution, and Toma was silenced abruptly.

By working the slack in the roll, he got to the point where he could just see Toma's face, which, like his own hands, was darkened by dust to an Egyptian hue, and when the one good eye opened it seemed as white and as large as a tennis ball.

"Can you hear me?" The eye blinked once. What else must he ask, do? Harwell knew only that he must not move him again: the thought of that sound made him flinch. The eye drooped shut. *Air,* he thought. *Water.*

He took his knife and slit the layers of silk one by one to a point where he guessed the breastbone must be, then peeled them back like the petals of a flower. Toma, his eyes still closed, took several deep breaths. The mouth twitched. Was that a smile?

"Water."

"Yes. Yes, water." Harwell spilled a good deal before he realized that Toma could not raise his head enough to take the flask to his lips, and when the water fell into his mouth he coughed weakly. By pouring water into his palm Harwell found he could make it dribble down his fingers, which he held right to the lips, so that Toma could take what he wanted, drop by drop. Harwell took a mouthful for himself of what remained in the bottle. He used a few more drops to wet his handkerchief, then bathed the muddy lacerations of the boy's face.

"Can you tell me where you are hurt?" There, that was most definitely a smile. "Tell me where you were struck, just now, I mean."

"The back, somewhere on my back. Something broke . . ."

"The stake that he struck you with . . . it was shattered."

"No, something broke." Toma held his breath, grimaced, sighed.

"But you have not lost the feeling in your hands, or your feet?"

"No, alas."

"And you can move them?" Harwell held his own breath.

"Perhaps, but not now."

"No, no. Now you must rest."

"Water."

Harwell put his hand gently under Toma's head and raised it ever so slightly to the water. Now it was gone. He took his eyes away from Toma to see what this place was, if a wall might by some magic translate to water, a concealed spring, and saw that the rough blocks of ancient stone towering above him here on the level ground ran away up a steep slope, angling to the features of the land until they vanished over the crest and reappeared there over his right shoulder where a low platform of rock looked out over the valley and the higher mountains to the west. In the trees below the crest of this bump of a hill he saw what might have been a tower and some roofless buildings. There would be water here somewhere.

Exhausted by the night's ride, he lost himself in these ruins, wondering what this place had been, and who might have built it, and how they had ended. "Horses," muttered Toma, his eyes closed again, and Harwell turned to find the mare and the stallion grazing peacefully on the dusty grass. "Horses."

He heard the sound then, horses indeed, and climbed onto the fallen stones to see over the wall. There, almost at the point where he had turned into the ruin, an Austrian cavalry patrol—six, eight riders—churned the dust of the road, and the strange light made halos around their plumed shakos. *Hussars*, thought Harwell, with a smile for his own lost soldiers.

They rode on, making a furious clatter that echoed from the hill, and Harwell breathed again. When they returned, at a walk, they would see in the dust the tracks of his horses leading to this place. He wondered how much time he had.

He left Toma then and walked unsteadily up the hill in the direction of the buildings, for his knees betrayed him at every step, as if the ride had lasted for twenty years. This was a fortress, and from such a height . . . But there below him was Toma, who could not be moved or hidden, and the horses. He sat down on the edge of the stone platform and sprang up again as if he had been bitten, or stung. His fingers found the stiffened patches of cloth on the seat of his breeches where the blisters had burst. He had not even been aware of them until now.

Below the platform he found a cistern that held some water, and as he was filling his bottle he heard the sound of distant gunfire, away up the road that the hussars had taken, a volley of shots, he thought, and then several more drawn out over the next half minute. By the time the shooting had stopped, he had run recklessly down the hill, fallen once, and torn the fowling piece from the mare's saddle with such violence that she reared away from him, and he cursed her. Toma glared at him with his one eye.

"Something has happened ahead. They will come now."

"I wonder," said Toma.

On the stones behind the wall he laid the fowling piece, each barrel double-charged with shot, and the wads and the powder, though he knew he would never have time to reload the awkward old thing. Beside it he put his pistol and all the extra bullets he had for it. Without reloading, then, he had exactly eight shots. It was possible that if they all came through the gate together, a perfectly unlikely event, he could disable several of them with the blasts of the shotgun. *Ah, Raymond*, he thought, *this is not at all how I thought it would end.* He looked again at his armory, at the glint of nickel plating on the pistol, the dusty brass-bound wood of the shotgun. If Raymond were here, or just over there on the other side of the gate, they might have had a chance. This is what they must have known inside the Sikander Bagh, those sepoys of the Mutiny, the guilty ones, awaiting the attack of the Sutherlands and the Punjabis: *if they make it through the wall we are as good as dead.* He smiled. He waited.

The horses came at a gallop, and as he crouched out of sight behind his rocks, Harwell wondered at the merciless energy of these soldiers and their mounts. So engrossed in the imagined sequence that must follow, the horses wheeling in his mind and in the dust of the gateway there, the sun behind them as he fired into that knot of terrified animals and cursing men, the sound and the smell of their dying and his own, his breath coming in great gasps . . . so utterly lost in this teeming vision of the end, he heard now the sound, the diminishing sound of hoofbeats, and made no sense of it at all. He peered over the wall, and the horses, six of them, were almost at the bend where they would vanish. Six riderless horses.

He built a bower of branches to shade Toma from the sun and rejoiced in that work, though he kept an ear cocked for the sound of those other horses. He gave Toma more water, and ate a tiny piece of chocolate that he found in the side pocket of his pack. On his second trip up to the cistern he found the nest of some bird in the grass against the rock, and he took eight of the ten speckled eggs and fed them to the boy one by one. Then he lay down in a shaded angle of the wall, thinking only to rest and to listen for hoofbeats on the road, and he slept.

He awoke late in the afternoon, startled by the mare, who stamped once to rid herself of a fly. The sun, about to sink behind the mountains, shone full in his face, though weakened by the haze, and for a few moments he could not remember where he was. There were the horses, hill and cistern, Toma asleep in his cocoon. He listened and heard nothing louder than the rumbling of his own stomach. He turned the situation over in his mind, raising outlandish possibilities, objections to his growing conviction that they were safe, at least in this place. The horses followed him up the hill, where he watered them out of his hat. Then he gathered wood for a fire, started some water for tea, and sat down by Toma to smoke and consider what must now be done.

When a gust of wind blew the smoke into Toma's face he awoke, and Harwell saw not just the one eye, but a sliver of the other that had been swollen shut. "Toma, how do you feel."

"I hurt. Everything hurts."

"The hands and the feet. You must tell me if you can move them." There was a silence while the boy closed his eyes in concentration, as if he were listening for something. Harwell sipped his tea and considered the haze, thought that the weather might have settled somewhat, hoped for a moon.

"I can do it, but there is a great pain between my shoulders."

"Well, I am sorry for it. But if you felt nothing at all I would not know what to do for you. As it is, I am going to put you back on your horse."

"Never."

"Yes. We cannot stay here. We must get to Morača."

"I do not think I can hold myself in the saddle."

"You won't have to." Harwell rummaged in his pack until he found the bag with his brushes and tooth powder, and unwrapped a small stoppered bottle of purple glass, the laudanum he had carried all this way against the toothache, for his teeth had always given him trouble.

"Drink." He held the bottle to the boy's lips. "Again." In a few minutes Toma closed his eyes and began to snore.

Harwell tied up the end of the carpet so that Toma was immobilized like a sleeping lunatic in a straitjacket, then he lifted him as gently as he could and laid him down across the horse's back in the same position as before. Toma groaned once, but did not wake. When Harwell had packed his weapons away and scattered the embers of the fire, he saw that the sky had taken a milky rose color, beautiful and strange, and the road he must follow led up into the mountains, towards the brightest patch of that color.

Beyond the apparently deserted village, where two of the houses lay in roofless ruin, he found the bodies of the Austrian patrol on a grassy bank, a soft and pleasant feature in that otherwise severe landscape. The hands were crossed over the breast, a mark of respect, perhaps, but the weapons were all gone, and the heads too. He looked again. It was the very last of the light, and he might be imagining this detail. He had often had to mend his soldiers after a battle, using glue and a stout matchstick to fix the head back on the body. But if the heads were lost . . . He tried to remember what these same fellows would have done to him, and the terror of that moment when he thought they were almost upon him.

The mare, of course, did not like the smell of this place, and Harwell had difficulty in holding her steady while he reflected. They must have galloped through the village and then turned back, realizing that they had overridden the fugitives. And when they reached the narrow place just ahead with stones on either side, the villagers were waiting for them. Perhaps the soldiers did not know the history of these mountains, believed a patrol of the emperor's horse to be invulnerable to such ragged shepherds.

And where were the victors now? Why no blaze of light, no roasting sheep in the village? He thought then of what Sofia had told him, her vision of the war that must come. Why not here? Why not now? The people of the village had withdrawn into the mountains to await retaliation. He imagined Sir Percy, shaking his head in disapproval of such barbarism and saying to him, "See what a mess you have made of things!"

He rode on, determined to put as many miles as possible between him and the border, but slowly too, for the sake of Toma. On the other side of the defile they crossed a shallow, muddy streambed where the hussars must have realized their mistake, the least of their mistakes. There was no moonrise, and no stars to be seen, but light suffused the sky long after the sun had set, and although Harwell could make out little of the road, it was enough for the horses, who picked their way among the rocks. At times he heard rushing water away to his left, and odd currents of dank air rose from below. After a couple of hours of slow progress, the mare came to a halt and would not be moved. He guessed that the road was blocked, and so he lifted Toma, still sleeping, down from his horse, and found a space for him among the rocks. Then he tethered the mare in the road and rolled himself in his blankets to sleep.

The first thing he saw when he opened his eyes was a patch of brilliant blue sky above him: the wind must have shifted sometime during the night. He heard a cough, assumed it was Toma waking from his drugged sleep, but when he raised his head he saw a man seated on a boulder in the road, staring back at him. A tall man, dirty and hollow-faced, wearing a long sheepskin vest with the fleece turned out, beneath it the usual array of bandolier, girdle bristling with weapons, and tired finery. What caught Harwell's eye and made him stare was the dusty horsehair crest with its bright clasp that adorned the bandolier, a trophy of yesterday's victory.

"Who are you?" The tone was neither welcoming nor accusing; the man had no weapon in his hand.

"Harwell. My name is Harwell, and I am English."

"Who is your prisoner?"

"He is not my prisoner, and his name is Toma Pekočević." The man made a sound that might have been disapproval, or disbelief, and so Harwell repeated his assertion, adding that the boy was the son of Danilo.

"And you have beaten him?"

"No, no. It was not I. I have rescued him from the Austrians. We came from the Sandžak, and the soldiers you fought with were chasing us, him."

"If you speak truly, then we have saved the son of Danilo, and our victory is the greater for that. The Vasojević will sing a song praising this day." Exhausted as he was, the man took delight in his thought.

"You are not of the Vasojević?"

"No, but I know them, have fought with them and against them, and Danilo is a hero, their greatest man. The son of Danilo may be a great man, him that we saved."

"It may be so."

"Have you any food? And where are you bound?"

"We must reach Morača, where the monks will help us, and I do not know what is in my pack, for we left in great haste. You are welcome to what you find there. And your name, sir?"

"Milutin. My name is Milutin," and though the man bowed as he spoke, it seemed odd to Harwell that he looked away and that he gave no patronymic, or family name. He turned and set about the task of emptying the pack, where he discovered the food that Harwell had taken up into the mountains just a few days ago. Milutin laid the other items on the ground: the wrapped books, journals, a shirt, the lantern. They were all familiar to Harwell, but distantly so, as if they were the details of a story that had happened to someone else. For when he had made that journey, Sofia had still been alive.

"*Scoranze!*" exclaimed Milutin, holding aloft the bag of little fish that had long since perfumed every other article in the pack.

"You are welcome to them. Take them with you when we part."

"Yes, good. But now we must eat." While Milutin busied himself with water and wood, Harwell coaxed Toma back to consciousness, fearful at first that he had given him too much of the laudanum. And when Toma woke at last he looked at Harwell as if he did not know him.

"Such things I have seen," he said, and slept again.

When they had eaten, had devoured the entire pot of rice and fish, Harwell asked the visitor if he thought the Austrians would come back.

"I believe they have already declared war, and that the earthquake was a sign to them, as it was to us, that the hour has come. And when they come there will be an army, and not just a handful of these fools. There was a funeral in the village yesterday, an old man, my uncle, who was killed by a rock that fell from the mountains when they shook, a single rock cast down by the hand of the Devil. The Austrians rode through this celebration, and a child who could not get out of their way was hurt. He will live, but they deserved their death." Milutin scraped the pot vigorously with his fingers, and licked them. "And not a single man of ours was killed. It was as they sing it in the old songs."

"Where are your people now?"

"In the mountains, where the Austrians cannot find us. We will have to see how many they are, and what help is available to us." Harwell looked up, saw the trees perched crazily on a jagged line against the deep blue of the sky, then dropped his gaze to the vast slide of gravel, boulders, and uprooted evergreens that blocked the road. The sun was now up over the steep wall, and a gentle steam began to rise from the wreckage before them.

"If the Austrians cannot find you, I'm afraid they will have no trouble finding us."

"There is a way that I will show you, and they will never find it. You will carry news of this to Cetinje, to Prince Nikola himself, and he will know what to do without delay. The army of Montenegro must be raised. Each family must send its fighting men."

"I did not say I was going to Cetinje."

"Where else would an Englishman go? Surely you do not live among the monks?"

"No, but I lived for a time with Danilo and his family, until . . . until the earthquake, and I would gladly go back."

"What happened to them? Does Danilo still live?"

"Yes, but his wife is dead."

"Sofia, she was called?"

"Yes, Sofia." How odd to speak that name aloud, how unbearable to confirm the fact of her death.

"It is said that she was, in her youth, the most beautiful of women, a woman fit for such a man."

"She was so until the hour of her death."

"And the boy?"

"There was some trouble, and he was taken by the Austrians. He escaped and killed two of them, one a captain."

"Then you must bring him to our prince, for he is a hero already. Two, you say?"

"He goes to America. It was his mother's wish."

A look of disbelief clouded Milutin's face, and when he spoke there was undisguised anger in his voice. "That cannot be so. If the son of Danilo leaves, runs away . . . What does Danilo say?"

"He honors the promise that he made to Sofia."

Milutin spat into the fire, as if to wash away the taste of this thought. "You have meddled in things that do not concern an Englishman, and when the boy wakes, pray God he will think again about his choice." They looked at Toma, who, having eaten a few handfuls of rice and taken some water, now dozed with the sun full on his face. "You were in love with this woman who is now dead."

"I too honor her wish." Harwell could not bring himself to meet Milutin's glare as he spoke these words. Milutin sighed.

"Well then, let us put the boy on his horse."

Harwell offered Milutin whatever food was left in his pack, for the monks would feed them in Morača. Then he made Toma swallow a little more from the purple bottle, not so much this time, as his forehead was warm to the touch. He found himself thinking again that even though Sofia had no power to save herself, she would not let her son die before coming to America.

This proposition was tested over and again by the track that Milutin found up and behind the slide: it was steep and tight, and he took the stallion's rope from Harwell, sprang like a goat among the broken rocks, and the horses followed him. At one point the wall of rock to their right, gleaming orange in the shadow, forced them so close to the edge where the mountain had faulted that Harwell could look straight down onto the broken trees and shattered stone that blocked the road. The mountain had moved once: it might do so again. Harwell closed his eyes.

When the way was safe again, when they had descended to a sunlit glade that lay like a cloth of gold in the mixed forest of beech and spruce, they stopped to let the horses eat, for the grass here was fresh and green and starred with flowers.

"Tell me," said Harwell, "why you gave your name as Milutin."

"There are many Montenegrins with that name."

"But it is not your name."

"No."

"Well then. What harm is there in a name? I would like to know the man who saved my life."

"I will tell you this. Danilo had three sons. The first was killed in the market at Berane, by the Turks, in a dispute over the weight of a sack of grain. The last one, this one, you say you are taking to America. But the other, the second son, I myself killed that one, with a shot in his heart, and every man who fired his gun that day lives in fear of Danilo and the Vasojević, even though it was the judgement of our prince, a just decision."

"But you have given him back a life. You have settled your account."

"Who knows how Danilo counts these things? If the boy goes to America he is as good as dead to Danilo. And if the boy stays he will know me as his brother's executioner, a blood enemy. Did you know him, too, the dead one?" Harwell shook his head, could not speak for the memory of that cave and its stench, for the thought of Toma living in that dream of death and vengeance.

"Go now. The road is not far below."

"Goodbye, Milutin."

"Remember that you owe us your life as well. You must not fail to send help, or to bring news of this victory to the prince. You have a debt to the living as well as your promise to the dead. Think on this." He raised his hand in a wave or salute, and ran away through the long grasses of the glade.

Because the weather had turned fine, and the wind through the gorge carried away the heat of the sun, Harwell did not fret at the slow progress they made towards Kolašin. There were trees down across the road, spruces with mats of dark moss trimmed in new growth that was the color of limes, and at one point a bottomless crack some two feet wide split the road, but the mare stepped across it as she would a mere rut.

The road rose at last out of the rugged canyons of the Tara, a place that he would always remember as the valley of the shadow of death, and the country opened out into broad uplands of evergreen forest mixed with pastures. No birds sang, and the stillness was complete and unsettling. Behind him the earthquake had toppled mountains into valleys, but here, on the even ground, was a stranger devastation: rocks catapulted from their walls; a broad swath of trees topped about a dozen feet from the ground; a pasture full of sheep lying on their sides, apparently dead.

In his excursions from the Hermit's Meadow into the high country he had sometimes experienced a nameless joy, from which sprang the conceit that he was viewing creation for the first time. That splendid flow of rock, so like a river, might just have cooled, and those drifts of gentians, unseen until this moment, might have been set in the bare stone for his sole delight. Now, lonely as ever but cut off from hope, he was Adam after the fall, journeying through the land east of Eden. In the grip of this thought he dismounted to make sure that Toma still breathed. He put his hand on the carpet, felt the slow rise and fall of it, and when he put his ear to the crimped end it seemed to him that the boy, in his dream or his delirium, hummed a song.

At Kolašin he found the fork where he and Janko had turned away to the southeast, knew now how far he had to go to reach the monastery, and thought they might make it just after the sun set. The road did not pass through the town itself, but close enough so that he could see the cluster of steep-roofed houses, and he was no longer alone: he encountered a man riding an ass, followed by two women bearing enormous burdens of firewood. Harwell pulled his hat down over his face, and no one asked him where he was bound. In the late afternoon clouds swallowed the sun, and by the time they came to the headwaters of the Morača they were enveloped in a fine, soaking drizzle.

The monks were either at their prayers or eating their supper when Harwell knocked at the gate, and it was a long while before he heard the slap of sandals on the stone. His hand ached where he had struck a bolt in the wood. Janko stood there, frowning into the gusting rain, annoyed with this visitor, whoever he might be. Harwell waited until the boy recognized the mare, muddy and wet as she was.

"And are you still pledged to silence, Janko? Have you no words for old friends?"

Janko almost dropped the torch in his amazement, then crossed himself. He ran back into the courtyard, bellowing as he went in a voice that cracked a full octave. "He has come back. The English has come back out of the belly of the earth!"

Other torches were lit, and Harwell supervised the careful unburdening of the stallion. He turned away for a moment to answer the greeting of Stefan, who held a lantern in one hand and a cloak in the other, and was surprised to find himself seized in an ardent bear hug. "Follow me," Stefan whispered urgently in his ear. Just then, behind his back, he heard Janko's thin squawk of amazement.

"Ehh! There is a dead soldier here, one of the Germans! Look!"

"He is not a German, Janko, and pray that he is not dead. That is your friend Toma."

"Never," said Janko, putting the light closer to the battered face. "Well, it may be so, but how he stinks. He has ruined this fine carpet."

"It does not matter. Put him in a bed as gently as you can and cut the carpet from him. I will come in a moment. Do nothing more, for we do not know what his injuries are." He entrusted Toma to three pairs of hands, then found Stefan waiting for him in the archway, his lantern turned low.

"Where are you taking me, Stefan? Not to the kitchen, by any chance?" He reached out a hand and patted the wall, rejoiced in its safety and solidity.

"Later you may eat," muttered Stefan, "but there is more pressing business first."

"How? Business you say?"

"You have a visitor, arrived no more than an hour ago. How it is possible to have come up the Morača today, and alone, I do not know. Nor do I know how you come here with the son of Danilo, half dead and rolled up in a carpet."

"A visitor," said Harwell, as if he had never heard the word before. Stupid with fatigue he repeated himself: "A visitor." Stefan led him down the passageway and stopped before a closed door. His lantern caught the anxious confusion on Harwell's face.

"You will come to no harm, I think. We will have much to talk about later, but for now there is this greater claim on you." He turned away, taking the light with him, and Harwell heard him mutter, "Such a journey . . ."

The silence beyond the door had a different quality to it now. There had surely been two of them, for there was a brief conversation, and then one went away, she thought it was only one, but perhaps they were both gone. She shrugged off the blanket and pulled her sodden cloak around her shoulders, so that she was again chilled, but at least properly dressed. What had possessed her to come away without a stitch of spare clothing? She had not been thinking clearly. Now, exhausted by her journey, she was less capable still of cogent thought. She could not know if there was someone on the other side of the door, and, if so, why that person waited there in the shadows. She was suddenly annoyed with herself: she had not come all this way, risking her life, let alone Sir Percy's horse, to be afraid of the dark, or of any man. She opened the door savagely.

For a moment they did not quite recognize each other: she because his head was bowed in anxious reflection, and the borrowed cloak—Lady Foote was a very substantial person indeed—blotted up the candlelight behind her; he because that same cloak so disguised her shape and her size, and the only other feature he could make out was the silhouette of her hair that stood out in an angry halo from her head and transformed her.

"Oh," she said, and her hands went to her hair, to smooth those damp, intractable frizzes, for she saw that he was staring at it. How gaunt he was; how changed from the person she had conjured from each letter, dream, and thought; how sad. She felt quite hopelessly stupid because she could think of nothing to say, and all the relief, joy, and thanksgiving that churned within her were distilled into the ludicrous wish that she had remembered to bring a hairbrush.

"I should have knocked," he said slowly, wondering at the sound of his own language. "I had no conception of who could have anticipated my arrival . . . I still do not believe it. How have you come here? Why have you come?"

She took his hands in hers and the faint heat there spread through her like a balm. "The how is a reasonable question and I shall attempt an answer. The other is so silly it deserves none."

"Help me," she said as she struggled to lift the boy's naked body and turn him over on the bed. Harwell and Stefan had been waiting for such a signal, conversing in low tones but distracted by the anxious spectacle of this examination. She had flinched neither at nakedness nor at filth, had insisted on her qualification as a woman, as the daughter of a doctor. She had seen such things, and worse.

They put him on his stomach now, and the shallow, fevered breathing continued as before. She moved the candle closer so that they could all see the mark, high on the back and between the shoulder blades, where the skin, purple but unbroken, bulged alarmingly.

"What do you think?" asked Harwell, as she palpated the swelling, gently, so gently, with her wrists arched like the leaf springs of a carriage.

"This is an appalling bruise, and there must be something broken there as well, the ribs or the spine itself, though he has movement in his extremities, as you have seen. If the lungs were punctured I think we would hear it in his breathing. That is what I think. Also that the carpet preserved him from a much greater harm. He will certainly live and walk. Have you something for his fever?" She looked up at Stefan. The candle picked out the lines in her face, melting Harwell's heart. "As you can see, I came here with nothing useful."

"We have a bark that we use against a fever."

"Fetch it, if you will, for I have almost finished bathing him, and then he must sleep. We must all sleep." Lydia rubbed her forehead with the back of her wrist, and Harwell saw how her shoulders slumped in this unguarded moment. He spoke gently to her.

"How long must he rest? How long before he can travel?"

"I am no doctor, but the only cure for the fever, and for this hurt to his back, is rest."

"But how much rest?"

"I cannot tell you that." There was an edge to her response, which she regretted. "I'm sorry. Tomorrow we shall know more."

He heard the door close behind him and wondered if he should tell her Stefan's thought, after he had heard the whispered tale of Harwell's flight through the Sandžak from the Hermit's Meadow: that if Toma was to leave the country it must be without delay, ahead of the wind bringing news of this disaster to the court, and ahead of any Austrian ultimatum. One could not know the mind of the prince. So often before he had found excuses for delay, for temporizing, when the moment had seemed ripe for bold action. And if Nikola now judged the Austrian strength to be too great, or the Serbian support doubtful in any way, then Toma might become a pawn sacrificed to avoid the greater calamity.

He watched her closely, saw the infinite care with which she applied the warm, scented water to the boy's body, and it was as if she smoothed away the hurts and fatigue he himself felt. Stefan had left the room once before at Lydia's bidding, after she had changed the fouled sheet, to fetch something that would clear the air. When she changed the dressing on the wound in his thigh, she grazed the private parts with her cloth, and Toma had moaned. She looked up at Harwell.

"Can you tell me, please . . . is this the normal state, or . . . ?"

Harwell saw the swelling, the discoloration, and shook his head. "No, that is not normal." *Christ, the boy's stones were the size of a goat's, or a bull's.* "They must have kicked him there."

She sighed and bent again to her task. Stefan had returned then with a small bottle of oil and a handful of twigs. When he put them in the warm water, the odor of the mysterious white-blooming shrub filled the close air of the cell and Harwell's mind as well, flooding him with such painful and irresistible recollection that he thought he would weep. Lydia had looked up at him with a private smile.

Now he knelt opposite her to help Toma again onto his back, and they covered him with the coarse linen sheet. They touched once, then again, and finally she surrendered her hands to his, laid them so warm and soft with the oil in his great rough palms. He felt the boy's chest rise and fall, felt the quickening pulse in her wrists, and gazed intently on the top of her bowed head, just a few inches from his own. Like a wanderer in prospect of a vast, untravelled, fruitful land, he was stilled by the revelation, or the rediscovery, of what might be love.

Chapter Sixteen

"DEAR GOD," exclaimed Harwell, half blinded by the glare of sunlight from the pale, treacherous rock, "what did you think you were doing? Had you no fear for yourself in this wilderness?" As he spoke these words he remembered that even last night, in the midst of his profound sleep, he had been awakened by a further tremor through the floor of the monastery, which rocked him in his bed.

Now he kept his eyes fixed on the back of Lydia's head, trusting the mare more than himself. He had forgotten how dreadful was the defile of the Morača, and the earthquake had rendered it more difficult still. But how prettily she turned her head, and the billowing hair, through a trick of light, was touched with fire at its very tips. Who would have thought there was so much red in it? Who would have thought . . . And here he was lost in admiration for all that had been dared on his behalf.

"I had no conception of mortal danger. How could I"—here she actually laughed—"as your letter was so very discreet, so manly, so understated. But do you know, I never was particularly worried for myself, although the noise of falling rock is quite the most terrifying thing I have ever heard. But the horse . . ."

"The horse?" What an extraordinary device the sidesaddle was. A perfectly ridiculous affair, he had always thought, awkward, unstable, unbalanced, and so on; and yet it might have been made for just this situation, as Lydia could quite easily twist around to carry on a conversation with him, almost as if they were sitting in her parlor. He did notice, however, that she never once looked down at what lay below the trail.

"Yes, you see it is Sir Percy's horse. We were out riding when the earthquake struck, and he was thrown. I'm afraid his leg may be broken."

Harwell made a sound of shallow sympathy. "I suppose, under the circumstances, it was very civil of him . . ."

"Oh, but I'm afraid I never asked, or never had a chance to ask. The rumor, so Draško said, was that we had both been killed in an avalanche, for the horse that Sir Percy rode ran straight home after the accident, and I was a good while seeing to him before I could ride back for help. Draško was very surprised indeed when I sent for him from the legation: he said that everyone at the school was sure I was dead. The Petrović girl, no doubt, is regaling them with the text of my dying words, unless the roof has fallen on her head and cut her tale short."

"And what do they think now?"

"With any luck they think I am still dead, and my return will be an event of Biblical significance. Draško is sworn to silence, and even though he brought me food he does not approve at all. And Lady Foote, of course, who has been so kind to me: I did not tell her what my plan was, but I think she rather sniffed it out. So I shall be very glad when I can return the horse, and very sorry . . ." Here her words were lost to the sound of the Morača, for a slide on the opposite wall of the gorge had forced it from its bed with a dam of white slag that created a pool and an angry waterfall. Harwell was left to admire her from this odd angle—she seemed no more than a child perched crookedly on that big, rawboned horse—to admire her and to wonder anew at what she had managed to do, with no more than his letter and Draško's grudging directions, not even a map to guide her. She had confided to him the night before, as they had walked arm in arm back to her room, that no power on earth, not even his disapproval, could have prevented her from attempting this, once she had got it in her head, once she had seen the road that ran away to the east from the pass above Cetinje. And the earthquake was the last straw. His letters had sounded quite desperate to her, did he see? and they had taken away her peace of mind. He was not unhappy that she had come? No, not in the least, he was not unhappy at all, but even as he delighted in the reassuring, determined pressure of her arm clasping his to her side, he tried to think what he could have written to her that might have ignited this dangerous fuse.

And now when the gorge opened out, and the sound of the water diminished, she looked back again from the trail ahead, encompassing Harwell and the waterfall behind him in the radiance of her expression. "Is it not grand?" she cried out gaily. "And look there." She pointed to where a great wind-riven pine tree stood out from the bare rock, its base bulging from the fissure where it had taken root. "Never in my life," she started to say, "never have I . . ." and then fell silent, not knowing how to approach such miracles with language.

Toma heard the voices behind him, and knew that the English woman was talking to Harwell, but most of their words were lost to him, for Janko still held the stallion's rope and led the way, keeping up a stream of fanciful chatter about heroes and old songs and golden-haired saints rising from the ground.

He was tied to his saddle by various ropes, so that even though he sat upright he could not shift his weight to ease the burning ache in his thigh. He had told Harwell, and Miss Wadham, that he was able to travel, even though he saw in her eyes that she did not trust his statement, and certainly there were times in this descent when, but for the ropes, he would have fallen, proud horseman that he was, for the fever had taken his strength from him, and the pain in his back was such that it made him faint.

"Do you not think that the *guslar* will mention me when he sings your story? If I had been there I too would have slain the Austrians, and many Turks besides." Janko's questions required no response from Toma, who had tired of the boy's adulation, even though he was grateful to him. Instead, he fastened his attention on the pool and the waterfall as he passed, and then on the memory of it, for it hurt too much to turn his head. There was at least a twelve-foot drop where the water shot out over a tree trunk and arced down to smash upon the rocks. Here and there freshets bubbled from the raw bank of shale and boulders below the pool, so that he knew this dam must soon fail, and all that water trapped there, twelve feet deep by thirty or forty feet long, must be released at once, scarring the gorge as it rushed down. When would that be? The fury of this thought, such an irresistible and destructive force of water, filled his mind.

He had no help from an earthquake in building his own dam, and there had been that one rock that almost broke him, but he had moved it nonetheless. There were pictures in the book, his mother's book, of such machines as could lift a score of those boulders as if they were feathers, could pile up ten dams like this one in the course of an hour. And this was where he was bound: he would see with his own eyes how such things were done.

He remembered the sun on his back as he lifted that rock which would anchor his dam, and how he had poured sweat into the water so cold that it numbed his legs. He had pretended not to notice how Aliye's gaze fell on him as she sat there with her bare legs in the water.

He had never again seen her as he had that first time, naked under the sun, though the glimpses of her on the moonlit nights were enough to keep every detail of her alive, a memory fed by the slow, certain knowledge of his hands. She had never refused him anything, had even, to his amazement, shown him how he might please her, stilled him with the touch of her hand to his chest so that it was no longer he that moved upon her, but she to him, her breath sweet and quick against his neck until she bit him there.

But at the edge of the pool something was different: there was a distance in her, a reserve, that he did not understand. Perhaps one of her aunts or her mother had told her that she must act and dress more like a woman, for going and coming she often wore her shawl pulled up over her head. Perhaps also she knew or guessed that she was with child, and was summoning the courage to tell him.

Aliye's death, and its echoes, had been stilled by the greater horror of his mother's death, which burned inside him like a smothered coal in the silence there. But Aliye had started dying from the moment his mother told him that they were not to marry, in spite of the bey's gracious visit, in spite of the fine carpet, in spite of the words he had whispered to Aliye and which he had thought were true words. He knew then how it must end for her, though his mother said it would be otherwise. He wished that there were one fixed thing in the world that would never change, or disappoint him, or leave him, but he did not know what that might be, unless it was the idea of God, which was a certitude without delight or consolation.

When he was hidden in the carpet, he had such strange thoughts that he wondered if this was a sign that he was about to die. The blow had knocked him unconscious, and when he was aware of himself again, of pain, and of the fact that he could not move and could barely draw breath, he imagined that he was the unborn child in Aliye's body. Later, after the English had given him the drops to make him sleep, he had dreamt of machines, like the ones in the book, that moved earth, spun wire, hammered metal, but unlike as well, for they had faces and souls and all their workings were revealed to him. The blades of the turbine were hands turning ceaselessly to take strength from the water and make electricity. The mill press that crushed metal into a different shape had corded shoulders and scowled in concentration. And the gun that could kill thousands had many nimble fingers feeding bullets into the breech faster than the blinking of his eye.

It was almost embarrassing to think these thoughts in the broad daylight, and yet he took a lonely pride in this knowledge that he could not impart. Miss Wadham would think that his vision was only the fever speaking, and Harwell's face would assume that kind, pained expression that meant he did not understand the words in the book. He thought of his father, who was so difficult to talk to. He could tell him about the miraculous gun that would make him master of his meadow against the armies of the sultan, but Danilo's interest would be in how fast and how many the thing could kill, how many men it would take to carry it, while his own thought was fastened upon the whispering of steel against steel that made a kind of language, or music.

He would never have this conversation with his father after all. It would be another one of the silences between them, a part of the greater silence that devoured the world he had known. It was as if something in him had died, for he could no longer remember clearly the joy of the horse between his legs when he had carried the prize at Rožaj, or the texture of Aliye's skin, or the touch of his mother's hand. And the things that were always present in his mind and could not be forgotten—the smell of the cave where he had carried Vuk, the sounds of his mother's ordeal, the infernal light in Schellendorf's death chamber—these things he could not and must not speak about.

In the middle of the afternoon they came to a spot where the river fell into a long, quiet pool, and they could see that not far ahead of them the foothills gave way to the gentle plain of the Morača. Here were farmhouses, and tilled fields, and the road was at last level, or nearly so. They bade farewell to Janko, for there was enough of the day left for him to reach the monastery by nightfall, and he capered back up the trail humming a tune that would help him compose his own version of the deeds of Harwell and Toma.

Lydia, too, sang to herself, would have sung aloud had Bron not been telling her something, for a great weight of anxiety had been lifted: Toma could manage his horse well enough on such a road, and Bron seemed quite another man with the gorge behind them. They must soon pass through Doclea, he said, where he had seen the viper—did he write about that in his first letter?—and not far beyond that was the spot by the river where he had made his camp with Draško, and the ass had ruined one of his new pots . . . and so on in this happy vein of tranquil recollection until he remembered with embarrassment that she had passed this way only the day before, and knew all the landmarks of their route as well as he.

She was sorry he had stopped, even though there were no surprises in his account, for she did love to hear him talk on any subject, and the letters had been so solemn, whereas this version was transformed by the thread of comedy that led through darkness to the happy ending of the tale. She remembered the pall of his face in the shadows the night before, what an exhausted, unhappy shell he had seemed of the man who had left her in Cetinje two months ago. She must make him laugh, she must make him forget. She must fix her mind upon her own happy ending and lead him there.

When they were encamped by the river, on that flat familiar to them both, on those grassy stones that signified in a more ancient context, the happiness of which she dreamt seemed almost within her reach.

They had helped Toma down from his horse, and unpacked their few belongings. When Bron was laying the blankets out on the grass—with a very discreet space between his and hers, she reflected—he found a hairpin, which he produced in smiling triumph, and indeed it was hers, lost the night before last, though it seemed half a lifetime ago.

Bron went off with his gun, trusting her to tether the horses out on the most promising grass, and although she had never put her hand to such a task she managed it well enough: the pins held against any stress except a vertical lift, and a horse would have to hold the rope in his teeth to achieve that. She looked up when she heard the shots, and saw a clutch of small bright ducks fleeing down the course of the river. She thought also that she heard a muttered oath, for Bron had jumped the ducks not far from their camp. She smiled: even his seriousness was now a joy to her, though she would wear a properly grave expression when he returned to camp empty-handed.

"I don't believe I have ever in my life missed two ducks at such a childishly simple distance. And not just two, mind you, but all six, the veritable broad side of the barn. You must forgive me." He threw the gun down in disgust, and she said that because she had kept ducklings as a girl, even though they were tame ones, she really did not enjoy eating this particular bird.

In any case, there was plenty of food, for the monks of Morača had supplied them with bread, and delicious vine leaves stuffed with rice and bits of meat, and a cake of baked meal with some herb in it. It was cold, and it might disappoint the appetite of the determined carnivore, but it went very nicely with the pot of tea.

The boy was the problem. She could have sat there all night quite happily, more than happily, with one or another of them feeding little bits of brush into the fire to keep it alive, smoking occasionally, watching Harwell's endearing, awkward way with the cigarette for which he was so grateful, he having smoked the last of his tobacco—her tobacco—in the aftermath of that moment when the hussars had threatened to overwhelm them. And had he driven them off? The details of that dreadful journey were all quite confusing to her. No, he said, showing her that little smile of his that made him seem like a boy himself, it was nothing so heroic as that.

"I could pretend otherwise, of course"—he looked across the fire at her—"but I have already compromised your opinion of my marksmanship, and I don't think you would be inclined to believe me."

She began to say how glad she was that he had not attempted anything heroic, anything more heroic, as that might have led to the gravest . . . And here he interrupted her with his achievement of three quite perfect smoke rings.

Through all of this Toma sat like a boulder at the edge of the firelight, withdrawn into some private reflection that wrote its grief on his face. It would not do to devote her attention exclusively to Bron, however strong her impulse to do exactly that, and so she made a point of asking Toma how he did, whether he would be more comfortable lying down, would he eat another bite of food? And to all of these civil inquiries she got barely any response at all, perhaps a grunt, or a shake of the head. This desperate, mute loneliness did not correspond at all to Bron's descriptions of his character. She would try harder. She must remind him that his place was here among the living, that he had his whole life ahead of him, that he would soon see his dear sister. Her courage almost failed her at the thought of Natalia: here was she, rejoicing in her private good fortune, in these feelings which overwhelmed every defense of reason and caution, and she had forgotten entirely about the child upon whom an awful truth was about to fall.

She stood behind Toma and gently raised his shirt so that she could examine the bruise on his back. The wound on his leg would have to wait until they got back to Cetinje, and his other injuries would heal of their own accord. As the days were still stretching towards the summer solstice, even at this hour they were enveloped in a luminous twilight that softened the lines on Bron's face as he sat staring into the fire. She needed no candle to see, and perhaps the swelling looked less angry than it did last night. The boy, who had not uttered a single word of complaint all day, said nothing now as she laid her hand on this spot, though the muscles in his back quivered in the anticipation of pain.

"There," she said, letting the shirt fall, "you will be as good as new in no time." She stood behind him, wanting to make some gesture that was tender instead of merely therapeutic, but was constrained because Toma had suffered the wounds of a man, had borne them as bravely as any man. She put her hands on his shoulders, kneading the muscles there very gently.

"I met your mother once, Toma. Did she tell you that? It was when Natalia was brought to the school, less than a year ago, though it seems so much longer now. Even then she told me of the dream she had for you, how you would study abroad and become a scientist, or an engineer. And it was the most intimate and pleasant of conversations, for she had taken me aside, not to speak about Natalia but because she knew your father could not approve wholeheartedly of such a plan. It was to be our secret, and I would send her the books for you to read. I was captivated by her, that is the only word for it, by those fine eyes, and more so by her spirit, her determination that goodness and learning should prevail. That is how I will always remember her: by the look on her face when she spoke of her hopes for you. That is how you must remember her, for then you cannot go wrong in life: you will know what you must do. Natalia, of course, must be told, and I do not know if I have the strength to break that heart myself, or to keep it from breaking. So we shall do it together, you and I, and . . ."

What indiscretion of hers had triggered this barbarous keening? It was as if her fingers had found some wound deeper than any she had known of, and its poisons came spewing forth. His shoulders began to shake, and his breath came in shuddering gasps, and when she fairly shrieked his own name at his ear to cut off the awful monotone wailing, he began to speak.

There was much in his tale that should have shocked her, but she took no offense, flinched neither at Sofia's terrible ordeal, which the boy had been powerless to prevent, nor at the more terrible revenge exacted upon the Austrian officer. More terrible, she supposed, because he had not been a helpless witness, but these arms . . . She must not draw back from him now.

"There, Toma, there . . ." The tale, disjointed enough, and shot through with extraordinary references to saints, and monks, and she knew not what, had been overwhelmed by his grief at last, and he wept silently now against her breast. There was so much anger in it, in him, and he was being consumed by what he had seen and done. How could she be offended or shocked by this? Saddened, perhaps. Yes, quite overcome by sadness.

Standing there with Toma curled against her, she had a view of Harwell as he stared agape into the fire, and from that expression, and the set of his shoulders, she knew that he had not heard these appalling particulars before. What had he said last night? *She died in the earthquake.* It was a perfectly plausible explanation, and he must have believed it, as she had. What did it matter? Was not the most awful and important fact simply that of her death? Could they not put this behind them, for the sake of the living, her children, as a way of going forward? "It is over, Toma. You did what you could, what you must, and now it is over."

And yet it was not over. She could tell that too from looking across the fire—it was almost out—at that face. "Bron," she called softly, and got no answer. He sat there, staring ever into the embers, but his thoughts were miles away, and he fingered an object on a chain or string hung around his neck. The earthquake itself could not have effected a more sudden, a more brutal change. She knew now, without having the slightest basis other than an intimation as keen as a knife thrust, that Bron had been in love with this woman.

As she helped Toma to bed, making a pillow for him of a saddle blanket, she thought, *I cannot be right . . . I must be imagining this.* And yet every glance she stole at his unmoving, unblinking figure confirmed her intuition: he seemed as lost as Toma had been, and utterly unaware of his surroundings, of her. "Bron," she said more urgently now, "will you look to the fire?"

He did as she asked, breaking a branch of the brush into very small pieces with those hands of his that might just encircle her waist, thumb to thumb, and fingertip to fingertip. How she had thought about those hands in the endless, cruel weeks of his absence. The firelight grew stronger now, or was kept alive, for Bron was content to feed it bits of wood one by one, tossing them in from where he sat. And she asked herself, *How have I deserved this?* She ran her fingers through the tangles of her hair, took satisfaction in the sharp sensation when she encountered a knot.

I have deserved this. She felt the tension drain away, and her shoulders sagged as she allowed herself this thought. *I have deserved it because I wanted him too much, and because I threw myself at him. What kind of a woman makes so bold a proposal?* She had not seen it in his eyes, because they were outside in the dark, but he had surely drawn back from her; the voice told her that. And all the gallantry and gradual intimacy of the letters, had that been merely kindness? an unwillingness to hurt her feelings? The letters. *And I should not have read his letters: that too must be accounted for.* Could she feel remorse for what she had done and felt, even as she was being punished for these things? She could not. She would admit no regret, could not imagine herself sitting meekly and patiently in Cetinje, doing nothing, pretending not to care whether he returned or no; still less could she imagine her life without this true and painful thing at the center of it. And why, then, when she had done all that was in her power to do for him, when she could not have behaved otherwise, could he not so much as speak kindly to her?

"Bron."

He looked up at last, reached out his hand and took hers. "I am sorry you had to hear that. I had no idea . . . It must have been a terrible shock to you."

"And to you. Shall I make you a cigarette?" How pitiful now were the things she had to offer.

"Thank you, no. No more cigarettes. Whiskey, though. Perhaps I shall have to be civil to Sir Percy when we reach Cetinje, especially civil."

"And what will you tell him?"

Harwell was silent for a few seconds. "Tell him? I shall tell him that I should have listened to him, that I ought never to have travelled to the Sandžak, that I ought to have stayed in London, for I have made the most appalling mess of everything I have touched, or meddled in."

She sat beside him, holding his hand, which suggested no intimacy. "Listen to me now." She could at least do this for him. "You have not failed. You have triumphed, or at least you can achieve some good out of all this misery, which would have fallen on them whether you were there or no. Do you think you caused her death? Sofia's death?"

Wordless, Harwell shook his head.

"I know you grieve for her, but would she not have given her life if her son could be saved, if he could do those things which she dreamt of, and for which you prepared him?"

"Yes. She told me that. These were perhaps the very words she used. But now I do not know . . . You heard his tale. And there was a man I met on the road, a man who saved our lives, who scoffed at the idea that a Pekočević would flee, that there could be any place for him other than with Danilo."

"And if he stays, have you considered what future he may have? Think what he has done. What sort of life will that be?"

"A short one. Or a bad one."

"And whose voice, then, will you listen to?"

"Hers. I will listen to hers." To Lydia, at this moment, looking at his profile, this seemed a very literal truth. "If we can get Toma to Cetinje tomorrow, I shall bring him to the coast the following day. But I must speak with Sir Percy, must I not? and explain what has happened? I must not abandon these people who have taken up arms on my behalf."

"You will leave that in my hands. I believe I have more influence with Sir Percy even than you." He smiled at her, a weak smile, but enough to encourage her to think that he would get through this ordeal.

He got up to water the horses, and she followed him down to the stream leading her horse, stood there looking up at the stars. She had not seen them since she left Cetinje.

They went to bed then, their blankets no nearer and no farther from one another than when he had first laid them out on the grass. Tired as she was she would not yield to sleep, for she did not know when, if ever, she would have such a mantle, a panoply of light to her bed.

"And if you had stayed in London," she asked softly, so as not to wake him if he had already fallen asleep, "what sort of life would you have had there?"

"No life at all, I think." She thought he might say something more, but she could not keep her eyes open any longer.

They reached the outskirts of Cetinje in the late afternoon. It had been a long, tiring, silent ride, and Lydia could imagine quite vividly the pleasure of her tea, in spite of the heat, tea taken in a proper cup with a handle, and a saucer, and blessed with a drop of milk. Did she want her tea first? or a bath? Tea before, and tea after.

They had stopped briefly at the summit of the pass to let the horses rest, and she was able to show Bron just where she had stood, dismounted, to view the country to the east, with plans and possibilities whirling in her head. A little farther on she could show him the place where Sir Percy had been thrown from his horse during the tremor—why not she?—and where she had known suddenly what she would do. Bron in turn showed her the vantage point from which he had spied their holiday procession descending the flank of Lovćen on the day that he left, when he had missed her at the school. This, put together, was more conversation than they had had during the preceding eight hours, and she was conscious of a forced gaiety in her voice when she touched on what she had done and what she had felt.

"Look, Toma," she said. "That is Cetinje. Have you ever seen it?" She could not tell if the boy was impressed with so many dwellings, or simply mute. "At the far end of the town, in that largest of buildings, Natalia will be waiting for us. What a joy it will be for her to see you."

Cetinje was a sullen shambles, with many of the outlying buildings showing cracked walls or a stove roof, and a greater devastation lay on the center of town. The Grand Hotel had a diagonal wooden brace across the front doorway and Vuko Vuletić, the innkeeper, ever in his green apron, stood on a strand of broken glass, staring straight past them without acknowledgement, his lips moving silently as he calculated his repairs. Across the road, the entire facade seemed to have fallen off the museum, and the pictures within hung at crazy angles on the walls. A guard sat on a straight-backed chair in the courtyard, disdaining the ruin behind him, deeply suspicious of these foreign riders.

They stopped at the British Legation, which showed no more damage than a few tiles fallen from the roof and a broken window on the upper floor. Through a narrow gap in the top of the garden wall Harwell saw a figure that must be Sir Percy, propped up in a comfortable chair with his bandaged leg stretched out on another. Lydia dismounted and pushed through the gate, calling out to him as she went. "Sir Percy, how do you do today? Forgive my intrusion."

"My dear, what an unexpected pleasure. I welcome the intrusion, if you will forgive my informality. I am better today. But my butler reported you dead, crushed by enormous boulders. I am glad to see he was mistaken."

"And your leg is broken?"

"Yes, but only the tibia, whatever that may be, and the doctor says I shall be up and about in a matter of weeks. Next time the carriage, eh? A therapeutic outing."

"Indeed, I look forward to it. I have a surprise for you: I have seen Mr. Harwell."

"Did you so? The chap with the flowers? Was he much hurt?"

"No, not hurt at all, but he . . . or I would ask . . ."

"Whatever is in my power, my dear."

". . . a bottle of whiskey."

"Yes, yes. Two, if you wish them. The doctor has forbidden me to drink so much as a drop." He called out to a servant to fetch a bottle for Miss Wadham, carefully wrapped. "Very sensible of you to think of the whiskey. I myself am defying the doctor to the extent of taking wine, and in no circumstances should you drink the water. Do you note that persistent smell?"

"I do. Dead animals, I should think."

"That at least. But there are reports of fever in the town: typhoid, cholera, who knows what? Anything can happen in such circumstances, so I beg you to take care."

"I will, and I have a matter of particular importance to discuss with you if you will allow me to return in an hour, perhaps two."

"My dear, I shall rise from my sickbed and dress for the occasion. Perhaps Walters can find us something to eat."

"Thank you, and I shall return your horse."

"My what?"

"The horse that I was riding when . . ."

"Of course, of course. I thank you, though I have no need of him just now. You will give my compliments to Mr. Harwell?"

"I will certainly do that, and I know he will greatly appreciate your gift."

"Well, well, it is nothing, really. I shall expect you when I see you, but it will be no great occasion. My household is turned quite upside down."

"And ours at the school, I expect. My love to Lady Foote."

Lydia closed the gate behind her and handed the bottle to Harwell. It seemed to him that she fairly glowed with her triumph.

The Girls' Institute had been spared the worst of the earthquake, perhaps because the masons employed by Maria Alexandrovna had built to such exacting standards, and only a single one of the roofs had collapsed. This wing, abutting the chapel, unfortunately housed the infirmary, and the spacious, sunny room that would have accommodated Toma was now a wreckage of beams and beds and plaster dust.

He was therefore carried by Harwell and Draško to Lydia's own rooms, and although the arrival of a young man, somewhat damaged, in such dramatic circumstances would ordinarily provoke a lively curiosity, it passed practically without notice. Where were all her pupils? asked Lydia. Gone home, was Draško's sour reply. And why, when the comprehensive examinations were only a week away? The director feared an outbreak of the fever, he answered, and also, perhaps, further tremors. All girls who lived within a day's walk of the school had been told to return home. Besides, he added with more than a hint of reproach, it was not at all clear that she herself would return.

"Yes," said Lydia. "Well, I have returned, as you see, and if not exactly in triumph, still not in disgrace. And Natalia?"

"She is here. She is in the schoolroom with her books. They did not know what else to do, the ones that are left."

"Then you must bring her here to me as soon as you can, and we shall need a great deal of hot water: for this boy, who is the son of Danilo Pekočević; for Mr. Harwell, who must stay with you, I think; and for myself. If you have any broth at all, give it to the boy, to Toma, but make sure you have boiled it. And the first of the hot water, if you would be so very kind, must be made into a great pot of tea." Lydia sighed with satisfaction when she came to the end of these particular instructions, and Draško left, repeating her words as nearly as he could remember them.

Harwell stayed long enough to realize that he was in the way. He greeted Natalia when she arrived, breathless, and saw in the instant she laid eyes on Toma that she had comprehended everything. She embraced him silently there on Lydia's bed, and it seemed almost as if she were older than he, almost . . . well, it was what Sofia would have done, and he was relieved when Lydia closed the door on this grief that was so near to his own. Draško reappeared bearing a tin tub in which the boy must be bathed, in which Lydia must bathe, before she dressed. Really, there was no place for him here, not even room to stand after the furniture had been shoved back against the walls.

"I am sorry about this commotion," said Lydia as she placed the bottle in Harwell's hands. "The bathhouse is apparently out of commission just now, and so you see . . ." She spread her arms to emphasize her point, managed a little smile.

"Please don't worry about me. Perhaps I shall see you later?"

"Perhaps, but there is much to do here, and I have no idea how long I shall be with Sir Percy. I must lead him gently to the idea of easing this crisis, by whatever influence he has, though it may be awkward if the Austrian, who is his friend, is operating under a contrary set of instructions. At least I will know what, if anything, he knows. You will be ready to travel in the morning?"

"Yes, if Toma is able. But how can I thank you for . . ."

"I have accomplished nothing as yet, other than your whiskey. You may put a jinx on my efforts."

"But you have thought of everything."

"I have had time to think, and shall again when . . . when this is over."

"Good luck with Sir Percy."

Lydia smiled wryly at this. "Sir Percy, it may safely be said, would do almost anything for me. He will have to."

He wandered off with his precious bottle, admired the coffered ceiling in the entryway and the curious form of the pilasters in the corridors. He reflected on the strangeness of this evening, when there was such busyness all around him and he himself had nothing whatever to do, no useful occupation other than reflection. Well, he could write in his journal.

Draško's shed had a sturdy bench which served as his writing table, and with his sleeve, his filthy sleeve, he wiped off a space for his journal and for those flowers he had taken for Lydia under the horned peak. He drank whiskey from his tin cup as he wrote, forgetting that he had eaten nothing since breaking camp, and he was very glad when a crooked serving woman brought him a tray of food. It was simple stuff, remarkably like what he had cooked for himself in the mountains, but there was a little glass of yellow flowers by his plate, and the serviette was held in an ornate silver ring.

It was after dark when Draško arrived, muttering to himself, bearing the tin bath, and on subsequent trips, buckets of steaming water. He lit a lamp over the bench, and placed a candle over by what must be the bed, and on this he spread a fresh sheet.

"There," said Draško in satisfaction. "Is she not beautiful?"

"I beg your pardon?"

"Is she not beautiful, the *gospodja*?"

"Miss Wadham?"

Draško stared brightly at him.

"Yes, I suppose she is. I have often thought just that myself . . ."

"And brave also."

"Certainly brave. As brave as any woman, or any man."

"Good," and here Draško's eye fell on the bottle and the mug, which he then took up. "To the *gospodja*." He drank and handed what was left to Harwell.

"To Miss Lydia."

Draško then set about tidying up his quarters, putting a few things in a sack by the door.

"I say, there's no need for you to leave. We can both sleep here. I am perfectly comfortable on the floor," Harwell lied.

Draško looked at him as if he were mad. "*Ne, ne!* Here is soap for you," he said, producing an object from his pocket. "Your water will be cold unless you hurry." And with that he took Harwell's tray and departed.

The supper with Sir Percy had gone as well as she had hoped, and she could not but admire the gallantry of his efforts. The right leg of his trousers had been split up the seam from cuff to waist, and then pinned back neatly in place to accommodate his cast.

"Mustn't stand on it too long," he said, wiggling his toes in the black silk stocking. "Please sit with me and have some sherry."

He would do as she asked, he declared over the cold fish, and if he wondered at her sources of information, or suspected that Bron had taken a part in all this, he betrayed nothing. The Austrians had quite clearly overplayed their hand, and some show of Montenegrin resolve—a discreet show—coupled with a crisp note hinting at the displeasure of His Britannic Majesty . . . that should pretty well do it. And would he himself be overplaying his hand? Not a bit of it, dear girl: a man in his position was expected to represent the interests of his country as he understood them. He would request an audience with the prince in the morning, and as for Baron von Tripp, he was quite certain that his colleague, his confrère, would take a sensible view of these matters. It was Bismarck, after all—a German, of course, but of enormous influence in Austria—who had said that the Balkans were not worth the bones of a single Pomeranian grenadier. Would they have the pleasure of Mr. Harwell's company in the near future? inquired Lady Foote. No, Lydia explained, alas no, for he was being called away on urgent business. But at the door, after Lydia had said good night to Sir Percy, Lady Foote pressed upon her one of Sir Percy's shirts. "For Mr. Harwell," she said simply.

It was this shirt that Lydia held to her breast as she climbed the echoing stone stairs to her room. There was no need for light, as her eyes had become used to the dark during the walk home. The euphoria of the evening, her triumph, had worn thin: Bron would be quite safe, she was sure, and Toma. They would leave in the morning. There on her own bed, by the light of a single candle, she saw both Toma and Natalia asleep, she curled against him with her arm thrown across his chest. She could imagine that they had slept together this way as children at home. She blew out the candle.

She sat on her settee and considered its unsuitability as a bed while her fingers, of their own accord, found the pouch of tobacco and rolled a cigarette. There was no point in pretending to herself that she would sleep on this wretched thing, and once that was decided, the rest followed quite naturally. She wanted some whiskey. She would have some whiskey. What, after all, did she have to lose? She stubbed out her cigarette on the sole of her shoe.

On her way down the stairs, and on the stone path to Draško's shed, Lydia attempted arguments against this course of action. She was past the point of blaming herself for the disappointment that would mark the rest of her life—how clearly she saw that much— and her frustration, her sense of impending loss, must necessarily attach themselves to Bron. She thought of what she had dared to do, out of love: was he not insensitive to this, even ungrateful? She thought of how single-minded she had been, attaching to him every hope and every desire: was he not inconstant, foolishly and unforgivably inconstant? She thought of him staring at the fire, wrapped in his grief, unable to reach out to the boy who needed at least a kind word from him: did this not bespeak coldness and a narrow soul? She framed the question to herself: *What on earth do you think you are doing?*

Through the window of the shed she saw him, legs splayed out over the sides of the narrow bath, head thrown back against the wall behind: asleep. How could she feel anything but the tenderest compassion for him now, exhausted by his ordeal? Would he not catch his death in that cold water? She entered, and poured herself a generous measure of whiskey in the mug. The undiluted strength of it brought tears to her eyes. Or were there tears there already? *Oh,* she said silently, *but he is beautiful.* Perhaps she should not wake him. Perhaps this moment was all she should hope for. She took another swallow of the whiskey, drew courage from it, and approached the bath, knelt there.

"Bron," she whispered in his ear. He awoke, looked around him in confusion, then focused on her face. "Bron . . ." she said again, and could not think of what else to say, but felt the whiskey burning its way down to the center of her. She bent a little closer to him so that he, by the very slightest exertion, might incline towards her and kiss her, which of course he did. There, it was done, this small point of honor satisfied. If he did not want her he would have turned away.

It had never been like this in her imagination, the delicate politics of this kiss, the abyss of broken hopes and disappointment on either side, now safely passed. Nor had imagination supplied the exquisite sensation of his lips on hers, so different from the fierceness of their first embrace. She thought he would pull away, but it was only to tilt his head a little, to return, to take possession of her mouth more completely. She held to the rim of the tub with both hands, with all her strength.

He moved, and the water splashed up onto her cheek and neck, shockingly cold. "Oh," she said, breaking away from him. "It is so . . ."

"This will never do," said he, looking about him for his clothes, a towel. He had begun to blush when he met her eyes. "What shall we . . . ?"

"I am becoming rather inured to naked men, for better or worse. Here," she said, taking the linen from the bed, "this will have to serve." She held the sheet up with her arms outstretched to preserve his modesty, and when he stepped from the bath she enclosed him in it, wrapped her arms around him, drew him to her, damp through and shivering. "You are my prisoner," she said against his chest, trying to make a joke, but her voice nearly failed her.

When he had rearranged the sheet so that he had arms again, he picked her up and carried her to the bed, where he stood her on that low platform of sacking, and her face was now on a level with his. They embraced, and those few inches yielded a new universe of delights: his shoulders there beneath her hands, her breasts crushed to his chest, her heart striving towards his. She pulled back when she thought she would faint, looked at him in that wonderful and ridiculous garment. "How Olympian. How very Olympian indeed. The gods themselves do envy us."

With this encouragement he put his hands to the little silk buttons at her neck and with a most solemn expression asked: "May I?"

She put her hands over his and pressed them to her. "I had better do it myself. There are so many of them." She began to shed her clothes, layer by layer, and to fill these awkward moments he turned to snuff the candle. "Please do not, on my account," she said, coloring at her own boldness. "I am content that you should see me as I am, and I have no shame in this."

She felt less brave when she was reduced to her camisole, and smaller too without her shoes. "Now," she said, "as you are wearing the one sheet we have, you must take it off and put it on the bed, and when you have done that you may take this from me. There are no buttons left." She stood again on the corner of the bed and raised her arms, not daring to look upon him. While she was still blind-folded by the reluctant camisole, she felt him like a flame against her, everywhere, and the smell of him was like incense. With her eyes closed she pressed herself to him, kissing his lips, his eyes, his neck, wondering at the heat, the fierce urgency of this thing, his male part, that rose impossibly, inexorably, to be crushed against her belly. Did she dare put her hand there? She did, and in a voice husky with desire was able to make a joke of her own ignorance: "Tell me, sir, is this the normal state . . . ?"

There were no jokes after this one, no conversation at all, but breathless and wordless discovery. Where she had imagined pain—this from the conversation, presumably informed, of a girl in Birmingham—or embarrassment—this, obliquely, from her mother—she found neither, or simply leapt over them, like the hunter sailing clear of the fence, to those unknown realms that had so fevered her dreams and which she now claimed as her own. There had been a moment of hesitation when she knew Bron would have wished for darkness, the moment when he took her, entered her. And yet she was glad for the light, because she knew that no shame or harm could come to her, and, as a surfeit to the sensations and emotions which flooded her, she was able to rejoice in the expressive pleasure that transformed his face.

He slept afterwards, slept with his head against her breast, like a child, while she, mindful of how short the night would be, took careful inventory of every feeling, every thought, even admitting the one rueful question that she knew was most dangerous: *Why must this end? Would perfect happiness not consist in an endless succession of such nights?* She would not dwell on this. She would make the best of what was granted to her, and never beg for what was not willingly given.

She glanced at the candle and saw that it was nearly spent, so she shifted her weight to look upon him as he lay there, his limbs entwining hers. This night was willingly given. She touched him then, with her hand and with her mouth making a slow, bold exploration of her conquest, and when he woke she was kneeling there beside him, holding his hand in both of hers. He disengaged that hand and put it to her breast, so slow and deliberate a movement that she could note how her flesh trembled in anticipation, how the nipple rose to his touch. He had made her body beautiful. She climbed astride him, no sidesaddle for this horse, this rider, and had just time, before the candle guttered out, to see his look of surprise and delight.

They both slept then, but she woke at the first hint of light in the east. She would not stay beyond her appointed time, wanted nothing to mar the perfect memory of the night. She could hope for everything, but she must expect nothing: she steeled herself against this bitter thought.

The lamp over Draško's potting bench had also gone out, but there was light enough for her to dress. She left the clean shirt for him there by his journals. What were those things? Ah, the pressed flowers. Well . . . and that curious object he wore around his neck. She looked closely at the cross but did not touch it. She knew for a certainty whose it had been, and what it meant. *This is the thing that binds him to her, the instrument of my undoing.* The morning air braced her, saddened her. As quietly as she could she closed the door on all her happiness.

Chapter Seventeen

THE DAY DAWNED hot and airless in Kotor, and Harwell was surprised to hear the bell striking eight o'clock. His hotel, the whole town, lay so close under the precipice of the mountain that the light did not reach it until long after the sun had risen. Toma was not in his bed, but sat over by the window, which gave an oblique view of the sea. Surely this curiosity, this energy were good signs.

They had missed the steamer the day before, the same old tub on which Harwell had arrived, and which would have carried Toma down the coast to Bar and Ulcinj, or Antivari and Dulcigno as they were shown on the Ungaro-Croatian schedule. Now they must catch the Austrian-Lloyd steamer—the name was hardly promising—which would take him, after a call in Bari, all the way to Naples, and there he would find direct passage to New York. "Repeat after me, Toma: 'New York. New York. Mi bisogna andare a New York.'"

The time had been well spent. Toma could hardly make an impression on the New World in those hand-me-down clothes of Janko's, which might burst at any moment, and so the first order of business was the purchase of a pair of trousers, which the tailor promised for this morning, a pair of shoes, and a tight-fitting jacket, peculiarly cut, that pleased Toma greatly. This item, said the tailor, had been made to the order of a young man who had died before he could wear it, and so he could let it go for a very reasonable price.

Next Harwell must do something about money, for although he had spent almost nothing since outfitting himself in Cetinje, he certainly did not have the price of the passage to New York in his pocketbook, and so he must negotiate Lord Polgrove's letter of credit, which gave him theoretical access to a considerable sum of money. He would settle his accounts later in London.

The bank was just closing when they arrived. The manager, after careful consideration of Harwell's papers, and some frankly curious glances at their attire and at Toma's face, declined the transaction. "I can do nothing," he said, flinging both hands in the air. "Come back tomorrow or, better, next week, and we will have made inquiries."

"A plague on Italian banks," said Harwell under his breath as he gathered back his papers. Lord Polgrove would be distressed indeed to learn that his seal and signature counted for so little here, whereas the Austrian foreign minister's . . .

It was by luck, then, that Harwell encountered another Englishman there in the elegant, claustrophobic alleys of Kotor, recognized him as such by his vulgar whistling of a dance-hall tune, and entertained him to several beers and an hour of very forced camaraderie. Grout was the name, and he was the agent of Hammer & Thomson in Podgorica—beeswax, pyrethrum, but principally hides—and in fact he had just put a great consignment of hides on a ship bound for Trieste. He was sure that the price he had struck here in Cattaro more than compensated for the difficulty and cost . . . Harwell nodded sagely at each of these crucial details, congratulated the cheerful Grout on his success, his undoubted acumen, and sympathized with his problems in dealing with the Austrian officials. As it turned out, Grout's transaction had left him with his pockets stuffed full of Italian currency, which he would be only too glad to exchange for sterling, allowing the proper discount, of course, as he was not really a banker himself, and would have to . . . Harwell did the sums in his head, and decided that if Grout was not a banker he had probably missed his calling. Still, he was in no position to debate the matter, and they shook hands on it.

"Come from up above, are you?" Grout wanted to know. Harwell took a slow swallow of his beer, wondering what connection the man had made.

"Yes. Interesting place, I found it, at least to visit."

"And did you by any chance encounter Miss Wadham, English girl who teaches at the academy in Cetinje?"

"I did have that pleasure."

"Ain't she a pip, Miss Wadham? Introduced myself to her at the residence there, and seen her a couple of times since, as I get to Cetinje every now and again. Real spirit, she has. Can't figure out how a girl like that gets stuck in such a place. Can you?"

"Can I what?"

"Can you imagine what is to become of her in such a godforsaken town? Why hasn't she met some bloke who would keep her from coming here in the first place? Or take her away? Why not you, Mr. Harwell?"

Harwell cleared his throat, tried not to meet Grout's greedy stare. "Well, I'm sure she has her own plans for the future."

"Don't think I haven't thought about it myself, not that she'd have me. Besides, I have a missus." He looked into his glass of beer, then raised it to Harwell. "But you, Mr. Harwell, you don't look married to me. I should think she'd be fairly praying for someone like you to happen by." Toma had sat quietly throughout this entire exchange, apparently engrossed in the curiosity of his iced drink, a carbonated extract, first of *framboise*, then of *cassis*. But at this point he too raised his eyes to Harwell's, as if he had been following every word and awaited some response.

It had been such an inappropriate, odious conversation that had Harwell not been in great need of Grout's cash he might have dashed his beer in the man's face. No, he would do no such thing, could not afford such self-indulgence, even though he had heard no rumor from the east beyond the fantastic reports of the earthquake that had levelled whole villages and killed scores of people. He smiled at them both, and shrugged.

And yet this inappropriate, odious conversation had stayed with Harwell through the evening, came back to him now as he lay in bed watching the light fill the room. *Why not you, Mr. Harwell?* He knew well enough from Lydia's letters what a lonely life it was for her there in Cetinje, lonelier still if she should lose Natalia, and the thought of her having to deal with Grout's attentions, or Sir Percy's, was either distressing or ludicrous. But was this his doing? Did one night of intimacy—what a pale word for what had passed between them!—require him to save her from these circumstances? He remembered what Sofia had said about Aliye, that no one had made her do this thing. But he also remembered how hard a lesson that had seemed at the time, and how his heart had gone out to the girl. Had Toma loved Aliye? If he had loved her enough, would she not still be alive? And Sofia too? He looked at Toma, who sat in the same position by the window, gazing out at the sea, and thought: *I must not judge him.* Did he even know who this boy was? In the shape of those shoulders, in the broad silhouette of the back, he saw Danilo, or how Danilo must have looked as a young man. And yet if he would turn his head, there would be Sofia's eyes.

His mind was filled with these impossible calculations of obligation and responsibility, and yet the greatest and most urgent responsibility was to get Toma safely aboard his ship, and so he arose from his comfortable bed and clean sheets—how evocative the smell of fresh linen had become!—and said to Toma that they had not much time to lose.

They breakfasted on the terrace under a striped awning, and with his hair combed and his new shirt sparkling white even in this shade, Toma was already transformed from the fugitive into the earnest student. "This," said Harwell, "is called a *croissant,* and I have no idea what it is called locally, or by the Austrians. We must give credit to the French." He also remarked that the coffee was a disappointment. Toma smiled and lowered his eyes, for they both knew that the standard against which this coffee must be measured was Sofia's.

"And the leg, Toma." Harwell was eager to move the conversation ahead. "Is that wound healing?"

"Yes. Miss Wadham saw to it before we left. She gave me a dressing for it, that herb you found in the mountains that is said to heal the wounds of the warrior. She said my mother would have known of this."

"And did she speak with you about this journey?"

"She set my mind at rest." *

"And you have the letter, the copy of the letter to your mother's cousin in Chicago?"

"I have it. Is Chicago far from New York?"

"Quite far, I should think. You may have to find work for a while before you make that journey. But do not forget that the end is an education, if possible a university education, and you must write to me if you need a recommendation."

"And where will you be? In Cetinje?" Toma had his mother's way of asking questions with the eyes.

"Most likely not . . . perhaps in London. I haven't thought much beyond today." Harwell touched his breast pocket, where he had put the schedule of departures for Trieste.

"Will Miss Wadham know how to find you?"

"Most certainly. And you must write to her often, for it is she who will know how to get letters to Natalia, and to your father."

"Yes." The boy stared into his coffee, and Harwell decided that any discussion of what was being left behind was dangerous. Only the future mattered, that dream, concocted from a book of exaggerations, for which Sofia had sacrificed everything. And he himself, viewed from this perspective, was about to become part of what was left behind, a figure dwindling on the quay. That was how Sofia would have seen it. The great adventure now belonged to Toma.

"Come," he said. "Mr. Grout will be waiting for us, and the tailor, too."

He did not think that saying goodbye would be difficult, for the boy was distracted by the sights and sounds of the busy ship, and even the gentle rise and fall of her deck in the harbor swell fascinated him. Harwell put the ticket in his hand, and half the money that he had received from Grout, which Toma wrapped into a cloth around his waist, under his shirt.

When the horn of the steamer sounded twice, nearly deafening them, Harwell shook Toma by the hand and asked if there was anything more he could do.

"The book," said Toma, almost shyly, "if you would give me the blind man's book."

"What, the Homer?" A great smile broke upon Harwell's face. "But you do not read Greek, how will you . . . ?"

"I have learned your language, and in time I will learn his. He walked in our mountains, it is said, and I will remember that when I read his poem."

Harwell rummaged in his pack, found the book, and was about to place it in the boy's hand when he had an idea that made him smile again. On the flyleaf, under his own name, he wrote, first in Greek and then in English, *We give you glory: it is yours to win.*

"What does this mean?"

"These are his words, and I no longer know for sure what they mean. I think you must find out for yourself."

Toma held the book with both hands, staring, like a blind man himself, at something unseen. "Farewell. Thank you for everything. I shall write to Natalia, and to my father, but you must give my particular thanks to Miss Wadham, and my love."

Toma embraced him then, took him by surprise, kissed him on the lips the way Harwell had seen men kiss each other at the feast of the archangel. His heart raced, and his mind was filled with a dazzling chaos that he could not articulate, a soaring joy. He embraced the boy on Sofia's behalf, but on the other hand, that was surely her face, those her eyes. Without another word, he took the silk cross from under his collar and placed it around the boy's neck. There, it was done. Then he stepped down the gangplank to the quay, where he was soon that dwindling figure on the shore, no longer quite sure if he could be seen from the deck of the steamer that cut a graceful curve in the waters of the Bay of Kotor.

Harwell had a whiskey at a café that commanded a view of the harbor and the bay beyond, now a blue void under the clear sky. The whiskey was not the equal of Sir Percy's bottle, did not begin to compare with it, and yet it would do very nicely to mark this moment. He had done his best—he even said this aloud—done what he had been asked to do, in spite of obstacles that could not have been guessed at when he made his vow. He raised his glass in the direction of the departed steamer. He drank, and was reminded how the whiskey had tasted on Lydia's mouth.

At that moment, with the bells of the town still tolling the hour of noon, the Austrian musicians took their positions on the little bandstand near the water's edge and struck up their anthem, *Gott erhalte Franz den Kaiser*. The music annoyed him. How could a man think with such a racket? He ordered another whiskey. A steamer for Trieste was due to arrive in two hours. It would be the simplest thing in the world to walk on board and have done with it, with everything. In a matter of days he could be in London.

This thought did nothing to cheer him. Of course he would very much like to see Raymond, to tell him all that had happened, to spend an evening over a better bottle of whiskey . . . But Raymond, he reflected, was now married, was he not? He drank to Raymond's happiness, and prayed for his success in arranging the matter in Shepherd Market. No, he thought, *there is no particular thing that calls me to London. I might as well stay here.*

He could go to Africa, to India, or China . . . The very names conjured an emptiness, that unsought isolation about which he had written to Lydia, and which he now might choose as his fate. He had written so many things to her, and how he regretted the loss of that order—the unhurried discovery of one's self and of another being that was possible in such a correspondence—which was now subsumed in the chaotic, unmanageable events of real life.

He could write to her again. Or, being a perfectly free man, he could also go back to Cetinje. Their parting had been strained and muted by circumstance: there was Natalia clinging to her brother's arm, trying her best not to weep anymore; there was Lydia, offering her hand, that firm grip, and smiling bravely at him. She seemed tired, but the color in her cheeks from yesterday's sun made such a fine setting for her eyes, somehow altered their color or aspect. She reminded him that he would need to make some arrangements for his luggage, but neither of them spoke of the possibility of his return. She laid no claim on him, asked nothing. Was he surprised? Was he disappointed?

To the very end she offered her encouragement, and her humor, resisted the dreadful solemnity of the occasion. She had done this for the sake of Toma and his sister, but also, surely, for him, as if she saw what was best in him, and would draw it forth. And he, fool that he was, had not even the wit to kiss her goodbye, but stood there shaking her hand until the bell of the monastery reminded them both of the hour.

Had he even thanked her? If Toma must thank her, must he not be doubly, trebly grateful? He looked at the empty bay, and at his watch, forgetting that it no longer told the time. He could not be moved by mere obligation, and it would not do to thank someone for her love. He had loved Sofia, and for the sake of love had done something that was a near impossibility. And all that Lydia had done and dared, had that not been for love as well? But if his mind now turned from Africa and Asia, those barren shores, and from what he used to call home, and if instead he remembered the smell of her hair on the sheet after she had gone, or heard again the question she had asked that night under the stars, and if the idea of her bending Sir Percy to her will made him grin like a lunatic, must this too not be out of love? He was tired of endings, and there was no salvation in something merely new. He must find a beginning, a true beginning.

The owner of the livery stable was surprised to see him so soon again, and disappointed too that the bargain on the horses must be undone, even though Harwell rewarded his trouble. The mare seemed unwilling at first, or uncertain of his intentions as they started back up that steep road with the stallion on a lead. But he spoke flatteringly to her, and by the time they reached the first of those glorious, grueling curves, she was stepping out with a will. Night would have fallen by the time they reached Cetinje, but there would be a magnificent sunset for them somewhere near the top of the pass, and he was now quite familiar with the way.